CW00431231

Praise for Karen

The Lightkeeper's Wife

'Absolutely sublime. One of the top ten books of the year.' —*Le journal de la santé*

'heart-wrenching and absorbing . . . *The Lightkeeper's Wife* is a story of love versus passion, right versus wrong, and ultimately, a story of forgiveness.'—*Bookseller & Publisher*

'Nature can both isolate and enlighten. Battling the elements can be as much about battling the storms within yourself. In *The Lightkeeper's Wife* . . . Viggers sets the scene in a family dynamic filled with regret, loss and love.'—*Australian Women's Weekly*

'a triumph'—*Le Figaro*

'This is a moving story of loss and love, and acceptance of the hand life deals us. It is truly unforgettable reading.'—*Woman's Day*

'Viggers shines in her descriptions of the wilds of Bruny Island and Antarctica.'—*Daily Telegraph*

'a song in two voices . . . Arguably the book of the summer' —*Femme actuelle*

'an emotional, engrossing read, gently but passionately told.' —*Sunday Herald Sun*

'Each page is impregnated with salty sea air, wild waves and rocky coasts, a thousand shades of grey. In the folds of the surf, Karen Viggers has written a beautiful story of loss, memory and the effect of time on our aching souls.'—*Lire Magazine*

The Stranding

'a poignant anatomy of loss. It is a memorable story of broken hearts trying to mend, of personal discovery and recovery. Her writing creates seductive land-edge experiences, light off the ocean, wind over sand, weather coming in.'—*The Australian*

'There is a raw saltiness to the writing that vividly conveys the wild moods of the ocean, the crippling nature of emotional baggage and the challenges of a whale rescue.'—*The Age*

'*The Stranding* aptly demonstrates how fiction plays a part in revealing the intricate and sometimes fragile bond that we share with nature.'—Wild Melbourne

'Steeped in natural beauty, it will have you longing for coastal sunsets and afternoons lost wandering empty beaches.'—Laurie Steed, Readings Carlton

The Grass Castle

'a story that will return to you time and time again'—*Sydney Morning Herald*

'quality commercial fiction for which Viggers deserves a strong following.'—*Books + Publishing*

'Karen Viggers weaves her tale against the backdrop of our love of the land.'—*Yours Magazine*

'Evocative and thought-provoking.'—*Newcastle Herald*

'a breath of fresh air that teaches us humility in the face of nature and the courage to face fears. Live rather than survive.'—Le petit crayon

Karen Viggers is a wildlife veterinarian with a passion for people, animals and wild places. As a biologist and researcher, she has worked with native animals in many remote parts of Australia from the Kimberley to Antarctica, and she brings a unique set of perspectives to Australian contemporary fiction. Her novels have been translated into several languages. In 2016, *The Lightkeeper's Wife* (*La Mémoire des embruns*) was awarded the *Les Petits Mots des Libraires* literary prize and was short-listed for the *Livre de Poche* Reader's Choice award. This novel was on the French national bestseller list for more than 42 weeks, going as high as No. 3. *The Orchardist's Daughter* is Karen's fourth novel. You can read more about Karen and her books at **www.karenviggers.com**

Also by Karen Viggers

The Stranding
The Lightkeeper's Wife
The Grass Castle

KAREN VIGGERS

The Orchardist's Daughter

ALLEN&UNWIN
SYDNEY • MELBOURNE • AUCKLAND • LONDON

This is a work of fiction. Names, characters, places and incidents are products of the author's imagination or are used fictitiously. Any resemblance to actual events, locales, or persons, living or dead, is entirely coincidental.

First published in 2019

Copyright © Karen Viggers 2019

All rights reserved. No part of this book may be reproduced or transmitted in any form or by any means, electronic or mechanical, including photocopying, recording or by any information storage and retrieval system, without prior permission in writing from the publisher. The Australian *Copyright Act 1968* (the Act) allows a maximum of one chapter or 10 per cent of this book, whichever is the greater, to be photocopied by any educational institution for its educational purposes provided that the educational institution (or body that administers it) has given a remuneration notice to the Copyright Agency (Australia) under the Act.

Allen & Unwin
83 Alexander Street
Crows Nest NSW 2065
Australia
Phone: (61 2) 8425 0100
Email: info@allenandunwin.com
Web: www.allenandunwin.com

A catalogue record for this book is available from the National Library of Australia

ISBN 978 1 76063 058 4

Author photo (p. iii) by Michelle Higgs
Set in 12/16 pt Adobe Garamond Pro by Bookhouse, Sydney
Printed and bound in Australia by Griffin Press

10 9 8 7 6 5 4 3 2 1

The paper in this book is FSC® certified. FSC® promotes environmentally responsible, socially beneficial and economically viable management of the world's forests.

For David,
who has dedicated his life's work
to studying the mountain ash forests of Victoria

and

For my sister Fiona,
who understands where the heart resides
within the story of life

Only the untamed forest
is home to that silence which
is union with the divine. And only
the forest creatures grasp that
being in the single moment is all.

Jane Baker, 'Church' (unpublished)

We dance to the echoes of our own gods.

John Karl Stokes, 'A River in the Dark', Chant No. 6,
Riverwater: Eight chants from the Clyde River

Prologue

She was asleep when it happened, so she didn't hear the embers collapse as the log rolled from the fireplace onto the floor. She was dreaming of escape: tearing off her apron as she ran barefoot down the long potholed driveway, past the lines of twisted apple trees and onto the gravel road that led away from here. In her sixteen years, she'd only been down that road once. It led to another world, where perhaps God was kinder and someone else helped with the jobs.

The others were asleep too, so nobody heard the clothes rack slump onto the log. Nobody noticed the flames licking at the crumpled clothes, stroking with liquid fingers, fizzing in the fibres. Nobody saw the fire ignite the faded carpet and the worn, sagging furniture, the pedestal with Father's leather-bound Bible.

In her dreams, she was walking towards a different horizon. A carpet of trees. Shifting shadow and light.

A voice floated around her, waxing and waning, warping, disintegrating. She struggled to make out the words.

Then the voice became clearer. Her brother shouting, 'Get up!'

Something crashed into her room and she opened her eyes. Smoke billowed like thick fog and a cough punched her chest.

Her brother loomed over her, his hands rough on her shoulders, shaking her, encouraging her to move. But she couldn't breathe. She was smoke-addled. Ragdoll loose.

An insistent sound rumbled through the house, vibrating and roaring; she felt it in her skin, in her bones, everything humming to its rhythm. The smoke had thinned and the light was surreal. Orange. Flickering.

Her brother pulled her from bed and she slumped to the floor. Around her, she heard crackling and hissing, and an evil heat radiated from the door.

Was this hell? Had God come to punish her?

Her brother hauled her across the room, wrenched open the window, and shoved her out, dropping her among the rosebushes. She landed on hands and knees, gasping, smoke scraping her chest, no air in her lungs. Thorns snagged her skin and tore at her hair as she dragged herself free.

She crawled to the driveway and hunched there, struggling against faintness until her throat released and she sucked in a lungful of air, a rasp drawn through her body.

The house was burning. Smoke poured from under the eaves, and flames clawed the sky. As she watched, a trickle of flame shimmied up the pine tree beside her bedroom, racing up the trunk, along the branches, through the needles, snapping and popping. Transfixed, she huddled, mesmerised, terrified, as the whole tree lit up.

But where was her brother? Her parents?

Stumbling to her feet, she ran around the house on the circular driveway, toes crimping on gravel.

No one.

There was no way back in. The house was alive with fire. She stood powerless, watching it burn. Flames in the lounge room, in their parents' room, behind the windows. Somewhere, the tinkling of glass. Clumps of ceiling were dropping like stones. Her brother was taking too long.

When it seemed the whole house had been converted to hell and that everyone must be dead, he lurched from a window. Flames danced on his back, and he tumbled to the ground, rolling frantically, then ripped off his woollen jumper and flung it away.

In the leaping light of the blaze, he staggered across to her, soot-blackened and gasping, eyebrows singed.

He was clutching something to his chest: Father's black leather folder.

When she looked in his eyes, she knew her parents were gone.

PART I
Seeds

1

Leon drove into town on a clear autumn Saturday. Blue skies, leaves turning golden, a hint of smoke in the air. He felt optimistic. New home, new job, new life—he was going to make this work. For too many years he'd been living on Bruny Island with his folks. He'd had his reasons for being there, but it was time to move on. This was a fresh start, and no matter what his dad said, Leon was up for it. Being a Parks ranger in a timber town would bring challenges, but there were ways to fit in—you just had to find them.

He would miss the island, there was no doubt. He loved its wild beaches, columnar cliffs and shifting winds. The sea frothing against the shore. The still waters of the channel with its hook-necked, red-beaked black swans. Dragging his kayak across mudflats alive with waterbirds and scuttling crabs. But he'd left all that behind and now he was here. At least he was still in southern Tasmania, and working among forests and trees, which were in his blood.

Pretty much everything he owned was in his old red car. Kayak on the roof-rack. Box of books in the back. A few folding chairs. Suitcase stuffed with worn clothes. Hiking boots. The down sleeping-bag he'd bought when he was studying in Hobart. Oh, the trips he'd planned: big multi-day hikes in southern Tasmania that never eventuated because he'd had to move home. It had been a necessity—his mum had needed him. He would never forgive his dad for wrecking his life and ruining hers.

But today none of that mattered. Twenty-five wasn't too late for a new beginning, and he was excited. This was the first opportunity he'd had in forever.

He drove slowly up the main street, surprised at how busy it was. Parking spots clogged with cars. Muddy kids in footy jerseys. People pushing trolleys and lugging shopping bags. Tourists spilling from a coach outside the visitor centre. He checked out the shops: post office, pharmacy, butcher, baker, bank, cafe, takeaway next to the supermarket, hardware at the top of the street. Back home in Adventure Bay where his parents lived, peak hour was twice a day for sixty seconds when the bus came through with tourists for the scenic boat trip around the coast. The only shops were the general store and cafe, so this place was a metropolis in comparison. He would be set here for most things he needed. Anything else he could buy down near the Parks office, in the last town he'd passed through. He could have rented closer to work, but he'd decided to live here, at the foot of the mountains—the springboard to his new future.

He crossed the highway into a quiet street lined by weatherboard houses with white window frames, walls of firewood piled along fences, smoke wafting from chimneys. Turning a corner, he headed uphill past a brick house half-hidden by rose bushes, a log truck parked on the kerb, a vacant block with a scarecrow in an overgrown vegie patch, then another weatherboard with an old blue car set on stumps down the side.

Further upslope were his new digs: a little pink house backing onto bush—he recognised it from the photos on the website. It was part of a deceased estate, cheap rent and semi-furnished, which suited him because he didn't have furniture. Before moving back in with his parents he'd been in a student house in Hobart with shabby old armchairs and a stained sofa, none of which had been worth keeping.

Pulling up on the gravel driveway, Leon assessed his new premises. The agent had said it was occupied until recently, but it looked closed-up and neglected. The grass was long. No front fence and no garden. The uphill boundary with the bush had five-strand barbed wire, and the low paling fence that divided him from his neighbours was bolstered by firewood, all on their side.

He slid out into cold air that was heavy with wood smoke and the sweet smell of cows in the paddock across the road. Next door, a red heeler with a big belly and long teats trotted to the fence and barked at him—the welcoming committee. Leon mounted the steps to the front door and poked the key in the lock. It was stiff and the door wouldn't budge, so he shoved it with his shoulder to get in.

The house was almost empty. Nothing in the lounge room except a pile of rubbish in the fireplace. Skewed venetian blinds at the windows. Mantelpiece thick with dust and possum shit. In the bedroom: a squeaky bed. He sat on the bed frame, and springs poked his bum. Underneath, on the floor, he found a rusty chamber pot. The old lady who'd lived here must have been incontinent. Suddenly the bed looked even less appealing.

He continued his tour of the house. In the kitchen, two vinyl chairs spewed stuffing from their seams, and possum shit was everywhere. He screwed up his nose. What had happened to *recently vacated* and *partly furnished*? This wasn't what he'd signed up for. He considered calling the agency and blasting them. Then he sighed. He wanted to be a new person here, the sort of man who didn't snap to anger, different from his dad. There were ways to sort things. He had a couple of days to clean up before starting work. Tomorrow he would use some savings and buy a new mattress, maybe find cheap furniture at garage sales. But it was a shame the place was such a mess. The irony of it almost made him smile. Three years of dealing with the emotional mess at home, and now this. The grime was daunting, but it would be easier than looking out for his mum whenever his dad was tanked.

Outside, he lifted his kayak from the car and stashed it alongside the house. Then he lugged in his gear and dumped it on the floor. Where to begin? He would start with the fireplace, because any bet the house wouldn't be insulated and he would freeze tonight if he couldn't light a fire . . . assuming there was wood.

When he searched out the back there was none.

In a cupboard he discovered an old radiator, so he plugged it in. The stench of burning dust permeated the lounge room, then the power snapped off; the radiator had shorted everything out. He checked the fuse box and switched the power back on, but there would be no heating until he organised a delivery of wood. He found a number on a fridge magnet and arranged for a load to be dropped off that afternoon.

After he'd carted the rubbish to the bin, he wiped down the mantelpiece with an old rag from the car, scrubbing away sticky dots of possum piss and shrivelled clumps of poo. When it was clean, he set his books on it: field guides and history books, then his favourite fiction, all set in Tasmania: *For the Term of His Natural Life*, *Death of a River Guide*, *The Roving Party*. Somehow the books made the house feel more of a home. They were part of him and their presence made it easier to tackle the rest of the chores. Each time he walked past, he imagined himself reading by the fire on cold nights—it was heartening. But the cleaning wasn't going so well. The damp rag wasn't sufficient to shift the dirt, so he traipsed down to the supermarket and bought a bucket and mop, bleach, disposable cloths, a scrubbing brush. Back at the house he began sweeping, mopping, wiping with his new gear. The whole place needed attention. And then there was the algae-stained loo.

His mum rang as he was tossing a bucket of scummy water on the grass. 'Leon,' she said, as if they hadn't spoken in months, 'how are you? It's quiet here without you.'

He thought of her standing at the tulle curtains, looking out across the lawn to the street. Yes, it would be quiet back home. Weekdays, she would be busy cleaning cabins at the caravan park. But weekends, she'd be stuck in the house with his pensioned-off dad. Minnie the cat would be curled on the couch or weaving her way around his mum's legs. In the main bedroom, his dad would be propped up with pillows watching TV: a footy replay, or maybe a golf tournament. Across the road, small waves would be tumbling onto the sand and hissing up the beach. Leon checked his watch—the morning tourist boat would almost be back.

'Is the house all right?' his mum asked.

He couldn't tell the truth or she'd be here tomorrow, trying to fix things, calling a friend to find him some furniture. 'It's fine,' he said. 'Everything's great.'

'Oh, good.' She sounded relieved. 'Hope all goes well at work on Monday. And don't forget to visit Grandpa. I told him you'd drop in, so don't leave it too long.'

Three years had passed since he'd visited the old man, so rocking up now would be awkward. Leon felt guilty. It was easy to forget people in aged-care homes, easy to assume they had all they needed: food, assistance, other ancient friends. But he'd learned a little about old people last year. He'd befriended an old lady on the island and checked on her every day, providing groceries and occasional conversation—a small commitment he'd been able to manage. She'd been interesting, full of tales of the past, lighthouse stories. And he'd realised old people had many memories to share. Maybe he could get Grandpa talking. Who knew what skeletons the old man might have in his closet? And Grandpa might be able to shed some light on why Leon's dad had turned out so badly. There was no love lost between the two men; Leon's dad never rang the old man. It was another fraught and fractured father–son relationship. The world was littered with them.

'Don't forget to eat properly,' his mum was saying. 'And you'll have to find a laundromat. You should change your clothes every day.'

'Mum, you don't need to worry. There's a laundromat in town.'

'I miss you, Leon. Come and see us sometime.'

Four hours since he'd left, and she was already inviting him back. 'I'll come when I can. But it'll be a few weeks. I have lots to organise.'

'All right then. I suppose I'd better let you go. Don't forget your lunch.' She'd made vegemite and cheese sandwiches on white bread, just like for school.

'See you, Mum.'

He fetched his sandwiches and sat on the front doorstep. The neighbours' dog came to the fence, weaving through bikes and balls on the lawn. It growled at him, ears pricked, hackles raised. In the backyard, a woman with streaky blonde hair was hanging washing on the line, and down the back in the tilt-door garage, a skinny man with jeans that sagged off his bum was tinkering with something at the workbench, the pre-game footy commentary blaring on the radio. Leon could hear them talking over the din: the wife paying the husband out. 'What are you doing, Shane, making love to that chainsaw? You've been working on it all day.'

'Chain's stuffed and I only sharpened it Thursday.'

'Buy a new one then. Don't cost much, do they? Chain or smokes, you choose.'

'Smokes. Can't do without them.'

'Can't do without a chain either, can you? Or we'll have no money at all.'

'I'll try sharpening this one again first.'

A scruffy boy in a footy jersey came pumping up the hill on a bike, no helmet. He wheeled the bike through the gate next door, dumped it on the grass then ran inside, reappearing soon after with a pack of chips in one hand and an iPhone in the other, the dog panting at his heels. He came to the fence and looked over at Leon. He was thin with a mop of mousy brown hair, hollow cheeks, pale skin.

'Hi,' Leon said. 'How are you going?'

'Good. Who are you?'

'Leon.'

The boy opened the chips and pulled out a handful, which he shoved in his mouth while the dog ogled him hopefully.

'What's your name?' Leon asked.

'Max.'

'Nice dog.' The dog curled its lip and snarled.

'She's Rosie,' the boy said, stroking the dog's back. 'She's Dad's dog, not mine. Dad takes her up to the forest to guard his ute against greenies. He wanted a boy-dog but Mum said we had to have a girl because boy-dogs piss on everything.'

'You like dogs, don't you?' Leon said.

'They're okay.'

Max ran a hand over Rosie's head while she panted up at him.

'She likes you,' Leon said.

'That's because I feed her chips.'

'What's with her teats?'

'She's had pups before. But she ate them.'

That didn't sound likely. Was the kid having him on? 'Why don't you get her spayed if she's no good as a mum?'

'Costs too much.'

Leon wondered how many litters the dog had delivered. More than one, judging by those dangly teats. Looking at the size of her belly, another one was probably on the way. 'How old are you?' Leon asked.

'Ten.'

'You're tall for ten.' The kid stood up straighter. 'You play footy too.' Leon pointed at the kid's jersey. 'What's your team called?'

'The Devils.'

'How did you go today?'

'We lost.'

'That's too bad. But you can't always win.'

'We *never* win.'

'Bad luck, eh?'

'Dad says it's nothing to do with luck. He says it's because we're crap.'

'Nobody's good when they're ten.'

'Callum's brother Jaden is good.'

'Is he ten?'

'No, twelve.'

'You've got two years to get good then.'

Max shook his head. 'I can't.'

'Why not?'

'I'm useless.'

Those were Max's father's words, Leon was sure of it. He could almost hear them echoing across the backyard. It reminded him of kicking footies with his dad down on the beach. His dad would yell at him whenever the ball bounced into the water: *Go get it out. Can't you kick straight?* But most of the time they'd had fun knocking a ball around together—it was the way they'd connected when Leon was small. Fishing hadn't worked because he kept tangling the line and losing his tackle on the rocks, so footy had been their best currency. Pity it didn't work anymore. 'I'm all right at footy,' he said to Max. 'I can help, if you want. A bit of practice and you'll improve really fast.'

Max shrugged and put his phone on a fence post so he could eat more chips. 'Are you going to live in that house?'

'Yep. I moved in today.'

'It's haunted, you know. Mrs Westbury died in there. Someone was supposed to check on her, but they forgot. Dad noticed the stink and called the cops. They said she was rotten. Like soup.'

Leon imagined the old lady dead in bed. A heart attack in the middle of the night? Or had she faded slowly away, waiting for help? It was sad no one had been looking out for her. Maybe it was better to be in a home like Grandpa. But, then again, maybe not—Leon hated the hospital-feeling of those places. Maybe Mrs Westbury had preferred to die in her own bed.

A small girl carrying a baby doll emerged from Max's house and came across the lawn. She was brown-eyed, dark-haired and snotty-nosed with a jagged home-cut fringe and a finger up one nostril. Obviously Max's sister: same face shape, same jaw.

'This is Suzie.' Max knocked the little girl's hand from her face. 'Stop picking your nose.'

The blonde woman was watching from the clothesline—she must have heard them talking.

Leon smiled and waved. 'Hi, I'm Leon. Just having a chat with your kids.'

She lit a cigarette and came over. Up close, Leon saw she was younger than he'd thought, not much older than him, only she'd lived harder and had kids. With her blonde hair and blue eyes, she was actually quite pretty, but she looked worn out. 'I'm Wendy,' she said, squinting at him through a curl of smoke. 'You moving in, are you?'

'Yeah. Six-month lease. Just got a new job.'

'Forests?'

'No. Parks. I'm a ranger.'

There was a short silence and Wendy's lips tightened. 'My husband's a logger. Cuts trees on slopes where machines can't go.'

That would explain the chainsaw, Leon thought. 'He's a rare species then. Not too many using chainsaws these days.'

Her mouth twisted. 'You know something about forests?'

'Family history. We go way back. My grandpa was a logger on Bruny Island, and his father before him, and so on. Dad worked at the mill till he nearly cut off his hand.'

'Shame.'

'Yeah. It's been hard on him. Hard on Mum too. Dad hates being on a pension. He'd rather be earning a proper wage.' Leon couldn't believe he was telling Wendy all this. And why was he defending his father? 'Anyway,' he added, 'I'll be cleaning loos and emptying bins.'

Wendy dodged his eyes and passed a hand over her daughter's head. 'I'd better get the kids in for some lunch. And you have to clean up your room, Max.'

As she herded the kids away, Leon spotted Max's phone, still sitting on the fence post. 'Max,' he called. 'You've left your phone. Better grab it in case it rains.'

Wendy clipped Max on the arm. 'If you don't look after that phone, I'm taking it back.'

The boy slouched to the fence and scooped the phone from the post. 'It's not going to rain today anyway,' he grumbled.

Leon felt sorry for him. 'Bring a footy over sometime and we'll have a kick.'

The kid nodded.

Wendy was watching from the front porch, and Leon thought perhaps there was a glimmer of surprise on her face. She slung an arm around Max's shoulders and guided him inside. Leon heard her say, 'How about that, Max? We can get Dad to pump up your footy.'

When they closed the door, Leon was alone again—except for the dog, which looked at him and wagged its tail.

He didn't trust it. He didn't know much about dogs, but he knew one thing: they could look like friends and then bite your hand off.

2

Max didn't want to tidy his room, because that was boring. He couldn't see the point when he was just going to mess it up again. Mum kept going on as if it was important, but the rest of the house wasn't tidy. Not like Robbo's house down the street. His wife, Trudi, kept everything neat. *Just like a display home*, Mum always said. Mum reckoned Trudi had nothing else to do because she didn't have kids and only worked part-time. But Mum didn't work at all, so she should have had plenty of time. Max sometimes wondered what she did all day. He and Suzie weren't hard to look after, so why couldn't she clean his room for him? Max had other stuff to do. Like take the dog for a walk.

He liked taking Rosie for walks on weekends to get away from Mum. He was sick of all the jobs. *Pick up your bike. Put the balls away. Dry the dishes. Put out the rubbish.* The rubbish was Dad's job, only he never did it. And why couldn't Suzie put the balls away? It was easy. And why did he need to pick up his bike anyway? He would use it again tomorrow.

He went out to the shed to get Rosie's lead.

Dad was still working on his chainsaw and he looked grumpy. 'Where do you think you're going?' he said, cigarette bobbing on his lip.

'For a walk with Rosie.'

'No, you're not. It's nearly lunchtime.'

Max dropped the lead on the floor. Rosie would be disappointed; she was watching him with her tail wagging and her mouth in a big happy smile. 'Later,' he said to her. 'Dad says we can't go now.'

Dad shot him a look, but Max just mooched back to the house.

In the lounge room, the TV was on as usual—Mum never turned it off. She said the sound of voices kept her company when no one else would talk to her. Max couldn't understand it. She was on her phone doing Facebook all the time. Wasn't that talking to people? Dad was in the forest all day, so of course he couldn't talk to her. And Max was usually at school. When he was home she kept giving him jobs, so he didn't have time to talk either. And Suzie was only little, so all she did was whinge and cry. What did Mum expect? She should talk to Rosie. You could say anything to dogs and they just listened.

He threw himself on the couch but there was only boring stuff on TV. Car racing and other sports. Max was sick of sport. Mum was banging plates and pots in the kitchen, cooking sausages for lunch—Max could smell them. She popped her head in at the door. 'You ready to eat? Go tell your dad and Suzie.'

Max sighed. Couldn't she see he'd just sat down? He was tired. All that running round at footy this morning. Up and down the field. Never getting the ball. Always losing. He was over it. Adults said winning wasn't everything, but Max knew losing was nothing. He could tell by the way Dad turned away from him after the game. Dad didn't have time for losers.

Lunch was quiet to start with. Dad served himself first because he was man of the house. Then Mum made a sausage sandwich for Suzie, and Max had to wait even though he was starving. When Mum gave him the nod, he grabbed a bit of bread and a sausage and squirted on tomato sauce.

'Go easy,' Mum said. 'You don't need that much.'

Dad frowned. 'Who do you reckon's paying for that sauce?'

Dad ploughed through four sausages, but Max didn't have space for more than two. Then Dad asked him to get a beer from the fridge. He said it all bossy like Max was his slave. Max got up slowly and fetched a can of Cascade for Dad, who opened it and took a swig.

'Who's that new bloke next door?' Dad asked Mum.

'Name's Leon,' Mum said.

'What does he do?'

'Parks ranger.'

'Bullshit.' Dad groaned. 'I don't need a neighbour like that. He'd better not expect me to be nice.'

Max wasn't sure what sort of neighbour Dad thought Leon was. Dad hadn't even spoken to him yet.

'He seems okay,' Mum said. 'He offered to help Max with footy—didn't he, Max?'

'Yeah.' Max was surprised Mum was saying good stuff about Leon. She hadn't been nice to him when they were talking; she hadn't even looked at him. That was what she always told Max to do: *Look at someone when you're speaking to them.* But she didn't do it with Leon.

Dad wagged a finger at Max. 'Don't you go talking to strangers.'

What did Dad mean? It wasn't like Leon was going to kidnap Max or something. And he was more interesting than old Mrs Westbury.

Mum said to Max, 'Ignore your father. Leon's all right. You should go over tomorrow. Take a footy.' She looked at Dad. 'Can you pump up a ball for him?'

'If I can find one. Can't find anything in all that long grass.' Dad was making another sausage sandwich. He squeezed on tons of sauce.

'What are you doing after lunch?' Mum asked Dad.

'Working on the chainsaw, then I have to go to the footy.'

'You said were going to mow the lawn.'

'No time today. Max can do it.'

'But I'm taking Rosie for a walk,' Max said. 'And I can't start the mower.'

'I'll start it up for you,' Dad said. 'You can take Rosie later.'

Max was sick of later. He hated mowing the lawn—that meant he had to pick up all the bikes and scooters and balls. Or maybe he could just mow around them. Wouldn't that be good enough?

Dad stood to go, but Mum said, 'What about all the other jobs you were going to do this weekend?'

'Tomorrow,' he said.

'But you were going to fix the drain and help with the shopping. And the toilet's not flushing properly.'

'Kids use too much toilet paper.'

'It needs to be sorted.'

'Call a plumber.'

'And pay with what money?'

Dad headed for the door.

'If you're not going to help, I'm not cooking tonight.' Mum's voice was getting louder. 'I'm on strike. You'll have to cook.'

The door banged behind Dad. 'It'll be takeaway then,' he yelled.

'Save some money and cook instead.'

'I'm saving money by fixing the chainsaw.'

'I suppose you'll still be fixing it tomorrow.' Mum was screeching now, and Max covered his ears. He hated them arguing. Always about money. That's why Max liked hanging out with Rosie. Dogs didn't make you do jobs or argue or tell you what to do. They were warm and happy and fun. The more he thought about it, the more he liked dogs better than people.

'Your dad's bone-lazy,' Mum muttered. 'Always tomorrow.' She pointed at Max. 'Don't you grow up like that.'

'I don't want to do the lawns,' Max moaned. If he sounded sad enough, maybe Mum would do it for him.

She shrugged. 'No one else to do it. You'd better pick up those bikes first. I don't want a patchy job like last time. And don't forget to tidy your room.'

Max finished his sausage and went to his room. He stuffed his pyjamas under the pillow then tossed some toys in the cupboard and shut the door. Hopefully Mum wouldn't look in there. If the floor was clear, that might be enough. He took some pocket money out of the drawer before fetching Rosie's lead. They would go down to the shop and buy lollies. That would make him feel better.

But Dad had the mower out and was checking the fuel. 'Empty,' he said. He pulled the fuel can from the shelf and shook it, but it was empty too. He shoved the can at Max. 'Go and get it filled up at the servo.'

'It's too heavy,' Max said.

'Take Suzie's pram. You can wheel it back in that.'

'Please, Dad, can you fill it up? Kids aren't allowed.' Max didn't want to be seen with Suzie's pram. Everyone would laugh. Suzie shouldn't have a pram anyway—she was big enough to walk.

Dad opened his pack of cigarettes and took one out. 'Haven't got time to get fuel today,' he said. 'We'll do it tomorrow.'

That sounded good. Mum might not like it, but Max hoped Dad would forget and then Max wouldn't have to do the lawns. He grabbed Rosie's lead, and she trotted up, ready to go. He snapped the lead onto her collar.

'What are you doing?' Dad said.

'Taking Rosie for a walk.'

'Make sure you're back in time for the game.'

'I don't want to go.'

'Bad luck. You're coming. You can watch the big blokes and learn.'

3

At five o'clock, in the takeaway shop in the main street of town, Miki changed her apron ready for the Saturday night rush. This afternoon between customers, she'd swept and mopped the floors, wiped the benches, scraped the grill, fished the burnt bits of batter from the fryer, restocked the fridges and shelves, and topped up the salads. Now there was nothing to do except wait. She leaned against the counter and looked out through the window, watching the world go by.

Her brother Kurt was in the rooms at the back of the shop, where the two of them lived. He was working on the tax and accounts. The tax had been due at the end of last month, but he was slow when it came to paperwork. Miki had offered to do it—she was good at numbers, thanks to all those hours muddling over maths in the kitchen with her mother. But Kurt said it was his job to look after her, and that was the way he planned to keep it. Men's work and women's work separated, just like on the farm. Miki had to use secret ways of keeping in touch with the finances. When they worked together in the shop, she added income in her head while Kurt took payments and counted the cash.

Miki's life had been jobs since she was small. On the farm, she and her mother had shared the domestics. Then Mother's arthritis had worsened, and she'd become heavy and slow, always tired, with sore joints that made kneeling for prayer difficult. Despite constant pain, Mother had still taught Miki's lessons during the week, still enjoyed untangling convoluted maths problems. Miki had spliced her chores between lessons: cooking, cleaning, milking, washing, tending the vegie garden, setting the fire, feeding the chickens, raking up leaves. She was used to working hard.

Now, though, she was nearly eighteen, and the shop was too small for her. She yearned for more involvement and freedom, but Kurt had constructed a scaffolding of rules all around her. She had to minimise interactions with customers. Avoid eye contact. Keep her head down and keep working. Kurt made sure she always had things to do, so the only time she could stop to take a breath was when he was out of the room. He was her guardian, older by a decade, and he was in charge.

Mostly Miki didn't mind the shop—she'd learned to accept it. She'd found it difficult at first, so much more confined than the farm, with less air and less light, and often her chest felt constricted.

On the farm she used to live for Sundays. When the jobs were done, she would switch her skirt for overalls and head for the forest behind the orchard where her heart lifted and freedom beckoned. Kurt always came with her. They would trudge in gumboots past the packing shed with its tractor, tools and cool-room, past the vegetable garden that fed them most of the year, beyond the compost heap of vegie scraps—which, in turn, fed the local wildlife—and into the orchard where old man apple trees raised their gnarled arms to the sky, and grass grew in lush profusion. At the boundary fence the forest waited: shadowy, secretive and inviting. Miki would slip between the wires, while Kurt climbed over a post. They would follow a faint trail up past the beehives and between slender grey-barked eucalypts. As the bush folded around them, Miki would feel lightness on her skin, happiness settling. She loved the swaying skirts of the leaves high above, the squeak of wood rubbing against wood, the sigh of air in the canopy, the crunch of sticks beneath her feet, the minty scent of the scrub. In the bush, she felt more alive, more real. The week fell away and her father's rules faded. She was somebody. Herself. A young woman with hope in the world.

They would walk across-slope to their favourite gully, clambering over fallen trunks laced with moss, crossing a creek where ferns splayed their fronds and large rotting logs made moist chairs to sit on. Often, it was quiet. Grey fantails tinkling. Time and space expanding. There, she and Kurt would become equals for a few hours. Miki would ask him questions. 'How's Father?'—always the same every week. She hoped for meaningful answers, but with Kurt you never knew whether it would be sunshine or storm. He would shrug his broad shoulders. 'Bossy,' he would say. 'His way or the highway.'

She would think of the road leading from the farm, imagine it joining with other roads and then the highway going all the way to Hobart. She'd only been on that road once, when she was seven and Father lost his fingers. But she'd always thought that one day she would walk away from the farm and never return. She hadn't expected it to happen so soon.

Sometimes, they would speak of Mother's arthritis. 'I'm worried,' Miki would say. 'Mother's getting slower. Do you think she needs treatment?'

Kurt would raise his eyebrows. 'You know what she's like. Won't take any poisons. She'd rather live with the pain.'

But that pain had been a rope for Miki. A rope that wound round and round her future, keeping her tied to the farm.

It had always been different for Kurt. The rules had been more flexible for him because he was a boy. He'd gone to school till he was ten, whereas Miki had been home-schooled from the beginning. He'd always had more freedom, driving to town from the farm, buying supplies, meeting people. But Miki hadn't been allowed to leave at all, because Mother and Father said the world wasn't safe for women. They'd spoken of drug addicts and thieves, people without morals or God, men who forced themselves on women, rich people stealing from the poor, women showing too much skin. All evil.

Now Miki knew otherwise. Kurt said the locals and tourists were wicked, but she had studied their lives. She wasn't allowed to leave the shop, but the world came to her. She learned by listening to customers, reading faces, absorbing talk, watching the way people moved, their language and interactions. She recognised regulars by scent. The farm had smelled of grass, mud and manure, the woody aroma of apple trees. Here, everything was more complex and layered. Body odours. Perfumes. Cigarette smoke and food.

Even so, Miki longed to escape. To walk wherever she wanted. Talk to people. Go to school. But Kurt wouldn't allow it. Whenever he went out, he locked her in. He said women needed protection and he was keeping her safe. It was what Father and Mother would have wanted, he insisted. The same applied to school. Kurt said education was overrated for girls. A waste of time. How could Miki explain that she missed her lessons with Mother because she'd enjoyed using her brain?

Eighteen months had passed since the fire, and not a day went by without Miki remembering it. Everything gone in one awful night: her parents, her home and her life. Her family had worked hard to serve God, so surely he should have given them some sort of warning. And yet she'd revisited the day of the fire so many times in her mind and could find nothing that hinted at what was to come. Kurt said this was evidence God didn't exist; if God was real he should have protected them. Her brother had given up religion after that. And, although Miki had felt lost without God at first, a small voice inside her agreed. Had all those hours of prayer counted for nothing? It made no sense to her. If the fire was supposed to be a test of her faith, it had been too much to ask.

How did you recover from a loss so large you could barely believe it? Grief crept up in quiet moments, swamping her like a river in flood. She missed her mother, who'd been patient and kind, so different from Father. He had always been hard and unyielding, but he'd loved her in his own way, and Miki missed him too. At night, she imagined her parents in their burning bedroom. Father trying to help Mother out of bed. The ceiling falling in. Mother's nightie catching fire. Their cries for help drowned by the voice of the flames.

The morning after the blaze, while the chickens pecked around on the lawn, Miki and Kurt had waited for the authorities to leave, then they'd picked through the ruins of the farmhouse, looking for something that had been spared. But there had been nothing left. The scorched chimney. Mounds of twisted tin. Rows of concrete stumps. Bits of molten metal. Glass, melted smooth. Among the rubble, Miki had found the tarnished face of the mantelpiece clock, a broken doll's hand, warped and dinted coins. Holding these things in her soot-smeared hands, she had wept. She could have been walking on her parents' bones.

She had been destroyed by the fire, but life was insistent. In the bed of ashes left behind, a small seed had germinated and fragile fronds of a new beginning had started to unfold. Miki likened herself to a young tree, finding its way to the light. Those first few days, she and Kurt had lived in the shed, eating eggs and tins of baked beans heated in a pan over the gas cooker the men used for melting wax to graft shoots in the orchard. Once or twice, Miki had seen a car drive slowly by, possibly neighbours. But no one came in. Visitors to the farm had never been encouraged.

On the third day, Miki had huddled in a nest of blankets, while Kurt pored over the papers from the black leather folder he'd saved from the fire. She'd asked to see the papers too, but he had waved her away, saying she didn't need to worry about such things; he would take care of it. But she kept thinking of Father and that folder, how important it had been to him, the way he'd carried it with as much respect as his Bible. He'd never left it lying around, and she hadn't known where he'd kept it—so how had Kurt known where to find it?

Here, Kurt kept the folder hidden away too, possibly in the locked room under the shop where the fizzy drink was stored, and where he liked to retreat for some peace. Kurt said the folder was their ticket to the future, so he had to look after it. Miki couldn't imagine what might be in there—maybe his chequebooks and the lease for the shop. What else could there be?

After the fire, Kurt had wanted to stay on the farm. He'd planned to transform the shed into a home and have Miki help in the orchard. But when he'd visited the bank and discovered the farm was in debt, the only solution was to sell. With barely any money after settlement, the lease on this shop was all they could afford. Since then, they'd been working five days a week, seven in the morning till eight-thirty at night. It was a source of income, which they needed, and close to the forest, which they loved. And the shop had been successful. Kurt had bought furniture, a large colour TV, a new ute, gym equipment. He said they had savings and were on their way to having a deposit for their own farm. She knew he was devastated by the loss of the family property and couldn't wait to take back what had been theirs.

He emerged now from the rear of the shop as the first evening customers came in: big tattooed Toby from the mill with his tribe of four children. Toby was a giant of a man, with a bald head and a bushy beard like a nest of lichen draped from his chin. Weekdays, he smelled of sawdust and sweat, but weekends he wore aftershave with a hint of oranges, just like the cleaner Miki used on the floors. At a nod from Kurt, she lowered her eyes and stepped aside so he could take the order. He was gruff: 'What do you want?'—Miki would have done it differently.

Toby didn't bother with niceties either. 'Family pack of fish and chips and twelve potato cakes.' He frowned. 'How many bits of fish do I get?'

'Five. Same as always.'

'But there's six of us. Me and Steph and the kids.'

'Want an extra piece then?'

'How much are you going to charge me for it?'

'Prices are on the board.'

Miki would have added an extra fillet anyway; this was a weekly argument. The men bristled like dogs in the street even when there was nothing to fight over. Kurt charged Toby for six fillets while Miki slipped in a seventh and sank the frying basket into the oil. When Kurt's back was turned, Toby winked. He knew she was neutral territory.

Miki liked Toby because, although he looked ferocious, he was kind to his children. He wore T-shirts even in winter so you could see his tattoos. An ink snake wound from one arm to the other across his shoulders; Miki had seen the whole thing one time when he'd come in bare-chested on a hot day. He had a tiger on one bulging thigh, a red devil on the other, and more tattoos filling the spaces between. Now he thumbed through magazines from the rack while his children eyed off the lollies and Kurt glared at them.

Hiding her smile, Miki watched the fish and chips frying, bubbles rising, the soft hiss of boiling oil. She hummed along with the drone of the fume hoods. When the batter was golden, she tipped the order onto paper, dashed on a shower of salt and wrapped it quickly so Kurt wouldn't see the extra piece of fish. Then she gave the bundle to Kurt, who handed it over to Toby.

Miki found it easy to carry out small deceptions like this. When Kurt was in the shop, he manned the counter, taking orders and handling the money to protect her from exposure to locals. With his back to her most of the time, it wasn't hard for her to manipulate orders. She did it to make up for the way he treated customers; her little gifts were surely one of the reasons people kept coming back to their shop.

The next customer was blond-headed Mooney with his two little daughters. He had a strong smell that no deodorant could disguise. Miki didn't understand how someone could look angelic when he clearly wasn't. It didn't make sense that this good-looking man with his smooth face, tanned skin and silvery blue eyes could beat his wife, Liz—whereas thug-like Toby was kind and thoughtful. Miki had heard the women talking while waiting for morning coffees after school drop-offs. *Mooney's up to his old tricks again. Have you seen poor Liz? A black eye this time, patched up with makeup. Last time it was bruises round her neck. I saw them under her scarf.* Miki never gave Mooney extras, saving them till Liz and their girls came in without him.

She had just lowered Mooney's order into the fryer when more people crowded in, and the Saturday night rush was on. Customers chatted while they waited, dissecting the footy and the weather. *See that screamer Toby took today. Bloody amazing. What about Mooney's goal just before half-time? The man's a champion.*

Saturday was known as Mum's Night Off, and for the men that meant buying takeaway. Most ordered fish and chips or burgers, but some even bought salad. Occasionally strangers would lob in, couples or groups in fleeces and beanies, people who'd been hiking up in the park. They were friendlier than the locals because they didn't know Kurt. He treated them the same, and when they fled with their orders Miki knew they wouldn't be back. That was why she courted the locals with extras. Fortunately there wasn't much choice for fast food—if you didn't buy here, it was twenty minutes to the next town. Saturdays, most of the men drank a few beers, and they didn't want to drive and risk getting caught. Miki had heard the women talking about how *the rot set in after the footy.* Sometimes it started down at the oval, sometimes in someone's backyard, sometimes at the pub. The local policemen weren't very strict—it was common knowledge that a warning was as far as it went. The police had to live in town too, so they let things slide, even when Mooney laid into Liz. Miki wished they would take action on that. But Liz was good at hiding things. And maybe the police didn't hear gossip. In a way, they were outsiders around here too, just like Miki.

Just as she was thinking this, one of the local policemen strode in: Fergus Connolly, with his boys, Jaden and Callum. He was out of uniform but a hush still fell over the shop. He loudly said hello, and everyone stood aside to let him through. During the week, he smelled of shaving cream and soap, but on weekends Miki always caught beer on his breath. Usually he was strict on his boys, but after a few drinks he stopped noticing their behaviour and the big boy, Jaden, had a tendency to get out of hand. Miki didn't like the way he pinched and hassled his younger brother.

A stranger slipped in during the rush—Miki noticed him because it was late for out-of-towners, who mostly came mid-afternoon. He was maybe mid-twenties, lean and fit-looking, with messy orange hair, pale skin, a snub nose and crinkles at the corners of his eyes. She saw him nod at Shane and Max, who were waiting for their Saturday night family pack. Max offered him a lolly, which was unusual—the boy generally held tight to his sweets. While she was measuring out chips and dipping fish in batter, Miki heard the stranger ask for a burger with the lot but no pineapple, and she had the meat patty on the hotplate before Kurt had even handed her the order. She was proud of her efficiency and liked being organised. But it was often boring in the shop. Five long days a week cooking and cleaning. Only one day out of here, when she and Kurt went up to the forest on Mondays. Tuesdays sitting around while he went to Hobart. No one to talk to.

As she cooked and wrapped and delivered orders, Miki noticed the way the men looked slantwise at the red-headed stranger and sidled away from him. Even in the busy shop he seemed lonely. She knew how that felt, so she made his burger with special care and slid a Freddo Frog into the bag before putting it on the counter. Hopefully the chocolate wouldn't melt. It would be a nice surprise when he opened his meal.

At eight-thirty, after the last customer had been served, Kurt locked the front door and started counting the money. This was Miki's signal to clean up. She turned off the fryers and fume hoods, covered the salads and slid them into the fridges, mopped the floors, wiped the counter, and restocked the drinks from crates in the kitchen. Then she made steak sandwiches for dinner, and they sat at one of the shop tables to eat.

This was their usual Saturday night routine. After their meal they would go to the tip. The garbage wouldn't wait till Thursday; they needed bin-space for tomorrow when the Sunday tourists flocked into town.

While Kurt carted the rubbish out and tossed it on the back of the ute, Miki collected the meat scraps she'd saved during the day and put them in a plastic bag. Then she changed into overalls and slipped the bag into her pocket.

The tip was on a gravel side street at the edge of town, and Kurt always drove the rough road too fast. This evening, he swung through the open gate and sped to their usual spot beneath the fluorescent light near a large mound of garbage, pulling up so sharply Miki jolted in her seat. Kurt was laughing as he jumped out and dragged the rubbish bags off, tossing them onto the heap where they split open and leftovers surged out, cans and bottles and wrappers. 'That was funny,' he said. 'You should have seen your face while you were trying to hold on.'

Miki hadn't been laughing, but now she smiled too. Kurt's moments of humour were rare since the fire, so it was important to make the most of them. It helped her survive darker times.

She clambered onto the ute with an old straw broom to sweep off the remnants of rubbish, while Kurt climbed a pile of dirt to make phone calls. It was the same every Saturday; he would spend nearly an hour up there, attending to his business interests in Hobart. Often she would try to eavesdrop, but he kept his voice low and scowled at her if she came too close. Investments and decision-making were for men, he said. Women were destined to serve.

Miki used this time to explore. Once the tray was swept, she took the torch from the ute and set off among the garbage. The stench of rotting rubbish was horrible, but she didn't mind. She was outside, away from the shop, and the food scraps at the tip attracted plenty of wildlife. Coming here was a highlight of her week.

As she wandered away from the ute, her eyes adjusted to the darkness, and she began to see small scurrying movements among the trash. When something rattled, she swung her torch to a spotty quoll dragging a piece of paper with its teeth. It froze in the light, eyes wide. Slowly, Miki pulled out a chunk of meat from the plastic bag in her pocket, and lobbed it towards the quoll, but it ran away, a shadow slipping over a mound. Then it reappeared, snatched the meat, gulped it down and glanced at her briefly before scuffling away again.

Quolls used to visit the chicken coop on the farm, but they killed the chickens and ate the eggs, so Father and Kurt shot them. Miki hated that the quolls murdered chickens and left them strewn in bits across the yard, but killing quolls didn't fix anything—they needed to eat too. After Kurt had shot the fourth quoll and strung it up on the fence, Miki had quietly spent a few afternoons roofing the coop with wire. She'd also filled the holes under the fence with rocks. Then there had been no more dead chickens or quolls.

She liked the quolls and their pretty spotted coats, but the Tasmanian devils were her favourites. They used to visit the farm too; she would hear them at night, shrieking and growling like monsters up near the shed and off in the forest. Father always complained about the mess they made of the compost heap. Devils sounded large and frightening, but they were only the size of a small dog. Miki liked them because they were feisty. They had black fur, bulbous noses, pink ears and whiskered muzzles, and a family of them lived here at the tip: two adults and three young. There used to be more, but last year the other two adults had developed sores on their faces then disappeared. Miki had persuaded herself they'd run away, but she was afraid they might have died.

Near the devils' hangout, she squatted and made a line of meat scraps on the ground, then turned off her torch to wait. If the devils came out, she would ride on the thrill of it for a week.

After a while she saw movement in the shadows and a black shape loomed from the darkness. It was the female devil; Miki recognised the white crescent moon on her chest. The devil loped closer and stopped, forepaw raised, then sniffed the air and yawned, wide jaws and white teeth. Three small black youngsters scuttled to join her and snuffed across to the meat, hissing and gurgling as they wolfed it down.

Cross-legged on the dirt, Miki switched on her torch. The devils moved off a little, then the mother lay down and the young ones played around her like puppies, climbing over her, biting her face, ignoring her warnings. They were like children in the shop, Miki thought, scrapping over lollies, hitting their siblings, dragging at their mums. The mother devil growled at her babies, but she put up with their nips and bites and squabbles. Her patience made Miki think of her own mother because, unlike the devils, Miki and her mother had got along well—working together in the kitchen, kneading bread, churning butter, baking cakes. Evenings they'd sat by the fire knitting, while Father read aloud from the Bible and Kurt carved pieces of wood he'd found in the forest.

Miki had been friends with her mother, but Kurt and Father had clashed frequently, arguing over everything—farming techniques, decisions, even minor procedures in the orchard. They were too much alike, Miki thought. Both keen for power.

A new rattling sound in the rubbish announced the arrival of the male devil. He was making a grand entry, like most of the men Miki knew. He hissed loudly when he saw Miki, but quickly grew bold and moved in on the other devils, grumbling and complaining. The female tucked in her head and shrieked at him, like the mothers in the shop telling off their husbands. But the male devil yelled back, startling the little ones. He was like Father and Kurt. Bossy and overbearing. *My way or the highway.*

The female devil took off with her young towards the rear of the tip while the male sniffed around in the torchlight. Miki saw scratches on his face and ears, a small sore on his lip—devils were always fighting. After a while he loped away, and soon she heard more screeching as he caught up with the others in the rubble. It sounded like a family argument, and Miki couldn't help smiling. Maybe that was the way of all animals.

4

When Leon opened his door Sunday morning, Max was on the doorstep with a football under his arm. Leon was still busy cleaning, so it was a bit inconvenient. And from the slumped way the kid was standing, Max didn't seem keen either—Wendy must have pushed him into coming over. But now Max was here, there was no dodging the fact that a ball must be kicked, and Leon had better make it fun—he was the one who'd invited the boy.

'All right,' he said. 'Front yard or back?'

Max shrugged. 'Somewhere Dad can't see.'

The slope of the block was a problem, but Leon figured the front yard was best because it was less visible from Shane's shed. If he took the downhill side, he could stop the ball from bouncing onto the road. Not that much traffic came along here; after Leon's place, the road turned to dirt.

They found a suitable spot to one side of the woodpile that the delivery truck had dumped on the driveway yesterday. Leon was lining up his first kick when his phone rang. He dropped the footy to the ground, mouthed *sorry* to the kid and tugged the phone from his pocket. It was his mum.

'Hi, Mum,' he said. 'Everything okay at home?'

She gave a small laugh. 'Same, same.'

'Great.'

A pause. 'Actually, do you know if we have any rat baits? I heard rats in the roof last night, so I'll have to put some baits in the ceiling.'

Leon felt bad. This was a job he usually did for her. 'There's a box of baits in the cupboard out in the garage. Any chance Dad could help you?'

'He's not strong enough to get out of bed.'

'Sorry I can't do it for you.'

'Don't worry, Leon. I can manage. I'm not completely incapable, you know.'

Leon smiled. 'Anything else?'

'No. That's it.'

'Okay. I'll be off then. I'm playing footy with the boy next door.' He slotted his phone in his pocket and picked up the ball.

'Let's start with handballing,' he said, knocking the footy to Max.

The kid managed to catch it, but his body language smacked of self-doubt, and Leon knew it would take some work to build up his confidence. He punched another easy pass, and this time Max fumbled the ball to the ground and was immediately downcast. 'See,' he said, 'I told you I'm useless.'

'No, you're not. There's a better way to hold your hands so you can catch it. Like this.' Leon showed him. 'Now let's try again.' He stayed close and passed short, looping balls that were simple to catch.

After a few successes, Max's face started to light up. Then he dropped one again and kicked at the grass. 'Bloody ball. It's such a stupid shape.'

'Yes, it is. But we can't change that, so we just have to go with it. When the ball hits the ground, you have to guess which way it's going to bounce—that's half the fun. Sometimes you it right. Sometimes you get it wrong. And when you get it wrong, you just have to laugh. Now pass the ball back to me.'

Max punched it high, and Leon feigned a miss. He let the ball bounce and did a dive to the wrong side, allowing the ball to roll down the hill. Then he leaped up and raced after it, scooping it up and punching a high lob back to Max, who was laughing. 'Get under it,' Leon called. 'That's the way. Get your arms ready and it won't hurt.'

The boy seemed to surprise himself by gathering the ball to his chest.

'See?' Leon said. 'When you get your hands right and get in position, it isn't so hard.'

They worked on handballs for a while, Leon gradually increasing the distance between them and the difficulty of the passes, so Max caught most of them and missed just a few. Then they moved on to kicking. Leon punted a short ball, which Max marked easily. Then the boy took hold of the ball, screwed up his face and rammed his foot at it, sending it curving and spinning way off to one side. Leon tried to defuse the kid's dismay by clowning around, but the bad kick was obviously a blow to Max's pride and Leon could see he was ready to go home.

'Hang on,' Leon said. 'Let's not finish like that.' He retrieved the ball and demonstrated the best way to hold it, hands wrapped around the contours, fingers spread. 'I'm going to show you some tricks. And if you're willing to work with me each day, then you're going to improve.'

'How soon?' Max asked, bottom lip jutting.

'A couple of weeks.'

'What if I can't come every day?'

'Then it might take a bit longer.'

The boy nodded. 'Show me again and I'll have another go.'

Leon set the kid up, and Max booted the ball over the fence and ran home after it, happy to be let off the hook.

Neighbourly duties completed, Leon strolled down the street to buy lunch. Last night's burger had been tasty, and there had also been that chocolate frog—he hadn't had one of those since he was a kid. The man behind the counter hadn't been friendly, so the girl must have given it to him. Had it been a mistake?

The takeaway shop was halfway down the street between the supermarket and the bank. *Mullers Takeaway* in yellow capital letters on the front window, and beneath that: *Good Food Fast.* Inside, it seemed very ordinary. Bain-marie and high counter. Salad bar. Stainless-steel fryers and fume hoods. A few tables and chairs. Fridges stacked with drinks. The mandatory racks of chips, chocolates and lollies. But that was where the ordinary ended and the unusual began. On shelves above the magazine rack were tubs of honey for sale, and carefully laid-out knitted goods with prices pinned to them—beanies, tea-cosies, socks, booties, doilies, baby clothes, tiny little dresses and jumpers, stuffed toys—the kind of things his grandma would have made when she was still alive. Leon had seen craft like this in country stores before, but never in a takeaway shop.

He scanned the chalkboard menu to see if he'd missed anything last night, but it was the usual takeaway fare: fish and chips, burgers, steak sandwiches, pies and sausage rolls. In the bain-marie: slices of battered pineapple, crab sticks, potato cakes, Chiko rolls. An array of salads at six dollars for a medium tub, nine dollars for a large. The young woman from yesterday was behind the counter, staring at him boldly with big blue eyes. Leon felt awkward. She looked very young—a teenager—with few social skills, apparently. And she was wearing a long, heavy, old-fashioned skirt and a shapeless pink blouse tucked in at the waist, like someone from a bygone era, plaits twisted on top of her head like a halo. 'Who's the knitter?' he asked, pointing at the shelves of woollen goods.

'Me,' she said.

This struck him as strange. Most teenagers were into phones, not knitting needles.

'How can I help?' she asked, wiping her hands on an apron tied round her small waist.

'I'll have fish and chips. What kind of fish do you have?'

She indicated the board. 'Flake, trevalla and flathead.'

'Anything fresh?'

'No, but the flake is good.'

'I don't want to eat shark. They're overfished. I don't want to support that.'

Her eyes widened. 'Maybe you could try the flathead. It's usually nice.'

'Okay. I'll have that.'

She measured out a serve of chips and dipped the fish in batter before lowering it into the fryer. 'You were here last night, weren't you?' she said, turning back to him.

'Yes, the burger was good. Oh, hey, and thanks for the Freddo.'

'Did the chocolate melt?' She seemed concerned about this.

'No. It was fine.'

'Oh, good.'

'Do you do give frogs to everyone?' he asked.

She shrugged. 'Some of the time.'

'Well, if we're on a chocolate-frog basis, I'd better introduce myself. I'm Leon. I've just moved into town.'

'I'm Mikaela,' she said. 'But you can just call me Miki.'

'Hey, Miki. Nice to meet you.'

She gave a small smile and swivelled to check the fish and chips.

'What's it like living around here?' he asked.

She glanced to the rear of the shop as if she was expecting someone. 'I like it,' she said quietly. 'The forest is nice. And the sky walk is supposed to be amazing.'

'You haven't been? Isn't that the main attraction around here?'

'My brother hasn't taken me yet. Maybe one day.' She turned back to the fryer and gave his order a shake.

'That guy yesterday was your brother?'

'Yes. Kurt.'

'What do you do when you're not working? Are you still at school?'

'No.'

'Wow, you look young to have finished.'

'I didn't.'

'But you went to school around here?'

'No. I was home-schooled.'

Leon couldn't get his head around this. 'All the way through?'

'I stopped when I was sixteen, when we came here.'

She turned pink, and Leon wondered if he'd overstepped the mark. 'Sorry. I didn't mean to pry.'

She drained the oil from the frying basket and turned his fish and chips onto paper. 'Salt?'

'Yes, please.'

She flicked it on, added a few slices of lemon, then wrapped the order with deft hands. There was a noise out the back, and she cast an anxious glance towards the rear door as it opened and her brother came in. Leon hadn't realised yesterday what a big guy he was, intimidatingly tall with hair cut short and eyes wide apart. He was muscular—maybe he worked out—and right now he was clearly unhappy. He glared at Miki, who dropped her eyes and picked up a cloth to wipe down the bench. Leon felt himself being inspected too, and knew he'd been judged and found lacking. But he met the big man's eyes and would not look away.

'Hurry up, will you?' Kurt grunted at Miki. 'You're taking forever.'

'It's okay,' Leon said. 'We're done. I'm just heading out.' Miki took his payment, her brother watching like a hawk guarding prey. It was unsettling. Leon pocketed his change and smiled at her as if nothing was out of the ordinary. 'Thanks,' he said. 'I'll see you another time.' Poor kid. Her brother didn't cut her much slack.

He ate his fish and chips on a bench seat further down the street, surprised to discover Miki had given him two pieces of fish when he'd only paid for one. He couldn't work out when she'd added the extra. Hadn't he been watching her batter the fish? He was sure he'd seen her every move.

While he was eating, Max came down the street with Rosie, whose belly seemed even bigger today. The kid tied the dog outside the takeaway, went inside and came out with a bulging bag of lollies. Leon waved, but Max didn't see him—he was too busy plunging a hand in the bag to pull out a sweet.

Two other boys arrived while Max was untying the dog: a skinny kid like Max, and an older boy with a pimply face. When the bigger boy tapped Max on the shoulder, Max gave him a handful of lollies. Then Max high-fived the smaller boy and took off up the street with the dog.

Something about Max's rapid departure made Leon think he didn't like the big boy. Looking at his smug face, Leon decided he didn't like him either.

5

The old people's home where Grandpa lived was down by the water, a fifteen-minute drive from Leon's new town. It was an imposing building that overlooked the wide silver stretch of the river: a view probably wasted on a good portion of its inhabitants. Leon felt bad that he hadn't visited in years, but he hated the place. It was the smell. When he opened the door, there it was: the stench of disinfectant, musty clothes and sour skin, exactly the same as last time. He hated the decor too—it tried hard to be cheery but was fake and depressing, just one step away from a hospital.

In the foyer, he realised he'd forgotten the way to Grandpa's room, so he had to ask at reception. The woman behind the desk was plump and middle-aged. Her name tag read Maryanne, and she was all red-lipstick smiles as she led him down the corridor. Leon ran a hand along the railing, which was there to help shipwrecked oldies who'd lost their sea legs. The walls were white, and it was deathly quiet. Was anyone alive in here? Maybe they were sleeping. Maybe it was that time of day.

Maryanne pointed out Grandpa's room, then retreated, her dimples deepening. 'He'll be so happy to see you.'

Leon tapped on the door. No answer. He knocked louder; Grandpa was a bit deaf. Still no response, so he opened the door and peered in. There was the old man, hunched on a large armchair with a checked woollen blanket tucked round his knees. He was thinner than Leon remembered, and his eyes lit up at the sight of a visitor. 'I thought I heard someone. Is that you, Leon?'

'Yeah, it's me, Grandpa.'

'Come on in.'

The room was as bland as a motel suite. Leon hoped never to live in a place like this, but Grandpa didn't seem to mind. After Grandma died, years ago, he hadn't coped on his own, so he'd moved in here where his meals were cooked and his washing was done and there was help if he needed it. It suited him, Leon supposed.

Grandpa was chuffed to see him and kept shaking his head. 'It's been a long time. Come closer, boy. Let me have a look at you.' He examined Leon through Coke-bottle glasses. 'You haven't grown any.'

Leon smiled. 'You didn't break any height records either.'

'No, and now I'm shrinking. Just you wait—it's all ahead of you.' Grandpa sniffed. 'Still got your red hair.'

'Yep. Walker through and through.'

Inspection over, Grandpa's eyes narrowed. 'Why are you here? Has somebody died?'

'No. I just came to see you.'

'What for? Do you want to talk about my will?'

'I'm being sociable.'

'Ha!' the old man barked. 'Nobody comes to be sociable.'

'*I* do. I'm turning a new page. Starting today.'

Grandpa grunted. 'Come to check me out, have you? Your mother says you've developed an interest in old people lately. It's about time. Can't remember the last time I saw you.'

Leon sat on the edge of the bed. 'Yeah, sorry. I've been slack.'

'I hear you've got a new job. Working in forests? Better be careful. It's dangerous.'

'You did it for years.'

'I was lucky. Survived some near misses. Your father wasn't so lucky, though. If he hadn't hurt his hand, he'd still be working.' He paused. 'Would you like a cup of tea?'

'Sure,' Leon said, 'why not?'

Grandpa's face creased into a grin. 'Good. You can make it. Jug's in the bathroom, and the tea bags are on that chest of drawers. I'll have one too. Tea always tastes better when it's made by someone else.'

The bathroom ponged of disinfectant and tacky air freshener. Leon filled the jug at the basin, which had bits of whiskers in it and a clump of toothpaste. He set the jug on to boil then wiped down the basin, straightened the towel and picked up the bathmat left screwed up on the floor. He couldn't help himself; when he was a teenager, his mother had insisted on tidiness. She'd said she was training him to be a good husband one day.

'Tell me about your job,' Grandpa called from his chair.

Leon went back to join him. 'Not working in forests. I'm with Parks.'

'Ah! And what does your father think about that?'

'He loves it.' Leon perched on the bed again.

'I don't believe you. He'd be saying you ought to be knocking trees down, not locking them up.'

'Yep. That's his mantra.'

'But the park's in the high country, so why would he care? Only wind and crows up there. Nothing worth cutting.'

'I'm breaking family tradition, Grandpa. Dad says I should have a chainsaw in my hands.'

Grandpa shook his head. 'But they don't use chainsaws anymore. It's all machines.'

'Who told you that?' Leon was surprised—the old coot couldn't have been up to the forest in years.

'I have a friend who keeps an eye on things,' Grandpa said. 'He's a bit more mobile than me, and he goes for a drive in the forest every month then calls me up and gives me the lowdown.' He shook his head. 'I wouldn't work in the industry now if you paid me. It's changed too much. Vandalism, if you ask me. My mate thinks so too. The forest is overcut, that's a fact. Young blokes these days don't know what it used to be like, so they can't see what they're doing. If they asked us old codgers, we'd tell them to stop. They've overdone it now.'

'Maybe they could switch to plantations.'

'Could. But won't.'

'Why not?'

'Ideology.'

'Isn't that politics?'

'Forestry is politics. Back in my day it was just a job.'

The kettle boiled, spitting water all over the basin, and Leon went to turn it off. 'You need a better kettle,' he said.

'That'd cost money. Unless it's totally broke, they won't fix it. That would be *unnecessary expenditure*.'

'I'll buy you one then. Next time I come.'

The old man snorted. 'You won't come again.'

Leon poured hot water over the tea bags. 'Yeah? Well, get ready. I'm close by, and I'm going to be your new best friend. I might even take you for a drive in the forest sometime.'

The old man perked up at the suggestion of an outing. 'That'd be good. I hardly ever get out. Your mother used to take me for a spin every now and then. More than I can say for your father.'

Leon paused. 'You heard from Dad lately?'

Grandpa's face fell. 'No. It's usually your mother who rings.'

'She rings me too,' Leon said, grinning. 'Sometimes I wish she wouldn't.'

'Still not weaned?'

'Not completely.' Leon sipped tea and changed the subject. 'How long have you lived in this place?'

'Best part of a decade. I've seen a few inmates come and go.'

'Inmates? It's not supposed to be a prison.'

'Not supposed to be, but it is. They lock the doors so the fruit loops can't get out.'

'Be careful,' Leon warned. 'You might become one.'

'If I do, you'll have to put me down.'

'And spend the rest of my life in jail for murder?'

'Either that or you could spend your life with a woman. Any girls on the scene?'

Leon scoffed. 'Yeah. Mum's cat Minnie.' It was supposed to be funny, but it sounded sad.

'I was referring to females of the human variety,' Grandpa said.

Leon shook his head.

'*I'm* on the lookout,' the old man said, eyes lively. 'This place is full of prospects.'

Leon was appalled. 'What about Grandma?'

'She's been dead a good while. I don't think she'd mind.'

'Good luck to you then.'

Grandpa peered at him. 'What will you do if you're not going to chase girls? How will you entertain yourself?'

'I'll find something to do. Maybe a bit of bushwalking.'

'How about footy? You could join the local club and meet a few chaps. You used to be good at it. Your dad said you were a handy winger.'

Leon shrugged.

'How is your father?' Grandpa asked.

Leon wasn't sure how much Grandpa knew. 'His liver's stuffed, you know.'

Grandpa nodded. 'An infection, your mother said. Some sort of virus.'

Leon hesitated. Obviously she hadn't told Grandpa the truth. 'Ah, I think it's more than that.'

The old man regarded him with interest. 'Yes?'

'He's been pissing on for years, Grandpa. He's got cirrhosis.'

'Hmm. I had my suspicions.' Grandpa eyed him keenly. 'Is that all?'

Leon wasn't sure he should reveal the rest. Not on his first visit. 'That's about it.'

But the old man was shrewd. 'It's not, is it?'

Leon sighed. 'How well do you know your son?'

'Not so well these days. He never talks to me. Must be allergic to the phone.'

'He's allergic to more than that.'

'Housework? I wouldn't be surprised.'

'No. He's allergic to being nice. To being decent.'

'To you or to your mother?'

'Both. I don't care how he treats me. But I care about him being a bastard to Mum. I was there to put myself in the way.'

Grandpa's eyebrows lifted. 'Has he hurt your mother?' Leon's silence was his answer, and Grandpa's lips flattened. 'Well, I'm not so sorry to hear about his liver then. Sounds like he had it coming.' The old man paused. 'So that's why you've been living at home. I should have guessed. I thought it was strange.' He shook his head. 'I never thought one of mine would end up like that. But let me tell you, boy, it didn't come from me. I was wild when I was young, and I did some fool things, but I never touched a hair on your grandmother's head. Don't know where your father learned that rubbish. I smacked him a few times when he was a boy. But it was only a tap on the bum. It wasn't abuse.'

Leon had often wondered where his father's violence had come from, whether it was genetic, and he'd spent years worrying it might be in him too. A person might not realise they had mongrel inside till they snapped. Leon had seen how it came from nowhere then disappeared. His dad's weakness was failing to acknowledge it, because that allowed him to avoid taking responsibility. Or perhaps that wasn't quite right. In the past, his dad had apologised to his mum, begging forgiveness and promising it wouldn't happen again. But it had, and that was what Leon feared most: snapping once and falling into his dad's habit. If he did, he would never forgive himself. That was why he didn't drink, a decision he'd made years ago.

He sipped tea in silence, grateful that the old man let him be. He was comfortable with Grandpa, so he would visit again. Maybe drop in once a week on his way home from work. They could get to know each other again.

A buzzer rang in the corridor.

'Supper's in ten minutes,' Grandpa said. 'You'll have to go. Can't miss out on my fruit cake.'

'That sounds all right. What's the food like here?'

'Good, if you have no teeth. They serve up slop. Except for the fruit cake.'

Leon smiled. 'Do you still have any teeth?'

'Yep . . . even a few I can call my own.' The old man shifted his tongue and popped out a denture.

'That's revolting.'

'Let's see how many you've got left when you're eighty-six.'

The buzzer sounded again, and Leon stood up. 'Okay. I'll see you next week.'

Grandpa's lips twitched and his face crumpled slightly. 'You don't have to come, lad.'

'Maybe I want to.'

Leon patted the old man on the arm, but Grandpa waved him off. 'Go on with you or I'll be late for my cake.' He sounded gruff, but as Leon paused at the door he noticed tears in his grandfather's eyes.

6

Monday was forest day, and Miki woke with lightness fizzing under her skin. Kurt wanted to check the beehives, so they left in the ute early. Miki was in overalls, and Kurt was in hunting clothes: dark-green knitted jumper, khaki trousers, black beanie crammed over his ears, rifle stashed in the back so he could go shooting later.

They drove towards the school, past a group of boys lugging schoolbags. Miki saw Max among them; he was walking with the policeman's younger son, Callum. As Kurt's ute roared by, Max looked up at Miki and waved. Behind him, Callum's big brother, Jaden, booted Max's backpack so it bounced up, hit his head and almost made him tip over. It upset Miki when Jaden hassled the younger boys. He did it in the shop all the time, using size to get his own way. His father should do something to keep him in line.

From town, the road rolled through open country and green hilly farms, past the sawmill where the whine of machinery and smell of sawdust hung in the air, and workers' cars huddled beside the corrugated-iron shed. Miki hated the mill because it ate trees. Every day, truck-loads of logs came down from the forest:

mostly skinny logs destined for woodchipping, but many large old trees too—ancient swamp gums that had been growing for centuries. Miki couldn't work out why the loggers kept cutting wood when endless piles of sawn timber sat at the mill, waiting to be taken away. Over weeks and months, she'd watched those piles slowly turn black and then silver.

The forest was close to town, not far from the sawmill, and when they drove into its misty shadows, Miki lowered her window to let in some air. Water swished under the tyres and the wet trees smelled minty and fresh. She was grateful to be out today. Kurt had been dour this morning, and sometimes when he was in a mood he made her stay home. She wasn't sure why he was so grumpy. Last night he'd worked late on the paperwork, and this afternoon he would go to Hobart for business, which always made him surly. But his current sullenness was out of character—usually their expeditions to the forest made him happy. Something was bothering him. Either it would blow over or he would erupt like a spring storm. Miki knew it was best to keep out of his way when he was like this; she had learned how to make herself small.

He was hunkered over the steering wheel, brow furrowed. 'Who was that guy you were talking to in the shop yesterday?' he grunted. 'The redhead at lunchtime.'

So that explained Kurt's anger. 'I don't know,' she said. 'I think he's new to town.'

'Making him feel welcome, were you? Having a nice little chat?'

Miki's skin tightened. 'He did the talking. I was only being polite.'

'Forget polite. You should have called me. Why didn't you?'

'You were doing the books.' Last week she'd been in trouble for disturbing him.

'I don't want you talking to scum, so don't.'

He glared at her and she felt herself shrivel. Her heartbeat accelerated and her palms prickled. 'I'll call you next time,' she promised.

She held her breath and waited. It could go one of two ways: either he would start shouting, or it would be suddenly over.

As the moments slid by, she realised he'd let it go.

They turned off the main road onto a gravel track that wound through regrowth forest crammed with tall, skinny saplings. Potholes jolted the car and, despite being locked in by her seatbelt, Miki had to cling on so she wasn't bounced around. Trees hugged the edge of the track, impenetrably dense. She could imagine getting lost in forest like this: you might never find a way out.

They came to a patch of old-growth with towering trees. Here, the understorey opened out, and the forest was park-like and stately. Miki loved the tall swamp gums jutting into the sky. Tree ferns splayed their fronds. Pockets of beech were just beginning to turn golden—the only deciduous trees in the forest. Over the next few weeks, they would yellow up then drop their leaves. Autumn was definitely here.

Further into the forest, she wound her window right down and leaned out so she could see way up to the wedge-tailed eagles' nest: a messy platform of sticks and bark woven onto a branch. Kurt said there weren't many wedge-tails left in Tasmania, so this nest was special. Miki thought the birds magnificent with their proud heads and hooked beaks. The view from their tree must be amazing: the forest stretching all around, layered and complex, like life. Last spring, the eagles had raised a chick; Miki had seen its doddery head just above the lip of the nest, peering out at the world. The adult birds were wild and free, but the chick was like her, watching from its nest, unable to join in till its wings were fully grown.

Driving on through the forest, they came to another patch of old-growth, where broad tree trunks reached high and lost themselves among clouds.

'These trees must be hundreds of years old,' Miki said.

Kurt sniffed. 'Only takes a few minutes to cut them down.'

Miki felt a surge of passion. 'I wish I could buy the whole forest and lock everyone out so all the trees could just do their thing and grow up to the light. No one ever chopping them down. Then everything could go back to how it was before white people came.'

'The Earth is here for us to use,' Kurt said.

'But not to wreck. Look at this!'

They'd crossed a boundary into a blitzed area, recently logged. More than a year since the loggers had finished their work, but everything was still a terrible mess. Barely a tree left standing. Only a few exposed spindly specimens and a cluster of scraggly tree ferns. Piles of bark and branches, waiting to be burned. The whole place was a scar on the landscape. And it was quiet, so quiet. Small seedlings had begun to push up through the soil, but not a bird to be seen.

They traversed the logged area then re-entered forest, where the track narrowed and roughened into dirt. Miki's shoulders eased. This was where she and Kurt liked to come: a place that spoke to her, a hidden patch of ancient trees. Their own private piece of forest.

Kurt pulled up near a grove close to where he'd hidden the hives. On the farm, they'd kept bees to pollinate the apple trees, and Father had stacked the hives up near the bush. Sometimes he'd let Miki help harvest the honey, which they'd sold in recycled jars at their self-serve roadside stall near the front gate. Here in the forest, the sweetest honey came from leatherwood trees, and Kurt knew where to find the best thickets. He said bees had their own language, their own way of talking to each other. One bee could dance out a story telling the others where to find food. All he had to do was put them near flowers, and the bees would do the rest. He admired the clever way they made honey out of nectar and pollen, and he liked the hierarchy of the colony in which every bee had a specific job to do.

Miki loved bees for different reasons—the way they were a huge family and cared for each other, sharing jobs and nurturing their young.

Now Kurt unfolded himself from the ute and tugged out the bee suit. They had only one, so Miki often had to stay in the car. Sometimes Kurt let her have a turn, and she would slide into the suit and slip her hands into the gloves. She loved being close to the bees and hearing the hum of the hive, the energy of it. She liked the excitement of lifting out the frames and peering in at all that activity, the bees crawling over each other.

'Can I do it?' she asked.

Kurt shook his head as he stepped into the suit, hitching it over his shoulders. 'Not today. It's almost the end of the season and the bees might be grouchy.'

'I'd be safe in the suit.'

'I don't want to annoy them. They might pack up and leave.'

During winter Kurt left the hives full of honey, and the bees hid inside because they hated the cold. Miki watched him stride off through the bush like a spaceman in his bee suit. He was carrying a large plastic box to bring back the honey frames. She pictured him lifting one out and shaking off the bees. They wouldn't like it, and they would spin and buzz around like noisy little satellites, until eventually they returned to the hive to get on with their work. At home Kurt would carefully scrape off the wax caps that sealed the honeycomb, then slide the frames into the extractor and spin out the honey. Miki would sieve out the fragments of wax then pour the honey into jars to be sold in the shop.

She waited in the ute wishing she'd brought something to read, but her three special books were on the bedside table in her bedroom. She and Kurt had found the books while going through boxes in the farm shed after the fire, searching for anything useful their parents might have left behind. The boxes had contained mainly old household items: cracked crockery and tarnished cutlery, salt and pepper shakers, vases, worn flannelette sheets. Miki had opened a box expecting more of the same, but beneath old folded camisoles, silky pantyhose and a pair of faded jeans, she'd uncovered three books: *Jane Eyre*, *Wuthering Heights* and *Tess of the D'Urbervilles*. She'd lifted them out and thumbed through the stained yellow pages; Mother's maiden name, *Heather Jones*, was inscribed inside each cover. Kurt had wanted to throw the books away, but Miki begged him not to, and in the end he'd let her keep them. On the farm, she'd grown up with only the Bible, so these books were exciting. They were from another time in Mother's life, and their existence made her a mystery. Miki wondered why Mother hadn't stored them in the house. And what had made her relinquish them for the Bible? Had she read other books? She must have given these ones up, but why had she kept them? Had she been saving them for her daughter?

Miki loved her three books. The main characters were all different, but she adored each of them and she envied their fascinating, complicated lives. She admired Jane Eyre's integrity and boldness, Tess's sweetness, Cathy's passion for the high moors above Wuthering Heights—just like Miki's love of the forests. Each heroine possessed certain strengths she respected. They took risks and ventured into the world. They accepted new challenges and succeeded or failed. They loved, made friends, lived: all things Miki longed to do. She yearned for Jane Eyre's freedom to go to school, then find a job as a teacher. She craved long stimulating conversations like those Jane had with Mr Rochester. She wished she could ask questions and seek answers, form her own opinions and be allowed to disagree. Just like Jane. She wanted to make mistakes, like Tess. She longed to see the world, and meet people, maybe find love as Tess had with Angel. She wanted to feel her emotions as wildly as Cathy—not always have to be careful like she was around Kurt.

She was still thinking about her books when he appeared in his white suit, carrying the plastic box. Several bees clung to his sleeves and Kurt brushed them off before removing the suit. The ute juddered as he hoicked the box onto the tray. Now it was safe for Miki to get out. While Kurt removed his gun from the lock box behind the seat, she slithered out and donned her coat.

'You carry the rifle,' he said, shoving it at her.

'No thanks.' She shrank away.

His brow furrowed. 'I need some help, so you can just bloody do it.'

She took the rifle, holding it tentatively as if it might go off. It was heavy, the metal shaft burnished and cold. She hoped Kurt would take it back, but he stuffed gear into his backpack and strode off up the track, so she was forced to follow, gingerly manoeuvring the rifle onto her shoulder. He only shot creatures that damaged the forest, like wallabies that ate the new growth, and lyrebirds, which had been introduced to Tasmania and weren't supposed to be there. But Miki still hated it. On the farm, he used to shoot rabbits because they chewed on the apple trees. Mother liked rabbit stew, and Miki didn't mind using them for food, but to simply shoot animals and leave them seemed such a waste.

They tramped up the overgrown track in the damp dripping forest. When they rounded the bend, she could see her favourite tree up ahead: an enormous swamp gum, fifteen strides round and ninety metres high, its crown lost in clouds. The trunk reared like a vast bark highway, and halfway up, small branches poked out like antlers. At the base of the tree, Kurt stopped and lit a cigarette. Resting his pack on a buttressed root like an elephant's foot, he leaned against the trunk and blew smoke in the air. Miki slipped the rifle from her shoulder but was afraid to put it down; she knew how paranoid Kurt was about moisture and rust. At home, he usually cleaned the rifle in his locked room under the shop, but sometimes he used the kitchen table; that was when she'd seen how gently he handled it, the way you might hold a baby.

He looked at her now and chuckled. 'Here, give me that thing. It won't go off, you know. It's not loaded.'

Relieved, she handed the rifle over then wandered around the huge trunk, running her hand across the woolly bark, listening to the hush of wind in the leaves. Around the far side, a fire scar had cut a chasm into the heartwood, an opening large enough for a human to enter. The tree reminded her of childhood visits to the bush up behind the farm on Sundays with Kurt. Beyond the back fence, among a bower of ferns, there had been a tall tree with a scar in it too. Miki used to like playing there with Kurt, acting out stories from the Bible. Once, they had been Samson and Delilah even though Miki thought it was sinful. Kurt had gone along with it until she produced a pair of scissors to cut his hair, snipping off a chunk before he realised what she was doing. He'd yelled and broken free of her poorly tied ropes and snatched the scissors, tossing them into the bush. She remembered the look of horror on his face, and it still made her smile. They'd spent hours searching for the scissors and arrived home late, covered in mud and leaves. Father had been furious.

Now she hooked a hand around the curved edge of the scar and ducked inside the hollow. Within the tree's thick skin, it was dark and quiet, dense with the sweet scent of rotting wood. Her feet sank in a soft bed of crumbled debris, and when she peered up she could just make out a small circle of light way above where the tree's crown had blown out. So far away. Closing her eyes, she heard a faint whisper: the tree sighing out secrets, breathy stories of ages past, wind and weather, black people sliding through the bush. If she held her breath, she could feel the heartbeat of the world.

Outside, a grey fantail flitted to the ground so close she could see its white eyebrows. Then it saw her and fluffed its tail, swinging it side to side and chittering. Miki loved the trees and birds, but what she loved most couldn't be seen. The way she felt in the forest. The scent of the bush after rain. The sound of bark crackling. Branches squeaking. The feeling of patience and agelessness, growth and renewal. The aura of trees. The sense of connectedness. Of everything having its place. She could stay here all day, breathing with the tree, drawing its life into her lungs.

But she heard Kurt's muffled voice calling her.

When she joined him, he was still lounging against the tree. 'What were you doing?'

'Just standing inside the tree.'

He shook his head slightly as if he thought she was mad, but she knew he shared her affinity for the forest. It was what bonded them—not the long hours in the shop or the endless evenings in front of the TV, not even her homely cooking or the snug tidy rooms behind the shop, but this: time spent in their world beneath trees. As they stood together in comfortable silence, a gust of wind rustled in the canopy, and the leaves shifted like schools of fish flickering against the sky. They looked up, watching clouds scud by.

'Lovely, isn't it,' Miki said.

Kurt's long exhalation indicated he was relaxing at last. 'All right then,' he said. 'I'm in a good mood. Ask me some questions.'

Occasionally when Kurt was feeling generous, he offered to share some of his memories. These opportunities were rare, so Miki stored questions for weeks. It was the only way she could learn about life before she was born and unearth who she was, where her parents had come from. This was knowledge she craved, and which Kurt kept under stringent control. She had to ask her questions with care; there was a fine line between his generosity and anger.

'Tell me how you used to get to school,' she said.

He sucked on his cigarette and smiled. 'You're so funny the way you want to know all these things. But I suppose it's nice to look back . . . Dad used to drive me.'

Miki felt the forest melt away as she tried to imagine Kurt's school. She pictured a small white building with green trim, a shady playground, gum trees up the back. 'What did you have for lunch?' she asked, hungry for detail.

'Cheese sandwiches on homemade bread.'

'Who were your friends?'

He puffed out a cloud of smoke and gazed up at the trees. 'A boy called Chris and a girl called Cherry. They were twins.'

'What games did you play?'

'We dug in the dirt and made roads and gutters for water to run down when it rained.'

'What did you do in class?'

'We read books and sang songs, learned how to write.'

'What were your teachers' names?'

Miki knew these by heart, but she liked hearing just the same. The only teacher she'd ever had was Mother. She wished she had gone to school. She wished she could go now.

She hesitated before her final question, because she'd never asked this one before. How would Kurt react? If she was out of line it could ruin the whole day. She felt the forest breathing around her; it gave her courage. 'Why did you stop going to school?'

'Because you were born.'

'Why did that matter?'

'That's when Father and Mother decided to retreat to the farm. They'd had enough of the church. Decided to go their own way. Do their own thing. Make their own rules.'

Miki was confused. Hadn't they always lived by God's rules? She hadn't known those rules were open to interpretation. 'I don't see what that had to do with me.'

'Timing, I suppose.'

'Why couldn't I go to school?

'Because you're a girl and they wanted to protect you.' He scraped the stub of his cigarette on the tree trunk and tossed it in an arc to fizz in a puddle. Then he stood and reached for his pack.

Miki felt that she was on the edge of something important so she pushed on. 'Why didn't we have visitors? And why don't we have any relatives? Are they all dead?'

Kurt dodged her eyes and shouldered his pack. 'I'm done with questions.'

Miki was frustrated. Why wouldn't he tell her? 'Please.'

His face clouded and he turned away. 'I'm off. Make sure you stay close to the tree.' He started up the track, pausing to toss her the car keys. 'Get in the ute if it rains. I'll be back in an hour.'

She watched him disappear into the forest: the thud of his feet on the trail, the swish and crack as he shouldered into the scrub. She knew he might glance back so she remained outwardly composed, but inside her questions rippled and seethed like the wind.

For a while, she stayed by the tree, turning over questions in her mind. Then the clouds condensed, the light faded and rain began to spill from the sky. She retreated to the car, still going over questions, preparing for an imagined day when Kurt might treat her like an adult and open in honesty towards her, impossible though this seemed.

Why hadn't her family had visits from friends? Where were their relatives? Didn't they have grandparents? Didn't Mother and Father have brothers or sisters? What was in Father's black leather folder? Why wouldn't Kurt let her see it? Why wouldn't he allow her into the storeroom under the shop? Why didn't he trust her to go out alone? How long until they would have enough money to buy their own farm?

The questions made her skin itchy, and she realised that mulling over them had stolen the pleasure from her day. Seeking distraction, she opened the glovebox, hoping to find something to read. Sometimes Kurt kept newspaper clippings in there: ads for new four-wheel drives or gym machines. But there were only car manuals. Miki was disappointed—even a street directory would have been interesting.

Poking around, she opened the ashtray expecting it to be empty, but in it she found several silver keys. She'd never looked in the ashtray before because Kurt never used it—when he smoked he tipped ash out the window and tossed his butts on the road. Now she wondered if these keys had always been there. Picking one up, she measured its weight in her hand then lined another alongside it, matching the teeth. They were exactly the same. She pulled out the other keys. All identical, but different from the car keys. Why did Kurt have so many duplicates? Had he had them cut for a reason? Was he worried about losing them? She considered the locks in the house and counted them up: front door, back door, Kurt's filing cabinet, the room under the shop, the gun box in the car, the ammunition box, the metal cashbox. She jingled the keys. Since they were all the same, would Kurt notice if she took one?

Her heart flipped as she contemplated deceiving her brother. Should she do it? Or would it be wrong? For a long moment, she sat looking at the keys. Then she asked herself what Jane Eyre would do. Jane was bold but she was also clever, and she had courage and lived by her principles. Would it be unprincipled to take a key? Miki thought of Jane at Thornfield Hall, investigating strange sounds at night. Mrs Fairfax had told her to always remain in her room, but if Jane hadn't ventured out Mr Rochester would have died when his bedroom was on fire. Kurt locked Miki in when he left her at home, but there might be times when she needed to venture out too.

There were so many keys here. Surely Kurt didn't need all of them.

Before she could change her mind, she slipped a key into her overalls pocket and zipped it up. Then she replaced the other keys in the ashtray and closed it.

7

Parks headquarters for the region was a twenty-minute drive from Leon's new town. The office was in the main street between the hairdresser and real-estate agent. Leon pulled up outside and sat in his car, watching rain slide down the windscreen. He was nervous. It would take time to get established in a new job but he was looking forward to working in a team and making friends with people who shared his passion for wild places and who liked the outdoors. He checked his watch. Ten to nine. Time to go in.

A buzzer sounded as he entered, but there was no one about. He heard a murmur of voices and the clacking of a keyboard behind a large opaque screen at the back of the shop. For a few moments he inspected his surrounds: shelves with books and maps for sale, a postcard rack, stuffed toys. Then he stepped up to the counter, which had a glass top with a map beneath it. He dinged the bell and a tall, lanky man emerged from behind the screen. He had short dark hair, a long nose, after-five shadow and questioning brown eyes. 'Hi, how are you? Need any help?'

Leon reached over to shake hands. 'I'm Leon Walker. Starting a new job here today.'

The man smiled and accepted the handshake. 'G'day, I'm Terry. Pleased to meet you.'

He led Leon behind the screen and introduced him to Brian, the boss: a big man hunched over a small desk in a pokey little office right out the back. Brian was frowning at a computer among a mountain of papers and several used coffee cups. From his doughy shape and double chins, Leon figured he didn't visit his parks very often—something he probably delegated to juniors like Leon. But when they shook hands, the grip was solid, just what you'd expect of a manager.

'Sit down,' Brian said, pointing to a chair.

Leon sat.

'So you've come from Bruny Island. Busy over there?'

'Yeah. I was on my own, so it was flat out.'

'You're used to working alone?'

'Yes. They didn't replace the other ranger when he retired. Not enough money.'

'Understood. Things are tight here too. No resources. The reality is we're understaffed and you'll be busy like on Bruny.'

'That's okay. I'm a hard worker.'

'Good. I appreciate enthusiasm. You'll have plenty to do. And not all of it will be outside. These days we only get up to the park three times a week, and mostly we only send one ranger because there's so much office work: manning the counter, answering questions for tourists, that sort of stuff. Any specialties you bring to the job?'

'I like talking to people, so if there's an opportunity I'd be keen to take guided walks and do nature interpretation. School visits, maybe. Back on Bruny, I used to look after the Scouts.'

'Sounds great, but to start with you'll be checking toilets and doing the rubbish and track maintenance. Sorry. But that's how it is. Once you've settled in, we can talk more.'

Leon hid his disappointment. After years of toilets and tracks, he'd been hoping for something different.

Brian was already focusing back on his computer. He glanced up at Leon from beneath bushy brows. 'Terry will get you sorted with a computer and uniforms, then he'll take you up to the park.'

The conversation was over.

They were on their way out of town in a white Toyota LandCruiser when Leon's phone rang. It didn't look good taking personal calls first day, but he thought he'd better answer it. 'Sorry,' he said to Terry. 'It's my mum—she might need something.' He pressed the phone to his ear and kept his voice low. 'Hi, Mum. What's up? Have to be quick. I'm with another ranger.'

'Stan's here.' Her whisper was urgent.

Stan was Dad's drinking partner who plied him with grog even though it was killing his liver. Stan would never have visited if Leon was home, so word must have got around that he was gone. 'What's he doing?' Leon asked.

'He's at the door.'

'Don't let him in.'

'The car's in the garage. I can't pretend we're not home.'

She sounded panicky. Even over the phone, Leon could hear the pounding on the front door. What was Stan doing? Trying to knock it down? 'Tell him to get lost,' Leon said.

Then his dad's voice, distant, muffled. 'Someone's at the door, Sylvia!'

'Don't go,' Leon pressed.

'I have to. Your father is shouting at me.'

'Don't do it. You know what will happen.'

The line went quiet. She was gone.

Leon felt as if he was hanging above an abyss. He'd counted on his dad being too weak to do anything—that was the strategy to keep his mum safe. But maybe this plan was delusional. If Stan got Dad drunk, it could go anywhere.

'Everything okay?' Terry asked.

'Yeah, yeah. It'll be fine.'

Terry shook his head in sympathy. 'Families.'

They drove along the silvery stretch of the river, whizzing past farms and dormant orchards. Leon was trying not to think about home. He couldn't do anything from here, so it was futile to waste energy worrying. And, yet, visions kept niggling him. His dad staggering into the kitchen and swiping at Mum with a hairy paw. His mum with a purple shiner under one eye, like the day Leon had first discovered his dad was hitting her. He would never forget her sad face as he tried to convince her to leave. It hadn't made sense to him when she said she loved his dad and could never go. He couldn't understand such blind devotion. Was that how women ended up fenced into inescapable situations? He hated his dad for the power he wielded over his mum.

Terry was trying to make conversation, so Leon made an effort to tune in.

'I couldn't help overhearing you talking to the boss,' Terry was saying. 'It's a tough time in Parks. Not many opportunities. I'm with you on public outreach, though. I'd like to see more of it. But the boss is concerned about money—things are so tight.'

'Same everywhere,' Leon said. 'It's a problem.'

'There are some good things going on in the wildlife scene, if you know how to tap into it,' Terry said. 'I can connect you with scientists doing fieldwork around here, if you like. There's a guy from Canberra looking for swift parrots in the forests. And a bloke from the uni working on Tasmanian devils. None of it pays, of course, but it might give you what you're looking for. A bit more stimulus than the usual work.'

Leon was grateful. Sometimes he wished he'd become a scientist himself, but ranger work suited him because he liked being outside. He couldn't imagine himself chained to a desk.

At the turn-off to the park, the road deteriorated to potholed gravel, and Terry slowed to navigate a particularly rutted section.

'They only grade it a couple of times a year,' he grumbled. 'Can't afford to seal it. Not enough traffic to justify the expense.'

The road climbed gradually, and soon forest gave way to heathland dotted with small gangly trees and buttressed peaks. Mist hung on the mountains, and the light was long and grey. It was hauntingly beautiful.

At the end of the road, Terry pulled up in a circular car park where the hiking trails began. Leon was excited. The light was soft and a blue haze hovered above the heath. 'Can we walk to the pass?' he asked. 'I wouldn't mind seeing the view.'

'Another time. Too bloody cold today. It'll be blowing a gale up there.' Terry led the way along a short boardwalk to a large shelter for tourists. Inside, he showed Leon the walking-intentions book. 'When you're on duty, you have to check this book to make sure no one's missing. Inexperienced idiots go hiking in a white-out and they don't stick to the trail. Then it's up to us to find them—full-scale search and rescue. Some of them walk in T-shirts and thongs. It's a shame we have to save fools.'

Leon had helped with search and rescue on Bruny Island too. Sometimes they found those who went missing. Other times it was a mystery. One young woman had hiked up Fluted Cape and never come back; a week of searching and they'd concluded she must have fallen from the cliffs. Leon didn't like to think of her crashing onto the rock platforms below. He'd spent his childhood exploring those cliffs; lost his virginity up there with a girl staying at the caravan park over summer; fed the white wallabies that grazed the grassy area at the bottom of the trail. That place was part of who he was. Maybe this place would become part of him too.

After they had cleaned the loos and restocked the toilet paper, Terry was ready to head back to the office. 'No point hanging round in weather like this,' he said. 'Nobody here except us, and we don't have any say in the matter.'

They were spinning through the forest back towards town when Leon saw the dog on the road: a red heeler with swinging teats. It had to be Rosie from next door. He called to Terry to stop. 'Hey, I know that dog. She lives next door to me. We should take her back home.'

As Terry pulled over, Leon noticed Rosie had a gash in her side. He wondered how she'd ended up here by herself. Had she run off, or had she fallen from the back of Shane's ute? He remembered her growling at him back home and wasn't sure if she would try to bite him, but he couldn't just leave her here—the wound was dripping with blood.

He spoke to her quietly as he approached. She was panting, probably in pain. 'Got a rope in the car?' he asked Terry. 'Something I can loop round her neck.'

Terry tossed out a length of cord that Leon hooked around Rosie's collar. She was compliant—maybe she sensed he was trying to help. He coaxed her to the LandCruiser and encouraged her onto the back seat. She tried to leap but winced, so Leon wrapped his arms around her and lifted her in. He felt those dangly teats against his skin, the wetness of the wound. So much for his new uniform—his hands and clothes were covered in blood.

When they arrived at Leon's place, the neighbours weren't home.

'We'll have to take her to a vet,' Terry said. 'The nearest one's near the Parks office.'

At the vet clinic, a buzzer went off as Leon pulled Rosie in through the door. The smell of disinfectant hit him and his boots echoed on the floor. Tugging the dog over to a plastic chair near the front window, he sat down to wait. The front desk was unattended, but someone must have heard the buzzer go off—it was certainly loud enough. On the desk, a sign in black capitals announced there was no credit to be had here and full payment was required at the time of consultation. Leon supposed he would have to pay the bill; no guarantees Wendy and Shane would do it.

A middle-aged woman with short brown hair emerged from a room down the back and assessed Leon and Rosie; her name tag read Frances. 'Hmm,' she said. 'That wound's nasty.'

'Are you the vet?' Leon asked.

'I'm nurse and receptionist. We have to multi-task around here . . . You been here before?'

'No. I found this dog up in the forest.'

'She's not yours?'

'No, but I'll pay for whatever needs to be done. I think she needs help.'

'You can say that again. I'll just get the vet.' Frances turned towards the rear of the premises and bellowed, 'Hey, Kate. Got a minute? Mind taking a look at this dog?'

A young woman in jeans, Blundstone boots and a teal-green gown appeared. She was slim and bright-eyed, and her blonde hair was pulled back in a ponytail, surgical gloves on her hands. She peered over the counter and Leon shifted the dog so the wound was visible. 'That will definitely need stitches,' she said. 'What happened?'

'I was just explaining how I found her up in the forest. She belongs to my neighbours but they weren't home. Didn't think I could leave it. I'm happy to pay—not sure my neighbours can afford it.'

Her smile was warm. 'That's kind of you.'

'Can we spay her at the same time?' Leon asked.

Kate's brow crinkled as she took in Rosie's dangly nipples and massive belly. 'It would be a good thing to do, but we can't without the owner's consent, especially when she's this far advanced.'

'That's a shame. The kid next door said she ate her previous pups.'

Kate's eyes widened. 'Really?'

'I'm wondering if the father might have drowned them.'

'That's awful.'

Frances was clearly disgusted. 'People like that shouldn't be allowed to own animals.'

Leon agreed. 'Look, sorry, but is it okay if I give you some details and get back to work? It's my first day on a new job and if I don't show my face soon, I'll get the sack. Then I won't be able to pay.'

After work, he collected Rosie from the clinic, all patched up and looking miserable with stitches in her side and a plastic cone around her head, tied to her collar. 'The cone of shame,' Frances said, handing Leon the rope connected to the dog. 'If she chews those stitches, we'll have to do it all over again. I'm sure you don't want to pay twice.' Leon had no idea whether his neighbours would keep the cone on or not. If Rosie pulled the stitches out, they'd have to pay next time.

He led the dog to his car and lifted her onto the back seat, but she weaselled into the front, bashing her way through with the cone. When he tried to shift her, she hunched down and dug her claws into the seat. Was she testing him, or was she used to getting her own way? He didn't think Shane would allow the dog much leeway, but sometimes you couldn't tell how people treated their animals. Maybe Shane was all bluster in public and a softie in private.

Leon put the car in gear and was about to drive away when he noticed he'd missed a text from his mum. *Can you drop in to see Grandpa on your way home? He has something to give you.* A wave of relief washed through him—she was okay. She hadn't mentioned Stan or his dad, so things must be sorted at home. But surely Grandpa could wait till tomorrow. Leon was already late heading home, and he'd seen Grandpa only yesterday. He didn't want to disappoint the old man, however, so perhaps he could leave the dog in the car for a few minutes and make a quick visit.

But in the car park at the old people's home, Rosie was determined to go with him. She leaped onto his lap, crashing the cone against his face and scrabbling at his thighs with her claws. Leon tried to calm her, but she yelped wildly and he couldn't shove her away. When he opened the door, she barrelled out too, and it was all he could do to hold on to her. The cone was clearly bothering her, so he took it off, keeping the cord coiled round his wrist so she couldn't escape. He tried to coax her back into the car, but she ducked and weaved and shrank onto the ground. Leon was afraid to force her in case he damaged her wound. Now he was faced with the problem of where to put her while he went inside. He contemplated tying her up but was frightened she would slip her collar. It would be a disaster if she ended up being hit by a car. He wondered if the receptionist might come out and hold her for a few moments, but there was no one at the front desk.

Exasperated, he stood by the sliding doors, waiting for somebody to emerge. Five minutes passed. The dog sat, panting up at him happily—she was a different person now the cone was off. In the end, Leon took her in with him. The foyer and front office were deserted—it was probably dinnertime—and maybe he would get away with a quick walk down the corridor to Grandpa's room to collect whatever the old man so desperately needed to give him. He might just pull it off.

Everything went well until he found Grandpa's room empty. Either Leon had to search for the old man, or give up. But having come this far, he was bold enough to go on. With Rosie trotting alongside, he slunk towards the lounge room where several old people sat slumped and half-asleep in massive armchairs. It only took one of them to notice Rosie, and suddenly the whole room was awake. 'Would you look at that?' a creaky voice announced. 'It's a dog.'

Leon was planning his escape, but all around craggy faces lit up and thin lips split into gaping smiles. Departure was not an option. Rosie was on display.

'Can you bring her over here, sonny?' a crinkled old woman called.

Leon shortened the rope and led Rosie across the carpet. He hoped she wouldn't bite anyone. She tugged him along, stopping when her head was under the old woman's hand. Leon watched those bony fingers grasping woodenly at the dog's head in a rough sort of pat. He noticed the bright look of rapture on the old lady's face, and the dog's equivalent of a smile. The woman's eyes sparkled. 'Oh, she's a bonnie doggie, isn't she, sonny? Those ears are like velvet.' Leon was surprised the woman could feel anything with those gnarly hands. 'What's her name?'

'Rosie.'

'Hello, Rosie. Aren't you a good dog? You've made my day.'

'Hey, what about us?' a man called out. He was a thin scrap of humanity with a camel's-hump back, sitting in a wheelchair on the other side of the room. 'We want to pat her too. You can't have all the fun, Glenys.'

The old woman laughed. 'You lot can wait. Rosie and I are already friends.'

'All right then,' the man in the wheelchair said, 'if Muhammad won't come to the mountain, then the mountain will come to Muhammad.' He yanked at his brake and started wheeling himself across the room.

'Good Lord, Duncan,' someone said. 'What are you doing? You know you're supposed to wait for a nurse.'

'Bad luck,' Duncan said, 'I want to pat the dog.'

Leon saw the wheelchair approaching and realised the old man had little control. Those thin arms were pecking at the handles unevenly and the chair was skewing wildly. To avert a crash, Leon grabbed the armrest and pulled the chair to a halt, bending to sling an arm around the old man so he wouldn't slither to the ground. It was a near thing, but neither Glenys nor Duncan seemed to register this. They were crooning over the dog, thin faces glowing, smiles like dark caves, semi-toothless.

'What's this?' a loud angry voice called, much younger and authoritative.

The excitement in the room held its breath, and Leon looked up. The voice belonged to Maryanne from the front desk, her red lips compressed.

'Sorry.' Leon dished out humble pie. 'I'm looking for my grandpa.'

Maryanne was proficient at haughtiness and she piled it on now. 'What's this dog doing inside? Is it clean? Has it been wormed? Is it registered as a carer dog?'

'Yes to everything,' Leon lied—the easiest way out. 'And look how much happiness she's giving. Everyone here's come alive!'

Maryanne scanned the room like a radar and her posture softened. The old people were no longer limp husks; they were all reaching to touch the dog. Fortunately, Rosie remained cooperative. While Maryanne supervised, Leon led the dog around the room, greeting each oldie one by one.

'Don't forget Hector,' Glenys said, pointing to a contorted fossil of a man in the corner, so bent he couldn't even raise his head.

Leon led Rosie over. The dog seemed to be revelling in her role; she walked straight up to Hector and put her head on his lap. Leon waited for the old man to say something, but the only thing that issued from his twisted mouth was a string of drool. For a moment, all was still: the warped body didn't move. Then the dog lifted her yellow eyes to peer at Hector, and his shaking purple-blotched hand pawed gently at her head. The room was silent, everyone watching Hector connect with Rosie. Only Leon saw the droplets of moisture that fell onto the dog's nose. When he looked more closely, he realised it wasn't Hector's saliva, but his tears.

When everyone had said hello then goodbye to Rosie, Leon asked after his grandpa. 'He's in the library,' Maryanne said. 'Do you think you could bring Rosie again sometime? She's been good medicine for everyone.'

Leon had dug himself into a hole. 'Ah, yes, maybe. I'll phone later on and make a time.'

'That would be wonderful. And, next time, could you bring her carer-dog papers with you? I'll need to make copies.'

'Sure.' Leon waved as he led the dog down the corridor. He was worried about all these lies, but there was a time and place for honesty, and this wasn't it.

He found Grandpa alone in the library, bent over a book at a large wooden table. Leon announced his presence with a short cough, and Grandpa looked up, eyes sharpening with surprise. 'It's you again.'

'Mum said you wanted to see me. So here I am. And I've brought a friend.'

Grandpa frowned at Rosie, then smiled. 'I didn't know you had a dog.'

'I don't. She belongs to my neighbours.'

'Looks like she's about to have pups. What's that in her side? Stitches?'

'You're the first person who's noticed. Seems like you're the only one with eyesight around here.'

'My eyes are pretty good for my age.' Grandpa pushed his spectacles up. 'How did you get a dog in here anyway? Maryanne allowed it?'

'She wasn't at the desk.'

Grandpa chuckled. 'Good to know you can get past her. Knowledge like that could be useful.' He waved Leon closer. 'I wanted to show you this book. It's about the logging history of this area. Written by a mate of mine from Bruny Island. I think you'll find it interesting.'

Leon leaned in to look. The cover had a photo of a large log on an old timber jinker with two men perched on top of it. Grandpa opened the book to a black-and-white photo of four axemen standing on boards notched into the base of an enormous tree.

'This is Bruny Island back at the turn of the last century,' Grandpa said. 'And this is my great-great-grandfather, William Walker.' He pointed to a bearded man just visible behind the broad trunk. The man's face was shadowed by a rough-looking felt hat, but Leon could see the nose was Walker, no mistaking it. Grandpa licked his index finger and flicked through the pages. 'I thought you might like to take the book home and read it. Lots of history in here—your mum says you're into that. There's a chapter on Bruny Island and one on bushfires. You might discover something interesting, if you read between the lines.' He turned to the chapter on fires and tapped the page.

What was the old man talking about, Leon wondered. Some sort of secret? 'All right, I'll read that chapter,' he said.

'If you have any questions, you can ask later,' Grandpa added. He had become twitchy and restless.

'Is there something in that book about you?' Leon asked.

Grandpa wouldn't meet Leon's eyes. Instead, he leaned down to Rosie and she sidled in for a pat. 'I used to have a dog like this,' he said. 'A blue heeler called Fred. He was hit on the Adventure Bay road. You wouldn't credit it. One car an hour back then, and the bloody dog gets killed. Best dog I ever had. And I've had a few over the years. You sure this one isn't yours? Dogs are good company.'

'No, I have to take her home now. Her owner will be wondering where she is.'

'Go on with you then.' Grandpa closed the book and handed it to Leon.

By the time Leon pulled up at home, it was after six-thirty. He fastened the cone around Rosie's neck then let her out of the car, and she dragged him through the yard, whining excitedly as he knocked at her front door. He heard rapid footsteps in the hall, then the door burst open and Max was there. His face lit up when he saw the dog.

'Hey, Mum,' he yelled. 'It's Rosie. And she's wearing the weirdest thing on her head.' He dropped to his knees and wrapped his arms around the dog's neck, staring at the stitches.

Leon caught the look of surprise and annoyance in Wendy's eyes as she ambled down the hall. 'What happened?' she asked.

'I found Rosie on the road in the forest with a cut in her side, so I took her to the vet.'

Wendy frowned. 'Why didn't you come here first?'

'I did, but no one was home.'

She looked at the dog and the kid.

'She has tons of stitches,' Max said. 'Twenty-two.'

Leon could sense Wendy's question hanging in the air. 'I fixed things up with the vet,' he mumbled. 'Least I could do.'

'What's this thing on her head?' Max asked.

'A cone to stop her chewing her stitches.'

'Cool,' Max said. 'She looks like an alien.'

At that moment Shane's ute roared up the street, headlights swinging towards the house, illuminating them all. Leon stood by helplessly as Shane strode up the path and checked out the dog. 'What the fuck?'

'She fell off your ute again, Shane,' Wendy said. 'And look what's happened.'

'She's fine now.' Leon couldn't help putting in.

Shane squinted at him. 'Did you have something to do with this?'

It was an accusation, not a thank you—but before Leon could respond, Max shouted, 'Leon saved Rosie, Dad. Look how big the hole was. And Leon got her fixed. She might have died, but he saved her.'

Obviously it was easy to be a hero for a kid.

'Should have bloody died,' Shane muttered. 'It would have been cheaper.'

'Don't worry,' Leon said. 'It's all sorted. The vet wanted to do it straight away, so I paid. I couldn't leave her with a great hole in her side.' He backed away, taking the moment of confusion to exit.

Shane was scowling, but Max's face shone with delight, and Wendy gave a quiet nod. At least she understood he'd done it out of compassion for the dog, even if Shane didn't appreciate it.

Later that evening, Leon sat on the floor in front of the fire with Grandpa's book on his lap. It was a hardback, a historical document outlining the story of the main sawmills that had existed in southern Tasmania. He flicked through it. The text was detailed and included anecdotes and facts about logging going all the way back to the mid-1800s. But what caught his eye were the photographs—they seemed alive to him, and they told the tales of the old timber cutters and tramways better than any words could.

The photos were mostly black and white. Some were faded and had deteriorated with age. And others were so clear, you'd think they'd been taken yesterday—until you looked at the people and the clothes they were wearing, the activities they were doing, the cars and trucks they were driving. There were photos of tramways being constructed from timber. Horses waiting patiently to begin dragging a log along a tramway. Steam locomotives hauling logs. Old timber-town settlements. Steamships that carried sawn timber to overseas markets. Timber cutters with their wives and families. Sawmills and bridges being built.

Leon studied the faces of the workers, and they all seemed like serious men. Nobody smiled for the camera—that must have been the way of the times, or perhaps they all lived hard lives. Most of them had moustaches and wore hats, dark trousers and jackets over light-coloured shirts. Leon noticed the way they stood, with arms crossed or cocked on their hips as if they had been carefully set up for the camera—he supposed fewer photos were taken back then, so every shot was important.

He read about the timber industry on Bruny Island at Adventure Bay, where he'd grown up. The book told the story of discovery and settlement, which Leon already knew—he'd been raised on a diet of history and explorers. It was interesting to read about sawmills on the island, however there were few mentions of names, and little that related directly to his family.

He finished by delving into the chapter that Grandpa had recommended, on bushfires and fires in sawmills and their impact on the industry. But he couldn't work out what the old man had wanted him to glean from all this information. Grandpa's discomfort was still a mystery. Leon supposed the truth would come out in the fullness of time—he would wait for the right moment to ask. He had a good feeling about his relationship with his grandpa. Weekly visits to the home were going to be interesting.

8

For Miki, Tuesday was the loneliest day of the week. That was when Kurt locked her in and went off to Hobart. Usually he left Monday afternoon, which was okay, because she would spend the evening knitting or reading a book. But Tuesdays seemed to last for an eternity. And here she was, yet again, perched on a chair in the empty shop, staring out at the street, watching life pass her by.

Kurt had been grumpy when he left yesterday—there was something about going to the city that always made him edgy. Normally Miki didn't worry about his mood when he drove off, but since she'd taken the key yesterday morning, she'd been tense, wondering if Kurt had noticed it was gone, and how he would punish her when he found out. But nothing had been said, so for now it seemed her secret was safe.

This morning, she'd risen early and ticked off her jobs: vacuuming the rooms, doing the washing, mopping the floors, cleaning the fryers. Changing the oil was a job she and Kurt generally tackled together. She detested doing it alone: draining the old oil into tins, scraping out the dead bits of batter, wiping away the scum, and then scouring the bottom of the fryers. After pouring in the new oil, she'd showered to get rid of the grease. And now she was watching the children on their way to school. She saw the policeman's sons go by: Jaden shoving against Callum and pinching his arm. Then Max dawdled past, focused on his phone. But he looked up, peered into the shop and waved—the only person who had seen her all morning. She was invisible to everyone else.

A log truck rumbled up the street, the shop windows rattling as it pulled in across the road, air brakes snorting. It was Robbo in his battered blue Kenworth, his name written in curly silver letters on the door. His load of slender logs was probably headed for the pulp mill. It seemed most loads were destined for pulp these days: so many thin trees, too young for sawing.

Robbo climbed down from the cab, hitched his jeans and crossed to the bakery. He wasn't supposed to park his truck in the main street but he was a law unto himself, and his wife Trudi worked part-time at the bakery, so he must have figured he had an excuse. Trudi was nice. Miki often served her in the shop, and she always smiled and said thank you. Miki had heard Trudi only worked part-time because she wanted to help out in the community, like delivering Meals on Wheels for old people who couldn't cook anymore. Trudi also assisted with reading at school because she liked to be around children. Apparently she couldn't have her own children, and the women said she had troubles with depression too. Miki didn't know much about depression, but she could see something mournful in Trudi's eyes. It was lucky Trudi had Robbo: Miki could tell by the soft way he looked at his wife that he loved her. Not like some men in town. Mooney's eyes were always hard when he looked at poor Liz.

Now Robbo appeared from the bakery with a cream bun and a coffee-to-go. Not the sort of food he ought to be eating: he was short and thick around the middle. People joked that he was carrying a spare tyre for his truck.

Miki liked Robbo; he always gave a nod when Kurt was looking away. Today, though, he didn't notice her. When the shop was shut it was as if she didn't exist.

Three teenaged girls walked by, talking and laughing. They were tall and elegant with long hair that swept around their shoulders like mist. Miki looked at the time: nine o'clock. The girls would be late for school, but they didn't seem to care. They had their elbows hooked and their heads close together. Miki wished she could have friends and go to school too. She was nearly eighteen. Kurt ought to trust her.

When they had gone, the street was quiet. Autumn leaves shuffled in the gutter, and a few used wrappers tumbled by on the breeze. Miki fetched *Jane Eyre* from her bedroom and read the scene where Jane's cruel aunt locked her in the red room and wouldn't let her out, not even when she was stricken with fear. Poor Jane suffered so much persecution. At school the principal, Mr Brocklehurst, labelled her deceitful, but Jane bore the insult with admirable resilience. If Jane could overcome oppression and unfairness to find a path in life, Miki could too. But right now she felt captive, like Jane in the red room.

She thought of the key she'd taken from the ute yesterday. Maybe now was the time to try it. Last night, she'd crept from bed and retrieved it from her overalls. Then she'd taken a sharp knife from the kitchen, made a small slit under her mattress and concealed the key in the padding where Kurt wouldn't find it. She fetched the key now and clutched it in her hand. The metal warmed quickly in the hot flesh of her palm. Jittery, she inserted the key into the front door, and her hand was shaking as she twisted it. What if it didn't work? But the lock released smoothly, and there she was with the door slightly ajar.

She stood still, breathing in the fresh air. She didn't know what to do next, hadn't thought that far ahead. She could walk up the street, but nobody had seen her out by herself before, and what if someone talked to her? They might say something to Kurt later: *Saw your sister out yesterday*. Then what would she do?

She wondered what Jane Eyre would do, but this time it didn't help. She would have to decide by herself.

Trembling, she collected the window-cleaning gear from the laundry. Then, tremulously, she opened the front door and set everything on the footpath. Her heart was a jackhammer in her chest, and her hands were so fluttery she could barely squeeze out the sponge. She drew breath and tried to concentrate on the windows; surely if she got on with the job, nobody would notice her.

The windows were certainly smeary. During the week, children pressed grimy fingers against the glass and made faces at their friends. Starting at one end of the shop, Miki began wetting down the glass with the sponge. It felt strange being outside when she wasn't meant to be. She was buzzing with excitement, as if the entire world was watching her even though nobody was there.

After finishing with one pane, she was shifting her ladder along when she saw Wendy strolling up the path with her little girl, Suzie. Wendy always looked tired, and she always had a cigarette in her hand—didn't she think about her children breathing in all that smoke? She was a good-looking woman, and today she wore tight jeans and a denim jacket over a close-fitting top. Whenever she entered the shop, men noticed her, and Miki was sure Wendy was aware of this—something about the way the blonde woman pulled back her shoulders and pushed out her chest. Now Wendy paused, with a wry smile, to watch Miki at work. Miki smelled Wendy's perfume, light and sweet like freesias, but the sour tang of smoke was still there, just underneath.

Wendy grinned. 'You can do my place next, if you like.' She was holding the little girl's hand, and Suzie was inspecting Miki with big brown eyes, the same shape as her mum's.

'Can I have a turn?' Suzie asked.

'Sure.' Miki dipped the cloth in the bucket, wrung it out and handed it to Suzie, who started wiping haphazardly over the section Miki had just finished.

'Kurt let you out for the day?' Wendy asked drily, raising an eyebrow. 'I'd run, if I was you. I'd hit the road and never stop. He's a controlling bastard, your brother. He's really got you under the thumb.'

Miki was uncomfortable. She knew people talked about her and Kurt, but she'd never been confronted like this and she couldn't think what to say, so she dodged Wendy's eyes.

'Sorry I'm a straight talker,' Wendy said. 'I've always been that way. I say things as they are.'

Suzie was wiping the window enthusiastically, water dripping down her pudgy little arm and onto her clothes.

'Where's Kurt today?' Wendy asked Miki.

'Out the back doing the books.'

Wendy sucked on her cigarette and exhaled a small cloud of smoke. 'Rubbing his hands over his money, no doubt. You should ask him to buy you some new clothes instead of that old skirt. He can afford it. This place does well for a takeaway. *Too* well, if you ask me.'

Miki wasn't sure what this meant. Did Wendy think their prices were too high? 'Suzie is getting very wet,' she said, to divert the woman's attention.

'Oh, that doesn't matter. She changes clothes four times a day. That's little girls, isn't it? We were all like that once.' Wendy smiled at Suzie indulgently, as if being a girl explained everything. But Miki had never changed her clothes four times a day. She hadn't owned four changes of clothes and, even if she had, Mother would never have allowed it. Wendy was looking at Miki appraisingly. 'How old are you now, love?'

'Nearly eighteen.'

'Almost independent, hey? Christ! I was pregnant at your age. Once you're eighteen, Kurt has no hold on you. You can go then, you know.'

This was news to Miki. Kurt had told her they needed to work together till she was twenty-one. And what about the farm they were saving for? That was a family thing.

'You should make sure the business is in your name too,' Wendy was saying. 'Otherwise none of it belongs to you. I wouldn't put it past your brother to keep it all for himself. Sorry to say it, but I wouldn't trust him as far as I could kick him.'

Miki was embarrassed now, and she wished Wendy would leave. Clearly this woman didn't understand Kurt. Yes, he was unpredictable, and Miki disliked his restrictions, but sometimes he could be quite considerate.

She was saved by Suzie. The little girl crouched to dip the cloth in the bucket and tripped, knocking it over as she fell and sending a small river running down the path, the bucket rolling after it. Miki was about to rescue the bucket when Suzie's face screwed up and a murderous scream came out, along with a good dose of tears. Wendy's sigh was exasperated as she helped Suzie up and handed the wet cloth to Miki.

'Sorry,' Miki said. 'It was meant to be fun.'

Wendy shrugged. 'It's always fun till someone loses an eye.'

Miki hadn't thought Suzie was hurt. 'Is her eye all right?'

Wendy laughed. 'Yes, she's fine. You're very literal, aren't you?' She wiped her daughter's cheeks with a handkerchief and helped blow her nose.

'My knees are sore.' Suzie pouted. 'And my tights have holes in them.'

Wendy checked Suzie's knees and planted a kiss on her daughter's mop of brown hair. Then she took Suzie's hand. 'How about we get a doughnut from the bakery? Will that help?'

Suzie nodded.

Wendy winked at Miki and led her daughter up the footpath. Miki watched them go, noticing how their walk was the same, the shape of their shoulders and the way their hips moved. She had wished them gone, but now she felt lonely. It was the intimacy between mother and daughter that moved her: Wendy's gentle care, the small things mothers shared with their children. Miki missed her mother.

Turning back to the windows, she started cleaning up the soapy mess Suzie had made.

When the windows were done, Miki locked the front door and hung the cleaning things to dry in the laundry. The rest of the day stretched ahead of her. Entertainment options were few. Kurt had disabled the TV and hidden the remote controls so she couldn't watch it without him. All she could do was knit or read. But now she'd been outside and tasted freedom, she wanted to do it again.

She let herself out the back door this time and left it unlocked—she wouldn't be gone long.

On the back steps, she hesitated with the key in her hand. Should she try the padlock for the storeroom under the shop? She held her breath as she attempted to slide the key in. But it didn't fit. Kurt must have other keys for his private hideaway.

In the street, she paused, unsure what to do. She saw her reflection in the window, and her eyes were wild. Out here she was somebody else: someone bold and exciting; she barely recognised herself. But she couldn't stand here all day, hovering in front of her own shop—that would attract attention. So, mustering courage, she walked down the hill, her boots striking the concrete.

She wasn't alone on the footpath: a man in a fluorescent work vest was coming the other way. Anxious to avoid him, she ducked into the visitor centre, pushing open the double doors.

She'd never been here before, and she stopped in the doorway and gazed around—all these new things were quite overwhelming. A gust of wind blew some leaves at her legs, so she stepped in and let the door close behind her. She was in a large echoing hall that had a wooden information counter to one side and all sorts of displays. It was warm inside. In the centre of the room, a pot-bellied stove pumped heat, and down the back was a silver log-truck cabin for children to climb on. A boy and girl were playing on it now—the boy hanging from the truck door shouting for his mum to come and look, while the girl bounced up and down on the seat.

Miki wandered around, trying to appear calm as she looked at the displays, but she was too agitated to take in more than a cursory impression. There was so much to see: posters and photos, landscape paintings, a massive cross-section of an old tree trunk, rusty cross-cut saws, old maps, ancient glass bottles and wooden boxes. Near the counter, a series of shelves displayed books for sale, polished pieces of turned wood, postcards, soft toys. It was very neat. Miki imagined there must be quiet times here, just like in the shop. She knew how in those moments you could tidy things over and over, trying to stay awake.

A woman was sitting behind the counter. She was soft-looking and middle-aged with a mushroom cap of grey hair. She smiled at Miki, and her eyes were like half-moons, her mouth kinked upwards at the corners. She seemed friendly, but Miki was too nervous to talk to her. Instead, she slipped behind a blue velvet curtain into a small room where a video was playing to empty rows of yellow plastic seats. Miki sat down. She felt safer behind the curtain where nobody could see her.

On the screen, a man with a rotund belly and bushy beard was talking about Tasmanian devils. Holding up a poster, he explained the breeding program at his private wildlife park. He spoke about an illness affecting devils called facial tumour disease. While he talked, the camera crossed to devils with sores and lumpy wounds on their faces. In some cases, the tumours had eaten away the devils' faces so the poor creatures looked like monsters. Miki felt sick. The man was saying how much he loved devils and wanted to save them. He said the tumours were caused by a disease passed on by bite wounds. Devils bit each other all the time; Miki knew how an argument over food could easily lead to a fight. She wondered, with a flash of panic, whether this disease had killed the other two adult devils at the tip last year. They'd had sores on their faces. The man said all the devils were dying—ninety per cent had already gone. He spoke of losing them forever. Miki was so distressed she couldn't listen anymore. She stumbled into the main hall and wove numbly through the exhibits, heading for the door.

'Are you all right?' The lady behind the counter was speaking to her. 'You look upset.'

Miki hesitated. Could she put her trust in this woman? 'I saw the film about the devils,' she said miserably. 'I didn't know about the disease.'

The woman tutted sympathetically. 'Yes, I know. It's awful, isn't it?'

Miki gravitated towards the desk. The woman had a kind smile and crinkles at the corners of her eyes. The name tag on her generous bosom said Geraldine; on the counter in front of her lay a thick, forked-open book.

'I think I've seen devils with that disease,' Miki said.

Geraldine looked concerned. 'Around here?'

'Yes. At the tip. Some of them disappeared.'

Geraldine's face twisted with worry. 'We need to tell someone. Devils are a Tasmanian icon. We're afraid they'll go extinct like the tigers.' She paused. 'I'm Geraldine, by the way.'

'I know.' Miki pointed to her name tag.

Geraldine smiled. 'And you're Miki, aren't you? From the takeaway.'

Miki was surprised this woman knew her. Was it possible that everyone in town knew everyone else, except her? What else didn't she know?

'I'm sorry I don't come into your shop,' Geraldine was saying. She patted her bulging waistline. 'Trying to watch my weight.' She opened a laptop on her desk and typed on the keyboard. 'There's a scientist in Hobart working on that disease,' she said. 'His name's Dale, and he's been asking whether anyone has seen devils around town. How would you feel about talking to him?'

'Perhaps he could find them himself,' Miki suggested. Kurt wouldn't want her talking to strangers.

Geraldine shook her head. 'I'm sure he'd want to speak to you. He'd want to hear about everything you've seen, especially about the devils that disappeared. Why don't I find out when he's going to be here again? He might make a special trip.'

Miki pretended to look through the postcards while Geraldine was typing. She wanted to leave, but that would be rude. She shouldn't have come here. Things were getting out of control.

'There you go.' Geraldine smiled. 'I've sent him an email.'

Miki's knees felt weak, so she put a hand on the counter to steady herself. Geraldine's book was there; Miki's eyes were drawn to the cover: *The Luminaries* by Eleanor Catton. 'How is your book?' she asked.

'It's very good. It won the Booker, you know.'

'The Booker?'

'The international prize for fiction.'

'Of course.' Miki tried to hide her embarrassment.

'You like reading?' Geraldine asked.

'I love it.'

Geraldine's smile widened. 'That's great. I do too. What books do you read?'

'I like classics,' Miki said, feeling safer.

'Me too.' Geraldine's face lit up. 'How wonderful. We can talk to each other about books—there's not much opportunity for that around here.'

Miki pointed to *The Luminaries*. 'Your book is almost as big as the Bible.'

'The Bible is an enormous book,' Geraldine agreed.

'I've read most of it,' Miki said.

'Really?' The older woman's eyebrows lifted so high they were lost beneath her fringe. 'That's an achievement.'

'It's the only book we had growing up.'

Geraldine tutted. 'People should grow up in a house *full* of books. Do you have many now?'

'Only a few, but I read them over and over.'

'You should join the library,' Geraldine said. 'You can borrow ten books at a time, and if they don't have what you want you can put in a request and they'll bring it across from another library.'

'I don't think that will work for me.' Miki knew Kurt wouldn't approve.

Geraldine frowned. 'What books do you have?'

'*Jane Eyre*, *Wuthering Heights* and *Tess of the D'Urbervilles*.'

'Good taste. Those are wonderful books. I used to teach literature at school and I loved teaching the romantic classics. These days they mostly teach modern stuff. Such a shame.' She sighed. 'I had to give teaching away when I moved here. Not many jobs at the local high school and I don't like to drive, so I'm doing something easier now, working here . . . although some days you wonder . . . especially when the children are screaming and you have difficult people.' She smiled. 'The books save me. I read whenever I can.'

Books saved Miki too.

'What I love about books,' Geraldine went on, 'is that they show you about life. You fall in love with the characters and see the world through their eyes. Then you realise parts of their lives are just like yours. Different setting and time, but the problems are the same. You just have to be clever enough to see it. Does it work like that for you too?'

'Yes,' Miki said. Hadn't she been thinking about Jane Eyre just that morning?

Geraldine picked up *The Luminaries* and slid in a bookmark. 'I'm sad you have only three books—that's not many. Fact is I have too many books at home, so next time you come here I'll lend you one. How about that?'

Miki didn't know what to say. A new book would be good, but how would she hide it from Kurt?

'What sort of book would you like?' Geraldine asked. 'Where shall we start? Another classic, perhaps?'

Miki nodded. That would be safest with Kurt.

'Good. I'll bring something tomorrow . . . Oh, look—Dale has written back already, and he says he can come in two weeks. What day would be best? You can choose.'

Miki felt paralysed. There was no way Kurt would allow it. And what if he found out about the key? She wouldn't be able to get out.

'How about 7 p.m. Monday?' Geraldine prompted. 'Does that work?'

'I don't know,' Miki said.

Geraldine's eyes softened. 'Is everything all right?'

Miki swallowed. 'Monday's okay. But if I'm not here, you'll have to go without me.'

Geraldine smiled. 'That sounds like a plan. Dale will bring a car full of traps, and then you can show him the tip.' Her smile deepened. 'How about I come too? We'll have fun. I'd love to see a Tasmanian devil in the wild.'

PART II
Germination

9

Max was looking forward to Rosie having pups. Every day her tummy grew bigger, and the other morning he'd even noticed a bead of milk on one of her teats. Since she'd gone to the vet with Leon nearly two weeks ago, Max had been looking after her. He'd made a bed for her in the shed and he put out her food every night: two cups of dry kibble. It couldn't be long now till the pups were born, and this time he wasn't going to miss it.

'Hey, Mum,' he said. 'Can we get a muzzle for Rosie so she can't eat her pups?'

It was just before dinner. Mum was at the kitchen bench, cutting potatoes. She frowned. 'I wouldn't worry about that.'

'But she did it before. Dad said she did.'

Mum stopped cutting and stared through the window. It was dark out there. Max couldn't imagine what she might be looking at. She sighed, but no answer.

'Mum, please. I want to see the pups this time.'

She scraped cubes of potato into a pot, half-filled it with water and set it on the stove.

'What if she has her pups up in the forest?' Max asked.

'Yes,' Mum said. 'That would be a problem.'

'I want her to have them at home.'

Mum sighed again. 'I'll tell Dad to leave her here instead of taking her to work.'

But later that night Dad was cross when Mum suggested Rosie should stay home. 'The dog guards the ute,' he growled. 'She always comes to work with me.'

'Maybe she shouldn't,' Mum said. 'It's not as if you're carrying anything worth stealing. And look what happened to her last time.'

'That wasn't my fault.'

'Of course it was. If you'd tied her up properly, she wouldn't have fallen off and cut herself.'

Dad had nothing to say to that. Max knew he was still angry at Leon for getting Rosie stitched up.

'If you leave her home, I can look after her,' Max offered.

Dad scowled. 'Are you two ganging up on me?'

'Wouldn't dream of it,' Mum said, laughing.

'When do those stitches come out?' Dad grunted. 'I'm not paying for it.'

'Leon said it was all covered,' Mum said.

'Do we have to take her to the vet?' Dad asked.

'Leon will take her,' said Max. 'But he can't if she's up in the forest.'

Dad was mad then. He stomped around the house cursing Leon. 'If I wanted him to take my dog to the vet, I would have asked for it.'

'You'd never take a dog to the vet,' Mum pointed out.

'I don't want to owe him anything.'

'That's easy to fix,' Mum said. 'He was asking if we knew anyone on the footy team. Says he's interested in playing. Maybe you could put in a word for him with Robbo.'

Dad glared at her. 'Why were you talking to him?'

'He was kicking a footy with Max.'

'Got a new coach, have you?' Dad stared at Max, and Max couldn't help squirming.

'He's more patient than you,' Mum said.

'But nowhere near as good,' Max added quickly. Mum was mucking this up. She was making Dad madder.

Dad gave Max a pleased smile and brushed a hand over his head. 'Good on you, buddy.'

'So you'll speak to Robbo?' Mum asked.

'And can Rosie stay home?' Max put in.

'I'll think about it,' said Dad, opening a beer.

Next morning when Dad drove off, Rosie stayed home. Max ran over to Leon's and knocked on the door. 'Rosie can get her stitches out today,' he told Leon.

Leon scratched his head. 'Oh yeah. I forgot about that.'

'Can you take her?'

Leon looked doubtful. 'I'm not sure. I can't leave her in my car all day. How about I ring and see if she can stay at the clinic while I'm at work?'

'What if the pups are born while she's there?' Max asked. 'Will the vet get to keep them?'

'No. The pups belong to you.'

Max sprawled on the doorstep while Leon made the call and talked to someone. 'Who was that?' Max asked when Leon was finished.

'It was the vet nurse. She was very kind to Rosie.'

'Is the vet nice too? Is he a good bloke?'

'He isn't a bloke,' Leon said. 'He's a lady called Kate. And she's very good.'

When Leon brought Rosie home from the vet that afternoon, Max inspected her wound to make sure all the stitches were gone. 'Did they make you pay?' he asked, because Mum had been going on about it since he arrived home from school. Leon said no, but he had that look on his face adults got when they told lies.

Max took Rosie home and fed her in the shed. She was restless after dinner, scratching around in her blankets and wandering about the yard, sniffing like she was looking for a bone. Maybe she was upset after having to sit in a cage all day. Max didn't blame her; it would have been like sitting in class.

Dad came home just on dark, and Mum called Max to dinner. It was meat and three veg again: barbecue chops with boiled potato, carrots and peas. Suzie was picking at her peas like they were poison, but Mum and Dad ignored her. If Max had mucked around with his food like that, he would have been in trouble. Nobody was talking much so he thought he'd better fill in the space. He didn't like it when Mum and Dad were quiet because that meant an argument might be brewing. 'Rosie got her stitches out,' he said, knocking his plate with a clatter that made Dad look up.

'Why is your fork in the wrong hand?' Dad said. 'If you're going to eat like an animal you can go out with the dog.'

That wasn't a bad idea. Max wouldn't mind being outside with Rosie. At least it was quiet out there. No arguments. And nobody telling him what to do. He picked up his plate and fork to go, but Dad yelled at him to sit back down. Max shook his head—he couldn't win.

'Did it cost anything to get those stitches out?' Dad asked, scowling.

'No. Leon said it was free.'

'Damn right, it ought to be free. Especially when I didn't want it done in the first place.'

'Her scar looks good. That's what Leon said.'

Dad glared at Max. 'What would *he* know? He's a bloody Parkie.'

Max asked, 'What's that?'

'Someone who works in the National Park,' Mum said. 'A ranger.'

'A Parkie is someone who locks up trees and steals people's jobs,' Dad snarled, leaning across the table towards Max. 'And don't you forget it.'

'Is that what Leon does?' Max asked Mum. Sometimes Dad got all hot about things that weren't true.

'He empties rubbish bins and fixes up trails,' Mum said.

'He's a damned greenie, that's what he is,' Dad insisted.

'His family were all loggers,' Mum said.

'Sounds like bullshit to me. You believe him?'

'Yes, I do.'

'Then you're just as clueless as he is.'

Max bent his head and got on with eating. The sooner he was done, the sooner he could get out of here.

After dinner he found Rosie in the shed, sitting in a funny position and pushing with her tummy. Max wondered if a bone had got stuck, then he realised she might be squeezing out a pup. He ran inside and fetched his torch so he could see. By the time he got back, Rosie had dropped something on the blankets and was eating a piece of red rubbery meat. Was she eating her pup?

Max shouted at her and reached to pull the pink stuff from her mouth, but it was slippery and Rosie rumbled at him. She gulped the last bit down and turned to the blankets, snuffling at the thing she'd left there. Out came her tongue, swiping. At first Max thought she was going to eat this too, then he took a closer look and almost burst with excitement. Rosie was cleaning a little white pup. She wasn't a bad mum after all.

He crouched and watched Rosie busy licking. She pushed the pup all over the place, and its head kept bobbing up and down. Its eyes were shut tight and its ears were funny little flaps of black skin.

Rosie started squatting again and pushed out another pup. She cleaned it, then a third one came out. Then she lay on her side, and the pups wriggled up to her tummy and tried to latch on to her teats. Two of them worked it out quickly, but the last one went the wrong way, right up under Rosie's nose.

Max couldn't handle it—on hands and knees, he gently scooped up the pup and pointed it onto one of Rosie's teats. Luckily Rosie didn't seem to mind. She lay back while Max helped the pup to hook on. It made him feel good to watch those pups sucking. Rosie looked like she'd done this before.

Mum came out when Rosie had six pups in total. Smiling, she sat down with Max to watch. 'She's really good at looking after them,' he whispered. 'I've been here the whole time and she hasn't had any troubles.'

Mum's smile faded a little.

'Look at her licking them,' Max said quietly. 'She's cleaning them up. Isn't she clever? What happened those other times? Didn't she know what to do?'

'I don't know, Max.' Mum's face had a crumpled look.

'What's the pink stuff that comes out with the pups?'

'That's the afterbirth.'

'It's gross. Why does she eat it?'

'To clean up, I suppose. Like all mothers.'

Max was horrified. 'You didn't eat the afterbirth, did you?'

Mum laughed so hard she had to lie down on the edge of Rosie's bed. 'Oh, Max,' she gasped. 'You're so funny. Of course I didn't eat the afterbirth. Only animals do that.'

Max looked at her, surprised. Didn't she know humans were animals too?

'Well, some people eat it,' Mum said. 'I've heard you can make it into lasagne.' She was snorting through her laughter. 'Imagine that. You'd never want to eat lasagne again.'

Max had never seen her so laugh so crazily. Part of him wanted her to stop, but it was fun to see her so happy. 'I'm glad you didn't do it,' he said. 'And please don't make lasagne this week.'

Then they were both laughing so much it made Rosie growl. Max had to tell Mum to shush up. Sometimes parents got carried away and forgot how to be sensible.

10

Thursday night, Leon pulled up at the oval for footy training and parked under the gum trees. Shane had told him the coach was willing to give him a run, but suddenly it didn't seem such a good plan. The weather was terrible and the field was a sea of mud. But that was footy, wasn't it? Rain or shine, you had to get out there.

Around the field, other team members were emerging from their cars: all twin-cab four-wheel drive utes with long aerials, which seemed to be the go around here. Leon tugged on the footy boots he'd bought that afternoon. The shoe shop in town had only a small range so it was lucky they'd had something resembling his size. As he squatted to tie his laces, some of the men jogged onto the field. Leon reminded himself this was just a small town and he should be able to hold his own here. When he was a kid, he didn't do juniors because Bruny Island was too small for a competition, but he'd played at high school and university, and he was a pretty good winger. He was quick on his feet and had solid skills. Now, he felt a rush of excitement. He was actually looking forward to knocking a ball around again. He didn't mind a bit of rough and tumble. And there was something therapeutic about putting yourself to the test. He ducked under the rail and headed across the field to join in.

Shane was standing alone, sucking on a smoke. In tracksuit pants and a black raincoat, he wasn't dressed for playing. When he saw Leon, he turned away, but Leon was relying on him for introductions so he strode up and offered his hand. Shane inspected it lengthily before shaking. 'Thanks for taking this on for me—I appreciate it,' Leon said, ignoring the snub.

Shane sniffed, and Leon figured Wendy must have pushed him into doing this introduction.

'You're not playing?' Leon asked.

'Nah. Did a knee years ago. I'm a runner now. And I help out with training.'

'Bad luck about the knee. Doctors can't fix it?'

'Nothing I can afford, other than tablets.'

'I've been lucky with injuries,' Leon said. 'A few knocks to the head, but nothing serious.'

Shane broke into a lopsided grin. 'Concussion, eh? Explains a lot.'

Leon smiled too. 'How's the team going?' he asked. 'Where are they on the ladder?'

'Near the bottom. Tough competition this year.'

'Maybe I can help.'

Shane glanced at him then spat on the ground. 'Got tabs on yourself, have you?'

'No. But I'll run my butt off. Maybe kick a few goals.'

'Maybe, eh?' Shane shook his head. 'Let's get this intro over and done with so we can get on with training.'

The coach was a stubby man with an enormous belly and beard, and an even bigger voice. 'Carn, you guys,' he was yelling. 'Get your arses into gear. You going to warm up or what?'

'Hey, Robbo,' Shane said. 'This is the bloke I told you about. Leon Walker. Wants to try out for the team.'

Robbo eyed Leon like a piece of meat. 'Not very big, are you?'

'No, but I can run.'

'You'll need to around here if you don't want to get squashed.'

Leon almost laughed. Robbo was a bowling ball crossed with a doughnut—what did he know about running? Shane had said Robbo drove the log truck Leon had often seen in the street: a big blue Kenworth. That was what you got from too much driving—a belly Humpty Dumpty would be proud of.

Robbo called the team in, and the men stared at Leon. They were a mixed bag: a couple of oldies in their thirties still trying to keep up, the rest in their twenties like Leon. Beards were the go and most had tattoos. Beside them, Leon felt like a cleanskin.

'Okay, fellers,' Robbo said. 'This is how it is. Walker here is trying out with us, and if he's halfway decent we'll let him in. We've had some injuries this season, so it won't hurt to have another player on the interchange bench.'

The men's faces were hard, and Leon heard murmurs of *Parkie* and wondered if they were all loggers. Robbo did nothing to stop the whispers and Shane wasn't saying anything, so Leon knew he'd have to show them he was good enough.

Then the rain set in, sheets of it rushing across the oval. He was used to bad weather, but this was still going to be tough.

Robbo sent them on a warm-up jog, and they took off, jostling, spitting and cracking jokes, rain needling their faces. Leon tried to hover at the edge of the pack, out of the way, but he wasn't going to get off that easy. A big bald bloke called Toby bumped into him and almost knocked him down. 'Ah, sorry, mate. Didn't see you there.' Toby's arms and legs were a tapestry of tattoos. 'Who do you barrack for?' he asked.

'Carlton.' Leon had chosen the Blues when he was a kid, even though most of his mates went for Hawthorn. He had no idea why he'd done it, maybe just to be different. Now Toby roared with laughter, and Leon knew he was done for.

'Did you hear that?' Toby yelled. 'He's a bloody Blues supporter. Fucken silvertails.'

The team jeered.

That set the tone for the session and there was no winning any favours. Leon worked hard, but no one would kick to him. They roughed him up, elbowed him, crashed into him, and wouldn't handball to him even if he was right alongside. A blond bloke called Mooney took an instant dislike and shoved him into the mud at any opportunity. Mooney's attitude was contagious, and by the end of training Leon was bruised and annoyed. One of the blokes proposed a visit to the pub, but they all avoided looking at him so he knew he wasn't invited. Just as well, because to admit he didn't drink would have been suicide.

When they left, Leon stayed back to have a word with Robbo, who glared at him with little pig eyes and no smile. Leon asked, 'Am I in?'

Robbo shrugged. 'Suppose so. We need you to make up the numbers.'

It wasn't exactly a compliment, but Leon decided it was enough. He would prove himself out on the field.

'How's your fitness?' Robbo asked.

'Not bad. I've been lugging sleepers up in the park. They're pretty heavy.'

'You realise the other lads come first. They've been training all season, so you'll be spending time on the interchange bench. The boys like to win. They don't take kindly to losing the ball.'

This was a bit harsh, given that nobody had passed to him tonight. 'Sure, I understand,' Leon said, 'but I hope you'll give me a chance.'

Robbo wasn't making any promises. 'We'll see how things go. Can you make it to the game on Saturday?'

'I'll be there.'

Leon shook hands and then left. But a surprise was waiting for him in the car park. While he'd been chatting to Robbo, the others had let down his tyres. At least he had a foot pump in the back, so he could sort things out. He supposed he'd better get used to self-rescue round here.

His mum rang as he was filling the tyres. 'How did footy go?' she asked.

'Fine,' he grunted, pumping with his foot.

'That's great, Leon. I'm so proud of you, making a go of it there.' He heard the smile in her voice.

'Any more visits from Stan?' he asked. He was concerned about the influence of his dad's old drinking mate. She was quiet, and worry welled through him like a fast-moving tide. 'What's going on, Mum? Has Dad been up to his old tricks?'

'No,' she said. 'We're good here.'

Leon thought her voice sounded strained. He would only know for sure if he saw her in person. 'Glad everything's okay, Mum,' he said. 'I'd better go. It's raining and I need to get home for a shower.'

On Saturday when Leon rocked up at the footy field for his first game, spectators were setting up folding chairs around the boundary fence so they could get a good view of the action. He sat in his car a few moments, psyching himself up. The big tattooed bald bloke—Toby—was walking across the oval with a woman, presumably his wife, while four kids gambolled around them like a small herd of goats. That nasty piece of work, Mooney, was there too, arguing with a thin blonde woman while two little girls watched on. The way the man stood over his wife, it was clear to Leon that the treatment he'd received from Mooney at training wasn't out of the ordinary. The guy was a prick. Leon would do his best to avoid him; he wasn't scared of the man, he simply didn't want trouble.

Seeing Mooney's behaviour bugged Leon so much, his nerves were replaced by fierce determination. But when he joined the team, the men stared at him blankly and he knew they didn't want him there. For a microsecond he considered walking away, but he wouldn't give up. This was his new beginning. No way was he going to quit. His dad would say, *I told you so*, and Leon wasn't having that.

Warm-up was the ritual jog round the oval then some stretches and sprints. Robbo was a hard taskmaster. He yelled and clapped and hurled abuse, especially at Leon. But as Leon jogged laps with the men, he realised it was all show. Sounding tough was about impressing the spectators who were watching from the boundary. Wendy was there, leaning on the rail with Max and Suzie. The little girl was dragging her doll around and Max was glued to his phone. As the team jogged by, Max looked up and waved at Leon. 'Rosie had her pups,' he yelled. 'I saw them being born.'

Leon gave him the thumbs up. 'How many?'

'Six. And she didn't eat any.' The kid hadn't worked out that Rosie had always been a good mum. 'Come and see them this afternoon,' Max yelled.

'Sure,' Leon called back.

Just before kick-off time, the men performed their final stretches. Then the umpire tramped onto the field. Leon was exiled to the bench, of course. Usually eighteen players were on the field and four on the interchange bench, and the coach subbed players on and off for a breather. Today, however, Leon was the only one on the interchange for his team, so they were seriously down on numbers and needed him more than they were letting on. He sat alone, perched on a plastic chair, telling himself that the best way to break into a town like this was through sport. Problem was, he could end up here for the whole game. He suspected Robbo would only use him if they were desperate. And if they let him on the field, he would have to pull out something spectacular, like walk on water. But he was up for it. He just had to stick it out.

The siren sounded, the umpire bounced the ball and the game was on. From the start it was brutal, neither side taking any prisoners. Robbo shouted and swore from the boundary, brandishing his fist at the opposition, the umpire, even his own team. Bodies thumped and clashed, men sweated and cursed, and everyone grovelled after that slippery mud-coated ball. Even though it looked like war, Leon couldn't wait to get out there. But as the minutes ticked by and his body cooled down, he realised he was just another spectator. He tried to convince himself it wasn't much of a game anyway, more like rugby than footy—a form of legalised murder. He didn't want to be killed or put in a wheelchair or smashed to a pulp. But excuses didn't make him feel better; there was no glory to be had on the sidelines.

At quarter time the men huddled on the field, bending over with hands propped on knees while Robbo yelled at them. They slugged from water bottles passed round by Shane, and jiggled their mouthguards and spat on the ground. Leon stood beside them and stretched, but he felt too clean. The men wore their mud and scrapes like badges of honour.

The second quarter was even rougher, and when the other team pulled ahead, the local crowd hissed and booed. At half-time, in the clubroom, Robbo roared at the men to start scoring goals. They glared at Leon in his clean blue shorts; they didn't understand how much he would give to get dirty.

Shortly after half-time, Mooney was thumped in a terrible tackle. From the boundary Leon heard the air go out of him as he collapsed to the ground. Outraged, the locals screamed and swore at the umpire, demanding justice, and Leon thought a fight was going to break out, maybe two—one on the field and one among the spectators. The umpire finally stopped the game and Mooney was carried off, blood streaming from his nose, groaning like he was in labour.

That was when Robbo looked at Leon. 'You're on.'

Leon had to go out there cold, but he wasn't going to pass up his chance. He jumped up and down a few times, did some quick stretches and jogged onto the field. The way the men looked at him, he wasn't sure which team was going to give him a harder time.

It was a battlefield out there. Nothing like schoolboy football. And nothing like footy in Hobart. Both sides were out to get him. Everyone crashed into him, and every collision hurt. Nobody looked for him. No one kicked or handballed to him.

Battered and bruised, he charged through the field, determined to do something useful. When the ball flew near, he sprinted and clawed for it, still running, and then he was scrabbling. But it was okay. He was out there on his own. The ball was his.

As he bore down on it, he heard heavy breathing on his tail. Without taking his eye off the ball, he snatched it into his hands, glanced up, looking for a pass, and tried to get his boot to it. Then something crashed into him and he slammed face-down in the mud. The breath whooshed out of his lungs and pain ripped through as a player thundered over, juddering him in his wake. Dogged, he thrust his feet under him and kept running. He had to be strong: they'd be judging him for this. But as he dug his toes into the mud and struggled to regain momentum, he saw a face scowling back at him and, with a jolt, he realised it was Toby who'd crunched him. Incensed, Leon burst after him, so angry he felt rocket-powered. But, before he could get close, Toby was brought down by a tackle around the neck from the other team. The opposition took possession, and it looked like they were going to score another goal—until Leon hammered in and snatched the ball again.

Suddenly, miraculously, he was clear. He tore down the field, bouncing the ball every few strides. The players were after him, but they couldn't get traction in the mud. Leon was in command of the ball. He sized up the goal, found his balance and swung his boot through. At the critical point of contact between boot and ball, his support foot slipped a fraction, but there was margin for error. The ball sailed through the air on trajectory for a goal.

Then it wobbled in a gust of wind and clipped the goal post, dropping through for a point.

Leon was crushed and so was his team. They were going for him, he realised. He'd almost made it.

'That was fucking bad luck,' Toby said. 'We could have used a goal.' He hoicked and spat on the ground, then grinned. 'I suppose that's what you'd expect from a Parkie.'

11

On the designated devil-trapping night, just before seven, Miki fetched her hidden key and unlocked the back door with shaking hands. She was wired with excitement. As she closed the door behind her and stepped into the blue light of evening her skin tingled with the sweet joy of freedom.

It seemed she'd been waiting for this day forever: a window of light in her ordinary week. She hadn't known until late whether she would escape or not. This morning she and Kurt had gone to the forest as usual, but when they came home Kurt had retreated to the storeroom under the shop and spent hours down there while Miki busied herself in the kitchen, lining up mugs in the cupboard, organising tins in the pantry, listening to him bang around and hoping he'd leave. All day, she had worried he might not go and her plans would be ruined. Maybe he knew about the key and was going to confront her. But nothing was said.

It was a relief when he'd finally locked her in the house and headed to Hobart. She had been sitting in the kitchen ever since, waiting in her overalls with a fast-beating heart.

Now, in the lane, she slid the key in her pocket and inhaled deeply. It was cold and dark, the air thick with wood smoke.

Up towards the mountains, silver stars blinked in the indigo sky. She glided along the laneway, where a crouching cat inspected her with green eyes and clawed its way over the fence. The main street was quiet—nobody about; everyone must be home eating dinner and watching TV.

Down the footpath she strode, springy with anticipation. But the visitor centre seemed deserted: the front door was locked, and only night-lights glowed in the windows. A wave of disappointment washed through her—maybe the whole thing had been called off. Around the back, a white Toyota LandCruiser stood in the car park, but the rear door to the centre was locked too. Unsure what to do, she waited for a few minutes.

She was about to give up and go home when the back door opened. Geraldine peered out, her face lighting up when she saw Miki. 'Oh good. We were worried you couldn't come. Dale's here, and a Parks ranger too. His name's Leon.' She called back into the building. 'Miki's here.'

Dale, the scientist, reminded Miki of a regrowth sapling: tall and thin with lined cheeks and wild grey hair. He was wearing overalls, and he nodded approvingly when he saw Miki's outfit—for once she was wearing the right uniform. She accepted his handshake even though she knew Kurt wouldn't like it.

Leon grinned as Geraldine introduced him. 'We've met before,' he said. 'Miki makes a mean burger.' Miki noticed scratches on his face, a lump over one eye—maybe he'd been in a fight. Then she remembered hearing he'd played footy on Saturday. Every week the walking wounded boasted about their cuts and scrapes in the shop. Now Leon was one of them.

Dale and Leon swung into the front of the Toyota while Miki and Geraldine sat in the back. It was awkward being with strangers—Miki was so nervous she almost forgot her seatbelt. The car smelled of vinyl and disinfectant. Behind the safety cage, mountains of gear had been packed: white pipes, plastic boxes and milk crates.

At the tip, they all clambered out. It was still and cold, and the rubbish was stinky. The men stood beneath the fluorescent light, hands in pockets, surveying the territory.

'I wouldn't have picked this as a hangout for devils,' Leon said. 'What's their usual habitat?'

'Dry forest and coastal woodlands, but there are good pickings in tips. Plenty of food.'

'There's shelter too,' Miki said. 'Places to hide.'

Dale's eyes settled on her as she pulled a bag of meat from her pocket. 'You feed them?'

'Yes. Sometimes they eat from my hand.'

He smiled. 'Devil woman!'

'Isn't that a Cliff Richard song?' Geraldine said.

Leon hummed a tune, and Miki didn't know what they were talking about.

Dale was still smiling as he extracted a spotlight from the back of the Toyota. 'Okay, Miki. Can you show us where you usually see these devils so we can put out some traps?'

She led the way through the tip. Now they were here, she felt apprehensive. She wanted to help the devils, but she didn't want them to be hurt. The devils trusted her, and her special connection with them had been built over time. It was fragile. If the devils were captured, the bond might be broken. They would be released again, of course, but they wouldn't know that when they went into a trap.

Rubbish racketed as two quolls sprang out from a pile. 'Hey!' Dale called. 'Quolls.' He swung his spotlight to find them, but Miki knew they were long gone. Quolls were sensitive creatures.

She trudged among the hummocks to the back of the tip. 'If you wait here near the excavator, I might be able to coax the devils out,' she told Dale.

He liked this idea, so she laid some meat at the far end of the yard then shifted a short distance away and sat down to wait.

For a while, nothing happened. Wind stirred pieces of plastic and loose bits of tin. Garbage creaked and moaned. Miki was beginning to think they would see nothing tonight, when a dark shape loomed from the shadows. It was the male devil, and he was suspicious. He stopped and sniffed the air then hunched and hissed and snarled, sound rising and falling in this throat like the noise of the takeaway's espresso machine. He must know strangers were present, but the scent of the meat was tempting, and eventually he scuttled forward and snatched it up.

Dale switched on the spotlight and the devil stopped chewing, squinting into the brightness. The sore on his lip had grown distinctly larger: red-raw and as big as a fifty-cent piece. Dale was beckoning to Miki, so she crept back to him. 'It looks like that devil might have the disease,' he whispered.

A stone rolled in her stomach. 'Could it be anything else?'

'I don't think so. They get some bad fight wounds but that looks more like a tumour. We need to catch him and take a sample.'

Dale started towards the Toyota, but Miki hung back, worried about using the traps. The devils wouldn't understand. It would be terrifying for them.

Leon waited to walk with her and Geraldine. 'Are you okay with this?' he asked.

She was unaccustomed to being asked her opinion—but if she didn't stand up for the devils, who would? 'I'd rather we left them alone.'

'Dale has trapped tons of devils. He knows what he's doing.'

Miki imagined the devil in a trap, butting wildly against the sides. She knew what it was like to be locked in, and the devil would be confused. She wished she hadn't brought people here.

Geraldine patted her arm and smiled reassuringly. 'I'm sure your devil will be okay. He's such a feisty animal. So much attitude for a little guy!'

At the car, Dale set up a folding table and jiggled it to find an even spot on the ground. He had an air of excitement about him as he laid out his gear, but Miki's stomach was still grinding with angst. Dale demonstrated how to set the Polypipe traps by attaching a chicken wing bait to a string that connected to a wire pin in the door. If an animal went in and pulled on the bait, the pin would be triggered and the door would fall shut. He made it all sound so easy but, to Miki, the pipe looked dark and confined, and her misgivings intensified.

'If we catch him, can you fix him?' she asked.

Dale's eyes locked with hers. 'I wish I could,' he said slowly, as if seeking the right words. 'But if he has the disease it's only a matter of time.'

A lump clogged Miki's throat. 'Till he dies?'

Leon was watching her. Something unspoken told her he understood what she was feeling.

'I'm really sorry, but yes,' Dale said. 'It's untreatable. A vaccine is being developed, but we're not there yet.'

'If you can't make him better, what's the point of catching him?'

Dale regarded her quietly and lowered his trap to the ground. His grey eyes were solemn. 'I know this is very confronting, so I'll try to explain. Facial tumour disease is a serious threat to devils and it could lead to extinction. We have several scientists working on different aspects of the disease, and my job is to map its distribution and the way it spreads so we can learn more about it. I can't save your devil, but the information we collect from him could influence our knowledge and plans and help other devils. We won't know what we're dealing with unless I collect a sample.'

Miki glanced away, not wanting to show how upset she was.

'I won't hurt him,' Dale went on. 'Handling wildlife is a privilege, and I study these guys because I care about them. They're quiet in these traps. It might surprise you. How about we give it a go? The chicken wings are in the esky. Devils love them.'

He handed Miki a trap, and Leon helped her fix a chicken wing in it. Then they set traps around the tip. Once the traps were in place, Miki sat in the Toyota with Geraldine while the men chatted outside. Geraldine unfolded a checked woollen blanket and spread it over her lap, then wriggled close and tucked it over Miki's knees too, saying, 'Cold out there, isn't it?'

This kindness reminded Miki of the way her mother used to come into her room at night and snuggle the blankets tight around her to make sure she stayed warm. It was a motherly thing: a concern for others that extended beyond self. Father never had it. Neither did Kurt. Maybe Geraldine was a mother too. Miki realised she knew very little about the woman sitting beside her.

Geraldine had been fossicking in her handbag, and now she pulled out a book and handed it to Miki. 'I promised to bring you one. Remember?'

It was *Far from the Madding Crowd* by Thomas Hardy, the author who had written *Tess of the D'Urbervilles*. Miki's pulse surged and for a moment she forgot about the devils. She examined the cover: a picture of a small flock of black-faced sheep being herded through a wooden gate on a snowy track. Behind them: a border collie and the figure of a man. Branches arched across the track, just like in the forest. A snow-covered farmhouse.

'I love sharing books,' Geraldine was saying. 'And I know you love *Tess*, but I think you'll like this story too. When you've read it, you'll have to come and visit me. I want to know what you think.'

Miki ran a finger over the cover. It was hard to believe the book was hers to discover, a whole story waiting to unfold from the pages. 'I don't know when I can come,' she said. Her escapes would end if Kurt found she'd taken a key.

'That's all right, dear,' Geraldine said. 'You come when you can.'

An hour later, they checked the traps. In the far corner of the yard, one was closed. When Leon shifted it, a loud shriek confirmed they'd caught a devil. Miki pictured the animal, hemmed in and frightened. But Dale seemed unperturbed. Businesslike, he covered one end of the trap with a hessian sack then opened the door and guided the devil in. He passed the bag to Miki, smiling triumphantly. 'Here's your devil. You can carry him back to the car.'

Miki accepted the bag tentatively; it was heavy. 'Will he bite?'

'Keep him away from your body,' Dale warned. 'Let's hope he's not hungry.'

In the bag, the devil remained quiet. 'He's very still,' she said. 'Could he be dead?'

'He's alive, all right. Don't put your hands on him.'

At the car, Dale took the bag from Miki and placed it on the table. With a special set of scales, he recorded the weight then showed Leon how to restrain the devil in the bag to avoid getting bitten. Leon knelt on the ground and settled the animal between his knees before carefully locating the devil's head and securing it firmly by the muzzle. Dale opened the bag and motioned to Miki and Geraldine to come closer. With the bag rolled back, Miki could see the devil's black rump. Dale slid a hand over the animal's coat. 'He's in reasonable condition. Good cover over the ribs. A decent amount of muscle. Do you want to have a feel?'

Geraldine kept her distance and crinkled her nose. 'He's a bit stinky.'

'That's because he's stressed,' Dale explained.

'I like the way he smells,' Miki said.

'Me too,' Leon agreed. He was doing a good job of holding the devil. He had good hands: firm but gentle—Miki could tell he cared about animals. With trepidation, she reached into the bag and laid a hand on the devil's fur, which was both wiry and soft. Dale's eyes were alight with excitement. He obviously thought it was a gift to touch a devil like this, even though the creature had no chance of escape. But Miki had stroked the devil here before with no one around. The devil had been wild and free, and he'd had a choice about approaching her. Contact hadn't been forced on him.

While Leon held the devil's muzzle closed, Dale measured the head and hind foot, and then shuffled the fabric around until the animal was sitting in one corner. He instructed Leon to slide a hand into the bag and grasp the muzzle directly. Taking care to keep the devil's eyes covered, Dale folded back the bag until the muzzle was just visible, nostrils quivering, whiskers pricking the air.

'How does it look?' Leon asked.

'Not the best,' Dale admitted. He measured the lump, took photos and made sketches.

Miki didn't need to be told it was bad—the wound looked nasty.

'I need to take the biopsy now,' Dale said quietly. 'It shouldn't hurt. Most of these tumours have a poor nerve supply.' He nodded at Leon. 'Hold tight anyway in case he moves.' From his pocket Dale produced a large needle with a circular tip that he pushed into the lump, twisting before pulling it out again. Blood dripped and Miki's heart thumped wildly, but the sample was done and the handling was almost over.

Dale transferred the sample into a vial while Leon closed the bag.

'When can we let him go?' Miki asked.

'Straight away,' Dale said. 'Would you like to do it?'

She carried the bag across the tip to exactly the place where the devil had been caught. Squatting, she turned the bag away from her and tugged it open, expecting the devil to bolt. But he didn't move. She could feel him shivering in there; he must be terribly scared. Slowly, she rolled the bag back until his head was exposed and she could see the dull red of his wound, his scarred pink ears and shiny black eyes. He was beautiful.

'Give him a little push,' Dale suggested.

She pressed gently on the devil's rump. She was humming—a hymn her mother used to sing to her when she was small and having trouble falling asleep. The devil's ears swivelled as if he was listening. For what seemed a long time, he sat while Miki hummed into the night until something clattered in the rubbish, and the devil sprang from the bag and raced away.

Miki rejoined the others. They were smiling. 'He's okay,' she said.

'He likes you,' Leon said.

Dale tossed a chicken wing towards the rubbish, and the devil loped out and snatched it up, apparently unharmed by his experience.

'That's the way to a man's heart,' Geraldine said. 'Just feed him meat.'

12

Max watched the pups growing, and it happened so quickly. Their eyes and ears opened at eleven days, and by four weeks they had transformed into small dogs. The bigger they grew, the more fun they were. Yipping at each other. Biting with sharp teeth. Pawing at each other's faces. Chewing on each other's tails. They were the best thing. Better than his iPhone, and even better than PlayStation.

But Dad didn't think so. Every time he saw the pups, he scowled and said they cost too much to feed. That wasn't true—all they drank was Rosie's milk.

There were four boys and two girls, and Max had names for them all: Bruiser, Footy, Diesel, Patch, Bonnie and Rosie Junior. For the first few weeks, they lived in the shed in a box that Mum made from a few wooden planks. She said she didn't want them getting in Dad's way, and Max agreed. When he let them out, they followed him around the yard and he was careful not to step on them. But Dad might not be so careful.

Max loved all the pups, but Bonnie was his special favourite. She always came straight up to him when he got home, and she liked to bark at him and play tug of war with his jumper.

She didn't mind when he put her in his schoolbag and carried it on his chest, so he started taking her around with him. On Saturday night, he took her down to the takeaway when he went with Dad to get fish and chips.

Miki noticed straight away and said, 'Wow! What a cute puppy.' Dad frowned and shook his head, but Miki was so excited to see Bonnie that she came out to pat her. Max hadn't seen Miki out from behind the counter before. She was tall and slim like a greyhound, and she wore a long flowing dress that looked like it was from an olden-day movie.

'How old is she?' Miki asked.

'Four weeks.'

'She's gorgeous.'

'Yeah, I know. She's the best.'

'How many in the litter?'

'Six.'

'Are you going to keep her?'

'Not bloody likely,' Dad growled.

Miki glanced at Dad then said quietly to Max, 'You'd better start trying to find homes. Maybe you could take them to school. You can put a for-sale sign in our window if you like.'

'Do you want one?' Max asked, hopeful.

'I wish I could, but I can't. No backyard.'

'You could keep her inside.'

Miki smiled, and Max saw sadness in her big blue eyes. 'Kurt won't let me have a dog. Maybe in a few years when we have our own farm.'

There was a bang at the back of the shop, and Miki hurried behind the counter and washed her hands at the sink just as Kurt came in. He and Dad stared at each other. Then Dad said, 'What does it take to get service in this place? I've been waiting for ages.'

Kurt frowned at Miki, and Max was annoyed at Dad for getting her in trouble. Kurt didn't say anything, but Max knew

Miki was in for it. He'd listened to Mum and Dad talking about Kurt at home. They didn't like him. They thought he was mean to her. *I think he locks her in*, Mum had said. *He treats her like a slave*. Dad had said maybe he'd better get some locks too, and then laughed as if he was making a joke. But Max didn't think it was funny—Miki was nice and always gave him extra lollies.

On the way home, Dad was grouchy. 'Those pups need to be gone in two weeks.'

'But they're so little.' Max ran a finger over Bonnie's domed head.

'They'll be six weeks old and ready to go.'

On Monday, Max convinced Mum to let him take the pups to school so he could find homes for them. He put them in the pram, but Suzie was upset and said, 'No,' very loudly and tried to take them out. Max shoved her away.

'You have to walk, Suzie,' Mum said. 'That's why you've got legs.'

In the street, Max asked if he could push the pram. Mum raised her eyebrows at him. 'I thought you didn't like wheeling the pram.' But this was different: Max felt important as he rolled it along. Kids came running to have a look and everyone wanted to pat the pups. It was lucky the pram had high sides. The pups kept trying to stand on their hind legs with their front paws on the edge, and Max had to keep jerking the pram to make them fall down so they couldn't climb out. By the time he arrived at school, he had about ten kids with him, all talking about how lucky he was. Even Lily Moon came over. 'They're cool,' she said. 'I wish I could have one.'

'They're free,' Max said, noticing how the morning sun turned her hair golden. 'You can have one if you want.'

'I'll have to ask my dad.'

'Does he like dogs?' Max asked. He wasn't sure if a pup would be safe around Mooney. He'd seen Lily's dad being mean to his wife and his kids.

'I don't know,' Lily Moon said, 'but I like them.'

In the classroom Max's teacher, Miss Myrtle the Turtle, was writing on the whiteboard. She didn't seem happy about the pups until Mum promised to take them home straight after show-and-tell. When the bell rang, the kids came rushing in and Miss Myrtle made them sit in a circle on the floor. Max removed the pups from the pram one by one and set them down. 'Tell us about your pups, Max,' Miss Myrtle said. 'How old are they? And what do you feed them?'

Max told the class everything. How he'd been there when they were born. How Rosie ate her afterbirth. How Robbo's dog was probably the dad. And how Dad said they had to go in two weeks.

'Free to a good home,' Mum said.

Miss Myrtle smiled. 'Does anyone think they might want one?'

Everyone's hands went up, and Max was stoked. There were twenty-four kids in his class. That made four possible homes for each pup—Max was good at his six-times tables.

Max's friend Callum didn't get to see the pups because he was late to school, so he came around to Max's place that afternoon. But there was a problem: he brought his big brother with him. Max didn't like Jaden, but what could he do when they both showed up? He couldn't tell Jaden to go away so he invited them in and gave them packets of chips from the pantry. Mum was down at the shops with Suzie, so she didn't see when Jaden took an extra pack without asking then drank milk from the bottle in the fridge, spreading his wet pink lips around the opening.

'So where are these pups?' Jaden asked, wiping his mouth on his sleeve and shoving the milk back in the fridge.

'They live in the shed.' Max didn't want to show Jaden the pups. Maybe he could get him to play *Call of Duty* instead. But Jaden was already heading out the back door. Max didn't like the way the big boy swaggered through the house like he owned it. For once, he wished Dad was home: he would have put Jaden in his place. But Dad was up in the forest cutting down trees, so Max would have to take care of things.

He hurried past Jaden into the shed and sat with the pups, lifting Bonnie onto his lap. 'Here they are,' he said. 'You can hold them, but you have to be gentle.'

Callum went straight for Rosie Junior, smiling and laughing as he rubbed the pup against his cheek. 'Oh, cool. They're so soft.'

Jaden picked up Bruiser, and Max wasn't surprised because Jaden and Bruiser were exactly the same. Bruiser was biggest because he pushed the others aside and claimed whatever he wanted. 'Let's take this one home, Callum,' Jaden said.

'You can't,' Max said. 'He's still drinking from Rosie. But in two weeks he'll need a home.'

'I don't want to give him a home,' Jaden said. 'I want to feed him to Prince for breakfast.'

Prince was Callum and Jaden's dog: a bony German shepherd that chased little dogs and bit kids. When Bruiser grew up he'd be a good match for Prince, but now he was too little. Jaden gave Bruiser a shake that made the pup cry, then he started throwing him in the air and catching him.

'Don't,' Max said. 'You're hurting him.'

'It doesn't hurt. I'm good at catching.' Jaden tossed the pup higher.

'Stop it!' Callum shouted at his brother. 'He's not a football.'

'Just because you two are no good at footy.'

Jaden kept doing it till Max was nearly in tears. 'Cry-baby,' Jaden said, thrusting the pup on the ground.

Rosie bared her teeth and snarled—she was a good judge of character.

'Keep your dog away from me,' Jaden said. 'Or I'll kick her.'

'She's only doing it because you were hurting her pup,' Max retorted. 'She's just being a good mum.'

'Bullshit. She's a mongrel.'

Jaden went outside and booted Max's footy over the fence into Leon's place. Then he chucked Max's bike over too. He was just about to give the same treatment to Max's scooter when Mum pulled up in the driveway. Max saw her through the windscreen: she was glaring at Jaden. The big boy stared at her for a moment then set the scooter back on the ground. Mum and Suzie came over straight away.

'I was just showing Callum and Jaden the pups,' Max said, hoping Mum could tell he was desperate for Jaden to go.

She looked at him, clear-eyed, and lit a cigarette, then turned to Jaden. He was leaning against the fence with his hands in his pockets, hair over his eyes. 'Fun's over now, boys,' she said. 'Max has jobs to do. Time to go home.'

Max wanted to hug her—she knew exactly what was needed.

Callum put Rosie Junior down gently and whispered to Max. 'The pups are cool—you're so lucky.'

Max would have liked to invite Callum over another time, but he didn't want Jaden near the pups ever again. He followed his friend to the gate and waved goodbye. Jaden was already gone, slouching down the street. When Callum caught up with his brother, Jaden turned back and gave Max the finger.

13

Sunday night, after closing time, Kurt announced he was going to Hobart. Miki was thrown. It was unusual for him to do things out of pattern; normally he went on Monday after they'd been to the forest. 'Why don't you wait till tomorrow?' she asked.

He was evasive. 'I have a business meeting in the morning, then I'll be home with a surprise.'

Miki was unsure how to read him. Since taking that key, she'd felt stilted and strange around him, always watching to see if he knew she'd been out. When he was quiet, she became tense; if he was grumpy, she was convinced he was about to explode. Now she stood in the hallway, watching him pack pyjamas and a change of clothes into his duffel bag. He unlocked the filing cabinet and removed the black leather folder, slipping it in his bag on top of his jeans. Why was he taking it with him?

'Can't you tell me about the surprise now?' she asked.

He glanced at her with hooded eyes. 'You'll find out soon enough.'

Ordinarily, his surprises weren't useful to her. Last time it had been gym equipment. The time before, a huge digital TV, which he controlled, selecting programs that didn't interest her:

sports replays, business videos, get-rich-quick schemes. When he was feeling upbeat, sometimes she was allowed to watch videos he'd chosen for her, like *Little House on the Prairie* and *The Love Bug*. But mostly he sat by himself watching shows that went late into the night. Occasionally she tried to open her door so she could see the screen, but Kurt had a sixth sense and he always caught her. She would try to listen from behind the closed door, but he kept the volume low so she couldn't hear.

When he was gone, revving down the lane in the ute, she sat in the shop looking out at the streetlights in the dark. A great stillness spread around her. She could hear the hum of the fridge, the buzz of the fluorescent light, the clock ticking on the wall. The shop was large and empty, but everything seemed close and confined. In the darkness, she was a Tasmanian devil in a Polypipe trap. Her skin itched. She decided to go out. Walking in the dark wasn't ideal, but now she knew the taste of freedom she was constantly craving it.

She fetched her hidden key and let herself out into the damp evening. It had been raining most of the day and water was still running in the gutters, the air fresh, grassy and rich. She roamed the streets, dodging puddles and spying through people's windows. She had begun to discover where everyone lived. Robbo's log truck was a giveaway, and Max's family was up the same street; Shane's rusty ute and Max's dog Rosie confirmed it. Leon lived just next door; the white Toyota parked out the front had a Parks logo on the door.

Down another side street, she watched TV through someone's front window until she realised that being on the outside, looking in, was as sad as being on the inside, looking out. Unless you engaged with people, you were still very alone. This reality sent her home again. It wasn't just freedom she longed for: she wanted companionship.

In the little lounge room behind the shop, she plumped the cushions and swept up some wood splinters Kurt had left on the floor when he carried in the wood. Then she lit the fire. When the embers were glowing and the room was warm, she fetched *Far from the Madding Crowd* from beneath the pile of home-knitted jumpers in her wardrobe. It had been more than a week since Geraldine had given her the book, but she hadn't dared read it when Kurt was at home. Now was a good time.

As she nestled on the couch with the book in her hands, a flush of excitement ran through her. It was like the first time she'd opened *Jane Eyre*: the thrill of hovering on the cusp of a new world. Miki remembered feeling anger as Jane was persecuted by her relatives and the school principal. She recalled the joy of watching Jane's friendship with Helen develop. Sadness when poor Helen died. The pleasure of travelling to Thornfield Hall when Jane began her job as a governess. Meeting Mr Rochester for the first time. Falling in love with him as his conversations with Jane unfolded. Miki had been inspired by Jane's strength, the way she stood up for herself, her dignity, the integrity of her beliefs. Racing through the pages, Miki had followed the evolution of Jane's relationship with Mr Rochester, the awakening of her passion, her horror at discovering Mr Rochester's secret, her terrible journey of escape across the high moors.

Now Miki was about to delve into a fresh story with new characters. New ideas. Her heart skipped. Kurt could keep her in the shop most of the time, but he couldn't control where she went in her mind.

She opened the book and flicked through the introduction.

Chapter One, first line: *When Farmer Oak smiled . . .*

The walls of the room melted as the story came to life.

Later, she wondered where the hours had gone; they'd slipped by so fast. That was the magic of books, having the secrets of stories buried in their pages. It was just as Geraldine had said:

Far from the Madding Crowd was wonderful. Miki liked Gabriel Oak from the start. She admired his steadiness, kindness and loyalty, and she was devastated when his dog herded his sheep over the cliffs. Losing everything had disempowered him; Miki knew how that felt.

She wasn't sure about Bathsheba at first; for a young woman she seemed so bold and independent. Miki was disappointed when Bathsheba turned down Gabriel's offer of marriage. She felt sorry for Gabriel because Bathsheba was so abrupt and insensitive in her refusal. But Miki could see it was too soon—Bathsheba wasn't ready for marriage. She was wild and free and didn't want to be tied down by expectations. She was so different from Miki, it was a little hard to relate to her. But as the book went on, Miki began to see that although their ambitions were different, they were, in some ways, alike. Bathsheba wanted more for herself, and Miki did too. She understood Bathsheba's craving for freedom. And she admired the way Bathsheba forced men to see her as an equal. When Bathsheba inherited fortune and property, she wanted to prove she was smart enough to run a farm, something women didn't do back in those times. Miki was impressed by the clever way Bathsheba persuaded men to help without ever bowing to them, never submitting. It was the opposite of what Miki had known. In her life—on the farm and in the shop—men had always been dominant. Bathsheba was proof it didn't have to be that way. The women in this town stood up to their men too—Miki had seen it when they came into the shop—and she knew most of the men respected the women. But it wasn't like that in Miki's home: Kurt made sure she knew her place.

Then there was Sergeant Troy, Bathsheba's lover: the scene in the forest where he whisked his sword all around her while she stood very still. Miki felt the power and tension of Bathsheba's emotions. She felt the breeze of the sword as it cut the air close to Bathsheba's skin. She felt the violent aftershock when Sergeant Troy cut off a lock of Bathsheba's hair with a sword he had told her was blunt. This was Bathsheba's awakening as a woman, and it moved and unsettled Miki. She was a woman too. But her feelings were all locked inside. Sometimes they knocked in her chest like a hammer.

As she read, Miki came to love Bathsheba and wanted to be like her. She read until she was exhausted and her mind was spinning. She read until she was full of words and ideas, all tumbling over each other.

By the end, she knew that she and Bathsheba had much in common. Miki wanted to go out into the world and meet people too. She wanted to get to know them. Be independent. Fall in love. Make mistakes. But she couldn't see when that might happen. For now, she would have to be happy with books.

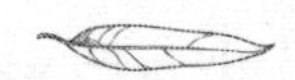

In the morning, Kurt arrived home in a new twin-cab, four-wheel drive ute. He parked it in the lane behind the shop, the shiny silver paint job glittering in the sun. Miki was stunned. They didn't need a new car—the other ute had been less than two years old and still in good condition. *Aren't we saving for a farm?* she wanted to say, but she was too afraid of his anger. From the kitchen she watched him fuss over a few squashed bugs on the windscreen. The new ute had yellow fog lights and a bullbar almost as big as a truck's. What did Kurt think he was going to plough into with that? And how much had the ute cost, enough for a deposit on a farm?

He was keen to take the new car up to the forest to try it out on dirt tracks, and Miki was invited because who else was there for Kurt to show off to? He drove fast, testing the steering and tyre grip around corners, while she sat quiet and still in the passenger seat. When he whooped and hollered and slapped the steering wheel, she smiled to appease him. But inside she felt ill. He should not have spent all their money.

He swung onto their usual side road, and they hadn't gone far when they came to a sign: *Logging Operations.* Miki's heart kicked. Ahead she saw open space, several four-wheel drives parked along the verge.

Kurt drove to the sign and stopped. 'What the fuck?'

Miki couldn't believe it. Beyond the sign, the landscape was unrecognisable. Where there used to be forest, a bomb might have been dropped. The tall trees and spreading ferns were gone, and now there was only wide-open space and white sky. The ground had become a rubbish-tip of stripped bark and broken branches, leaves wilting in hummocky piles. The air was heavy with crushed eucalyptus and freshly churned dirt.

Miki was devastated. Everything had been normal last week, but now her haven had been converted from peaceful trees to ruin. Part-way up the hill, she could see the perpetrators: two huge growling machines that crawled around, knocking down trees. As she watched, the falling-machine grasped a tree with a mechanical claw and cut through the trunk as easily as a knife through cheese. Miki felt as if she'd been cut in half too. She shuddered as the tree whooshed to the ground with a thump. The machine topped and tailed it like a carrot before the skidder took over, skimming off the side branches and dragging the tree down the hill, revving and clanking as it grumbled over mounds of debris. It was appallingly fast: in a matter of minutes, a tree had become a log. The machines would eat their way through the forest until nothing was left.

Further along the road, Miki saw Robbo's truck parked on a recently bulldozed landing. He was supervising as a loader stacked logs onto the tray. Way uphill, where the block steepened, the forest was untouched. Miki hoped the machines wouldn't make it up there.

Behind the steering wheel, Kurt sat grim-faced, staring at the wreckage. 'Bastards,' he mumbled.

'Why are they here?' Miki's voice caught in her throat.

'Some idiot in an office marks an X on a map, and that's where they go.'

'But there were so many old trees. How could they do this?' She wanted to turn back time and restore the forest. This was vandalism. There was so much forest out there—why couldn't the loggers go somewhere else? She thought of the eagles; their nest tree wasn't far away. Would the machines knock that down too?

Kurt drove around the sign, manoeuvring past the workers' vehicles. Shane's rusty ute was among them. There he was, in hard hat and safety vest, tinkering with a chainsaw at the back of his truck, a cigarette between his lips. He scowled at Kurt as they passed—it was no secret they didn't like each other—and Kurt matched the scowl, muttering *fuckwit* under his breath. As Miki watched, Shane lifted the chainsaw and started uphill, stepping over the chaos of fallen branches. She remembered hearing that he cut trees on steep slopes, so the trees uphill weren't safe. In a few weeks, the whole place would be wrecked.

Kurt continued on in jaw-clenched silence, following the track through the clearing. The open space was a vast emptiness: sky, logging-slash and dirt. Downhill in a gully, the skeleton of a lonely tree fern waved its battered fronds and three skinny trees stood in a sad cluster, exposed to the wind. Miki saw a currawong eject skywards from the forest edge—at least something was still alive. But it didn't give her much hope.

As they drove away from the logging site, the shriek of machines gradually faded, but Miki felt bruised. It was only when they slid into forest again that her tension began to ease. They passed the eagles' tree, and then it wasn't far until they were in their beloved patch of forest where the trees closed in and shrubs scraped the car as they whipped past. Kurt was still rigid with fury. When they stopped, he leaped out and slammed his door, then yanked out his rifle and loaded a handful of ammunition. 'Bastards,' he spat. 'I wish they'd piss off. I bet they're going to log through to here.'

Miki's anxiety escalated. If the loggers came this far, what would happen to her favourite tree? To those men, a forest was just logs to take out on a truck. Money in the bank. Food for their bellies. A payment on a large-screen TV. Petrol in the tank. Her tree would be worth nothing because its core was rotten; they would hack it down. 'What can we do?' she asked Kurt. 'Should we move the hives?'

'We won't need to worry for a while. It'll take weeks for the loggers to get here.'

'Isn't there some way we can stop them?'

Kurt nestled the butt of the rifle to his shoulder and swung the muzzle back the way they'd just come, tilting his head to squint through the sights. 'I could shoot them,' he said.

Miki's skin went cold. 'You wouldn't.'

He lowered the gun and inspected her with cold eyes. 'Of course I wouldn't. We haven't worked this hard to throw it all away.'

What about the new ute, she thought. Wasn't that throwing it all away?

Kurt spent a long time in the forest that morning while Miki huddled in the car, fretting about her trees. Around her, the forest shifted and sighed as if nothing was different. It felt wrong that everything could seem normal here when it definitely wasn't.

On the way home, Kurt was grimly silent and refused to be drawn into conversation about the loggers. He disappeared into his room under the shop for an hour, then took off to Hobart in a terrible mood.

As soon as he was gone, the knot in Miki's chest eased. She was still feeling wretched, but she knew a way to make herself feel better. She fetched her hidden key and let herself out, sucking in a lungful of fresh air as she closed the door behind her. Being outside somehow loosened her mind. She needed to figure out what to do about the logging, and the best way to think was to walk.

Her feet took her down past the primary school and onto the road to the forest, her pace quickening as she felt the pull towards freedom. Walking felt good. Cars whizzed by, blasting her with wind, but she didn't mind. She liked the beat of her boots on the ground, the warmth that crept through her despite the damp cold, the fact that Kurt didn't know where she was. She passed small green farms and houses with smoke threading from their chimneys. Dogs dashed out to bark at her, hackles raised. She avoided eye contact and carried on.

On the crest of a hill, she heard a car coming and glanced back to see a large white four-wheel drive roaring towards her from town. Instead of passing, it slowed and stopped beside her. Miki noticed the Parks logo on the door.

Leon rolled down the window. 'Hey. Where are you heading?'

'Nowhere in particular. Just out for a walk.'

'I'm going up to the park to drop off some gear. Want a lift?'

'I'm not going that far.'

'That's okay. I can drop you wherever you want.'

Miki shook her head. Kurt would be incensed if she accepted a ride. 'I'm fine,' she said. 'Have you heard anything from Dale? Have the devil's test results come through?'

Leon's smile faded. 'Hang on. I'll pull over.' He drove past and drew up on the verge then walked back to her, hands in pockets, brow knitted in a frown.

From the look on his face, Miki knew the devil must have the disease. She felt herself sinking. This made a bad day even worse.

Leon had an air of awkwardness about him as he delivered the news. 'Dale emailed the other day . . . The results aren't good . . .'

She glanced away, looking to the mountains for strength. But then she remembered what was going on up there—the trucks and the machines—and her heart plummeted.

'After we dropped you and Geraldine off, we went back to the tip and got a glimpse of the female,' Leon was saying. 'We couldn't see any wounds.'

This was a relief, but a nod was all Miki could manage.

'Dale reckons we should move her and her young to a safe place so they won't catch the disease.'

Did that mean the male devil would be left behind? Miki couldn't bear the thought of his loneliness—it was something she knew about. 'What about the male?'

'He would have to stay. There's nothing Dale can do . . .'

Miki dodged Leon's eyes. There was too much kindness in them. If she looked at him, she might cry. 'Where will Dale take them?' she asked.

'He wants to shift them to a sanctuary where they breed devils in captivity. They can be part of a program to release clean devils back into the wild.'

Miki had imagined the devils in a coastal forest with other healthy animals, a tribe they could interact with. She looked at Leon, shocked by this solution. 'So they'd be in a zoo?'

He paused. 'Kind of. Dale says the enclosures have plenty of room. And the devils would be well looked after. They would have food and company and space. No disease.'

'And no freedom.' Miki didn't want her devils locked in. If they were stuck in a zoo she would have betrayed them. Their wildness was what she loved most about them. They were strong and confident. Freedom was important. No fences. No locks.

'It's not freedom if they catch that disease,' Leon said. 'All it would take is one bite and the others could catch it.'

When Leon put it this way, the sanctuary seemed necessary. But Miki still felt trapped. How would the devils cope with being closed in? She wouldn't wish it on anyone. 'When can Dale move them?'

'I don't know. I'll ask him. You should come along and help catch them. Are Mondays still good?'

She hesitated. Could she pull off a second trapping trip without Kurt finding out? 'Yes, Mondays.'

'How about I slip you a note over the counter?'

She couldn't think of any other way. 'Okay. Just make sure Kurt doesn't see . . .'

Leon shot her a look that showed he wasn't fond of her brother. Miki was used to it—no one liked Kurt except her. They didn't know him, she told herself. But a small niggle reminded her that he was hard to like, even for a sister.

'It might not be soon,' Leon said. 'Dale's trapping over in the Tarkine for a few weeks. I'll let you know when I hear from him.' A car whizzed by and he glanced at the Toyota, parked precariously on the roadside. 'I'd better go.'

Miki had been focused on the devils, but now she thought of the trees. 'Hang on,' she said, 'I want to ask you something.'

Leon turned back, eyebrows raised.

'Kurt and I were up in the forest today and we came across some loggers cutting old trees. I don't think they should be there. There's a wedge-tailed eagle nest too.'

'I'm pretty sure they're allowed to cut old trees,' Leon said. 'But that nest would make a difference. Wedgies are a protected species. Where were they logging?' Miki gave directions while Leon wrote them on a notepad. 'It would help me to see it. Can you take me there now?'

This sounded logical, but Kurt would be furious if someone saw her with Leon. 'The loggers are working up there,' she said. 'I don't want them to see.'

Leon nodded. 'It wouldn't be good if they saw me up there either. Things are hard enough as it is.' He paused. 'How about we go this evening, after knock-off? Six-thirty?'

'It'll be dark,' Miki pointed out.

'I have a spotlight.'

She hesitated. 'Kurt wouldn't like it.' Now that she'd put it out there, Leon should understand.

'Of course,' he said. 'I could ask Geraldine to come too. She seems to enjoy an adventure.'

'Maybe.' Miki felt her options shrinking.

'If you can't do tonight, could we go tomorrow?'

'No. Mondays are best.'

'Let's do it then. I'll whizz back to town and line it up with Geraldine. How about I pick you up behind the visitor centre? Like last time. It'll be okay. See you then.' Leon smiled.

14

Leon's mum had a knack for choosing the wrong time to phone him. Occasionally it was about something important, such as reporting Stan's visits. Leon had tried to take action on that—he'd called Stan to warn him off, but his dad's dodgy mate was refusing to pick up his phone. Mostly, though, when his mum rang, it was something trivial, like telling Leon the oven light had stopped working or that the neighbour's dog had been killed by the tourist bus. 'Do you want me to come home?' he'd asked once or twice. But she'd turned him down, saying, 'That's kind, Leon, but it's too far.' She rang to tell him the bins hadn't been emptied. 'Maybe you should call the council,' he'd said. 'They'll be able to tell you what happened.' He knew she couldn't discuss things with his dad, but he wished his father would make more of an effort to engage.

She rang when Leon was in the Parks Toyota with Miki and Geraldine, driving the winding road to the forest, headlights spearing the darkness. He wasn't allowed to use his phone while driving, but right now he didn't really care. He wasn't supposed to carry passengers either, but nobody would see them at night.

'Hi, Mum, is everything okay?' he said quietly, acutely aware of Miki and Geraldine in the back seat.

'Your father is vomiting,' she said. 'Do you think I should take him to hospital?'

This wasn't the first time Leon's dad had gone down in a heap. There had been intermittent episodes of vomiting ever since he'd first crashed and turned yellow. It was to be expected: his liver rebelling against constant abuse.

'Maybe,' Leon said. 'But it's hard to know from here. You're probably the best judge. The last ferry is at seven-fifteen. You can still make it if you leave now.'

'I have to get him dressed.'

'The doctors won't mind. Take him as he is.'

'All right then. I'll go.'

He hung up and focused on the dark road, swinging the curves and watching out for wallabies and wombats with a suicide wish—at night, they could barrel under the wheels at any time.

'Is everything okay?' Geraldine asked him.

'Yeah, it'll be fine.'

'Somebody sick?'

'My mum's cat.' They must have known he hadn't been talking about a cat, but for some reason it was important to save face—he didn't want to share his troubles from home.

Following Miki's directions, he turned onto a side road, and within a few hundred metres the logged area opened before them. The headlights had a limited reach, but he could see the devastation and raw open space. Cut stumps. Piles of branches and bark. Discarded crowns. Bulldozed tree ferns. An abrupt wall of shadowy trees where the logged area ended. 'Wow, they've hammered it!' he said.

'It's horrible,' Geraldine agreed. 'No wonder you're upset, Miki.'

'I'm worried about the eagles,' Miki said. 'It's not far to their tree.'

The cleared area seemed to stretch forever as Leon drove through it. Landscapes like this were not new to him—his family had been knocking down trees for decades. But this kind of ruin had made him diverge from family tradition. It might have been possible, years ago, to think people couldn't overcut forests, but now it had gone too far. Tasmania still had big trees, but areas of old-growth were declining. Leon didn't know why they needed to cut old-growth at all. The large old trees were hollow inside or they split when they fell, and were basically useless for sawn timber. What was the point? They might as well leave the old trees behind. But loggers liked clearfelling because it was similar to mowing grass, safer and easier than selective logging, and they didn't even have to get out of their machines. Tasmania had some of the best old-growth left in Australia. In a civilised country they ought to stop cutting it altogether. Back home on Bruny, they only cut pulp because there was no old-growth left. The same would happen here if things continued unchanged.

Leon was relieved to drive from the clearing back into unlogged forest. Out of sight, you could almost pretend the logged area didn't exist. In the darkness, trees seemed to close around the vehicle, eerily lit by the headlights. This was how it was meant to be: forest like a blanket covering the earth.

Further on, Miki pointed out the eagles' tree and Leon pulled up beneath it. When they slid out into the cold night, the trees seemed to lean towards them, shadowy and dense, branches reaching like arms, leaves rustling with invisible life. Leon thought of the tales he'd heard growing up, stories that demonised forests: Snow White being chased by the huntsman, Red Riding Hood stalked by the wolf, the hostile woods in *The Lord of the Rings* and *The Hobbit*. Those stories instilled fear that evil lurked among trees—but no dark forces hovered here, waiting to destroy people. The creatures of the forest were busy doing their thing: bush rats and marsupial mice fossicking in the understorey, possums nibbling on leaves, owls hunting prey.

If people learned to love the forest instead of fearing it, they might want to save it.

Leon fetched his spotlight and switched it on, shooting the beam up the trunk. There was the nest: a convoluted tangle of sticks and twigs, high on a branch.

'Not exactly artists, are they?' Geraldine said.

'It's been there more than two years, and it hasn't blown down,' Miki said. 'I think that's clever. The wind gets really strong up here.'

In the glow of the spotlight, the white arms of the trees stood out like bones, and silvered leaves shivered. Leon wondered if the eagles were around. He probed the canopy with the light to see if they were roosting nearby, but there was no sign of them.

'Maybe they've been scared off,' Miki said, her face doleful in the dark.

Her passion for eagles was unusual, Leon thought. Most birdwatchers were nature freaks, like him, or twitchers from ornithologist groups. But there was something off-beat about Miki. She was young but old at the same time, shy but direct, surprisingly observant. She'd been home-schooled—perhaps that was why she was a bit odd. Maybe she'd spent time watching birds because she hadn't had other children to play with. He tried to imagine her life in the shop with Kurt. It was clear she'd been afraid to come out tonight, like on the night they'd trapped devils. Leon suspected Kurt wasn't always kind to her. It was hard to tell from the outside, but Leon sensed she needed a friend—someone to talk to. 'Sorry I can't find your eagles,' he said. 'They must be camouflaged among all those leaves.'

Miki was disappointed. 'Maybe they're sleeping.'

'They're endangered, aren't they?' Geraldine said. 'Why are there so few of them left?'

'Farmers think they kill sheep,' Leon explained, 'so they shoot or poison them. And sometimes they fly into powerlines.'

'How awful! How many are left?'

'About three hundred pairs.'

Geraldine shook her head. 'They're so big you think they're invincible, but nobody is.'

Miki said, 'While we're here, can I show you another tree? It's further along the track. We'll have to take the four-wheel drive and then walk.'

They packed themselves back into the Toyota and drove on. The track narrowed and became overgrown, shrubs scraping the sides of the car. Leon hoped he could find somewhere to turn round when it was time to go back; it seemed no one came here except Miki and Kurt.

Miki showed him where to park near a thicket of beech trees turning golden. They got out and she led the way along the track, walking slowly so Geraldine could keep up.

The tall tree loomed out of the darkness: the most enormous swamp gum Leon had ever seen. He stood with the others at its buttressed base in awed silence, gazing up the trunk to the shadowy crown that seemed to graze the star-dusted sky.

'Can you switch off the spotlight?' Miki asked. 'I love just listening to the forest at night.'

Leon complied, and as his eyes adjusted he could make out the faint outline of stumpy branches high up. Everything seemed amplified in the gloom. The hum of mosquitoes. Creatures rustling in the undergrowth. Frogs and tree crickets chirruping.

Something snapped in the canopy, so he turned the spotlight on again and directed the beam towards the sound. There, sitting on a stubby branch, was a fluffy grey possum with pointy ears and a brushtail. It stared down, inspecting them closely, tail hanging like a hook, eyes flashing red in the spotlight. Then it started to move. Digging sharp claws into the bark, feet stretched wide, it scratched its way down the trunk then sprang into the understorey and scuttled off, using trees and shrubs like a trapeze artist.

Miki's face was luminous. 'Aren't possums wonderful?'

She was obviously crazy about all forest creatures. Leon thought it was great to see someone so passionate about animals.

Geraldine laughed. 'I hate possums at home because they eat my roses and vegie garden. But, up here, they're amazing. Do you come here often?' she asked Miki.

'Every week. I sit under this tree while Kurt goes bush. It's peaceful.'

'What does Kurt do out here?' Leon asked, curious.

'He goes shooting.'

'Every week?' Leon couldn't conceal his surprise; Kurt couldn't be much of a hunter if he kept coming back to the same place.

'He doesn't shoot things every time,' Miki said, frowning.

Leon was astounded that she was sticking up for her brother. Surely it was clear the guy was indefensible. But there had been times when Leon had defended his father even though it wasn't deserved. Blood was thicker than water.

Miki was looking at him expectantly. 'It's a beautiful tree, isn't it?' she said. 'Do you think we can save this one as well as the eagles' tree when we stop the logging?'

Leon sighed. He was just a lowly ranger. But he promised to see what he could do.

15

At school on Thursday, Callum came running up to Max at lunchtime and told him Jaden wanted to see him behind the toilets after school. Max didn't want to. After Jaden had thrown Bruiser in the air, Max hated him even more. A kid could run away from Jaden's bullying, but the pups couldn't protect themselves.

When the school bell rang at the end of the day, Max fetched his bag and considered going straight home. If he ran fast, he could get there before Jaden realised he wasn't going to show up. But what if Jaden came around again and said he wanted to play with the pups? If he was mad at Max, this time he might drop a pup and kill it. Max didn't have any choice. He sloped behind the toilets where Jaden and Callum were waiting.

Jaden had a nasty glint in his eyes. 'How are those pups going? How's Bruiser?'

'They're good.'

'Big enough for my dog's breakfast? Prince is very hungry.'

Max tried not to show his horror. 'They're too small. I can bring dog food instead. It'll fill him up more.'

Jaden sneered. 'Forget dog food. Bring something else. Get me cigarettes. Your mum and dad smoke—you can nick some from them.'

Max was panicky. How was he supposed to do that? If Dad caught him stealing cigarettes, he would kill him. 'I'll try, but I don't know if I can.'

'Just open a pack and take some out. I want them tomorrow.'

'Tomorrow?'

'Yep. Or I'll come and take one of your pups.'

At home, Max ran into the shed and was relieved to see the pups were all there. Rosie leaped out of her box and jumped at Max's legs for food, so he filled her bowl. Then he took some kibble into the kitchen and soaked it in milk for the pups. They all yipped excitedly when he came back, and bounced up and down, desperate to eat. Normally it was funny when they did this, but tonight Max wasn't laughing. He put the bowl down and leaned against the door, watching them eat. When the bowl was empty, he let them out on the lawn; they galloped around, stopping to chew grass and have play fights. It didn't take long to wear them out, then Max put them away and went inside. Usually he hung out in the shed for hours, but he was miserable so he went inside and played *Call of Duty*. Before the pups were born it had been his favourite game. Everyone at school still talked about it, but he was bored with it now.

He was still killing zombies when Dad came home. After a four-week break, Max was way down on points and didn't feel like going to dinner. But Mum told him to *get off that bloody thing*, and Dad frowned at him from the table, so Max had to go. It was chops and three veg again, and Mum had forgotten to buy tomato sauce so he had to have barbecue sauce instead, which was disgusting. He got in trouble for eating too slow and then for using his knife and fork wrong, and then for not chewing the meat off his bone. Why couldn't everyone just leave him alone?

During the meal, he kept trying to see what Dad had done with his pack of cigarettes. Sometimes he left them on the kitchen bench or out in the shed, but mostly they stayed in his pocket. Mum was in a bad mood, so she told Max to wash the dishes. 'What about Suzie?' he said. 'She never does anything.'

'Just do it,' Dad said, 'or I'll knock you into next week.'

Dad didn't smack him much but when he did, it hurt, so Max put on Mum's pink rubber gloves and squirted dishwashing liquid into the sink. He took ages washing the dishes because it was fun playing with the bubbles and sometimes Mum got so fed up she couldn't help taking over. But not tonight. Mum put Suzie in the bath and then, in the lounge room, she and Dad started arguing. Dad was watching the news and drinking beer, and Mum was folding the washing.

'We're out of money again,' she was saying. 'Why's that, Shane?'

'Dunno. You must be spending it.'

'Rubbish. Look at you with your beer. Pissing it up against the wall.'

'I work my arse off all week. Man's gotta wind down.'

'How am I going to pay the bills?'

Max didn't know what they were on about. They said they had no money, but they were always buying cigarettes. Mobile phones cost heaps too, and Mum and Dad both had one, so they couldn't be broke.

'Where's all the money gone?' Mum said. 'You still haven't told me.'

'Bought a round of scratchies this week. I was feeling lucky.'

'You blew it on scratchies? What a waste.'

'I put a hundred on a horse too. Tip from Toby.'

'Did it pay up? Bet it came stone fucking motherless.'

Dad was quiet. Then he said, 'I'd had a shit day, darlin', and I was trying to cheer myself up.'

Mum wasn't having it. 'What sort of shit, Shane?'

'Haven't you heard? Greenies took photos of the site we're working on and they must have reported it. They found a wedgie nest up there and the department has stopped us logging till they can sort it out. The department stuffed up. They should've known about the nest.'

Max liked wedgies. They were cool birds. Maybe Dad would take him up there to see them.

'Did you know about the nest?' Mum asked.

'Yeah, I saw it when we first started logging the site. We shouldn't have been there. I thought about reporting it, but it's not my job. That's what those government bastards are paid for.'

'Where are they going to send you instead? Have they got another site lined up?'

'Don't know.'

'I hope they keep paying you. We have to eat, and there's nothing in the bank.'

Max had noticed the dog food in the shed was getting low too.

'Time to get rid of those pups,' Dad said.

Max tensed. He hadn't found homes for them yet.

Now it was Mum's turn to go quiet. 'I don't think we need to do that yet, Shane,' she said, more gently. 'They give the kids so much pleasure.'

'We can't keep them forever.'

Max felt sick. He'd stopped washing the dishes, and Mum called out, 'You finished yet, Max?'

'Nearly.' He slopped water over the last of the plates and shoved them on the rack. He needed to check the pups again.

They were fine. Still six of them, all curled up with Rosie.

When he went back inside, Mum was drying Suzie in the bathroom and Dad had disappeared somewhere. In the lounge room, Max saw Dad's pack of cigarettes on the coffee table. He could hear Dad in the loo. Holding his breath, Max opened the packet, took three out and shoved them in his pocket. His heart was thumping like mad, but luckily the pack was almost full, so hopefully Dad wouldn't notice.

He'd done it! Tomorrow he could give those cigarettes to Jaden and it would be over with.

At recess next day, Max was tugging his playlunch out of his bag when Jaden grabbed him by the arm, shoved him against the lockers and snarled, 'Have you got them?'

That wrecked the rest of the day for Max—he was so scared he couldn't do his work in class. He kept thinking about what would happen if he got caught giving cigarettes to Jaden. But he had to, or Jaden would bash him.

After school, he went behind the toilets where Jaden and Callum were waiting. 'So,' Jaden sneered, 'did you bring matches?'

'Yeah.' Luckily Max had thought of that. He gave Jaden a box of Redheads he'd taken from the fireplace at home. Then he produced the smokes from his pocket. 'One each,' he said, handing them out. They were a bit squashed, but Callum seemed to think he was cool.

Jaden took the best cigarette and put it between his lips. Then he tried to light a match, breaking six before he managed to get a flame. 'Crap matches,' he said. 'Get better ones next time.'

Max knew there was nothing wrong with the matches: Jaden was just useless at lighting them.

'This is how you do it,' Jaden said. 'You've gotta suck as you bring the match up so the smoke catches alight.'

Jaden was dragging on the smoke like an expert, and the tip of the cigarette went red. But then Jaden started choking. Max almost laughed, but stopped himself just in time.

Then it was Max's turn. He was worried he would cough too. It couldn't be that hard; he'd seen Dad and Mum do it a thousand times. Sticking the next-best cigarette on his lip, he lit a match. He was good at matches because Mum let him light the fire at home. In front of Jaden, he squinted his eyes, trying to look pro. Then he made the match touch the cigarette, concentrating hard so his hand wouldn't wobble. He was nervous. The cigarette hissed and he sucked on it a bit, but kept the smoke in his mouth without pulling it into his lungs. The tip of the cigarette went red and smoke came out of his mouth. It was like he was on fire on the inside.

Jaden was watching him. 'Hey, why aren't you coughing?'

'He's a natural,' Callum said, excited.

Jaden was pissed off. He kept looking at Max, waiting for him to cough. 'You're not doing it properly.'

'Yes, he is,' Callum said. 'Look at all the smoke coming out of his nose.'

Max stayed cool. When he finished the cigarette, he chucked it on the ground and squished it in the dirt with the toe of his shoe, like Mum and Dad did. Then he picked up the stub.

'What are you doing?' Jaden said.

Max gave him a look and said, 'I'm going to chuck it in the bin. If the teachers find it, we're dead.'

He was ready to go home, and he thought it was over, but Jaden gave a twisted smile and said, 'More.'

'What do you mean?' Max asked.

'I want more smokes.'

'What if I can't?'

Jaden grinned. 'You will.'

Max felt sick. Every time he tried to steal smokes it would get harder. And if he couldn't get cigarettes, Jaden might hurt the pups. He would have to find homes for them fast. But what if the bullying didn't stop when the pups were gone? What would he do then?

16

The men were calling the closure of the logging coupe *a complete fucking disaster*. Miki heard them going on about it in the shop. At first, there were rumblings and whisperings. Then the real action started on Friday when Robbo came in after work. Normally on Fridays, he went straight home to have dinner with his wife Trudi before going down to the pub. This afternoon he parked his truck in the street, defying the rules, and strutted into the shop to meet Toby, Mooney and Shane. They ordered a large serve of chips and sat at a table, obviously settling in for a chat. Kurt mumbled something about wanting them gone but, after he'd taken their money, he went out the back to do paperwork. A wise move, Miki thought. He wasn't always wise when it came to avoiding conflict with customers.

While she cooked the order, Miki listened to the men talking, which was tricky over the hum of the exhaust fans and the hiss of the oil. Robbo's voice was easiest to hear, deep and resonant. 'Forest wars are on again,' he said. 'And all because of some fucking birds.'

'The wars never stopped,' Toby said. 'This mob have always been out to get us.' He was in a T-shirt as usual, arm muscles popping so that his tattoo-snake seemed to be writhing.

'Wedge-tailed eagles, eh?' Mooney scoffed. 'We should go out and shoot them.'

'They're protected,' Robbo said. 'We can't shoot them or the department will come down on us like a ton of bricks.'

'We could knock the tree down,' Mooney said. 'Nest destroyed. Problem solved. Shane, you've got a chainsaw.'

But Robbo wasn't having it. 'Mate, they'd know it was us. We just have to wait.'

'Where are they going to send us instead?' Shane asked. 'I can't wait six weeks for a decision. I've got kids to feed.'

'Who fucking knows?'

'They'll have to pay compo, but that could take months to come through.'

'We need to hold a meeting,' Robbo said. 'Get everyone together on this.'

'We're already together,' Mooney said.

'Sure, but we need a plan. We have to make noise. This eagle nest will be all over the internet and the newspapers, and it'll be conservationist views. We need to put our case. Stand up for ourselves. Get some heads to roll. The department fucked up on this.'

'What do we do? Start a Facebook page? Email the newspaper?'

'Yeah, maybe. But who's going to do it? I'm no bloody good at technology.'

'I'll get Steph onto it,' Toby said. 'She's better at that stuff than me.'

'I can't do it,' Shane said.

'Why not?'

'I'm no good at English.'

'You can talk, can't you?' Robbo said. 'That's English.'

They all laughed.

'What about the pollies?' Toby said. 'Should we email them too?'

'Good idea,' Robbo said. 'And I'll think about a meeting. We can hold a rally in the main street and block it off to traffic. Get a loudhailer. Tip off the media and get some coverage.'

'"Loggers Strike Back"!' Shane said. 'I can just see the headlines. We'll be a household word.'

The men guffawed then looked glum.

Miki lost the thread of their conversation while she checked the chips in the fryer. When she glanced back, she noticed the men had fallen silent. Then Mooney spoke, a hint of menace in his voice. 'Who do you reckon dobbed us in?'

The silence lengthened, and Miki accidentally locked eyes with Robbo. The men were looking at her. Did they think it was her, or did they think Kurt was guilty? She tensed.

Mooney started pushing back his chair. 'If you think it was him, I'll have him now. Take the fucker down on his own territory.'

Miki edged towards the rear door in case she needed to warn Kurt, but Robbo had placed a restraining hand on Mooney's arm. 'Calm down, you crazy bastard. We don't know who it was.'

'Who else goes up there?' Toby asked. 'Didn't you say you saw the two of them driving through a few days ago?'

'Yeah, but I'm not convinced it was them. The girl's not a troublemaker, and neither is he. Apart from being a bastard, have we had any issues with him this past year? No.'

'Who then?' Shane asked. 'Parkie?'

Miki was worried she might have got Leon in trouble, but Robbo was shaking his head. 'Nah. He doesn't do much more than track maintenance and toilets, from what I've heard, all up in the park. Nobody's seen him snooping around. It was probably greenies, or a tourist having a poke around off the road. Maybe some birdwatchers.'

'What do we do then?' Toby asked.

'Nothing for now.'

'We could keep cutting the forest,' Shane suggested.

'Then we'd have greenies on our backs and a big fucken demo on our doorstep,' Robbo pointed out.

'Since when has that stopped us?' Mooney said.

'Never,' Robbo agreed. 'But I say we should let sleeping dogs lie for now. It's the department's job to find us somewhere else to log and they have to do it fast. Maybe they'll set out a buffer round that tree and let us back in.'

'Not likely,' Shane said gruffly. 'There's a lot of big trees in there. When they have a closer look, they'll pull us out for sure.'

'You reckon it's a breach?' Robbo asked.

'Could be.'

'Why can't you just knock the trees down?' Mooney said. 'You've already skittled heaps of them so they won't know what was there.'

Robbo snorted. 'Except for all the massive cut stumps poking out of the ground. Ever heard of satellite photography? Greenies can look that stuff up on the internet and count the trees from the photos.'

'We're fucked then, aren't we?' groaned Shane.

Miki lifted the order from the fryer, drained it and tipped it out onto paper. She'd been so busy listening, it was a bit overdone and she hoped the men wouldn't notice. Nervously, she doused the chips in salt, wrapped them, then carried the parcel over and put it on the table. She hadn't added extras today because she didn't want to draw attention to herself. A gift might be read as a peace offering and taken as proof of guilt.

'Ta, love.' Toby fired a wide grin at her and swiped a broad hand bashfully across his bald head. 'Best chips in town.'

'*Only* chips in town,' she said.

Toby laughed as she slid back behind the counter, and Robbo continued as if she wasn't there. That was good, Miki thought, because obviously they didn't suspect anything.

'I heard they might send us south down Cockle Creek way or back up north near Maydena,' Robbo was saying.

'Who's paying to shift the equipment?'

'Guess they'll sort that out later.'

'Wendy won't be happy,' Shane said. 'That's a lot of driving.'

'I still reckon we should do something,' Mooney put in. 'I don't like just sitting around.'

'It's not affecting you,' Robbo pointed out. 'You've got plenty to do at the mill. Just settle down, for once. It might all blow over.'

Mooney's phone rang and he answered it, then cursed and hung up. 'Liz wants me to pick up some stuff at the supermarket. Have to go.'

Robbo wagged a finger at him. 'Don't you go meddling with the nest, do you hear?'

Miki was worried about this too. Shooting the eagles or damaging the tree was something Mooney might do.

'I've got a few ideas under my belt,' Mooney said with a grin.

'Don't shoot the birds,' Robbo reiterated, shaking his head. 'Just you keep out of it.'

Saturday morning, Liz slunk into the shop to pick up sausage rolls for her girls on the way to netball. Leon was there too, waiting for a serve of hot chips. When Liz ordered, Miki caught the waft of her perfume: sweet and slightly stringent. Liz had a graze on her forehead and couldn't look Miki in the eye. Leon must have noticed it too, something about the gentle way he looked at Liz and stepped aside to give her space at the counter.

As Miki slipped the sausage rolls into bags, she saw Liz trying to spread her bitty blonde fringe over the bruise, fingers fluttering nervously. A knitted beanie would cover it, Miki thought, but it would be too obvious to give Liz one for free. Instead, she slipped three Caramello Koalas into another bag and handed them over with the sausage rolls, hoping to give Liz a little bit of pleasure later in the day. She deserved it for putting up with Mooney.

17

Tuesday, grey clouds sank over town, seeping rain. Home alone, Miki sat in the shop watching raindrops weep down the windows. Hardly anyone was about, and those who had to be out were huddled under umbrellas, heads bowed against the wind-driven downpour. Despite the weather Miki was keen to get some fresh air, so she retrieved the key and unlocked the back door. Weeks had passed now without Kurt mentioning anything and she'd begun to relax.

Before going outside, she fetched *Far from the Madding Crowd* from its hiding place in her bedroom. It was too wet for a walk so she settled on the visitor centre. If Geraldine was there, they could talk books.

Geraldine was crouching by the wood fire, feeding logs into its belly. When she saw Miki, she clambered to her feet, grimacing, and brushed sawdust from her trousers. 'Knees aren't what they used to be.'

The pot-bellied stove rumbled as wind whipped the smoke from the flue. Geraldine turned her bottom to the fire and swung slowly back and forth, warming herself.

'Cold in here,' Miki said. 'Not good for your bones.' She remembered how stiff Mother used to be in winter. Miki had heated hot water bottles for her, and knitted extra-long pairs of thick socks, but nothing had worked with such bad arthritis. Operations had never been discussed, and yet Miki knew from talk in the shop that knee replacements might have been a solution. Isolated as they were on the farm, options from the outside world hadn't been contemplated.

'It'll warm up once the fire gets going,' Geraldine said.

'Leave the stove door open a little,' Miki suggested. 'That'll help it draw.'

'I'm not much good with fires,' Geraldine said. 'I've got a gas heater at home. It runs off a big bottle out the back. Gas is more efficient than wood, but wood's cheaper.' She limped to her desk and sat down. 'Terrible weather, isn't it? Not good for tourists. They all hide in this rain, and who can blame them? I wouldn't want to go sightseeing in this. I'd rather stay home with a book.'

Miki put *Far from the Madding Crowd* on the desk.

'Oh.' Geraldine's smile lines crinkled. 'Did you read it?'

'Yes. I loved it.'

'I thought you would. What did you like about it?'

'I liked that it was set on a farm in the countryside.'

'Hardy's Wessex. It's just like here in the winter—very rainy. But lush and green in spring. You'd like to live on a farm?'

'My family used to have an apple orchard.'

'That must have been lovely. I've never lived on the land, but I've always thought it must be a great way of life. The rhythm of seasons and weather.'

Miki nodded. 'Father used to say everything had its time. Pruning and grafting in winter. Training and spraying in spring and summer. Harvest in autumn.'

'Did you have sheep like Gabriel Oakes?'

'We had some for a while, to graze in the orchard. But dogs got them and Mother was upset.'

'As you would be. Any poddy lambs?'

'Only one. I raised her on cow's milk.' Miki remembered the little white lamb in the kitchen, snuggled in a box near the stove. She'd named it Mary and fed it from the same bottle her mother had used when Miki was a baby. There had been something satisfying in that: the cycle of life, the versatility of reusing things instead of throwing them away. Her family had been good at that. They had to be creative with so little money.

'You could relate to Bathsheba's life on the farm, then?' Geraldine said.

Miki smiled. 'Not exactly. Bathsheba was rich, and we definitely weren't.'

'It's hard for farmers, isn't it?' Geraldine picked up the book and flicked through it. 'Any bits you didn't like?'

'Yes, the fire in the barn . . . I lost my parents in a house fire.' This was the first time Miki had told anyone about her family, and she felt a tide of emotion rising under her skin. She looked away. She didn't want condolences; they wouldn't help.

'I'm sorry to hear that,' Geraldine said.

Miki didn't trust herself to look up.

'Bathsheba lost her parents too. Like you.'

'It wasn't real.' Miki was surprised by the harshness of her own voice. '*Far from the Madding Crowd* is a story. Thomas Hardy made it up. Bathsheba isn't a real person. It's not the same.'

'I know,' Geraldine said slowly, as if feeling for words. 'But sometimes fiction can help us explore life. We can imagine how things might be in certain situations.'

'I don't want people imagining how it was to lose my parents in a fire,' Miki said. 'It's too sad.'

Geraldine nodded. 'Yes, good point—that did sound a little insensitive. I'm not trying to trivialise what you went through, Miki—it must have been terrible. What I'm trying to say is that books can help us to empathise with other experiences. Do you see what I'm getting at?'

Miki nodded, but she didn't see at all. Why would you want to recreate suffering?

'It's a way of examining life and the world,' Geraldine went on. 'Books show us the lives of others, because we can't live all those lives—we can only live our own. Books can take us back in time or into the future. They expand our thinking. They show us new worlds. That's what fiction is, what it does. It's so powerful.'

Miki smiled uncertainly, still confused. But Geraldine was right: Miki had learned through reading her books.

'I thought Bathsheba would have benefited from the guidance of a mother,' Geraldine was saying. 'It might have helped her avoid several mistakes.'

'Bathsheba needed to make those mistakes,' Miki observed.

'We all need to make mistakes,' Geraldine agreed. 'But it's hard for a young woman without a mother, isn't it? How do you cope?'

'I miss my mother,' Miki admitted. 'She was my friend.'

'I was thinking of other ways that mums are important. Like being there to talk to and ask questions about the world. Showing daughters how a woman should behave. Sharing information about feminine things.'

Miki blushed—she wasn't used to speaking frankly like this. Mother had taught her that her body was sacred and that purity was important, but everything else had been shrouded in silence. When Miki had her first period at fourteen, Mother had handed her a bundle of rags. Miki thought she was dying until Mother explained it was her monthly fertility cycle. *You're carrying sacred eggs that could become babies and grow into God's servants, like you.* That was all Mother had said—the rest Miki had learned in the shop, listening to the women. She knew now that there was nothing sacred about her eggs because all women had them. She'd also heard about sex and condoms, diaphragms, the morning-after pill—the women discussed everything. It had been education by stealth, but Geraldine didn't need to hear that. 'I make do,' Miki said.

Geraldine's eyebrows lifted, but she let it go and Miki was grateful. 'Bathsheba is a great character, isn't she?' Geraldine went on. 'Different from Tess, but tragic in her own way. Her judgement wasn't always good.'

'Like not marrying Gabriel Oakes in the first place,' Miki said.

Geraldine smiled. 'Do you think they were ready for each other in the beginning? Bathsheba certainly wasn't, wild young thing that she was. And did Gabriel have the maturity and understanding to handle someone like her?'

Miki thought about this. 'Gabriel needed to learn about himself too. He was proud. He shouldn't have assumed Bathsheba would say yes when he proposed.'

'No. One should never assume. How do you think she handled herself when she inherited her fortune? It was certainly a change in circumstances, wasn't it?'

Miki said, 'Bathsheba was strong, even if she did make mistakes. She tried hard and that has to count. Trying is important. That's how you learn.' She was thinking how she would give anything to live and make mistakes rather than sit in the shop. Maybe she was making a mistake now, being here with Geraldine, but it felt good. Conversation made her feel larger and wiser.

'What about Bathsheba's love interests?' Geraldine asked. 'Did she conduct herself well?'

'No.'

'Foolish, perhaps.'

'Yes. Sergeant Troy was bad and she couldn't see it.'

'Love is blind, they say. What about the way she treated poor Mr Boldwood? She ruined him, didn't she? He was such a vulnerable soul.'

'She shouldn't have led him on.'

'I agree. But how could someone like him keep themselves safe?'

'He was who he was,' Miki said.

'You're saying there's no keeping safe?'

'Maybe.'

'Perhaps we all have to take risks, or we'd end up staying home and never experiencing anything.' Geraldine looked at Miki pointedly. 'Mr Boldwood was a little impetuous and far too passionate, but I suppose Thomas Hardy had to get rid of him somehow, or Bathsheba couldn't have ended up with Gabriel. Prison was a dramatic place to put Mr Boldwood, don't you think?'

'Bathsheba married the right man in the end,' Miki said. 'I like Gabriel.'

'A better ending than *Tess*?'

'Happier.'

'And we all like a happy ending.' Geraldine pushed the book across the desk to Miki. 'It's yours to keep. Remember? I gave it to you.'

Miki didn't know how to explain she couldn't keep it. 'We don't have room for it at home.'

'That's a shame,' Geraldine said, but in the quiet depths of her eyes Miki could see she understood. 'I have another one for you.' Geraldine produced a small thin book from her handbag and handed it to Miki: *The Little Prince.*

'Thank you,' Miki said. But she wasn't quite sure what to think—the picture on the cover looked childish.

Geraldine smiled at her reticence. 'Don't be fooled. This book is magic. One of my favourites. For a little book, it contains a whole lot of wisdom.' Her eyes shifted to a group of tourists, milling just outside the door. 'Back to work,' she murmured. Then she smiled at Miki. 'Don't get too wet out there or you'll turn into a mushroom.'

At home, Miki curled up on the couch in front of the wood fire with *The Little Prince.* When she opened it, she felt a familiar thrill as she gave herself over to the story. *Once when I was six years old, I saw a magnificent picture in a book, called* True Stories from Nature, *about the primeval forest.* This was a wonderful beginning; Geraldine knew she loved the forests and had hooked her with the very first line. It occurred to her that perhaps her friend wasn't choosing books randomly.

She devoured the book in two hours, falling in love with the little prince and his fresh, unusual way of seeing the world. She could picture his tiny planet, which was ordered and predictable just like her shop. The prince loved his home and tended it carefully, just as Miki did hers. But he wanted more. His best friend was a rose, a demanding companion, and the prince felt burdened by her endless requests. He loved the rose. And he loved the beauty of the sunsets that he watched from his planet. But they were always the same, just as life in the shop was the same every day for Miki: always on the inside looking out.

Eventually, the little prince decided to leave his planet so he could discover the universe. He left behind everything he knew and loved to find what he needed and who he was. This was where the book had become exciting. The prince travelled to other worlds and met many strange people, and he learned something from each of them. He asked questions, searched for answers, made mistakes, nursed regrets. But he did it! And this was what Miki admired most. To find his own truth, the prince had left his cosy, habitual world. This had taken courage and Miki respected him for it. She feared for him during his journey, stressed over his vulnerability. Wept when, in the end, he faced death so he could return home to his rose.

She wanted this for herself too. Not to die, but to go out into the world in order to live. She wanted this even if, like the prince, she discovered in the end that everything she'd ever needed was already here. The prince had to confront the universe to know this, and she knew this was vital for her too. If someone had given the prince all the wisdom of existence in a box, he might have accepted it, but he wouldn't have understood because he wouldn't have lived it; he wouldn't have felt the knowledge of it in his bones.

Miki yearned for knowledge too. She wanted to break away from the shop walls and windows. The key she'd taken from Kurt had given her freedom, but she wanted more. She wanted to make choices and to try things: school, study, friendships.

Even if she failed, she needed to do this. And, like the prince, she wanted to do it on her own.

18

'Go on, Max. Get the ball. Get in there. Big kick. Big kick.'

Max was playing footy with the Devils and it wasn't going well. He'd improved, practising with Leon, but he was having a bad day. And it didn't help with Dad standing on the sideline shouting at him like that. He slipped in the mud, then he was down on the ground, and two boys ran over him, their studs digging into his leg.

'Get up!' Dad yelled. 'You're no use to anyone down there.'

Shut up, Max wanted to shout at him, *just bloody shut up*. But he couldn't say it, because Leon had come along to watch too, and Max didn't want to sound like an idiot. He picked himself up, scraped the mud off his jersey and flicked it away. Yuck.

'Come on, Max,' Mum called out. 'Keep going. We can hose you off after the game.'

Max glanced over at Leon, who grinned and gave him the thumbs up. It made Max feel better. What was it that Leon had said when they were kicking balls over at his place the other day? *Sometimes it all goes to shit no matter what you do*. Yep. Max was having one of those days.

By now all the other kids had reached the far end of the field, and Max stumbled after them so he could join in again. He hadn't quite caught up when the ball flew through the air and plopped in the mud at his feet. He couldn't believe his luck—no one else was even close. He grabbed the ball and ran with it towards the goals.

'Bounce it,' Dad yelled. 'Bounce the bloody thing.'

Max wasn't going to try bouncing the ball because he knew it would stick in the mud and then someone would catch up and snatch it. He ran as fast as he could on the soggy ground till he heard the other kids gaining on him, then he took a shot for goal. It wasn't a champion's kick, but at least he remembered to hold the ball like Leon said and sink his boot into it. He stopped to watch the ball spin through the air. He could see it wasn't going to make it as far as the goal, but he'd kicked it straight and that was good enough.

Then Dad was whooping and hollering because when the ball hit the ground it kept going, head over heels, and rolled between the goalposts. Max had his first-ever points on the board. He stuck his hands in the air like footy players on TV and sprinted around the oval high-fiving the boys in his team. Callum gave him a bearhug, and the other Devils were leaping up and down because Max's goal had put them in front. They were winning.

Back in the centre of the field, waiting for the umpire to do the ball-up, Max looked at Leon and saw a huge smile on his face. Leon wasn't standing with Dad and Mum; he was off by himself on the opposite side of the field. Max didn't blame him—Dad was embarrassing. Max would have liked it if Leon could be friends with his family and come over to dinner, but Dad was always saying stuff about *Parkie* with a sneer in his voice, so Max knew he didn't like Leon. Max did, though: Leon was the best adult around.

Max was still thinking about Leon when someone kicked the footy down the field, and he was left behind again. Sometimes this game got at him. All the running was annoying. Back and forth. Up and down. He hated it when he ran out of breath, and he hoped the game would be over soon so he wouldn't have to run anymore. Maybe Dad would buy him a sausage sandwich for being a football superstar. He deserved it, didn't he? His first goal of the season!

Now he was scoring goals, he could see himself playing for Hawthorn or Essendon when he was grown up. One time he'd overhead Robbo say that Dad used to have *loads of potential* and could have *gone all the way* if he hadn't busted up his knee. Whatever had happened to Dad's knee must have been serious to stop him playing for one of the big-time teams in Melbourne. Maybe Max could *go all the way* too. Then he could earn tons of money and buy food for Rosie and the pups, and keep them forever. He could also pay for cigarettes and not have to nick them for Jaden. Life would be a whole lot easier. Max couldn't wait to grow up.

He didn't have much luck for the rest of the game, but that was okay because he'd done his bit by scoring the goal, and his team was still in front. There wasn't much time left anyway. A few minutes later, the umpire blew his whistle, and it was over. They had won!

Max was glad to stop. He went up and shook Leon's hand because it seemed like the proper thing to do, like the footy heroes who won the Brownlow Medal each year.

'Great work,' Leon said. 'You kicked the winning goal.'

Max hadn't thought of that—he'd just been excited to kick his first goal.

Dad was watching him, so he went and shook Dad's hand too so he wouldn't get jealous of Leon. Max could tell from Dad's smile that he was proud for once. 'Good on you, my man,' Dad said. Max was proud too.

He was so stoked about his goal he didn't want to take his jersey off, even though it was covered in mud. It was like when the men played and got mud all over them. The more mud on their jerseys, the better they'd played—that was what Dad said. Leon was always muddy after a game, because he kept getting mushed on the ground. But he kicked heaps of goals too and never stopped running. Nobody on the men's team ever said nice things to Leon, but maybe that was okay. It was a whole lot better than bad stuff; Max knew about that from Jaden and the school playground.

Dad was so pleased with Max's goal he took him to the canteen and said, 'What do you want?' Normally, after a game, Dad stalked off and wouldn't talk to him because he was too mad. Mum said Dad got cross because he was *too damned passionate* about the game. Dad said he just wanted Max to do well, and *was that too much to ask?*

Until Leon came along, footy had been terrible for Max, but now things had changed. Maybe Dad would be happier now that his son was a football champion.

Max took ages choosing what to have from the canteen. In the end he decided on a sausage sandwich, a can of Solo and a killer python. It was a bit greedy to ask for so much, but how many weeks had Max missed out when all the other kids got sweets? He shoved the python in his undies because he couldn't carry everything in his hands; it would keep for later and didn't take up too much room.

While Dad was buying the food, Mum and Suzie had wandered across to talk to Leon. Leon was laughing and Mum looked happy too. Max wondered if it was because of the goal he had scored. Then he felt worried because he didn't know if he could ever do it again, and maybe he would never be a real footy star, and maybe Dad would be disappointed next week, and maybe Max would wreck his knee in the mud and that would be the end of his great footy career.

Dad was talking to another parent, so Max went over to see Mum and Leon. When Mum kissed him on the head, he ducked away.

Leon laughed and patted him on the back. 'You were in good form today. I knew you could do it.'

Mum was frowning. 'Did you say thank you to Leon for coaching you?'

'No need,' Leon said. 'He caught on really quick.'

'Thank you, Leon,' Max said in the same singsong voice he used at school to say good morning to Miss Myrtle.

Mum swiped him over the head, right where she'd just kissed him. 'Cheeky bugger.'

'He's okay.' Leon's hands were in his pockets and he looked awkward. Max hadn't realised Mum could make Leon feel that way, and he felt sorry for Leon. Hopefully Leon would kick goals today and win for the men's team, so he would get some praise too.

On the way home, Mum dropped in at the takeaway to buy hot chips for lunch.

'Hey, Max,' Miki said, 'how did you go today?'

'We won. I kicked a goal.' He felt himself grow a few centimetres taller.

'Good for you.'

'Leon's been coaching him,' Mum explained. 'He's good with kids.'

'Yes, he seems very nice,' Miki said.

Max noticed Kurt staring at Miki and looking unfriendly. Mum noticed it too; Max could tell by the way her smile faded into a frown. 'Your brother could take a leaf out of his book,' Mum said quietly to Miki. 'Looks like he's been eating lemons.'

Max knew Mum was trying to be funny, but Miki's eyes went tight and she didn't laugh.

'You poor thing,' Mum murmured. 'Kurt needs to get off your back.'

At home, Mum wanted to put Max's muddy jersey in the wash, but he wouldn't let her because he wanted to wear it to the men's game.

Mum shrugged and said, 'You're wet, and you'll get cold in the wind.' Max didn't care. Six points he'd scored for his team today. He'd helped them to get their first win.

But when they were down at the oval watching the men's game, Max wished he'd taken Mum's advice. The wind was blasting like a tornado, and it cut straight through to his skin. Mum shook her head at him and pulled dry clothes from her bag. Max put on a jumper and coat and a beanie, and felt better straight away. After that, he hung on the rail and swung upside down while the men warmed up on the field. All that running around this morning had made him thirsty, so he plucked a can of Coke from Dad's esky. Suzie wanted one too, so he gave her Fanta because orange was her favourite colour. He didn't notice she was shaking it up, so when she asked him to open it for her it squirted everywhere—and Mum told him off. Couldn't she see he was trying to help?

When the men ran past, Max waved to Leon who gave him a wink. He heard Toby say to Leon, 'Know anything about eagles, Parkie?'

'Yeah,' Leon said flatly. 'They're a footy team from Perth.'

'Not talking *West* Coast eagles, Parkie. I'm talking *wedge*-tailed eagles.' And the rest of the team laughed.

Max wondered why this was so funny. Hadn't he heard Dad and Mum talking about eagles the other day? Now it seemed everybody was talking about them. The men were out of hearing range then, but Max saw Mooney jostling up against Leon. Instead of shoving him, Leon turned his shoulder and dodged out of the way. Max would have liked to see Leon hit Mooney because Mooney wasn't a nice man; Max had heard him yelling at his kids and their mum. Somebody should stop him being such a bully. But maybe it was best for Leon not to get into a fight. If he slugged Mooney all the men might lay into him. So maybe Leon was smart.

Dad was over near the clubhouse, organising the water bottles for the team. Last week, Max had hung out near the goalposts and chatted to the goal umpire, but he couldn't today because Jaden was there. Max wanted to stay away because he was sure the big boy would ask him to nick something else. Jaden kept catching Max's eye and pointing at the clubrooms, so Max knew he wanted him to go there. But Max was safe with Mum, so he acted dumb and pretended he didn't understand. He was relieved when the siren went and the game got under way.

All through the first half, Max tried to focus on the game, but Jaden's eyes made him itchy. He kept trying to distract himself by drinking more Coke, and by half-time he needed to pee. He didn't want to go to the loos because Jaden would follow him, but he had a stomach ache from a full bladder.

The loos were empty, and he had a pee, shooting it at the yellow balls and dead flies in the urinal. Then Jaden was beside him, having a pee too. 'Get more cigarettes and bring them to me after school on Monday,' Jaden said.

Max thought fast. 'Mum said I have to come straight home from school for a doctor's appointment.'

'Bad luck.'

'What if she picks me up and takes me in the car to the doctor's?'

'Then I'll steal one of your pups and feed it to Prince.' Jaden smirked, leaned forward and dribbled piss on Max's shoes. Then he zipped up his pants and said, 'See you on Monday.'

When Max came out of the loos, Robbo was going off at the team. Dad called it *Robbo's half-time chat*, which was kind of weird because Robbo didn't talk, he yelled. Max noticed Leon standing off by himself and nobody talking to him. Max didn't get it—these days, Leon scored nearly as many goals as Mooney. Whenever Mooney kicked a goal, the team went nuts, jumping on him and giving him hugs and slapping his back. But when Leon scored a goal, the men just nodded and said *good work*, like he'd done an okay job but not as good as Mooney. In the games, Max had seen the other men push Leon off the ball. At least they kicked and handballed to him now, which they never used to. Max knew how awful it felt to be ignored, because it happened to him all the time.

Dad came off the field carrying the crate of drink bottles and called out to him, 'Hey, Max, can you give us a hand?' That meant Dad wanted him to refill the bottles while Dad watched the game. Max wanted to say no, but he knew Dad would get angry. It was easy lugging the bottles into the clubroom but not so easy bringing them out, full and heavy. Max went into the kitchen where the ladies were brewing cups of tea and coffee and selling them through the window. Robbo's wife, Trudi, gave him a smile and let him use the kitchen sink. 'Heard you kicked a goal today,' she said. 'Good on you.' Max puffed up with pride. Word was getting round. He was already halfway famous.

He had a hard time trying to haul the rack of full bottles back outside, so Trudi helped him. She grabbed one side of the crate, while he gripped the other. She was older than Mum, with black hair and sad eyes—Max didn't know how he could tell this about her, but he knew it was true. When she looked at you, it was as if all the sadness of the world was locked inside and couldn't come out. But she liked him; he knew that too. If she was outside watering her roses, she always waved when he walked past down the street.

'How are the pups going?' she asked.

'Good.'

'Found homes for them yet?'

'No.' The kids at school had been keen, but their parents weren't so excited.

'That's bad luck.' Trudi's eyes were even sadder.

'What's the time?' he asked as they put the crate of bottles on the ground near the interchange bench.

'Four o'clock.'

'I'd better go home and feed them.'

Trudi put a warm hand on his shoulder. 'You do that,' she said. 'And give them a pat for me.'

That night, Dad came home at nine o'clock after footy and the pub with the smell of beer on his breath. Max was in the shed when Dad came out to get a can of Southern Comfort and Coke from the spare fridge: one of those white cans with curly black writing. Max didn't like it when Dad drank that stuff because sometimes he got mean. Tonight, he was wobbly on his feet and his words were all slippery, like he couldn't quite sling his tongue around them.

Mum called out for Dad to come and kiss Suzie goodnight, and he grumbled and sloped off, leaving his packet of cigarettes and his can on the workbench. As soon as Dad was gone, Max saw his chance and tried to take some cigarettes for Jaden. But Dad came back while Max had the pack open, and he roared so loud Max jumped in the air. 'What the fuck are you doing, you little cunt?'

Max was so shocked at Dad using the c-word, he dropped the packet and all the cigarettes fell out—and that sent Dad crazy. He clouted Max over the head and made him pick them up. 'How long have you been nicking my smokes, you little shit?'

'This is the first time,' Max said, and Dad hit him again, a whack on the back that would leave red fingerprints.

'Bullshit.'

'Honest, Dad. I don't smoke. I don't even like it.'

'So you've tried it then! You little liar.'

'No, I haven't, Dad. I promise. Not ever.'

Dad grabbed him by the arm and dragged him inside. 'Did you hear that, Wendy? This little prick has been stealing my cigarettes.'

Mum's hands cocked on her hips and a worried frown creased her face. 'Is that true Max? Have you been smoking?'

He looked down and shook his head miserably. His day was wrecked. 'I haven't,' he said. 'Honest, I haven't.'

Dad's fingers hooked into his cheeks as he made Max look up at Mum. 'Say it again and look Mum in the eye.'

Max couldn't, and Mum said, 'Give me your phone and go to your room.'

Max handed over his phone and ran off to his room.

There was an argument then, a massive yelling match between Dad and Mum, all because of Max.

'Maybe it was his first time,' Mum said, trying to defend him.

'Bullshit, Wendy. You can see he's guilty.'

'How about I deal with it in the morning?'

'No way! That kid deserves a good hiding.'

'Since when did smacking ever teach him anything?'

'I don't care. Whacking his arse will make me feel good.'

'I don't want you to belt him, Shane, not when you've been drinking.'

'Why not? You scared I'll lose control?'

'Maybe.'

'Christ, Wendy. I'm not a child-basher. I just want to teach him a lesson.'

'What if someone put him up to it?'

'Not bloody likely. He knew what he was doing. Told me he didn't like cigarettes. How's that for guilty?'

'Maybe he's tried one, but so what? How old were you when you started smoking?'

'Too bloody young, and Dad whacked me so hard I couldn't sit down for a week.'

'Did it stop you?

'For a while.'

'Not tonight, Shane. That's all I'm asking.'

'Well, I'm saying now's the best time. Come on, Wendy. Get out of my way.'

'Over my dead body!'

Max heard scuffling in the kitchen, and he hoped Mum wasn't getting in trouble because of him. He opened his door a crack to have a look, and Mum and Dad were kind of wrestling. Then Dad chucked his can of Southern Comfort at the wall with a crash and it fizzed everywhere. Mum said, 'Look what you've done. Now I have to clean up.'

Dad stomped outside and came back with another can. He sat on the couch in front of the TV with a mad look on his face, and Max knew it was up to him to sort things out. He slunk out of his bedroom and stood in front of Dad and said, 'I'm really sorry, Dad. I won't take any more cigarettes.'

But Dad's face was cold, and he wouldn't look at Max. 'Have we got a cardboard box somewhere?' he called out to Mum. 'I'm going to deal with those pups.'

Max panicked because he didn't know what Dad was going to do. Dad put down his can and stood up, and Max yelled, 'No!' Dad took a swipe at him. But Max dodged under Dad's arm and ran outside. He was crying as he raced to the shed.

The pups looked up with their little ears pricked and their black eyes all frightened. Max jumped into the pen and tried to grab them, but they kept squirming away. He picked up Bruiser and then tried to grab hold of Patch, but the pups were too big to hold two at once, and he dropped them and they yelped. Rosie was standing up too with her teeth showing because she didn't know Max was trying to save her pups. He heard the back door bang and figured Dad must be coming. He had to do something, but what?

'Shane, please don't,' Mum was saying. 'Please let's talk about this.'

Max dropped to his knees and tried to scoop up the pups, but they were all wriggly. He dived randomly among them and wrapped his hands around one like a footy. It was Bonnie.

Then he heard Dad. 'Put that pup down.'

But Max wasn't going to let go of his pup. He slid under Dad's reaching arm and ran as fast as he could down the driveway, through the gate and into the street in the dark. Down the footpath he raced, sobbing. He didn't know where to go, but his legs took him to Robbo's front door, and he banged on it with his head because he couldn't use his hands, which were full of struggling pup.

The outside light came on and Trudi opened the door, eyes wide with alarm. 'What's happening?'

'Dad's trying to take the pups.' Max's words came out in scratchy sobs. He thrust the pup at Trudi. 'Can you look after this one while I go get the others?'

She took the whimpering pup, and Max didn't wait to hear her say yes. He sprinted back out into the street and fast up the footpath.

But it must have taken longer than he'd thought to run down to Robbo's because Dad was coming out of the shed carrying a big cardboard box, and little puppy heads were looking over the top. 'No, Dad, no,' Max cried, reaching for the box.

Dad held it high and pushed Max away with his hip.

Rosie was following too, leaping at the box. 'Piss off, dog,' Dad said, kicking at her. 'And you too, Max. Get back inside.'

'Where are you taking them?'

'Where I should have taken them right at the beginning,' Dad said, eyes icy cold. 'Where's that other pup, Max?'

'I don't know.' Max sobbed.

'Go and get it.'

'I don't know where she is.'

Mum was on the front doorstep with her pink cardigan wrapped around her shoulders, arms clutched tight across her chest. 'If you take those pups, Shane, then I don't want you back here tonight.' Her voice shook with anger and tears.

Dad wasn't listening. He tossed the box in the back of the ute, and Max saw the pups lurch and heard them yelp with fright. They couldn't know why Dad was taking them away or where he was taking them. Max didn't know either. He tried to scramble onto the back of the ute, but Dad shoved him down to the ground.

Then Dad was in the ute, backing into the street.

Sobbing, Max raced after him. Maybe he could grab the box while Dad was turning around. The terrified pups were crying over the roar of the engine. Rosie was barking.

Max reached for the tailgate, but Dad jerked the ute round so fast Max had to let go or he might get run over. Then Dad revved the motor and took off, accelerating down the street in the dark.

Max sank onto the road. He huddled there till Mum came out, slid her arm around his shoulders, helped him up and silently led him inside.

19

Sunday morning, Leon was taking his time over coffee and toast when he heard a knock at the door. When he opened up, Max was there with a pup in his hands. 'You still carting those puppies around?' Leon said.

The boy's face crumpled and he burst into tears. 'Dad took the pups away last night and he hasn't come back. Bonnie's the only one left. I managed to rescue her.'

Leon felt sorry for Max—it was clear what Shane had done with the pups. 'Maybe he's gone to Hobart to sell them,' he suggested, trying to comfort the kid.

Max shook his head. 'Mum thinks he's killed them.'

Leon patted the pup on the head. 'How did you save this one?'

'I took her down to Robbo and Trudi, and they looked after her.' Slumping on Leon's front porch, Max cried into the pup's fur, tears running down his face.

Leon had never seen anyone cry so hard. He sat down and put his arm around the boy's skinny shoulders, which were shaking with sobs. 'Hey, hey,' he soothed. 'You've still got this pup.'

'But I can't keep her. When Dad gets back, he'll take her too.'

Leon let the kid lean against him. It was a long time since he'd held anyone—not since he'd hugged his mum goodbye back on Bruny Island. Leon was sad for the boy. For weeks he'd been watching Max take care of those pups; Max was only ten, but no one could have done better. Last night, Leon had heard shouting next door, but that wasn't unusual for Shane and Wendy so he'd turned up the TV to drown it out. This was the same trick he'd used back home when his dad was going off. His dad used to go drinking then stagger home, rampaging and looking for a fight. It had taken Leon a while to figure out what was going on. In the beginning, he'd been living in Hobart and didn't know why Mum was being evasive on the phone. Then, one weekend, he'd dropped home to see his folks and was surprised to find the curtains drawn and nobody around. He'd hunted for the key that usually hung in the hedge but it wasn't there, so he'd gone for a walk on the beach. When he returned, he'd spotted his mum cringing behind the lounge-room curtains and he'd yelled at her to open up because, for God's sake, he'd come home to see her and why the hell wouldn't she let him in? She'd timidly opened the front door, and Leon had known straight away what was happening—the evidence was clear. After that, he'd made arrangements to move home and take a job on the island instead of applying for one of the bigger parks.

Now, breathing into the misty morning, he sat on the step waiting for Max to cry himself out. But the pup was getting sick of it, wriggling and whimpering in the boy's arms. 'Why don't you put her down for a bit,' Leon proposed, 'so she can have a run while I make some hot chocolate?'

Max shot him a look loaded with fear and desperation. 'Can I come inside with you? If Dad comes home and sees Bonnie, he might take her too.'

Clearly, the boy was traumatised; he was clutching that pup like a life raft. Leon wasn't sure he wanted a dog in the house, but the kid looked so mournful, what could he do? 'Take her around the back and wait for me on the doorstep,' he said. 'Your dad won't see you there. I won't be long.'

In the kitchen, he boiled milk in the microwave and broke into it some chocolate he'd been saving for a cold day up in the park. Oh well, this was a time of need. That was what chocolate was for.

Max was waiting on the back steps as Leon had instructed, thin shoulders rounded with dejection. Bonnie was on his lap, licking his face with her busy pink tongue; the kid was so down he didn't seem to notice. The pup was quite a cute little thing, Leon supposed, with her patchy red and grey coat, uneven ears and gangly legs. He sat beside the boy and handed him a mug. 'Here. Tuck into this.'

Max put the pup on the ground and took the drink listlessly.

'How old is she?' Leon asked, trying to draw him out.

'Seven weeks.' The boy turned moist eyes to Leon and said, in a shaky voice, 'Maybe you could keep her. You need a friend.'

The truth of it hit Leon like a tackle on the footy field. He'd been living in this town for weeks now, and who could he really call a mate other than this ten-year-old boy and Grandpa? He hadn't exactly been a screaming success, had he? But he *had* made progress, he told himself. He *was* getting to know people. No invitations to dinner, but the blokes were getting used to him on the footy field. And Wendy waved to him when he went out to chop wood. Dale, the scientist, had been friendly too. And Geraldine at the visitor centre was kind—Leon had chatted to her several times. He was sort of friends with Miki too, through the Tasmanian devils and the eagles' nest. And, courtesy of local garage sales, he'd almost converted this dingy old place into a home. He'd bought a TV, second-hand couch, two old armchairs, a few kitchen chairs. Didn't furniture and friends make him almost a local? It was a pretty good start.

Max was still eyeing him hopefully. 'What do you think?'

'I don't know, mate. I know nothing about dogs.'

Max was suddenly gushing with excitement. 'I can help train her,' he said. 'I can come every night and feed her and play with her.' He jumped up, knocking over his hot chocolate and stepping on the pup's paw, making her yelp. 'Oh, Bonnie,' Max cried, picking her up and burying his face in her ruff, 'I didn't mean to hurt you.'

Leon's guts twisted. The pup was sniffing around on the lawn now, tail up and wagging—she had no idea her future was being determined. But what would he do with a dog? He didn't need one, even though the pup needed a home. He was away working all day; wouldn't a dog require company? 'I don't have a fence,' he pointed out.

'I'll help you make one,' Max said. 'Or maybe Bonnie can stay inside.'

'She's not house-trained, so she'll shit and piss everywhere.'

'That doesn't matter. It's not your house anyway. And Mrs Westbury's dead. She won't mind.'

But Leon would mind.

Max sighed and looked at him seriously. 'Okay, then. I'll clean up the poo.'

This made Leon laugh because, from the look on Max's face, he could tell this was a significant commitment. 'Really?' he said.

The boy nodded. 'Really. And we'll build a fence next weekend. Mum will help. She's good at that stuff. She used to live on a farm.'

Leon felt himself melting. What else could he do? He wished he didn't have a conscience. 'All right, then, I'll give it a go. But if it doesn't work out, I'll have to give her to someone else. And remember, you said you'd help train her and clean up her poo.'

The kid leaped in the air, punching at the sky with his fist, even more animated than when he'd scored that goal yesterday. Clearly this was more important. But Leon had a sick sensation. A pup! How the hell was he going to manage that?

'Oh, I've got this for you too,' Max said, pulling a piece of paper from his pocket. 'Mum said to give it to you. It's for the forest festival. In case you want to go.'

Leon took the brochure; it had a picture of a log truck on the front. 'Are you going?' he asked.

Max shrugged. 'We have to.'

'Is it good?'

'It's all right.'

'Okay then. I'll go too.'

The boy's smile was as big as the sky. 'I'll go get some dog food—Mum said you could have some.'

'What about a collar?'

'We don't have one small enough. Mum said you could get one at the supermarket.'

Leon had the distinct feeling of being ambushed. The boy had an answer for everything.

After Max went home, Leon felt the full extent of his error. As soon as he took the pup inside, she peed on the floor without looking the slightest bit guilty. Luckily Leon didn't have carpets but his heart sank. He mopped up the wee with paper towels, realising just how uncomfortable he was with this new situation. Was this how people felt when they came home with a new baby? A small thing became a big thing, then your life changed and you couldn't go back?

He tipped some kibble that Max had given him into a bowl, then set it on the floor with a pot of water. While he made coffee, Bonnie worked her way through the kibble, crunching it with little sharp teeth. Then she lapped water, splashing it everywhere. Leon wiped up and threw down a rug for her to sleep on.

In the lounge room, he turned on the TV to watch a replay of last night's footy. He was just beginning to relax and forget about the dog when she started whining. Didn't she have what she needed? The whining grew louder, so he took her outside and she had another wee. Maybe that was the problem. Dogs liked being outside.

He tied her to the back door with a piece of rope then slipped inside, but she started whingeing again and scraping at the door. Leon tried to ignore it, but the whining turned into a howl so he let her back in. She sat on his feet and looked at him and licked at his jeans while he watched TV. He pushed her gently away with his foot, but she came straight back, shoving at his hand with her wet nose. Next thing she was flinging herself at his legs and scratching to get up, but no way was he going to let her on the couch. He deflected her again, but she took no notice and returned for more, still whingeing. Leon turned up the TV and refused to look at her. She paced the room restlessly then took a run-up, hurled herself up on the couch and crawled onto his lap. Leon shoved her off again. No dogs on the couch. On, off, on, off. Finally, the pup gave up and curled in a circle on the floor.

Leon looked down at her. He knew nothing about dogs, but he'd promised to give it a go for the boy's sake. He sighed. He could go online and search up advice for new dog owners, but he was already feeling tired.

Then he had an idea. Maybe his mum might know somebody who wanted a dog—she was connected with everyone in her community. Or perhaps she wouldn't mind taking Bonnie herself. God knows, Leon's dad wasn't much company. A dog might be perfect. He fetched his keys, scooped up the pup, and put her in a cardboard box in his car.

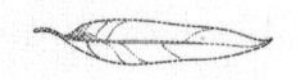

Bonnie was asleep when Leon pulled up outside his parents' place at Adventure Bay, Bruny Island. It had been tough trip.

Bonnie had spent the first hour howling and trying to jump out of the box until Leon's nerves were jangling. Then she'd finally fallen asleep. It was clear she didn't take after Rosie, who'd been a much easier passenger.

On the ferry across to the island, Leon had left Bonnie in the car so he could stand up front watching the light shift over the silver-grey water, just as he'd always done on this passage. It had been peaceful until someone tapped him on the shoulder and told him the puppy was crying. When he'd returned to the car, Bonnie had launched herself onto his lap and insisted on staying there. It hadn't been easy driving the island's rough roads with a dog draped over his legs.

He hadn't called ahead to tell his parents he was coming, but he figured they would most likely be home—they never went anywhere these days because of Dad's health. Mum's small white car was in the garage, the curtains were open, and there was Minnie the cat, surveying her world from the window. Leon hesitated. He hadn't thought of the cat; Mum might not appreciate a canine companion for Minnie. But he was here now, so he might as well give Mum the chance to say no.

He transferred the sleeping pup onto the passenger seat then got out of the car, closing the door as quietly as possible so as not to wake her. The scent of salt air greeted him. The soft hiss of waves on the beach across the road. The clacking of a yellow wattlebird in the trees. Everything so still, you could almost hear the grass growing. He'd forgotten how drowsy and peaceful it could be here, how the hush settled as soon as you arrived.

His mother was frowning when she opened the door, probably expecting Stan—but her wrinkles dissolved into smiles when she saw Leon. 'What a lovely surprise.' She hugged him, and he inhaled her familiar scent of coffee, flour and perfume. 'Come in,' she beckoned. 'I've just baked a cake. I'll put the kettle on so we can have tea with your father.'

The house was as if he'd left yesterday, but the kitchen seemed smaller and darker—he'd forgotten how it lost the light mid-morning because of the shadowy pine trees.

Minnie came trotting down the hall, tail erect and jerking. She came up confidently and was about to bunt her head against his leg when she paused and sniffed his trousers, probably smelling the pup. Then she rubbed her head against his calf. Maybe she didn't mind dogs. Some cats were okay with them, Leon had heard. He dragged out a chair and sat down. 'How are things?' he asked his mum.

She smiled tiredly. 'We're managing. Your father has good days and bad. The illness never really lets up.'

Leon was sliding into a hole. He'd had a break from his folks and their daily struggles with illness, yet the moment he stepped into this place he felt drained. He'd given so much to support his mum these past years; now he had nothing left. 'Any more trips to the hospital?' he asked, trying to be conversational.

She laughed feebly. 'Not this week. We had some check-up tests a few weeks ago to see how his liver is going—that time when I rang you because he was vomiting—but it's much the same.'

'How about Stan? He still coming around?'

'A bit.'

'What's been happening? Dad getting into the grog?'

She bypassed the question, took a knife from the drawer and started slicing the cake. It was chocolate, he noted, with a slick coat of icing.

'Mum?' Leon probed. 'Has he been hitting you?'

Her eyes darted to his face and away again. 'No, he's too weak.' Her mouth was small and tight.

'But he's tried?'

She lifted a slice of cake on the knife, put it on a plate and pushed it across to Leon. 'Here. Try this.'

'Mum, has he hurt you? I need to know.'

She met his eyes levelly. 'I know you worry, Leon, but it's okay. I don't need you to come and live with me again. It's not necessary. I'm at work most of the week, and when he gets out of hand, I go for a walk. He can't chase me anymore—he's too sick.'

'You need to lock your bedroom at night,' Leon said. 'Have you still got that padlock I organised for you?'

She nodded and watched in silence while he tackled the cake. When the kettle boiled, she poured tea.

'Why don't you go and see your father?' she suggested. 'I'll be down in a minute.'

Leon didn't want to see his dad after what his mum had just told him.

'Please, Leon,' she said. 'Do it for me. I want you two to get along.'

What choice did he have when she put it like that? Resigned, he headed down the hallway, scooping up the cat on the way.

He smelled his dad before he saw him, and so did the cat. Just outside the bedroom, Minnie stiffened. Leon held on, murmuring, 'Sorry, cat, we're in this together.' She shot him a foul look with wild eyes and tried to escape, but he secured a handful of scruff and clung on.

Dad was yellow and thin. He registered Leon briefly before turning back to the TV.

'Hey, Dad,' Leon said, trying to sound more upbeat than he felt.

Dad gave a sour smile. 'Well, well. Look what the cat's dragged in.'

'It's vice versa.' Leon carried Minnie forward. It took some effort to unplug her claws from his sleeve, and when he put her on the bed she tried to bolt. Dad stretched out a hand to pat her but Minnie hissed, and when Leon released her she pelted into the hallway. Leon sat on a chair, waiting for his dad to start talking—which, of course, he didn't. It would be up to Leon to get things going, as usual. 'How are you?' he asked.

'All right.'

'Mum said you've had a few tests.'

'Yeah. Same old bullshit. No miracle cures.'

'Stopping the grog would help.'

'I have.'

'Mum said the blood tests don't show it.'

His dad said nothing.

'What about Stan?' Leon went on. 'What's he been giving you? I'll guarantee it's not water.'

Dad eyed him sourly. 'Why are you here?'

Leon sighed. So, that's how it's going to be. 'You're not exactly pleased to see me, are you? I thought it'd be nice to drop in.'

'What's a man supposed to do?' Dad scoffed. 'A highland jig? You know I can hardly get out of bed.'

Leon was grimly pleased that his dad was stuck in bed—that kept Mum safe. 'I've been visiting Grandpa every week,' he said. 'He's not a bad bloke. We've been getting to know each other again.'

'Putting on a show, is he?' Dad grunted.

'I like him. He's good for a chat.'

'He's a troublemaker, that's what he is. Has he ever told you how he used to keep his hands warm in summer?'

'You don't need to keep your hands warm in summer.'

'Exactly. Tell him I told you to ask.'

'Sure. I might drop in and see him on my way home.'

'Give him my love,' Dad said.

Leon ignored the sarcastic tone. 'You should call him sometime. He'd like to hear from you.'

'Like hell,' Dad snorted.

'He's decent,' Leon added. 'You used to be like him before you got hooked on the grog.'

Dad scowled; clearly he didn't take this as a compliment. 'How's your job? Converting any lost souls to conservation?'

'Mostly preaching to the converted.'

Dad sniffed. 'That's how it goes. Just like religion.'

Mum tiptoed in with a tray on which she'd carefully arranged her best cups and saucers and teapot: the special Wedgwood set with the floral design and gold trim. 'How are my two favourite boys getting on?' she asked. Her smile had a tentative edge to it.

'Like a house on fire,' Dad said. 'Just as you'd expect.'

She poured tea through the gumleaf-shaped strainer Leon had given her for Christmas one year. She was funny like that, the way she trotted out the gifts he'd given to prove she remembered. She got stuck on objects as if it was *things* that mattered, not the way people behaved. The tea set and strainer were evidence of how much she wanted Leon to get along with his dad. *I'm trying*, he tried to tell her with his eyes.

They all made a reasonable attempt at pretence—up until Leon introduced the pup. Then things went pear-shaped.

Before letting Bonnie loose in the hallway, Leon had shut the cat safely in the kitchen. But Minnie had learned a new trick since Leon had left home—she had worked out how to open the door. Now she hunched in the corridor, hissing and spitting as the pup skittered up to her, yipping excitedly. She reacted by racing down to Dad's room and leaping onto the bed, knocking his teacup, which went flying onto the carpet. It would have survived if Bonnie hadn't bounded into the room and accidentally bounced on top of the cup, splitting it into pieces as she leaped at the bed, scrabbling with her paws and trying to reach Minnie. Leon wasn't sure who yowled louder: the cat or his mum. He grabbed at Bonnie, spilling his own cup onto the floor and shattering it. Then it was Dad's turn to yell as Minnie dug her claws into his belly and launched for the curtains. The pup barked shrilly. Leon cursed. And Mum was in tears, counting the fragments of her special crockery on the floor.

'Where the fuck did that dog come from?' Dad wheezed, grasping at his scratched abdomen.

By then, Leon had the pup in his arms and was trying to contain her frantically paddling legs. 'I thought she could be a get-well gift,' Leon said, grasping for a way to appease his dad. 'A nice surprise for you.'

'She's a fucking surprise, all right,' Dad spat. 'Just look what she's done to your mum.'

Leon clutched Bonnie to his chest and tried to calm his weeping mother. 'Mum. Sorry. It's okay. I can replace those cups.'

But his mum just picked up the tray and rushed from the room.

'Get rid of that dog,' Dad yelled. 'Get it out of here.'

Leon felt himself imploding. 'Back off, Dad. I'm taking her out.'

'No, *you* back off. You come in here and mess up our lives—'

'It's you who's been wrecking lives, Dad.'

His dad picked up a coffee cup from the bedside table and hurled it at Leon, who sidestepped neatly, allowing the mug to crash into the wall. Leon wanted to stay and rip in—he wasn't finished with his dad yet—but Bonnie was whimpering, scared by the raised voices so he carried her out and returned her to the car. When he went back into the house, his mum had gone out, which was good; it would give him free rein with his father.

There was something satisfying about storming down the hallway and into the bedroom where his dad was captive. A healthier man might have done a runner or stood up to confront him. Leon knew Mum wouldn't want them to argue like this, but there were things that had to be said. How could she feel sorry for such an arsehole? How could she tolerate his drunkenness, even now, with his liver shot to pieces?

At the bedroom door, Leon let loose. 'You leave Mum alone, do you hear me? If you touch her again, I'll kill you.' His dad snivelled, eyes dark with anger and impotence. 'And no more Stan,' Leon went on. 'If I hear he's been here again, I'll personally organise a restraining order.' He ran a hand through his hair as his fury suddenly dissipated into something else, a sort of sadness. 'I can't believe we have to go over this again. Three years of bashing Mum because of the grog and you still can't leave off, even when your liver is cooked. Do you want to die?'

Dad's jaw jutted. 'Man might as well be dead, if he can't drink.'

'That's not what you used to say,' Leon said. 'You used to have values.'

Dad slumped, bitterness in the twist of his mouth. 'As I said, might as well be dead. Not the man I used to be.'

'I was hoping to find the pup a home,' Leon said. 'That's why I came. The rest of the litter was drowned, and I thought you and Mum could use the company. She certainly could.'

'Are you trying to make me feel bad?' Dad croaked. 'Because let me tell you, it's not possible to feel worse than I already feel.'

'A dog might make you feel better. Dogs are good like that.'

'What would you know? It was a stupid idea. Take the dog and go. She's not wanted here. And neither are you.'

Leon stood up. His father was right. His plan had been ridiculous, based on a selfish desire to escape responsibility for the pup. A dog would be too much work for his mum. She had enough to do, caring for his dad.

He walked away, nursing an uncomfortable feeling that his dad had won again. Nothing had changed.

On the way home, Leon felt down. He shouldn't have bumbled in there, ruffling his parents' quiet lives. He felt guilty about the whole thing, so he stopped in to see Grandpa at the old people's home. Who better to talk to than someone who'd known Dad since birth and followed the trajectory of his life: the good, the bad and the ugly.

Irish Anne, the weekend receptionist, was on the front desk. She was a big woman with a *generous bosom*, as Grandpa liked to put it, and apparently she was a softie and you could get almost anything past her. 'Just dropping in to see Grandpa,' Leon said, passing the desk swiftly in the hope she wouldn't notice Bonnie in his backpack.

Anne smiled with crooked teeth. 'He'll be pleased to see you. It's always a good day when your grandson comes in.'

Grandpa's door was shut, and Leon was tempted to shove it open and barge in like a nurse, give the old man a surprise. But something held him back—maybe fear of causing a heart attack. He knocked, and a rustling, scrambling sound came from inside, then Grandpa's voice calling imperiously, 'Who is it? Can't a man have some peace?'

'It's me, Grandpa. Leon.'

There was a brief delay before the old man opened the door, naked except for a towel around his midriff. Leon was horrified to see all that loose, saggy skin. Worse still, beyond Grandpa, perched on the bed with his green-checked dressing-gown clutched around her shoulders, was an old woman with a blue-rinsed perm. Under the gown, she was clearly naked too.

Leon tried to back away. 'Looks like I've interrupted something. I'll drop in another time.'

Grandpa grinned crookedly. 'No, lad. Come on in. I want you to meet Glenys, my new best friend.'

Leon edged into the room, looking everywhere except at Glenys whose arthritic hands were doing a poor job of keeping her body concealed. 'I remember you,' she said, lighting up. 'You're the one who brought the dog to see us.'

Leon nodded. By this time, Bonnie was fed up with being squashed in the backpack and she let out a whimper.

'What have you got in there?' Glenys asked, excited.

'Live cargo.' Leon put the pack on the floor and pulled out the pup. 'This is Bonnie.' He set her down and she capered around, bouncing at Leon's trousers and then at Grandpa, her sharp claws raking his skinny old legs, drawing beads of blood. 'Watch out, she's scratched you.'

'I don't care.' Grandpa lifted the pup.

Glenys cackled with delight and reached for Bonnie. 'What happened to your other dog?' she asked Leon.

'Rosie isn't mine. She belongs to my neighbours. This is one of her pups. I saved her from drowning.'

Grandpa nodded approvingly. 'Good decision. Every man needs a dog. She's just what you need—especially since you don't want a girlfriend.'

'Oh, he'll find a girl now,' Glenys said. 'Women love a man who's good with dogs. Can I hold her?' Grandpa settled Bonnie on Glenys's lap, and the old woman curled her hands around the pup and raised Bonnie to her face. 'Oh, she smells good. Just like a puppy should. You'll bring her in to see us again, won't you? Everyone here loves dogs.' She turned to Grandpa. 'I never knew things would be so exciting when you came into my life.'

'Oh, I'm full of excitement,' Grandpa said, winking.

Leon patted his back pocket, seeking tissues to wipe the blood from Grandpa's leg, but he found Max's brochure instead; he must have shoved it there during the discussion over keeping the pup. He handed the brochure to Grandpa. 'What do you think about this? It's in a couple of weeks.'

The old man fumbled the flyer in gnarly hands. 'Forest festival, eh?'

'Do you want to go? It'd be a day out for you. Glenys can come too. We can have a look around then go for a drive in the forest. Maybe up to the park. See some nice country.'

Grandpa squinted at the brochure then gave it to Glenys, who was craning to see.

'What are all these events?' Grandpa asked. '*Bush Push* and *Truck Pull*. I've never heard of them.'

'Me neither. But it could be fun.'

Grandpa's eyes shone. 'I think we could do it.' Then he became serious. 'Where do they hold this thing, in a paddock? I won't be able to walk round for long.'

'We can take folding chairs so you and Glenys can sit down for rests. Soon as you've had enough I can bring you both home.'

Grandpa looked doubtful. 'Are you sure?'

'I'm sure. Give it some thought and let me know.' Leon picked up the pup. 'I have to take Bonnie home for some dinner. It's been a big day and she's hungry. See you, Glenys. Nice to meet you.'

Grandpa followed him into the corridor. 'Where have you been?'

'Home to Bruny.'

'How did it go?' Grandpa had a knowing gleam in his eye as if he'd already guessed.

'I had a run-in with Dad and I didn't hold back.'

'Might have done him some good.'

Leon shrugged. 'I don't hold out much hope. He's beyond redemption . . . Anyway, it was nice to meet Glenys. Sorry for barging in on you like that.'

'Minor interruption. We can pick up where we left off.'

'Aren't crosswords more appropriate this time of day? And I'm not sure it's legal to sleep with other inmates.'

Grandpa grinned. 'You ought to get yourself a girl too.'

Leon rolled his eyes. 'Bonnie's my main girl now.' He tapped the pup on the head as she peeped out of the backpack. 'Oh,' he added, remembering, 'Dad said to ask how you used to keep your hands warm in summer.'

Grandpa's smile shrank and he hesitated. 'He'd have been referring to the summer of '67 when a fire destroyed the mill on the island.'

'A bushfire, you mean?'

'Bushfires everywhere in the south-east that year—but, no, not in this case. It was deliberately lit. The last big mill on the island burned down, and it wasn't rebuilt. Had a big impact on the local industry and the family who owned it.'

Leon thought of the history book Grandpa had lent him. He remembered reading about a fire at a sawmill on Bruny Island. Was that the one Grandpa was referring to? 'Did they ever catch the person who lit it?' he asked.

'No, he got off scot-free.'

Leon detected a glint in Grandpa's eyes and began to understand. 'You know who did it?'

'Yes, I know him quite well.' The old man's lips and eyes flattened. 'The boss was imposing himself on your grandmother and he had to be stopped. A woman's honour is important. And a man in a position of power shouldn't be allowed to take advantage. That's why I did it. To make my point clear.'

'But you didn't even work at the mill.' Leon tried to keep the shock out of his voice.

'No, but your grandmother wasn't the only woman over the years. That man was a predator. I saw it as a strike for the community.'

If Grandpa had been so protective of his wife, Leon thought, it must have been particularly hard for him to hear of his son's domestic abuse.

'How did you do it?' Leon asked.

'At night, when no one was around. Threw some petrol over a timber stack and struck a match.'

'How does Dad know?'

'Your grandmother told him.'

'She knew too?'

'A man shouldn't have secrets from his wife.'

'Was she upset?'

'Of course, but she forgave me and stood by me. That's commitment. That's marriage. I was a bit of a hothead back then, but she understood.'

'How do you feel about it now?'

Grandpa's lips compressed. 'There are some things in life a man looks back on with regret, and that's one of them. I made my point, but it affected the whole town. I should have handled it differently and confronted him. It would have been enough. It would have stopped him.'

An uncomfortable silence fell between them. The pup sensed it and started wriggling. 'Thanks for telling me, Grandpa,' Leon said.

Grandpa nodded. 'I hope you don't judge me too harshly.'

'No. We all make mistakes.'

'The important thing is to learn from them. And cultivate the art of forgiveness—like your Grandma. It's a generous act. You could use a bit of forgiveness with your father.'

This caught Leon off-guard. 'Forgive him for hitting Mum? I don't think I can.'

'Is he still doing it?'

'Mum says not.'

'Has she forgiven him?'

'She's still living with him.'

'I suppose that's forgiveness. Maybe you should let it go.'

Leon wasn't ready for forgiveness. 'I'll think about it,' he said, inclining his head towards Grandpa's door. 'You'd better get back to Glenys or she'll give you up for dead.'

A twinkle returned to Grandpa's eyes. 'Not likely. We've still got an hour before dinnertime.'

20

After the logging was suspended, strangers started passing through town. They stopped in the takeaway shop: city people in khaki-coloured clothes with binoculars strung round their necks. Miki heard their murmurs about the eagles' nest. Word must have got out. And the *bird nuts*—as Kurt called them—were coming to find it.

Kurt didn't like the thought of people snooping around in the forest. It made him edgy. He wanted to check the beehives hadn't been tampered with, so on Monday they rugged up in coats and beanies, and piled into the new ute, hoping the weather would lift on the way.

The logged area was misty and desolate as they drove through it, curtains of rain sweeping the wide open space. To Miki, it still felt like death. She couldn't stop thinking about the animals that had lived there: birds and possums hiding in old hollow trees. Where had they gone when the machines came through? Some of the birds might have flown away, but what about the nocturnal creatures? Likely they had been crushed as their trees were knocked to the ground. It made Miki feel ill.

The ute sloshed over wet ground, squelching through divots and puddles. The machines were still there, upslope; Miki saw them through shrouds of drizzle. They were halfway up the hill, wet and silent: great hulking metal skeletons waiting for drivers to bring them to life. Miki couldn't wait for them to be gone—while they remained, there was a possibility they might resume their work.

At the eagles' tree, Kurt pointed out tyre marks in the mud and footprints where people had trampled around the base of the trunk. The tyre marks disappeared after that, so it seemed nobody had ventured further into the forest. Miki hoped her large old tree was still safe.

They parked in their usual spot, and Kurt agreed to check the big tree before inspecting the hives. They walked towards it through the dripping forest. And there it was, rearing unharmed into the clouds. But something small and silver glinted at its feet. A Turkish Delight wrapper. Miki's gut clenched.

Grim-faced and silent, Kurt stuffed the wrapper into his pocket then strode back to the car, Miki scuttling anxiously behind him. He lurched in behind the steering wheel. 'Get in,' he said. 'Let's go to the hives.' He backed the ute down the disused grassy track that led to the hiding place, braking with a jolt that sent Miki into the dashboard. 'What the fuck?' he barked.

He leaped out and, panicking, Miki followed.

The hives were scattered on the ground in pieces: boxes broken and frames strewn. No bees.

Kurt stared at the ruined hives, hands on hips, nostrils flaring. He was quivering, and it seemed to Miki that he was buzzing with all the angry energy of the bees that had lived in those hives—and that, at any moment, he might erupt and bees would pour out of him.

He kicked at the fragmented pieces of wood with his steel-capped boot. 'Fucking bastards,' he yelled. 'Rotten, fucking mongrels.' He laid his boot in several times, then picked up a slab of wood and hurled it at a nearby tree with a crash. Miki cowered. It reminded her of Father in a rage. Sometimes when things had gone wrong on the farm, Father had gone off, just like this. A blockage in the water pump. A car or tractor that wouldn't start. Once, he'd spent hours methodically taking the lawnmower apart and putting it together again, and it still wouldn't go. Miki had watched him trying to start it, pulling the ripcord again and again, becoming more and more jerky and violent, until he'd flung the mower in an arc across the lawn. Thank goodness it had fallen on soft grass and hadn't been damaged; they never could have afforded another one.

Now Kurt grabbed a second piece of wood and threw it wildly into the bush, then another, with the intent of slamming it into the ground. But a yell curdled in his throat, and suddenly he hunched over. Bees were attached to his hand. He slapped at them, brushing them off and yowling with pain. The bees must have been hiding among the bits of wood, left behind when the rest of the hive departed. Kurt nursed his hand, anguished. He'd been stung before, but never like this. He was panting. 'I'll kill the bastards who did this to my bees.'

Miki was relieved it wasn't the bees he was angry with, but she was worried about his hand, which was already starting to swell. 'We need to get you to a doctor,' she said.

He let her lead him to the car. His face was scrunched with agony, and his eyes were dilated and dark. He shuffled into the driver's seat, right hand clenched like a claw. 'Put the keys in the ignition,' he gasped. Miki fumbled but couldn't find the right key. 'The big square-topped silver one,' he said. 'Yes, now turn it to the right.' She did as he said, flinching as the ute roared to life. 'Okay, now get in. Fuck, it hurts.'

He drove bent forward, grimacing with pain, using only his left hand, the fat-looking right one folded across his chest. It was lucky he'd reversed down the trail because that meant they didn't have to turn. The rear wheels spun in wet grass, then they were jerking through the bush.

It seemed to take forever to reach the main road. Kurt pulled up on the verge. His face was puffy now. 'You'll have to take over,' he said. 'My vision's gone blurry.'

Miki was terrified. She'd never driven a car. 'I don't know what to do.'

'Get behind the wheel,' he ordered.

She sat in the driver's seat but her feet couldn't quite reach the pedals.

'There's a lever beside the seat,' he said. 'Grab it and pull yourself forward.'

She struggled with the lever, eventually dragging the seat into a better position.

'Now, the clutch,' he said.

When the ute finally took off, lurching along the road, Miki was afraid to switch gears, but Kurt made her do it. She was whimpering with the stress of it. Panic burned in her chest. She was scared of the ashen colour of Kurt's bloated face, the swelling of his hand.

A car overtook from behind, blaring its horn because she was swerving all over the road. Her stress morphed into anger. She could have learned how to drive years ago on the farm; it would have been easy for them to teach her on the tractor. But Father and Kurt had restricted her to the vegie patch, the cow and the kitchen.

Without changing gears and with the engine screaming, she drove into town, barely slowing to make a wild turn into the medical centre, bouncing the car over the kerb. She had no idea where to find the brake so the ute stalled in the driveway. Kurt was beyond caring. He was groggy, his breathing harsh. She jumped out and tugged at his arm. 'Come on, we need to get inside.' His lips were fat and his bloodshot eyes barely open as she dragged him to the door.

The receptionist gasped as they stumbled inside. 'Oh my God. I need a doctor here, right now!'

They took Kurt out the back while Miki sank onto a chair in the waiting room. She could hear urgent voices behind the closed door, calling for oxygen, adrenaline, antihistamine, icepacks. Was Kurt going to die? How would she cope on her own? What would happen to the shop?

'He'd be better off in hospital,' a female voice said.

Then a deeper tone: 'No time for that now. Give him a second EpiPen.'

'Listen to his breathing. Does he need intubation?'

'We're not equipped for that here. Oxygen will have to do.'

'Do we need to get him airlifted?'

'Keep your voice down.'

Miki wanted someone to tell her Kurt was okay. He might be difficult, but he was all that she had.

While she perched there, anxiously waiting, a blonde woman came in and stood at the counter, tapping pink-painted fingernails on the bench. Miki was so addled by stress it took her a few moments to recognise Mooney's wife, Liz.

'Nobody about?' Liz glanced shyly at Miki, who noticed the bruise on her brow was now gone.

'They're out the back, looking after my brother.'

'What happened?'

'He was stung by bees.'

'Ouch! Anaphylaxis? Is he allergic?'

'I don't know.'

'I know how scary it is,' Liz said. 'But he should be okay. One of my girls is allergic to peanuts. The doctor here has helped her before. She was all swollen and could hardly breathe, but she came through it all right. Your brother will be all right too.'

'I hope so.' Miki didn't quite believe it.

Liz smiled. 'Thank you for the Caramello Koalas the other week. The girls and I really enjoyed them.'

'That's okay.'

'You've given us treats before, haven't you? It's really nice.' Liz swept a strand of blonde hair behind her ear.

A nurse came out, red-faced, a sheen of sweat on her skin, and directed Miki into a consulting room so the doctor could speak to her. He was a tall, narrow man with grey hair at his temples and pale serious eyes. He said Kurt would be fine but would have to remain under observation for the rest of the day. Miki's brother was sleepy, the doctor said, which wasn't unusual after treatment for a multiple-stinging event. They had him on a bed where they could keep an eye on him and give more adrenaline and antihistamine if needed. The doctor said Miki could go home, but she couldn't bear the thought of sitting in the shop alone, looking through the windows and waiting. So she stayed, watching people come and go. There was no more talk of hospital.

She leaned against the wall, remembering how she had visited the hospital in Hobart years ago. It had been her first taste of the outside world, and the memory was vivid. Closing her eyes, she pictured her younger self and sank into the past.

There she was: seven years old and skinny as a stick, long dark plaits, grey overalls and red jumper. She was clomping along in pink, muddy gumboots through the winter orchard, carrying a pan of softened beeswax as she followed her father down a row of apple trees. He put down his toolbox and kicked a bare patch in the soft soil with the toe of his boot. Then he set the stove on it, turning on the gas and lighting the flame, adjusting it low. Miki placed the pan over the flame before trailing her father to a tree.

He flicked his secateurs from his pocket and got to work, snipping off twigs from last year's late shoots, cutting them into pencil-lengths. When he'd gathered a handful, he passed them to her and she clutched them in her sticky palm. She liked it when he let her help in the orchard, because most days she was in the kitchen doing lessons. She was old enough to go to school, but her parents were giving her an education in God, which was best done at home. These lessons were delivered at the kitchen table from the large old Bible with its black leather cover, worn by use. There were many dog-eared pages to mark the important bits, and that made the Bible even thicker because every page was important.

Little Miki learned about God while she sat in the house, but he was outside too, she knew this. Mother said God was everywhere, a presence inside her, closer than her breath. But Miki didn't feel God inside her; she simply felt herself. She was sure God hated the stuffy kitchen as much as she did and preferred to be outdoors where a soul could rise into the sky. She suspected God was in the trees and the wind, in the flowers, in the birds that flew overhead. He would be happier outside than he would be living between the dog-eared pages of a heavy old book full of hard words.

Miki loved being out among the gnarly old-man trees, and she loved to watch her father with his knife, the precise way he performed his cuts. He pulled a handsaw from his toolbox and hacked a branch from the tree and let it drop to the ground. With his stone-sharpened work knife, he made a notch in the fresh-cut stump. Miki passed him a twig, which he whittled to a sharp point and inserted into the notch then wrapped the join with tape. As he sawed off another branch, she handed over her last two twigs.

It was time to fetch the pan of molten beeswax so Father could paint the grafts to keep the water out. Miki turned off the gas knob and picked up the pan, making sure she didn't spill any wax while she carried it to her father. As she walked, the wax swirled in the pan, making pretty patterns. She held the handle with both hands and tried to stay steady as Father dipped his brush in. He dipped and painted, dipped and painted, making neat white collars around the grafts. Miki struggled to be strong, but the pan grew heavy and her hands began to tremble. She asked God for help because Mother always said he helped those who were weak and in need. In her mind Miki was yelling, *God, make me strong.*

Then Kurt yodelled to let them know he was near. She didn't mean to be distracted, but her head jerked up when she heard his call. At the same time she dropped the pan, spraying hot wax onto Father just as he had his knife out and was about to make a new cut. She heard his raw cry and saw a ruby spurt of blood pumping from his hand like a fountain. One of his fingers was dangling. Another was on the ground, a stumpy white thing, and the blood kept coming from his hand. She watched him fumbling at his loose finger, trying to put it back on as if forcing it in place would make it regrow. The blood was shooting in an arc. She saw Father's grimace, heard his yowl, the rough grunt of his breathing superimposed over the airy patter of her own puffy breaths.

The world became woozy and the grass was rippling. She looked again at the finger on the ground, nestled in a bed of grass. It was weird and white and lonely. Wrong. Meaty. A dark blanket spread over her, and time swelled and became no time at all.

What she saw next were the gangly branches of dormant apple trees reaching into the sky. She was in Kurt's arms, the rough wool of his jumper rubbing her cheek. He held her tight against his chest as he strode along the row of trees. She felt tired, but if she closed her eyes Father's detached finger was there—she couldn't shut it out—so she kept her eyes open and watched the branches jolting by.

At the house, Father was sitting on a chair in the driveway beside the big old pine tree, his face as grey as the clouds. Mother was bent over him, wrapping his hand in a tea towel, a red stain radiating through it like spreading ink. Kurt set Miki on the gravel, and she stood there watching silently. But the congealed strands of blood on Father's overalls made the world shimmer again. Kurt pressed her to the ground, and there she remained while the others had a discussion. Father's face was pale and tight. Kurt was standing alongside, listening intently. They were trying to work out how to get to hospital. With his finger cut off Father couldn't drive, and Mother had never learned, because driving was a man's job. Kurt was too young to have his permit, but he'd driven the paddock bomb and tractor around the orchard for years. He would have to drive the car. It was a long way to Hobart, but there was no other solution.

They had all clambered into the old brown Commodore: Father and Kurt in the front, Miki and Mother in the back. On her lap, Mother carried an esky with the finger inside. Miki was still reeling from the smell of blood, so she leaned against Mother while Father sat in the passenger seat and held up his hand, covered by the towel which was dark red and saturated. Mother reached forward with another towel and rolled it over the first, saying quietly, 'Put some pressure on it.' Miki wondered why God couldn't make the bleeding stop. Weren't her parents praying hard enough? Mother's lips were clamped in a flat line, and Miki knew she was angry—Miki felt a hot stab of guilt because she knew it was her fault. She was the one responsible for this disaster, as if she had cut off those fingers herself. But despite her shame, she felt excitement rising, because this was the first time she had ever left the farm.

In the driver's seat Kurt started the car and clunked it into gear, taking off jerkily and bouncing down the driveway through puddles and potholes and ruts. Father groaned with every bump, every clumsy gear change. Then they were through the gate onto the gravel road, entering territory Miki had never seen before, driving past paddocks and orchards, half-hidden houses with letterboxes and driveways, gates and sheds.

They came to an intersection where Father barked instructions, and Kurt slowed the car and turned onto another road that was smooth and black with no bumps. The car went so fast Miki thought they might take off and fly. It was scary but exhilarating.

They took another turn and already she was lost. They came to a place with many houses and buildings close together lining the street, cars parked nose-out on an angle, people, signs, rubbish bins, footpaths, children on bicycles. 'What is this place?' Miki asked. 'Town,' Mother said. This was where Miki's parents came shopping; she had always wondered what it looked like. She wished she could see inside all the shop windows. She knew her parents bought flour and sugar, broomsticks, soap, clothes, wool for knitting jumpers. But there must be other things too. She leaned forward, trying to see out, but Mother snapped at her to sit back and be still. Miki knew she should focus on her guilt and the chopped-off fingers and ask God for forgiveness, but it was hard. There were so many new things, and everything was rushing past: a school, a park, children playing on swings, a lady walking a dog. Her heart was beating quickly because she had to remember it all. She had to seal it in her hungry mind. The world was bigger than she'd ever imagined, full of fields and farms, fences, cars, people, buildings. She used to think everything was made up of apple trees and forest because that was all she could see from the top of the tallest apple tree on the highest hill on the farm.

They passed out of town and drove over hills, and the road widened. All was quiet in the car. Mother was still as stone, and Father was silent in the front seat with the blood-red towel wrapped over his hand. Kurt was concentrating on driving, and Miki stared through the window, taking it all in. Soon there were cars going in both directions. Big noisy trucks. Tourist buses heading up to the hills. They passed an enormous wooden apple shed. Poplar trees with brown leaves lining the road. Purple mountains in the distance. Green signs with white writing.

It was a long drive, nearly an hour, and Miki was exhausted from looking and seeing and storing things in her memory. Her brain was like a pot of hot water boiling over, hissing and fizzing on the stove.

Just when she thought she couldn't take any more, they drove around the shady side of a dark mountain, and craziness exploded all around: rushing cars close and noisy, crisscrossing roads, crowds of houses, tall buildings, red-and-green-eyed lights, people on paths, women in smart suits and high-heeled boots, men in black coats. Rain started to tumble and umbrellas appeared like mushrooms popping skywards.

The shadow of the mountain reared above everything, clouds low on its stern black brow.

At the hospital, they went through magic glass doors that slid open without you touching them. Mother talked to a lady behind a white desk, then Father was taken into another room to be seen by a nurse. He came back, closed-faced and quiet, and they went into a room full of people sitting in plastic chairs. The people were blank and stiff. Children rolled restlessly on the floor. Miki wondered how long they had all been there, waiting for who knows what. She hadn't seen other children before, only the boy who came every few months with the wood-delivery truck, sitting high on the front seat and staring down at her. Here in the hospital waiting room the children were fidgety and wild, and they argued with each other and moaned at their parents. A small boy tugged his mother to a large-windowed metal box in the corner; she plugged coins into it and pressed buttons, then something dropped down. The boy put his arm through a flap-door, pulled out a crackly packet and opened it, releasing the smell of salt and oil. 'What has he got?' Miki asked Kurt.

'Chips.'

'Are they good? They smell good.'

'Shh.'

Miki kept looking around. On the wall, a screen shifted with constantly changing pictures. She was transfixed by it; she clutched Kurt's hand and ogled. She wondered who made the pictures, and how they moved on the screen. She was so busy looking, she almost forgot the esky on Kurt's lap containing Father's finger.

A man in a green uniform called Father's name, and they followed him through a door into a wide room lined with white beds and people with grey faces and sagging eyes. They were shown to an empty bed on which her father sat, and a blue curtain was pulled around. The man in uniform had a weird thing made of black tubes hanging round his neck. He said he was a doctor, and Father explained what had happened to his fingers. The doctor opened the esky and peered in, then he unwrapped the tea towel on Father's hand and his face tightened. He reached towards Father's bloodied hand with a pair of scissors—and then, in the palm of his hand was another finger.

Miki felt floaty again. The room was swaying. She heard the clickety sound of shoes and wheels on lino floors, felt darkness descending. But there was no time for dizziness. The doctor barked for assistance, and another man in uniform came through the curtain and wheeled Father away.

They sat again in the waiting room. For a long time, Miki was alert: looking at everything, thinking about what had happened. What if Father's fingers couldn't be fixed? Would she get in trouble? Was it her fault? And what about everything around her right now? How could she make sense of it all?

Despite her fluttering mind, she must have fallen asleep with her head on Kurt's lap, because later Mother shook her awake. The doctor had come back to talk to them. Miki was so tired she barely heard him say the operation to save Father's fingers had failed. While Mother cried and Kurt sat in silence, Miki looked around at the new people who had arrived. A fat man who smelled of cigarettes and looked like a frog. A little girl with a snotty nose and a doll like a real baby. A boy with a noisy toy that jingled and talked.

Miki knew she should feel guilty and sad because those fingers were gone. She should be asking forgiveness from God. Instead, she was caught up in the world.

Her senses in overdrive. A disaster unfolding in front of her. Opportunity riding on the crest of that disaster. Her mind tingling with thoughts of what might lie ahead.

There she was: then and now. A young person waiting for the world.

PART III
Growth

21

Max didn't know how the kids at school found out about the pups, but at the start of the week it was all they could talk about.

'What happened? Did your dad kill them?'

'Lily Moon says your dad drowned them.'

'Why is your dad living at Mooney's?'

'Why is he sleeping on Lily Moon's couch?'

'Because Mum wants to kill him,' Max yelled. 'And I want to kill him too.'

He made himself sound tough on the outside, but inside he was crying. He didn't want to think about the pups. He didn't want to think of their little faces and how they must have looked when Dad was pushing them under the water.

Max knew now that Rosie had never been a bad mum. Dad must have drowned her other pups too, when they were just born. That was why Max never saw them. In the school toilets, he cried his eyes out. He hoped Dad stayed living at Mooney's forever, because Max would never forgive him.

Everyone was sad for Max—except Jaden, who had a big smirk on his face as if he'd been hoping the pups would die all along. 'Poor Maxie. Can't stop blubbering over the little puppies. Big pussy cry-baby. Now they're all dead.'

Not all of them, Max thought.

He didn't want Jaden to know about Bonnie. She was living with Leon, and that was the next best thing to Max keeping her himself. Every day before school, he went over to see how she was going. In the afternoons he fed her and played with her till Leon came home. Her training wasn't going too well, but Mum said he had to keep working at it. Bonnie was as good at concentrating as Max in the classroom. He figured they were almost the same.

Home was quiet without Dad. No yelling. No arguments. Max heard Mum talking on the phone to Trudi. 'How can Liz stand it? . . . Can you imagine Shane and Mooney in the same house? . . . You're right. Poor Liz doesn't have a choice . . . Imagine all the beer those men are going through. All that drinking and bloke talk . . . What? He asked to stay at your place? What a nerve . . . No, I don't want him back. Let him stew.'

But Max could see Mum was wearing herself out without Dad. Max had more jobs to do, like chopping the wood and carrying it in, and putting out the rubbish.

Sunday night, when he got up to pee he noticed Suzie's room was empty. He went searching for her with his torch and found her in bed with Mum. There wouldn't be room for Dad when he came back, so maybe he would have to sleep out in the shed with Rosie—Mum had said that to Trudi a few times.

Max wouldn't mind sleeping with Rosie. He would take his sleeping-bag and pillow and, if it wasn't raining, they could lie out under the stars. Rosie was better than a hot water bottle, and it was nice outside at night. When there were no clouds, the whole sky was dusted with stars and you could look up at the universe which went on forever, and all the sadness would slowly dissolve and you could be nothing and nobody, and problems melted away. Thinking about this helped Max manage at school. And it helped him to forget Jaden, who was still his biggest issue. The pups were gone, so Max didn't need to worry about Jaden hurting them, but he was still scared. Jaden was strong and kept threatening to bash him.

At recess and lunch, he tried to avoid Jaden by keeping his head down, but the bigger boy always found him. Thursday, Max spent lunchtime sitting on the loo hoping Jaden would get sick of hanging round and go away. Eventually he did. Then, when the bell went at home time, Max tried to get out of class fast and run for his bag.

But Jaden was waiting for him. He poked Max in the ribs. 'Did you get more cigarettes?'

'No. Dad caught me. That's why he killed the pups.' Max wanted Jaden to feel guilty, but his eyes showed that he didn't care.

'You still have to get cigarettes.'

'I can't.'

'Come behind the loos then.'

Max had to follow, and Callum came too.

'If you can't get smokes you have to steal something else,' Jaden said. 'Smokes are too easy anyway.'

Max's skin went cold.

'Like what?' Callum was all excited, the stupid idiot. He was supposed to be Max's friend.

'Something from the shops,' Jaden said. 'A bag of chips.'

'No way,' Max said. 'Too noisy. It'll be a dead giveaway.'

'Chocolate, then. Or lollies.'

Callum stared at Max with big eyes, scared for him. Max was scared too. 'I'll nick it from the supermarket,' he said, relieved to think of this. It wouldn't be too hard. Almost a cinch.

But Jaden's eyes were sly. 'No, you have to get it from the takeaway.'

Max felt sick. If Kurt caught him, he'd be dead. And he didn't want to steal things from Miki because she always smiled at him and asked how things were going. 'The supermarket,' he said again. But he was stuck—he'd have to do it. 'Next weekend.' He was trying to buy time.

Jaden spat on the ground and clicked his knuckles menacingly. 'No. Do it now at the takeaway or I'll smash you.'

There was no way out.

They picked up their bags and walked to the shops. Max dawdled and made excuses to stop, like tying his shoelaces, but Jaden kicked him to make him keep going.

Then they were across the road from the takeaway, and Max was feeling terrible. How could he do this and not get caught? If he had money he could buy lollies then steal something while the cash was going into the till. 'Have you got fifty cents?' he said. 'If I don't have any money they'll guess straight off.'

Callum nodded. 'He's right. Kurt'll kill him. Like *really* kill him.'

Jaden sniggered. 'Bad luck.' He pushed Max onto the road. 'You'll think of something.'

Max went into the shop. No one else was there. Only Miki behind the counter. This was better than Kurt.

'Hi,' she said.

'Hi.' He mooched around, looking at the fridge and the shelves. Then he checked out the lollies and chocolates and bags of chips. How was he going to do this?

'Are you okay?' Miki asked. 'It's so sad about the pups.'

Max ducked his eyes away. 'Yeah, I know.'

'Sorry I couldn't give one a home. But I heard Leon's got one. That's nice. Can you go over to see it?'

'Yeah, every day. I'm helping him train her.'

'I bet that isn't easy.'

'Yeah, she just wants to play. She misses the others.'

'I bet you miss them too.'

Max did, but right now he had other things on his mind. He scanned the shelves as if he was going to buy something.

Miki watched him. 'Can I help?' she asked after a while.

'No thanks. Just having a look.' He peeked out the window and saw Jaden and Callum still waiting across the road. Why couldn't they just go away? He took a can of Coke from the fridge and put it on the counter. 'How much is this?'

'Three dollars.'

He pretended to feel for money in his pocket. 'I haven't got that much.'

'How about a packet of chips?'

He shook his head. 'Haven't got enough for that either.'

She smiled. 'You're not having much luck today, are you?'

She was right. Max didn't know what to do. He couldn't go back outside with nothing. Maybe if he kept talking to Miki she might get distracted, and then he could nick something. 'What days are you shut?' he asked.

'Monday and Tuesday.'

'I'll tell my mum. She asked me to check.' This was a lie and Miki knew it—Max could tell from her face. 'Why do you wear those plaits on your head?' he asked.

Miki touched her hair and her cheeks went pink. 'I don't know. I've always done it. My mum wore her hair this way too.'

She turned away to check the fryer, and Max took his chance. He grabbed the nearest thing, a packet of Fruit Tingles, and shoved it in his pocket. When Miki turned back, Max wasn't sure if she'd seen. He said, 'Thanks, see ya,' and walked out of the shop.

He crossed the road and went fast up the hill, Jaden and Callum following.

'Did you do it?' Callum asked.

Max said nothing. His heart was banging so hard he couldn't speak. He went around the corner before he stopped. Then he opened his hand and held out the Fruit Tingles.

Jaden sneered, but Callum was excited. 'Sick! You did it. You did it, Max.'

Max felt all weak like he might fall down, but he'd got away with it—at least he thought he had. Miki might have seen him, but she hadn't said anything; she hadn't stopped him.

Jaden snatched the packet of lollies and tore it open and stuffed some in his mouth.

'Hey,' Callum said. 'Those are Max's. He stole them.'

Jaden smiled and chucked two lollies on the ground. 'There you go. I'm sharing.'

Max picked up a Fruit Tingle and put it in his mouth, but it didn't taste right. Maybe it was off. Or maybe he just felt awful for stealing from Miki.

'What next?' Callum said, and Max could have killed him.

Jaden grinned nastily. 'A can of Coke.'

This wasn't too bad because Max could get a Coke from the fridge at home. He tried to look scared so Jaden wouldn't choose something trickier—but the smile on the older boy's face told Max he wasn't going to get off that easy.

'A cold one,' Jaden said. 'You have to get it from the shop while we wait, like today.'

'That's too hard,' Callum said. 'They'll see him get it from the fridge.'

Jaden's grin widened. 'You'll work it out, won't you, Max? If you don't, I'll punch your lights out.'

Max stared at the footpath, trying to hide his fear. He would have to come up with a plan. There had to be a way.

'Have you ever nicked anything from that shop?' Callum asked his brother.

'Shut your face, Callum. Or you'll get it instead.'

Max kept his eyes down. 'I'm going home,' he said, and walked off without looking back.

22

On the morning of the forest festival, Leon collected Grandpa from the old people's home and helped him into the car. It took a bit of juggling to settle him in the passenger seat, but it was worth it just to see the old man smile. Glenys had decided not to come. 'She has trouble walking,' Grandpa explained. 'She wants us to have a good time. A boys' day out—that's what she called it.'

They drove along the water, then through farmlands and orchards, then back to the water, Grandpa leaning this way and that, taking everything in. 'Why do they have nets on those trees?'

'Cherries, Grandpa, worth a fortune.'

'And that ship—why do they need one so big?'

'Salmon farming. It runs up and down the river all day. They must be supplying the universe.'

'Salmon's good fish. Wish I got to eat it more often.'

'I can't afford it,' Leon said.

'Glenys likes it.'

Leon smiled. Grandpa was like a love-struck schoolboy.

They passed through Leon's home town, and from there followed the signs to the festival. It was in a big field. The adjacent paddock was being used as a car park and it was packed. Vehicles were also parked in lines along the road. At the gate, a Rotary rep in a fluoro vest jingled a bucket, and Leon wound down his window and dropped in some coins. The rep pointed to the far side of the car park. 'Can I drop my grandfather somewhere closer?' Leon asked. 'He can't walk very far.'

The rep grumbled, but when he saw Grandpa's lively face he broke into a grin. 'Hey, old-timer, looking forward to a fun day?'

'Sure am. They don't let me out often, so I'm going to live it up.'

'You do that,' the rep said. Then to Leon, 'Let the old fella out near that big white tent over there, then try your luck for a parking spot.'

Leon deposited Grandpa at the tent. When he came back after parking the car, Grandpa was sitting on the walker, easy to spot in his grey suit, collar and tie, and old trilby hat with a feather in it. 'Took your time,' Grandpa said. 'A man could die waiting.'

Leon folded the walker and hooked it under his arm. They made their way onto the field, which was teeming with people. It was quite a set-up. Tents and gazebos in rows. Log trucks and utes along fences. A central wood-chop arena near a tall pole rigged for tree-climbing. Draught horses dragging loads. Food stalls. Big-bellied men in Akubras and flannelette shirts. Kids running around, while their mums failed miserably at keeping them under control.

Leon led Grandpa towards a crowd around a four-wheel-drive ute in a roped-off ring. A driver sat in the cab and three men stood behind it; Leon recognised Toby and Mooney from footy. 'What's going on?' he asked a man beside him.

'It's the Bush Push, mate. Just about to start.'

'Want to watch?' he asked Grandpa.

'Yup. I want to see everything.'

Leon set up the walker near the front, and they were just in time; the start-gun went off and the men shouldered into the tailgate of the ute, faces screwed up with effort while the crowd shouted encouragement: 'Carn. Get into it, boys.'

At first nothing happened, then the ute started to roll forward. It moved slowly—but somehow the men pushed it a full thirty metres to a white line sprayed on the grass.

Leon thought it was over, but then Mooney donned chaps and a helmet from the tray of the ute, grabbed a chainsaw, slapped on goggles and earmuffs, and cranked up the saw. Near the white line, a log had been racked on a frame, and now Mooney zipped off two rounds of wood before killing the motor and tossing his safety gear over to Toby. With muscles and tattoos popping, Toby dragged on the gear and grasped a shiny silver axe and split each wheel of wood into five pieces. The last team member loaded the wood onto the back of the ute while the crowd roared. The men were red with exertion as they pushed the ute back to the starting line.

Leon couldn't help laughing. What a crazy competition! When one team finished, the next one lined up. He and Grandpa cheered with everyone else; Grandpa, bouncing on his walker, waving one spindly arm.

Afterwards, they watched the gumboot-throwing competition. Then they followed the racket of chainsaws across the field to a cordoned-off area where men in earmuffs and safety glasses were lined up at numbered racks bearing logs, clamped horizontally. When the starter dropped a flag, the men stepped to their blocks, chainsaws screaming, and deftly zipped off wheels of wood: the first with an up-cut, the second with a down-cut, and the third by inserting the saw into the log and slicing outwards.

Shane was in the second group; Leon recognised his neighbour's bony bum and workman's cleavage. Balanced and relaxed, Shane cut his wheels quickly and accurately, leaving small piles of sawdust on the ground. Wendy was watching with the kids; Suzie had her hands over her ears to block out the noise. When Shane won first prize—a meat tray donated by the butcher—he sidled over to give it to Wendy, but she turned away. Leon overheard Shane pleading with her. 'Come on, Wendy. It's for you. I want to come home.'

She cast him a glare that would have stopped a truck. 'Give it to Liz. It'll help pay your board.'

'Wouldn't have to pay board if you'd let me come home.'

'Should have thought about that before you killed those poor pups.'

Leon caught Max's eye and waved, and the boy waved back. He seemed to be having a good time: hot-dog in one hand, phone in the other. He slouched over.

'Hey, Max,' Leon said. 'This is my grandpa.'

'Hi.' Max bit into his hot-dog.

'Any good' Leon asked.

The boy shrugged. 'Not enough sauce.'

'This is the boy who gave me Bonnie,' Leon told Grandpa.

'Ah, yes.' Grandpa squinted at Max. 'You look like a boy who knows about dogs.'

Max puffed up proudly. 'She's a good dog, isn't she? I'm trying to train her.'

'Just as well,' Grandpa said. 'A dog's no good unless it's obedient.'

'We're making progress—aren't we, Max?' Leon winked at the boy.

Max nodded. 'She knows how to sit now. And I'm trying to teach her to drop.'

'*Come* is the most important command,' Grandpa said. '*Come or I'll give you a hiding.*'

Max looked confused. 'She won't come if she's scared.'

Grandpa nudged Leon. 'See. I told you he's clever.'

A roar of voices from across the field distracted Leon. 'What's going on over there?'

Max glanced in the direction of the noise. 'Truck Pull. I'd better go. I want to see Toby and Mooney.' He took off on skinny stick legs.

Leon and Grandpa ambled across the field to join the crowd. Robbo's Kenworth was in the ring with Toby, Mooney and Shane standing in front of it, a thick rope hooked across their chests. When the starter gave the signal, the men started pulling, heads down as they leaned into the load. Heaving and grunting, they eventually shifted the truck off the start mark and dragged it ten metres, eyes bulging. At the finish line, Robbo was waiting; he punched the air and slapped the men on their backs.

Grandpa was shaking his head. 'The things people do for a prize.'

After that, Leon and Grandpa watched draught horses pulling a truck. Then they watched a tree-climber shimmy up a tall timber pole.

Next, Grandpa wanted to see the carving competition in which sculptors created works from large blocks of wood using chainsaws. Robbo was moulding a log truck out of a swamp-gum block; Leon hadn't known he knew how to use a saw. Toby was there too, shaping a koala in a tree. Then Shane turned up, cigarette in his mouth, and got to work. Leon hadn't figured Shane for an artist and was surprised to see the sculpture emerging from his neighbour's hands: some sort of owl. Grandpa wanted a closer look, so Leon introduced him. 'Hey, Shane, this is my grandpa, Thomas Walker.'

Shane sucked on his smoke, staring at Leon. He looked the old man up and down and must have liked what he saw, because he offered his hand. Grandpa shook it enthusiastically.

'This is bloody amazing, Shane,' Leon said. 'I didn't know you were so talented.'

'I'm oozing talent.' Shane grinned. 'Do you know what it is?'

'Masked owl,' Grandpa said. 'You can tell by the beak.'

Shane studied the old man with interest. 'You know about this stuff? Spent some time in the forest?'

Grandpa's back straightened and his eyes shone. 'Retired logger. Cut trees for years on Bruny Island. Cut a few down this way too. Big ones. Not so many left now.'

'Still plenty of big trees,' Shane said.

Naturally loggers would defend their industry to the last old-growth log, Leon thought, just as cod fishermen had defended their right to take cod until there were none left.

Grandpa was eyeing Shane keenly. 'Tough job, working on the saw. Not like those men on machines.'

Shane nodded. 'Makes me laugh when they say they've done a hard day's work.'

'Those machines cut the forest too fast,' Grandpa said. 'Friend of mine says they're bad for the industry. You fellers are cutting yourselves out of a job.'

Shane shrugged. 'Not me, old man. I cut the trees on steep slopes where machines can't go, so my job's safe.' He slapped his arse. 'That's why I'm so frigging skinny. Walking up and down hills all day. But blokes like me are few and far between. The day of the chainsaw is over.'

'Shame,' Grandpa said. 'It's because of those machines, isn't it?'

'Yup. But it's no good being upset about it. That's just how the industry is nowadays. The machines cut more trees in a day than I'll ever manage.' He tilted his head. 'Have you seen what they can do? If not, you should take a look. There's a demo over the far side of the field.' He stubbed his cigarette butt on the ground. 'Better get on, I suppose.'

Grandpa wanted to see the machines, so they meandered across the field to where the metal beasts stood, claws folded, stinking of oil and diesel. There was no one around. Leon unfolded the walker and Grandpa sat down to wait. 'Your neighbour was good,' the old man said. 'I liked his owl.'

'Yeah.' Leon didn't want to compliment Shane. 'I suppose you get good with a saw, if that's all you do.'

Grandpa was onto him. 'You don't like him much, do you?'

'He hasn't exactly been welcoming . . . And he's a puppy killer.'

'So he was the one, was he? He has different values from yours, and that's hard for you.'

Leon shrugged. 'People who can't look after animals shouldn't be allowed to own them.'

'You didn't expect it to be easy fitting into a new town, did you?'

'No. That's why I play footy—to meet people and find a way in.'

'Is it working?'

'I'm trying my best to be neutral.'

'That might be your problem. Maybe they can't work you out. A man has to stand for something or he's nobody.'

'It's a timber town, Grandpa. No one will kick to me if I tell them I want to save trees.'

'You can't let them walk over you.'

'Nobody's walking over me.'

Grandpa cocked an eyebrow. 'Are you sure?' He switched his gaze to the machines with their specialised claws. 'Don't know where the industry's heading.' He frowned. 'It's all woodchips now.'

'High turnover for quick cash,' Leon said. 'The loggers say trees are renewable so the government ought to give them access to more forest so they can get enough sawlog.'

'That's bull,' Grandpa said. 'Trees for sawlog take a lifetime to grow. Don't they want jobs in twenty years' time?'

While they were talking, Leon had noticed a small group of people striding across the field towards them: three young men and two women. The men wore fleece jackets and jeans, and one was carrying a medium-sized camera with a microphone attached. One woman was older and grey-haired, in a stylish beige coat, while the other looked much younger, probably mid-twenties, and she was dressed more like the men. Leon's mental radar started beeping. They didn't look like loggers—something about their clothes and their determined way of walking. Instinct told him to move away. 'We need to go,' he said, tugging Grandpa to his feet and packing up the walker. 'We can come back later.'

Grandpa resisted. 'I want to see the machines in action.'

As the group passed them, Leon saw the men toting backpacks. 'That lot are up to something,' he said. 'And we don't want to get caught in it.'

Then he wished he hadn't said anything, because Grandpa wouldn't budge after that.

The group arrived at the machines and the men slipped off their backpacks, pulled out bundles of fabric and unfolded them. Two men climbed the machines, then the women passed the fabric up, helping to drape it from the mechanical arm—two large bedsheets with messages painted in black capital letters: *Machines Cost Jobs. Save the Eagles, Save the Forests.* The man with the camera started recording while the young woman produced a loudhailer and began shouting through it. 'Can I have your attention, everyone? All eyes this way, please.'

Leon glanced across the field and saw people in the crowd turning to look.

'I am the Lorax and I speak for the trees.' The girl's voice was shrill and metallic. 'It's time to stop raping our forests. We have the best forests in the world, and they belong to the taxpayers of this country, not the timber industry. The forests are our lungs. They give us oxygen, and they lock up carbon. It doesn't make sense to cut them down. Loggers aren't making money from trees—they're subsidised by our taxes. We're paying them to destroy our heritage. It has to be stopped.'

'Who are these people?' Grandpa said. 'They don't look like greenies.'

'They are, Grandpa,' Leon said. 'Used to be dreadlocks and ratbags. Now they're office workers and grannies. Mums and dads.'

The older woman produced a small drum that she began to beat while the young woman continued to shout into the loudhailer. 'These machines are the enemy. They're eating their way through our forests and nobody knows the damage they're doing. There are no jobs anymore. We have to ban them.'

'She's right, you know,' Grandpa said. 'I never thought I'd say this, but she's right.'

Leon tried to persuade the old man to leave. 'Come on, Grandpa. There's going to be trouble.' But Grandpa was far too excited.

Now burly men in fluoro vests were running across the field; Leon recognised Mooney among them.

'What's happening in our forests is a crime,' the young woman yelled. 'It's time for the loggers to get out. These machines cut the forest so fast the trees have no time to regrow. Enough is enough.'

'Fuck off,' someone yelled, and the entire crowd began to swarm towards them, shouting: 'Get rid of them.' 'Why are they here?' 'Who let them in?' 'This is our festival.' 'Fucking greenies.'

Mooney arrived at the machines first and tried to pull down the banners, but the men tugged them out of reach. 'Take that sign down,' Mooney shouted. 'Take it down now or I'll—'

'You'll what?' sniped the cameraman. 'Beat us up like the thugs that you are?'

'Get down and get the fuck out of here,' Mooney snarled. 'You're not welcome.'

'This is a family day,' the cameraman said, waving a brochure at him. 'It says: *All welcome.*'

'Yeah, well, that doesn't include you.' Mooney stretched up and grabbed at one of the men on the machines.

The cameraman was filming as his teammate tried to push Mooney away with his foot, yelling, 'I'll go you for assault.'

The young woman had shimmied aside, and now she went on with her commentary. But Mooney knocked the loudhailer out of her hands. Then he reached for the other woman's drum.

'Shit, Mooney,' Leon shouted. 'Be careful.'

Mooney swung his way and scowled. 'You on their side?'

'I don't want you to get in trouble.'

'This lot are trouble.' Mooney snatched the drum and tossed it away. It bounced on the grass and cracked. Then he turned back to the men on the machines. The cameraman was still recording.

Shane was there now too. He scaled the skidder like a monkey, hooked on to the demonstrator's leg and pulled. The guy attempted to shake him off but Shane didn't let go.

More men were sprinting across the field, rushing past Leon and Grandpa.

'Call the police,' someone yelled. 'The cops can get rid of them.'

Somehow the young woman fastened on to her loudhailer again and ran to one side, shouting, 'You don't like hearing this, do you? Because you know we're right. You've been trashing our forests for years. Of course you don't want to stop. You've had it good for too long.'

Leon was worried that things were about to get worse. 'Come on, Grandpa, we have to go.'

'No, wait. Look.'

The greenies were being hauled down from the machines. Mooney had the sheets and was tearing them up. But the demonstrators weren't going to stand by and watch. Both sides began yelling and pushing, grabbing each other's shirts, the two women shrieking. The man was still filming.

Grandpa was suddenly anxious. 'They won't hurt those women, will they?'

'Sorry, Grandpa,' Leon said. 'We can't stay to find out.' He grasped Grandpa's arm and led him away.

'We should call the police.' The old man was overexcited. 'That might protect them.'

Leon glanced back. 'Someone might get done for assault. And it won't be the greenies. Those loggers are angry.'

They worked their way through the crowd towards the exit, and it was slow going against the flow of people. Near the entry, Leon left Grandpa and went to fetch the car. It was a good time to be gone before people started pointing the finger and calling him Parkie.

23

On her eighteenth birthday, Miki woke to the tinkling of water in the downpipes. The music of rain on the roof had been her favourite sound at the farm. It reminded her of cosiness and warmth, the smell of bread and stew in the kitchen, the sweet aroma of baking cakes, trickles of rain running down windows. She wished Mother and Father were alive so they could see her today. But would they be proud? She wasn't perfect, nobody was, but she had been as good to Kurt as she could. She had tried to smooth things for him, the way Mother had for Father. And she hadn't complained, even when there had been a lot to complain about. Mother would have admired her for that.

It was early, but she showered and washed her hair. Out of habit, she started to plait it then stopped. She was eighteen and it was time for something different, a fresh start—she pulled her hair back in a ponytail. It felt strange to her unpractised hands, but looking at herself in the mirror she saw a glow of excitement. Girl yesterday. Woman today. Her eyes were lively and brimming with hope.

Kurt came out at six-thirty but didn't say anything. She cooked breakfast, and placed it in front of him with coffee.

All the while, she was hoping he would mention her birthday, maybe even comment on her new hairstyle. But breakfast spun out in silence, and she felt her spark fading. Kurt was buried in the newspaper, dipping his spoon into the porridge and lifting it absently to his mouth. She listened to the click of his spoon on the plate, the gurgle as he sipped his hot coffee. He had forgotten.

When his plate was empty she removed it. From the sink, she asked, 'What are our plans?'

'It's Monday so we'll go to the forest.'

'And tonight?'

'I'll be in Hobart. You know the routine.'

She said, 'It's my birthday.'

He glanced at her, but his eyes were blank. 'Is it? What's the date?' She told him, and he folded the newspaper. 'So it is.'

She waited for him to say something more. Air locked in her throat as the moments rolled by. She remembered his eighteenth birthday. Chocolate cake with his baptism candle and singing to celebrate his transition into adulthood. Mother's smile, bright and warm. Kurt looking serious. New lines of responsibility on his brow.

'You could make a cake,' he said eventually. Perhaps he was remembering too.

But bake a cake for herself on her eighteenth? Miki couldn't speak.

'Maybe a chocolate cake,' he went on. 'I like chocolate.'

Yes, she knew. 'I wondered if maybe we could go out,' she said.

'We're going up to the forest.'

'Somewhere different,' she tried.

'I thought you liked the forest.'

'I do. But it's a special day. I feel more grown up.'

'That's good.' Nothing more.

She said, 'I'm an adult now.'

He smiled with amusement. 'You're only a day older than yesterday. It doesn't happen that fast.'

In the ute she sat small and silent, curled around her disappointment. Kurt had to know she was hurting, but he refused to acknowledge it. She deserved something more. Yesterday, she had worked hard to feed all the customers coming through town for the festival. She always worked hard for Kurt and he never commended her efforts. He should appreciate her more, she thought. When Mother and Father were alive, birthdays had always been important in their family. Since their deaths, Miki had continued to make Kurt's birthday special. She didn't mind him overlooking her previous birthdays, but he should at least make a fuss for her eighteenth.

He was quiet as they drove to the forest. The rain had stopped, and the road was damp and dark, walls of trees leaning in—it matched her mood. They turned onto the side road and Kurt drove through the logged area where the sky yawned above, pearly and grey. Then he stopped the car and got out, leaving his door open. 'Your turn,' he said.

'What?'

'You're driving. This is your birthday present. A lesson.'

Trembling, she inserted herself in the driver's seat and adjusted it so her feet reached the pedals. The fearful memory of last time sank over her. 'I don't know if I want to do this.'

'Bad luck,' Kurt grunted. 'If I get stung again, I want to be sure you won't kill me on the way to get help.' Suddenly, unexpectedly, he was smiling, and it was as if the sun had come out even though the sky was overcast. 'You were scary,' he said, chuckling. 'How did we survive?'

Miki contemplated the gearstick and the dashboard. She couldn't remember what the pedals were for. She couldn't remember anything except the overwhelming power of the car and her previous lack of control. 'I can't do it,' she said.

'Yes, you can.' He gave instructions and she tried to listen closely. Left foot on the clutch, right foot on the accelerator. Pressure on the accelerator as she let off the clutch. Kurt cursed as she misjudged everything, and the ute took a leap and shuddered to a halt, stalling. 'Try again,' he said.

His patience held for the first few goes, then she started to hear the humming of bees deep inside him. His smile had been replaced with a frown. She wasn't sure whether she was more scared of the car or her brother. 'It isn't easy,' she said.

'Not for some.'

She tried again, and they worked their way along the track: starting, revving, jerking, stalling. She felt the ute getting angry. It growled when she pressed the accelerator and grumbled each time she made a mistake. Finally, she managed to do something right: the ute rolled forward. The front end jarred in a pothole, but they were off and running at last.

'It's going to take a bit of practice,' Kurt said, gruff.

'But I'm doing it, aren't I?' she said, elated. 'When I get the hang of it, I can get my licence.'

From the corner of her eye she saw his mouth twist. 'No need for that. This is just in case of emergency.'

'But if I have my licence, I can help you more.'

'You have your jobs, and I have mine. Driving isn't for women.'

All the women in town drive, she wanted to say.

The car stalled.

'Try again,' Kurt said. 'And stop being so demanding.' But he was smiling again.

After they'd driven back and forth across the clearing several times, Kurt took over and drove into the forest; the lesson was over. He parked at the usual spot then took off up the trail with his rifle and backpack, telling Miki to stay in the car. She was miffed that he should expect her to sit there on her birthday when the forest was all around and she could come to no harm. As she watched him striding away, a tiny robin with a small splash of red on his chest and a patch of white on his forehead swooped down to inspect his reflection in the side mirror, tilting his head. Miki was convinced this was a sign—the bush was calling to her. She slipped out into the cold morning air and the robin fluttered away, flashing his tail at her.

She walked up the trail, following Kurt's boot prints in the mud. At a large blown-out stump, his prints stopped, and she saw the suggestion of a faint trail leading into the bush. She'd never come this far before, but now she was here she was curious. What was Kurt doing in there? She hadn't heard any rifle shots.

Pushing into the scrub, she made her way uphill, following a vague trail. The going was tricky, crisscrossed with roots and sticks and slippery logs. She took her time, placing her feet quietly. Kurt would be cross if he saw her. The bush folded around her, and she knew how to embrace it. Navigating the understorey was a knack—if you didn't fight it, the forest let you in.

After a hundred metres or so, the track steepened through young skinny trees in a close-packed area of regrowth. Another two hundred metres and she came to a boundary with open country, logged sometime during the past couple of years. Tiny seedlings and woven wire grasses were pushing up through the clumpy soil. Ahead, Kurt was picking his way over the uneven ground, obviously not in a hurry. He stopped, one foot resting on a stump, a puff of smoke rising from his cigarette. He looked relaxed, the usual tightness gone from his shoulders. Miki felt awkward encroaching on his private moment. She knew him well, yet it surprised her to detect relief in his posture, a hint of softness in his face. Maybe the forest spoke to him as it did to her, gave him space to leave behind his public self and go inner. She hadn't thought about the impact of the daily drudge on him. Maybe looking after her was a kind of pressure and responsibility from which he enjoyed a break. As she watched, he bent and fiddled with his rifle, then took aim at something uphill. A loud crack, and bark sprayed from a stump. He finished his cigarette then strode off, disappearing into the forest.

Miki waited, afraid to go further. After a while she heard hammering some distance away. The clang of metal striking metal rang through the bush, then a knocking sound. In the clearing, a currawong poked around on the ground, looking for grubs in rotting logs. He hopped towards her, staring with sharp yellow eyes.

Silence had fallen, and Miki tensed. Was Kurt about to come back this way? She couldn't risk him finding her here, so she hurried downhill.

At the ute, she paused then continued walking. She had plenty of time: Kurt wouldn't return for an hour, so she decided to look for the eagles. Their chick had fledged months ago, but the forest was more than a place to nest, it was also their home; they might still be about.

The nest tree was a ten-minute walk back through the forest. Miki drew cold air into her lungs and her pace quickened as she strode along the track. It was exhilarating going where she wanted, under her own steam.

When she was close to the eagles' tree, she began searching. If the birds were there, her movements might startle them, so she slowed. The canopy was high above, but she knew the eagles often perched on branches down in the wattles, which were just starting to flower—spring was not far away. The forest was dense with dangling blanket leaf and minty *Pomaderris* so it was possible she might not see the birds, camouflaged in the foliage.

But there they were. Three massive shaggy eagles roosting in a patch of silver wattle: two dark adults and their lighter-brown offspring. The chick sat slightly separate from its parents, even though he was as large as them now, and as strong. Miki remembered the first time she'd seen him, his bald head bobbing at the edge of the nest, his body all soft with white down. Living so high, he could easily have fallen, but somehow he'd known not to move from his nest. In three months he'd changed from a fluffy chick to an enormous fierce bird with hooded brow, ragged cloak and hooked beak. What amazed Miki most was how he'd known when it was time to leave the nest. Had his parents told him, or had he just known his wings were ready? She wondered if humans could know too.

Near the nest tree, she sat on the damp ground to watch the birds and listen to the forest. The eagles knew she was there; they observed her carefully, peering along their severe black beaks, then jerking and swivelling their heads to check other sounds. The trees shifted constantly. Breathing. Sighing. Squeaking when two pieces of wood rubbed together.

Miki heard a sharp crack somewhere and a loud rustle as a branch fell. Simultaneously, the eagles gathered themselves, crouched forward and launched into the air, feathery legs trailing. With heavy wingbeats, they climbed skywards, finding gaps between branches as they gained height. For several moments they disappeared, then Miki saw them aloft against the grey clouds, their finger-tipped wings spread wide, wedge-shaped tails like rudders driving the arc of their spirals on the wind. Free.

She was euphoric. The eagles were the best birthday present ever.

24

At Tuesday night footy training after the forest festival, the vibe wasn't good, and Leon felt as much on the outer as when he'd first joined the team. Negativity was coming off Mooney in waves, and Leon figured they were blaming him because he'd been there when the tussle broke out over the machines. They had to blame someone, he supposed. But it annoyed him—was he always going to cop it just because they needed a scapegoat?

To avoid Mooney, he positioned himself on the far side of the pack during the warm-up. But the blond man was crazy, and tonight he was boiling with the kind of fury that could end in a broken nose—Leon's, not Mooney's. Evasion was a fine plan, but throughout the session Mooney kept bumping into him, shoving and muttering, 'What's wrong, Parkie? Can't stay on your feet?' Leon picked himself up and went on as if nothing had happened, but inside he was seething. When Mooney blatantly thumped him in the guts during a drill and nobody said anything, it was the last straw. 'Fuck off, Mooney,' Leon said loudly when he'd regained his breath.

The whole field came to a stop.

'You got a problem?' Mooney queried, lip curling.

'Yeah, I have. I'm sick of your crap. It's time you started playing the ball instead of the man.'

Mooney moved closer, and Leon felt the air contract. Everybody was watching. If the coach didn't support him, his season was over. Leon wouldn't fight this arsehole, so he'd be forced to walk away and leave football behind. He waited, the silence thickening. He couldn't believe the other bastards were all going to stand there and let Mooney rip in. It was poor repayment for the work he'd done to drag the team up the ladder. Hadn't all those goals earned him even a pinch of respect?

Mooney's fists were curled, his square jaw jutting, and he was close enough that Leon could smell him; the blond man's scent had always been rank. Leon was wired, senses sharp, the night alive around him.

'Hey, Mooney,' Robbo said at last. 'Leave off, will you? We're here to train. We've got a big game this weekend. Don't want any injuries.'

'I could punch you into next week,' Mooney snarled at Leon. 'And you'd bloody deserve it. Tree-hugging greenie.'

Silence hovered over the field again.

'I had nothing to do with those demonstrators,' Leon said.

'What about the eagles' nest?' Mooney barked. 'I'll bet it was you who reported it.'

'Why would I?'

'Because you're a Parkie.'

'Yeah, well, I didn't. But maybe I should have.'

The men's faces tightened and Robbo growled, 'What do you mean?'

'It's an asset for this town,' Leon said. 'It'll bring in the tourists.'

The stillness opened further, like a ditch, and Leon saw how he could fall into it. All it would take was one wrong word. He was trying to stand up for himself, like Grandpa had suggested.

And he was suffering the consequences. Maybe now wasn't the time. Him against the team. Not good odds.

'How so, Parkie?' Robbo's words fell like stones into a pond.

'Tourism brings money and jobs,' Leon pointed out.

'Cutting trees brings jobs,' said Robbo, steely.

The word *yeah* bounced around Leon.

'You'd better shut up, Parkie, if you want to walk out of here alive,' Mooney said.

Leon saw the sourness in Mooney's stare, felt anger radiating from the others. This was not a battle he could win. He'd made his point and they hadn't mashed him yet, so maybe that was enough for tonight. He pasted on a tentative grin. 'Sure. You're right. This is not my brief. I'll stay out of it.' He was trying to sound light-hearted, but his voice came out squeaky with adrenaline.

Toby guffawed. 'Is your voice breaking, Parkie?'

The tension released. The men cracked up and Leon had to smile too, in spite of himself.

'Okay, guys.' Robbo clapped his hands. 'Let's get on with training.'

Afterwards, Leon walked back to his car, feeling weary. He threw his boots in the back then went round to get in. On the driver's side, in black capital letters, were spray-painted words: *Piss Off Parkie.*

His whole body sagged as he slid in behind the steering wheel. Standing up for what you believed didn't pay around here. No prizes for guessing whose artwork it was, but a paint job would fix it. The only problem would be driving to work tomorrow—maybe he would leave in the dark.

25

Dad might never have come home if it wasn't for Trudi. She came to see Mum on Wednesday night when Max was in bed. Mum must have thought he was asleep but he was trying to work out how to dodge Jaden tomorrow at school. Jaden wanted him to steal chocolate now. The other day it was an icy pole. Max was getting more and more nervous about the stealing. He must be good at it—Miki never said anything. But sometimes she looked at him strangely and it made him feel bad. He didn't know how to stop.

He heard a knock at the door and Mum's footsteps going down the hall to see who it was. Then she said, 'Hello, Trudi.'

'Hi, Wendy. Can I come in? I've brought you some soup.'

There was a pause before Mum responded. 'That's nice. But you didn't have to, you know. I can cook.'

'I know, but you must be so busy looking after two kids on your own.'

'Better than having to look after three.'

Max wondered what she meant.

'I made a big pot tonight, and I had plenty to spare,' Trudi said. 'Thought you could use it.'

'That's kind. Come on in.'

Max heard the floorboards creaking as Mum and Trudi walked through to the kitchen.

'Kids are in bed,' Mum said.

'Okay. I'll keep my voice down.'

He heard the scrape of chairs being pulled out. The swish of the tap running. The hiss and rumble of the kettle. The low murmur of voices. But he couldn't hear what they were saying, so he slid out of bed and crept down the hallway.

'Are you going to let Shane come back soon?' Trudi was asking.

'Why would I after he killed those pups?'

'It was a terrible thing. But he's done it before and you didn't throw him out.'

'It's different this time. The kids were attached. And he did it to get back at Max. Who's supposed to be the adult here?'

'I thought he looked miserable at the festival.'

'Didn't stop him from getting into a fight with those greenies.'

'That was just pent-up emotion. All the boys have been upset about the eagles' nest.'

'Shane doesn't need an excuse.'

'He's been asking to stay at our place,' Trudi said.

'Got a cheek, hasn't he?'

'Liz is getting sick of him. Three weeks is a long time to have someone on your couch.'

Max heard Mum sigh. 'It's been peaceful without him. Easier. Maybe I don't want him back.'

'Of course you do. He's the father of your kids.'

'I know, but he's a pain in the arse. Drinking, smoking, gambling. It costs too much.'

What was Mum talking about? Max wondered. She smoked and drank too.

'Maybe you could take control of the finances and give him a weekly allowance so things don't blow out.'

'That's an idea . . . but I don't know if I can stand having him around.'

'Sometimes Robbo drives me mad too. But what about when you two were first going out? There must have been something that attracted you.'

Mum laughed, but it wasn't a happy sound. 'Booze and parties. It was fun back then. It's no fun anymore.'

'Come on. It can't be that bad. Tell me how you two got together. I wasn't living here then. That was pre-Robbo.'

The kettle clicked off and Max heard Mum pouring tea. He knew he should go back to bed, but he hadn't heard this story before.

'I knew Shane from high school,' Mum was saying. 'But we didn't hit it off till after we'd left. He was sexy. Good at footy too—you should have seen his muscles. And he told the best jokes. Had everybody in stitches.'

Max wondered why Dad didn't tell jokes anymore.

'All the girls had the hots for him,' Mum went on, laughing quietly. 'But he chose me. I was a bit of a looker in my teens . . . He said I had the best legs.'

'You're still pretty.'

'He doesn't appreciate it now.'

'I bet he does. Look at you—you've still got a good body.'

'Crumbling, if you ask me.'

'The men still think you're hot.'

'Nobody's hot after two children.'

Max agreed. What was Trudi talking about? Mum was old.

'When did you actually hit it off?' Trudi asked.

'I was eighteen,' Mum said. 'Shane was working in the forest and I was at the hardware store. We were down at the pub after a footy game and everyone was off their faces. Shane scored the winning goal, so he was the hero. We were playing pool, then he brushed past me and I lost concentration.' Mum laughed. 'Maybe he did it to put me off, because I lost with that shot—I went in-off the black. But he kissed me, and I liked it. We went up to the park and it was on for young and old. On the bridge with the creek running under us.'

'How romantic.' Trudi had a smile in her voice, but Max thought it sounded soppy.

'We were the hottest couple in town,' Mum said. 'Couldn't get enough of each other—you know how it is when you're young.'

It would've been good to see Dad with all those muscles, Max thought.

'You two had a lot going for you,' Trudi said. 'Can you use that to make it work now? Kids need a father.'

'It's been a while since I felt good about Shane.'

'Find something you like doing together. Maybe go out to dinner.'

'Can't afford it.' Mum sounded sad. 'We're up to our necks. Life's not cheap when you have kids.'

Trudi went quiet.

Mum said, 'Sorry. I didn't mean it like that.'

Max wasn't sure what she was sorry for. Then Trudi said, 'That's okay. Just forget it.'

Mum was quiet for a bit too, and Max thought he'd better get back to bed in case Trudi was about to go home. He didn't want them to find him, because Mum would go off. His bum was cold anyway, from sitting on the floor.

In bed, he lay there thinking about Mum and Dad playing pool at the pub, and Dad brushing up against Mum. Who'd have thought that would make Mum like him? It must have been all his muscles.

Next day, Max was on his PlayStation when he heard Dad's ute pull up outside. The door banged then Dad tramped through to the kitchen with a bunch of flowers. Max saw him pick Mum up and give her a bearhug. Mum squealed. Then she and Dad laughed and kissed.

That was it. Dad was home.

Max wasn't sure whether it was good or bad having him back. Dad seemed happy—it must be better than sleeping on Lily Moon's couch. And Dad and Mum seemed to be getting on, for once. But every time Max looked at Dad, he still thought of the pups.

Rosie didn't seem upset anymore. In the morning she followed Dad to the ute and jumped on the tray, and he hooked her up to the chain. One good thing had happened while Dad was away: he'd had a chain fitted to the ute so Rosie wouldn't fall off. But Robbo's dog went to the forest every day too. Wasn't that how Rosie got pregnant last time? Max remembered Leon saying there was a way to stop dogs having pups.

After school Max went over to play with Bonnie and wait for Leon, who didn't come home till nearly six o'clock. By then Max was hungry. Leon brought out a bowl of dog food for Bonnie and a packet of Savoury Shapes to share with Max. They sat on stumps of firewood and ate while Bonnie scoffed down her food. Then they kicked an old chewed-up footy for the pup to chase on the lawn in the semi-darkness.

'What was that thing you said to stop Rosie having puppies?' Max asked.

'You could get her spayed,' Leon said. 'I'm going to the vet soon to have Bonnie vaccinated. I could ask about it for you. Find out how much it costs.'

'Can I come with you?' Max asked.

'Sure. I'll make an appointment one night after school.'

Bonnie was running around like crazy, chasing her grotty old ball. It had her spit all over it and Max didn't want to touch it, but Leon didn't seem to mind.

'How are things at school?' he asked, tossing the ball for Bonnie.

Max shrugged. 'Okay.'

'How are your friends?'

'All right.'

'What about that big kid I've seen you with in the street sometimes?'

Max went cold. He didn't know anyone had seen him with Jaden. What else had Leon noticed?

'That big skinny kid,' Leon went on. 'What's his name?'

'Jaden,' Max said cautiously. 'My friend's big brother.'

'What's he like? Is he okay?'

Max shrugged again. 'He's all right.'

Bonnie put the ball near his feet, and suddenly Max didn't care about the spit. He picked it up and waved it in front of her face, so she grabbed one end with her teeth and they had a tug of war. He could see Leon watching, and it worried him. Maybe Miki had seen him steal something from the shop. Maybe she had told Leon. Maybe Max should get out of here. 'I have to go home,' he said, throwing the ball again for Bonnie. 'It's nearly dinnertime.'

'Okay, but if anything's bothering you, make sure you tell me, hey? Then we can fix things.'

Max nodded, but he was wondering what Leon meant. Fix things how? By telling Jaden's dad that Max had been stealing stuff and get him sent to jail? Did Leon know Jaden's dad was a policeman?

Leon gave him a ten-dollar note. 'Buy something at the shop. Lollies aren't cheap these days, not like when I was a kid. Buy yourself an ice-cream or something, and one for your friends.'

'Thanks.' Max put the note in his pocket. Mum wouldn't be happy about him taking money from Leon, so Max wouldn't tell her. He could secretly leave it in the shop for Miki, to pay for some of the stuff he had stolen. It might not cover everything, but it would be a good start.

26

Leon managed to get an appointment for Bonnie on Friday evening. He knocked off work early and went home to collect Max and the dog. As they spun down the highway, he was pleased to have Max there to hold Bonnie; she was so excited she was bouncing around like a jackhammer.

At the clinic, Leon realised he had forgotten the name of the woman at the front desk. Bonnie leaped around so much he could barely say hello. She wanted to sniff and touch everything, and then she launched herself at the counter. When Leon had her under sufficient control, he glanced at the woman's name tag: Frances. She was regarding him with an amused smile. 'Haven't I met you before?' she asked.

'Yes. I came in with a dog called Rosie. She had a cut in her side.'

'That's right. She was pregnant, wasn't she?'

'This is one of her pups.'

'Her name's Bonnie,' Max added.

'And who does Bonnie belong to?' Frances asked.

Max looked expectantly at Leon, and Leon realised the kid was waiting for him to confirm ownership. 'She's mine,' he said.

Frances peered down at Bonnie, who was panting fast and ogling her with a mad gleam in her eyes. 'She's lively, isn't she? How many pups were there?'

'Six,' Max said.

'That's a decent litter. How did you go finding homes?'

Leon caught Frances's eye and shook his head. 'Let's talk about that later.'

She took the hint and busied herself creating a record for Bonnie. Then Kate came out: the young vet with the long blonde hair—Leon hadn't forgotten *her* name. She led them into the consulting room and lifted Bonnie onto the table. The pup sank on her belly, ears and eyes drooping with fear. Max was worried about her, but Leon quite liked her this way.

'So, you've got yourself a puppy,' Kate said brightly to Leon. 'What about Max—is he yours too?'

'No. He's my neighbour,' Leon said.

'My dog is Rosie,' Max said.

'I remember her,' Kate said, smiling at Max. 'Is this Bonnie's first vaccination?'

'Yeah,' Max said. 'We don't want her to get sick.'

Bonnie cowered on the table while Kate examined her, poking and prodding here and there, listening to her chest with a stethoscope. 'She has a good heart,' Kate said. 'She's very healthy.'

'How much does it cost to get a dog fixed?' Max asked.

'Max is interested in having Rosie spayed,' Leon explained.

'Good idea,' Kate said. 'It's around three hundred dollars.'

Max looked stunned, and Leon realised this must seem like a million dollars to him. 'We'll chat about it on the way home,' he murmured to Max. 'I might be able to help. Maybe I can pay you to mow my lawns so you can save up.'

When Leon turned back to Kate, he saw warmth in her eyes. She finished her inspection of Bonnie and drew up the vaccination in a syringe. Max hid his eyes while she gave the injection, but

Bonnie didn't even flinch. 'There you go, it's all done,' Kate said. 'She's a very brave puppy.'

In the waiting room, Leon paid the bill, then Frances took Max and Bonnie on a tour of the surgery.

'That's so nice of you to adopt the puppy,' Kate said to Leon.

'Kind or crazy. I'm not sure which.'

'Kind, I would say. Not everyone would do something like that.'

'What's a bloke meant to do when a kid turns up crying on his doorstep?'

Kate's face fell. 'What happened to the other pups?'

'Drowned. And I gather it wasn't the first time.'

'Oh, that's grim. How about I give you a discount on desexing Rosie?'

'Really?' Leon was touched. 'Would you do that? I'd appreciate it.'

'It's my clinic. I can do what I want.'

'You own the clinic?'

Kate laughed. 'No, the bank owns it. Only the doormat is mine . . . But I could do the desexing for two hundred dollars? Would that help?'

'That would be fantastic. But I'll have to discuss it with Max's family first. Wish me luck. I think money will be an issue, even with the discount. But we'll find a way. I suppose you get that a lot around here, people unable to pay . . .'

'It can be a problem.' She smiled again. 'Fortunately Frances is very persuasive. She won't hand over medications till everything is paid up.'

'I'll make sure I have my visa card loaded when Bonnie's turn comes around.'

Bonnie gambolled back into the room, Frances and Max just behind her. Frances flashed Kate a meaningful look. 'I think Bonnie's ready to go.'

Kate smiled. 'Okay.' Then to Leon, 'We'll see you for her next vaccination. Give me a call if you want to book Rosie in.'

27

Miki was wiping down tables when a new-looking four-wheel drive pulled up in the street. It was too clean to belong to anyone around here, like something straight out of a showroom. Four men climbed out: three in smart-looking suits; the other, tall and thin, in a fleece jacket, checked open-necked shirt, black jeans, polished hiking boots. Miki wondered who they were. They looked too important to be tourists. They hovered on the footpath for a while, talking among themselves, before heading towards the visitor centre.

Ten minutes later they were back, and the tall man came into the shop. He had short grey hair and looked somehow familiar, but Miki couldn't place him.

'Hello,' he said, smiling. 'Thought I'd buy myself an early lunch. What would you recommend?'

Miki was serving today because Kurt was out the back with the Coke rep. 'We have some good salads,' she said, indicating the display fridge and inspecting the man while he inspected the salads. She still couldn't work out who he was, but she recognised his high forehead and straight nose and those sad, washed-out grey eyes. She blushed when he caught her looking at him.

'I'll have a medium serve of couscous salad,' he said.

Eyes down, she spooned a generous portion into a tub.

'Nice town, isn't it?' he said. 'Do you get out to the forest much?'

'Once a week.'

'I'm going up there today.'

Miki glanced at him, unable to contain her curiosity. 'Have you come to see the eagles' nest?'

'Yes, but there's another tree they want me to look at too. An old forest giant not far from the nest.'

Miki's breath caught. 'Why do you want to look at it?'

The man smiled again. 'I'm into big trees, and this one might be the tallest in Tasmania. We're waiting for a film crew to come with us. If you watch the news tonight, you might see the tree.'

'I know that tree,' Miki said.

'You do? Well, I'm going to make sure we save it for all Tasmanians. It's part of my life's work to fight for trees. And I get the impression you might understand. Am I right?'

Miki nodded. She had worked it out at last: this was Bob Brown. He loved nature, like her, and he wanted to stop logging. He wanted to keep wild places wild and stop humans from destroying the Earth—she'd heard him say something like that on TV one time.

He winked as he left with his salad

That night, Miki's tree was on the news as Bob Brown had promised. She was in the kitchen spooning stew into bowls when she heard the story come on, and she rushed in to see him standing in front of her tree. Kurt was scowling at the TV, arms folded across his chest, a dark frown on his face.

Bob Brown was staring into the camera, hands clasped in front of him, fingers interlaced. 'It's fantastic to find this big tree so near to town,' he was saying. 'It'll help raise awareness of forest issues. Because it's time for us to do more to protect our forests. This tree is a symbol of our past and our future, and it belongs to all of us. To our children, and to our children's children—that's how far ahead we should be thinking. A tree like this has been here longer than whitefellas have been in Tasmania.'

Kurt's lips tightened, but he didn't say anything. When the report was over, he switched off the TV and went to his room.

Miki wasn't quite sure how to read her brother. Since he'd been stung by those bees, he'd been more unpredictable than ever. She knew he must be concerned about strangers invading the forest, but was that the only reason for his present bad mood?

She boiled the kettle and made a coffee to appease him, approaching his room with a shiver of fear. He was at his desk, papers spread before him, Father's black leather folder to one side. As she came in, he snapped the folder shut. 'What do you want?'

'I made this for you.' She offered the coffee.

He ignored her and picked up a coloured brochure, waving it about. 'I'm thinking about buying a boat.'

Stunned, Miki stood with the mug held out in her hand. 'What for?' Kurt had never been into boats.

'To go boating.'

'But we never go boating.'

'We will when we have a boat.'

What about the farm they were saving for, their future escape from the shop? It would never eventuate if Kurt kept spending their money. 'How much will it cost?' she asked.

'I don't know . . . I want a good one, maybe twenty thousand.'

Knots tangled in her stomach. She couldn't hold back. 'What about our farm?'

'What farm?'

'The one we're saving to buy.'

Kurt shrugged as if he'd forgotten it. 'A farm is a big investment. Saving that much money takes time.' His eyes narrowed. 'What are you going to do with that coffee?'

She set the mug on the desk, trying to still her tremoring hand. Her eyes were drawn to the brochure with its glossy picture of a gleaming white boat. 'Where will we go boating?'

'On the river.'

'Will we stop going to the forest?'

'I don't know. Too many people hanging round there right now.'

'But I like the forest.'

'You'll like the water too. Now get lost. Too many questions.'

On the cusp of crying, Miki withdrew to her room. What was Kurt doing? First the new ute and now a boat. Where was he getting the money? Had he taken out a loan? She'd heard the women discussing finances over coffees in the shop. They'd said you could be in debt and keep borrowing if you could convince someone to lend you more money. Was that what Kurt was doing? Why wouldn't he include her in decisions? She was eighteen now. Would he ever give her a chance?

Dejected, she slumped onto her bed. What could she do? Her brother controlled everything and told her nothing. And now he might force her away from the forest. The thought brought forth tears, and she dashed them away with her sleeve. She must not let him destroy her. Staying internally strong was her one small triumph.

She lay on her bed staring at the ceiling, and gradually her breathing slowed and her angst eased. It was best to think about other things, like the fact her tree had made it onto the news—another type of victory. It changed the status of her secret forest forever, but if this was required to save the tree, it was worth it. Her sacrifice was everyone's gain.

As she lay there, she could hear Kurt shuffling papers next door; every time he shifted in his chair, it made a soft squeak. She wondered if feelings could penetrate walls too, whether he sensed her frustration. If he did, it wouldn't bother him. He never seemed to care what she felt. She heard him grunt to himself, then the rumble of drawers opening and closing; he must be packing his papers away in the filing cabinet. His footsteps plodded down the hall, paused outside her room. She held her breath. He walked on. Soon she heard the fridge door open and close, then the TV—a sports commentary of some sort. She peered out, tentatively testing the waters. 'Can I watch too?' She wasn't interested in sport, just wanted to ensure he wouldn't disturb her.

'Stay in your room,' he growled. 'I don't like the way you speak to me.'

She closed her door quietly. She was safe now. Punishment by banishment, except it was exactly what she wanted tonight.

She changed into pyjamas and snuggled up in bed with *The Old Man and the Sea*—the latest novel Geraldine had lent her. A small book, only one hundred pages. She flicked to the beginning. *He was an old man who fished alone in a skiff in the Gulf Stream and he had gone eighty-four days now without taking a fish.* A book about fishing! How ironic when she and Kurt had just been talking about boats. She sighed. Geraldine couldn't have known.

Two hours later, Miki had finished the book. Kurt was asleep, but she was alive and awake. The book had surprised her; like all of the novels Geraldine had lent her, it was full of revelations. It was a story about an old man, a boy and a swordfish, which sounded simple but wasn't. She hadn't imagined she would like a book such as this, but the writing was magical—it had made her feel as if she was there with the characters. In the fishing village where the old man lived, she could smell the salt air. She could see his squalid home and imagine him rolling his trousers to make a pillow, padding them out with newspaper. When he went fishing on his small boat, it was as if she was with him on the sea, chasing the swordfish, watching the light shift on the water. She could see flying fish leaping into the air, which seemed impossible; they crossed from water to air and then back again, unfettered by walls or windows or locks.

As she read, she felt like she was fighting the swordfish with the old man, the line cutting into her hands. She loved the swordfish as he did. She saw the changing colours and moods of the sky and the sea.

When she closed the book at the end of the journey, she realised with a jolt that the swordfish was not just a fish—it was meant to represent life. Suddenly, she could see parallels. The old man fought to catch the swordfish, just as she would have to fight to claim her life from Kurt sometime in the future. The swordfish was invisible in the water, just as everything she wanted was out of reach. She was the one in the boat, trying to hook on to life. The old man's fishing trip was about patience, hard work, perseverance and skill. But it was also about striving for what he believed. The swordfish had resisted being caught, even when it was dying. With a hook in its mouth, it had clung to freedom because freedom was worth fighting for, worth dying for.

Miki understood that she was the swordfish struggling for freedom, while Kurt held her in check on the line. She was his captive, but hope bubbled under her skin. She thought of the life she would lead one day, and it was so much more than this shop: large and free. She would visit the sea. Watch sunrises and sunsets. Walk in the rain. Finish school and go to university. Be independent. Own a dog. Her own home. Read books. Make choices. Meet friends. Maybe even find love and have a family.

Geraldine had given her this book for a reason: Miki saw that now. Geraldine wanted to give her the world, and she wanted Miki to strive for it.

Miki slid the book under her mattress and lay back, resting her head on her pillow, eyes closed. In the vast unfenced freedom of her mind, she could see a clear star-crusted sky spreading over the sleeping blanket of forest.

One day, she would be free to go. The time was coming—she could feel it.

28

Leon should have known that troubles always come one after the other. The demonstration at the forest festival. The run-in with Mooney. The graffiti attack on his car. And now this: he knew something was wrong as soon as he heard his mum's voice on the phone. 'Leon,' she said quietly. 'Your father's in hospital. We're in Hobart.'

Leon had just arrived home from a long day of work up in the park. He was tired and didn't feel much sympathy for his dad, but his mum sounded worried. A cloud of concern sank over him like weather descending on the mountains. 'Stan again?' he asked.

'I don't think so. He hasn't been round in a while—not since you visited with the dog. But things have gone downhill. A couple of weeks ago, your father's belly blew up and his legs went all puffy.'

'Did you take him to a doctor?'

'He wouldn't go. Then today, his belly was sore, and he started having chills and fevers.' Her voice was tight. 'He soiled himself in bed, Leon. It was a terrible mess. I had to clean him up. He was too sick to help.'

'Oh, Mum. That's awful.' He imagined the smell as she walked in, imagined her getting a bucket of water and gently cleaning his sickly father. It was too much, after all she had borne.

'Can you come, Leon? They've got him on a drip and they're doing tests. They think he might have an infection. They have to find the right antibiotic.'

'Okay, I'll have a quick shower then I'll be on my way.'

'Can you bring Grandpa?'

Leon paused. 'Is it that bad? Is he dying?'

'It might help your father. Grandpa's so strong.'

'So positive, you mean.'

'Yes, that too.'

'All right. I'll be there soon as I can.'

Leon rang ahead to warn Grandpa, and the old man was waiting in the foyer of the home when Leon arrived. He was dressed up in collar, tie and trilby, but he'd fallen asleep and was slouched in a chair, head tipped back, mouth open. He looked small and vulnerable, hollow-cheeked, lips caving in, barely alive. Leon wondered how much lifetime his grandfather had left. Normally Grandpa's vibrant personality made him seem large, but now Leon could see his fragility. The ageing process was confronting.

Leon tapped the old man on the shoulder and watched him wake, eyes widening with surprise, lips smacking, a blast of bad breath. Leon forgave him for that—a blotch of toothpaste on his lapel showed he'd at least tried.

In the car, Grandpa talked while Leon drove. He spoke of Leon's dad as a boy, how wild and cheeky Reg had been, always pushing boundaries, always getting into trouble. Reg had never really left the island except for a few years when he was at high school, and even then he'd caught the bus home every night, just as Leon had when he was a teenager. Reg had left school at fifteen and taken a job at a mill where he'd worked for twenty-something years until the accident.

Leon remembered his dad coming home each weekday evening, sweaty and with wood shavings stuck to his socks, fine grains of sawdust in his hair. Sometimes during the school holidays, Leon had been allowed to tag along to the mill. Reg had given him a pair of earmuffs and allowed him to wander around, so long as he didn't get in the way. It was interesting to see how they carved up the logs. Leon used to like watching the dripper trickle water onto the saw so it wouldn't overheat. He liked to watch the mounds of sawdust growing, the logs turning into timber for building houses. It seemed useful work.

As he'd grown older, he'd seen the industry change. Mills had become few and far between. It was hard to get sawlog because most trees were downgraded to woodchip. Leon had started looking more closely at the process, trying to understand what was happening. His dad hadn't liked it—the Walkers had always been loggers or sawyers, so he was furious when his son turned greenie. It was a betrayal.

But betrayal was a double-edged sword where Reg was concerned. When the accident had ruined his hand, and Reg could no longer work at the mill, his self-esteem had plummeted and he'd slid into drink. Alcohol had been a problem back when he was young, and he'd become a teetotaller to control it. After he'd lost his job, depression had struck, or something very much like it—the drink had been the simplest solution. But it brought out the buried aggression in Reg, and Leon's mum was an easy target. Right now, people might say Reg had run out of luck, but Leon believed you made your own luck. There were many things his dad could have done other than surrendering to violence. Losing his job might have challenged his manhood, but beating his wife was no way to reclaim it.

At the hospital in Hobart, Leon and Grandpa followed the receptionist's directions to the critical-care ward. Reg was strung up on a drip and had oxygen buds looping into his nose. He looked yellow, and for a moment Leon felt a flash of sympathy. His father's eyes were hollow and sad, as if perhaps he might have taken a different path had he realised it would come to this. Under the covers, his belly domed like a pregnancy, and the foot that was hanging out was pallid and swollen.

Mum was sitting by the bed, and she rose quickly to hug them, Grandpa first, Leon second. Her face was puffy and she had tears in her eyes. Her embrace made Leon feel like a bollard with a rope wrapped around it, but he let her cling to him. He sensed the shifting of responsibility as she foisted onto him a burden he didn't want to bear. Grandpa, meanwhile, had taken a seat by the bed and was talking to Dad, so Leon followed Mum out into the corridor.

'He has peritonitis,' she said, 'an infection in his belly. He could die. They're going to suck out all the fluid in his abdomen and put him on antibiotics.' Her face crumpled, and she leaned against Leon's shoulder.

Leon put his arms around her and held tight. She was so wracked with pain for that man—didn't she remember what he'd done? Leon hadn't forgotten her bruises, the loss of light in her eyes. Even now he couldn't kick his old habit of checking his watch at four-thirty each afternoon, because that was the time he used to start driving home so he could be there when his dad arrived, tanked and on fire, ready to lay into his mum. This illness was karma, Leon thought. What goes around comes around. If there was a god, then he had come to get his dad at last.

He unwrapped his arms from his mum and gently held on to her shoulders so he could look into her face. 'How long is he going to be in here?'

'A few days, maybe a week . . .'

'Well, you can't live here with him.'

'No, I'm going to check into a hotel.'

Back in the room, Grandpa was sitting on the bed, holding Reg by the hand. Was it that serious, Leon wondered? Was his dad going to die?

Driving home with Grandpa, Leon probed himself to detect any softening towards his dad, but it seemed his heart had turned to stone. Grandpa knew it, the discerning old bastard, and Leon sensed he was about to be attacked with a pick. When they pulled up outside the old people's home, Grandpa laid in. 'The last man as perfect as you walked on water,' he said.

Leon was offended. 'What's that supposed to mean?'

'You have to forgive, lad. Nobody's perfect.'

'Some are less perfect than others.'

'Your father is sick as a dog. Where's your heart?'

'You didn't see what he did to her.'

'And I'm glad I didn't—I'm sure it was a terrible thing. But she's forgiven him, so why can't you?'

'She shouldn't.'

'But she has. So you have to too.'

'I can't. This is what he deserves.'

'Live in anger. Die in anger. Live in peace . . .'

'Yeah, all right . . . Die in peace.'

'Think about it, lad. Promise me you will.'

'I'll think about it.' Leon gripped the steering wheel. He was still living in anger. There was no peace in sight.

'Can you take me again tomorrow?' Grandpa asked.

'Can't go till the weekend now, after Saturday's game.'

'What if he's dead then?'

'He won't be. Only the good die young.'

He waited while Grandpa punched a code into the security pad and the front sliding doors eased open. Grandpa looked back and waved. 'Just climbing the stairway to heaven,' he called with a crooked grin.

It's *buying*, Leon thought.

But as he pulled out of the car park, the lyrics of 'Stairway to Heaven' started up in his mind. He whizzed along the highway beneath the pale light of the moon, which reflected white on the water, and he sang the words out loud. It was as if he was hearing the song for the first time. He wondered how it was, after all these years of singing the lyrics that it had only occurred to him tonight what they were truly about. He'd never really thought about the words before, simply shouted them at parties and around campfires as part of mateship and having fun.

No doubt the song spoke differently to everyone, but for him, tonight, it was about many things. The journey of life. Making choices and getting it wrong. Facing death. Gaining wisdom. Confronting the past. Forgiveness and redemption.

He sang the song again, tipping his head back as he blasted out the words, knowing that somewhere deep inside him a change of path and forgiveness of his father might one day be possible.

29

When Leon arrived at the football ground for the semifinal, it seemed the whole town had turned out. The car park was crammed with utes and four-wheel drives, nose-in around the boundary. Leon felt a surge of excitement. After a slow start to the season, it was amazing the team had made it this far. He'd been partly responsible for their success—he had that much to be proud of.

Players in tracksuits migrated across the oval to the clubhouse, while fans hung over the rail, waving scarves and streamers, calling: 'Carn boys.' 'Carn the Lions.' 'You can do it.' 'Give 'em heaps.' Leon saw Wendy waving at him from over near the goalposts. He grinned and waved back. Suzie was there too, but no Max; Leon wondered where he was. Shane was at the door to the change room, high-fiving everyone as they entered. His smile faded a little when he slapped hands with Leon . . . or was Leon imagining it?

In the change room, the men sprawled on the benches and it was crowded and rowdy, thick with the fug of sweat and Deep Heat. Leon tossed his bag on the floor and sat to pull on his boots. Mooney arrived a few moments later, swaggering in as if he'd planned a grand entry. The team gave an encouraging roar—just what that man didn't need. He already had too much of an ego.

Now that everyone was present, Robbo puffed like a peacock and strutted round the room, red-faced and excited. 'First time in a decade we've qualified for the semis,' he said. 'And it's thanks to Mooney's star goal-kicking efforts.' He didn't mention Leon, even though he'd scored at least as many goals as Mooney. Mooney was most-valued player, they all knew it. But he was erratic: one week on fire, the next caught up in brawls.

Leon sat slightly apart from the others. While the men bantered and talked big, he rubbed liniment into his thighs and calves where he still had a few tight spots from collisions with Mooney at training. He glanced up to find Robbo staring at him, and was surprised when the man nodded. This was the recognition Leon needed. Robbo might not say it in front of the team, but from that small gesture Leon knew the coach was glad to have him out there today. Leon would give all he could. The only problem was whether Mooney would pass the ball to him.

Robbo slipped into psych-up mode and started building the tension. His passion was contagious, and when he sent them jogging onto the oval to warm up, Leon was as fired up as the others, bursting into spontaneous grapevines and high kicks to loosen his hips and stretch his hamstrings. The crowd shouted encouragement and the team was jittery. Leon felt the collective edginess as they jostled and jibed and ragged one another, fizzing with nerves. Spirits were high.

But when Leon leaned over to stretch his calf, Mooney clamped his neck with a vice-like hand. 'You'd better put that ball between the posts, Parkie, or I'll tie you to that fucking big tree and set it alight.'

Leon was so hyped he felt like hitting out, but he shook loose and stared the blond man in the eye. 'That tree has nothing to do with me. I've told you before.'

'Have to take your word for it,' Mooney sneered. 'But I don't have much confidence in your word.'

Toby shifted closer and Leon wondered if the two of them were going to lay into him right there on the field. But Toby broke into a grin. 'Confidence, Mooney? That's a big word. You been reading dictionaries?'

Mooney guffawed. 'No, mate. Didn't you know I'm full of vocabulary?'

Leon was grateful to Toby for defusing the situation, but Mooney wasn't done yet.

He jabbed Leon in the chest with a finger. 'Keep your fucken feet under you today, right, Parkie? Then we won't have to work so hard.'

Leon glared at him. 'We're all going to have to work, mate.'

Mooney spat on the ground and leaned close. 'Don't call me *mate*. And just remember—it doesn't matter how many goals you score, you'll always be Parkie.' He spat again, the mucus landing on Leon's boot, and added, 'You're lucky the boys put up with you. You wouldn't be here if I had my way.'

The game started well after the mandatory fights had settled. It was tense out there—the slightest shove and everyone was chesting each other like a bunch of oversexed bulls. Fortunately the umpire wasn't taking any rubbish. 'Oi, oi, you. Get back. Leave him alone. Back off so I can do the ball-up. Come on. Proper distance. You know the rules. If you don't back off, I'll have to give a fifty-metre penalty.'

It took a while for everyone to move beyond the scrambling at the beginning, when they were uptight and twitchy and wanting to sink a boot into the ball. There were pile-ups: men all over the ground, a few sly punches thrown in. Leon kept clear and hovered round the edge of the action, waiting for the ball to spit out. If he could get a hand on it and sprint clear, there would be no stopping him.

When things levelled out, the real game began. Leon's team started stringing a few kicks together. Leon looked for space and ran into it, shouting for the ball when his teammates had possession. He took his first mark, not particularly elegant; it was just good to get his hands on the ball and develop a feel for its bounce, put in his first big kick.

The field was wet from early spring rain, pockmarked and uneven, soft underfoot, good for falling on. And fall they did. Toby sent a ball spinning Leon's way and he leaped for it, but a ruckman from the other team charged in and wiped him out. It was a rough knock, but Leon was resilient. He sucked air into his lungs, spat phlegm and ran on, shaking his head and looking for the ball.

The other team scored first—a great doozey of a goal that set Leon's mob moaning. 'Fuck that.' 'Carn, guys. Heads up and get moving.' The opposition celebrated like they'd won the Olympics, and it was only the first goal.

Back at the centre for the ball-up, Leon nodded at Mooney. The blond man scowled but shouldered in on the mob and flicked the ball Leon's way. Leon was onto it. He scooped the ball mid-bounce and took off—he was away.

The field was clear so he took a few bounces as he ran. The defenders were charging after him, boots thudding on dirt. How long did he have before they launched a tackle and he lost the ball? He was going full pelt; just a few more strides would bring him within range of the goal. He heard heavy breathing behind and tried to balance himself and take those last two steps to get his boot to the ball. A hand clawed at him and caught his jersey, hooking under his arm. He faltered but swung his foot hard, connected with leather, and it felt good. The ball sailed between the posts for a goal.

He'd equalised. They were on the scoreboard.

Mooney offered a bearhug of elation, knocking him over, and the boys stacked on. It was supposed to be a celebration, but Leon was at the bottom of the pile—they were crushing the air out of him. Didn't they realise what they were doing? Or maybe that was part of Mooney's plan: to kill him on the field. Murder by stealth.

Things remained pretty even till half-time. One team inched ahead, then the other. Leon had been running hard, so he was grateful for the half-time break. In the change room, he drank then splashed water on his face and towelled off. Another fifty minutes of play to go and he already felt like an old man.

Robbo was going on about this and that, but his instructions didn't mean much, really. Out there, plans and structure helped, but the ball had a mind of its own. You could put yourself in position and then it would take off on an unanticipated trajectory.

The third quarter was their best. Toby excelled in back pocket, and Mooney motored in the centre and on the wing. The others did their bit too, playing out of their skins. They scored a ton of goals and pulled well ahead—the supporters for the other team were hanging their heads.

Then Mooney was mashed in a terrible tackle. Leon saw a giant of a man deliberately thump into him, and Mooney's mane of blond hair flicked back as he went down. He landed headfirst, and by the sound of the crunch Leon knew it was bad. Mooney was sprawled out, unmoving.

The umpire shrilled his whistle to stop the game and they all began to run. Toby and Leon were there first, kneeling beside Mooney.

'Fuck, he's out to it,' Toby said.

Mooney was like a sack of spuds, eyes rolled back, unconscious.

Leon took control, thankful for his remote first-aid training. 'Get him in recovery position.' With Toby's help he shifted Mooney onto his side. Blood dribbled from the man's nose and his breathing was rattly. Leon flicked out Mooney's mouthguard and looked round as the team crowded in. 'Someone call an ambulance,' he said.

Robbo reached them. 'What's up?'

'He's unconscious. Can I have your watch? I need to check his pulse.'

Robbo whipped off his watch and put it in Leon's hand, and a chill fell over the field.

'Ambulance will be here soon,' someone said. 'They're just finishing a call. Only five minutes away.'

The other team stood quietly, shaking their legs out. They had started jeering when Mooney went down, but now they realised that tackle had been over the top.

Mooney's wife, Liz, ran onto the field, trying to get through to him. 'What's wrong?' she cried, panicky. 'What have they done to him?' Leon was appalled a big brute like Mooney could be bashing her.

Toby took her by the arms and held her back. 'Settle, Liz. He's out to it. Nothing you can do.'

She was sobbing, mascara streaking down her cheeks. 'Will he be all right?'

'Sure, he's just knocked out.'

She glanced around wildly. 'Where are my girls?'

Over at the fence, Wendy had corralled Liz and Mooney's daughters, and they were both crying shrilly. 'Mummy,' one of them called out. 'What's happened to Daddy?'

Leon kept watch over Mooney, whose heart rate was fast. But he'd been running, so wasn't that normal? Leon wished the ambulance would arrive so someone else could take over. He was the outsider here, and they trusted him to look after Mooney—if something went wrong, he'd be scum.

Mooney started to kick and jolt in a convulsion. Liz sobbed hysterically, and Toby led her away.

'What do we do?' Robbo leaned over, face twisted with concern. 'Shouldn't we pull out his tongue?'

'No,' Leon puffed, trying to restrain Mooney's limbs. 'That's an old wives' tale. We have to keep him on his side so he doesn't choke if he throws up. Can someone get me a handkerchief or something? He's frothing at the mouth.' Everyone seemed paralysed, so Leon ripped off his jersey and wiped the saliva away.

Mooney stilled, then his eyes opened and he moaned and tried to sit up.

'Lie down,' Leon said. 'You've had a knock to the head.'

'Where the fuck am I?' the blond man mumbled, groggy.

'At the footy, mate,' Toby said. 'Semifinal. Remember?'

'What day is it?' Mooney glanced around wildly, obviously disoriented, but he allowed Leon and Mooney to lower him back down to the ground. Then he closed his eyes again, his face deathly white.

Leon was relieved when he heard the siren wailing. Someone opened the gates and the ambulance bounced across the field. The paramedics shifted Mooney onto a stretcher and slid him into the ambulance. They let Liz climb in and then they were away.

After that everyone stood round discussing whether to go on. The team didn't feel right playing without Mooney. Some of them wanted to call it quits—their will to win had driven off in the ambulance. But Toby's jaw jutted. 'Mooney would want us to finish. He'll be pissed off if we pull out.'

'We'll have to forfeit if we stop now,' Robbo said. 'It's up to you, boys, but it'd be a shame when we're so far in front.'

Toby glared at them all. 'Come on. Get your arses into gear and win the game for Mooney.'

Reluctantly, the team agreed.

Leon didn't have a jersey anymore—his was covered with blood and saliva. For the past fifteen minutes he'd been bare-chested and now his sweat had dried cold. He offered to take a spell on the interchange bench, but that went down like a lead balloon.

Toby pointed a finger at him. 'You're on, Parkie, whether you like it or not. Someone give him a jersey,' he yelled at the bench. One of the younger blokes, recently back from injury, did as he was told—a jersey came over the fence.

They took a quick jog round the field to warm up, and then it was on. But the team was more shaken than they'd realised, and there was desperation in their play that didn't help their game. Leon had stiffened during the break and couldn't find his pace, and Toby was out for revenge and kept giving away free kicks. The other team took advantage and started kicking goals.

In the end, the opposition won by three points, a total injustice. Leon's team came off dejected and sore. They were in the dressing-rooms when word came through that Mooney had a nasty concussion but should be okay—he'd had a brain scan and they'd ruled out anything more serious. But it was a sombre team that trailed from the field and headed home instead of the pub. It didn't seem right to drown their sorrows without Mooney.

Leon was limping across the oval to his car when Toby rocked up beside him. The big man looked rattled. 'Everything okay?' Leon asked, stopping.

Toby ran a hand over his bald head and shuffled awkwardly. 'Hey, Parkie. Thanks for helping with Mooney today.'

'No worries. I hope he's all right. It was a shit tackle. That guy ought to be suspended. Robbo should put in a report.'

'Good point. I reckon he should.'

Leon adjusted his bag on his shoulder, wondering what Toby wanted.

'Mooney was a bastard to you today,' Toby said. 'It was good of you to help.'

'Not a problem.'

'Nah, he was a prick. I wouldn't have helped him if I was you. You're a bloody hero.'

Leon didn't see himself as a hero. He'd assisted Mooney out of a sense of duty, but it was really Liz and the kids that needed help. He felt a twinge of guilt—he ought to have done something about that by now, given he'd known about Mooney's domestic antics for some time.

But Toby was grinning. 'Reckon you'd help a leper,' he said.

Leon smiled. 'Yep. I reckon I would.'

Toby reached out and grabbed his hand in a solid shake. 'Fuck off then, Parkie. You're a better man than I am.'

30

Max stayed home from the footy because he didn't want to run into Jaden. It had been a bad week—he was sure he'd soon be going to prison. After school yesterday, Jaden had shown him a little black book with a list of all the things Max had stolen. Jaden had written everything down in his messy, leaning-back writing.

Cigarettes
Fruit Tingles
Coke Cola x ~~2~~ ~~3~~ 4
Snickers x 2
Mars bar x ~~2~~ ~~3~~ 4
Mentos
Packet of lolly snakes
Cadbury's chocolate block
Icy pole
Picnic bar
Tic Tacs
Twisties
Jubes

Freddo Frogs x ~~2~~ 3
Violet Crumble

A two-page list with a word on every line. When Max saw it, he felt himself melting into the ground. Had he really stolen all that stuff? Jaden had made him do it, but that wouldn't matter when the cops got him.

'Five years is what you'll get,' Jaden had said. 'Five years behind bars.'

Max looked at him fearfully. What did kids do in jail? Did they have TV and PlayStation? Would he be allowed to use his iPhone? And did they eat porridge every day? The food wouldn't be like Mum's spaghetti, and no way would there be ice-cream.

'They put people like you in solitary,' Jaden said.

Max wasn't sure what that was. He decided not to ask.

Jaden flapped the notebook in his face. 'This is your death sentence. You have to do what I say, or off you go to jail. Do not pass Go. Do not collect two hundred dollars.'

Max's ears pricked. Two hundred dollars would be enough to get Rosie fixed. 'Where do I get two hundred dollars?'

'It's Monopoly, you idiot. Monopoly money is play money. Nobody's going to give you two hundred dollars. You have to rob a bank to get that much money.'

Max's knees went wobbly. He hoped Jaden wasn't going to make him rob a bank. To do that you needed guns and escape cars and balaclavas.

Jaden poked him in the ribs. 'Didn't you hear me? I want you to get me some beer.'

Max shook his head. Beer would be harder than cigarettes.

'Your dad has heaps,' Jaden said. 'He's an alco, and alcos always have beer.'

Max was cross that Jaden had called Dad an alco because it wasn't true, but he had to think quickly. 'Dad's given up beer.

Mum made him stop.' It was a good lie: everyone at school knew Max's dad had come home and was *in the doghouse*, as Mum put it.

Jaden did a Chinese burn on Max's arm and made it go red. 'If I see your dad drinking beer at the footy then I'll know you've got some at home.'

So Max didn't go to the footy, because this morning Dad had put beers in the esky. And now Max was home alone. He didn't like being home by himself, so he'd locked all the doors and played *Call of Duty* until he got sick of it. Now he looked at the clock on the microwave—just after five o'clock. The game would be over. He wondered who'd won.

Rosie started barking so he let her in and locked the door again. She wasn't supposed to come in, but Mum wasn't here so it didn't matter. He sat on the couch, patted the cushions, and Rosie jumped up. He put his arm around her neck and laid his head on her fur. She was panting as if she was smiling. Did that mean she was happy?

There was more barking outside, so Max went to the window to see what was happening. Bonnie was yapping like crazy at the fence. She usually didn't bark much. What could be upsetting her? Max was about to open the window and shout at her to shut up, when he saw someone on the footpath in front of his house. Someone tall and skinny.

Max's stomach knotted, and he ducked down so Jaden wouldn't see him. He heard clomping on the front porch. A knock at the door.

Rosie went nuts and ran to the door, snarling and barking, but no way was Max going to follow her. He would pretend no one was home.

He stayed out of sight, crouching behind the couch, listening while Jaden kept knocking. Max's heart was banging wildly. What would Jaden do? Did he know Max was home? Would he break a window to get in? And what if he came inside? Where could Max hide? Maybe he should get a rolling pin to protect himself. Or a cricket bat. Or maybe Rosie would attack Jaden—she had sharp teeth and she hated him because of what he'd done to her pups. She must remember him throwing Bruiser up in the air.

Everything went quiet, and Max chanced a peek from behind the couch. Jaden was at the window. He had his hands up like goggles so he could see in. Max's heart almost stopped. He sank back to the floor.

After a while, he heard footsteps leaving the porch. He checked the window again. Jaden had disappeared.

Now Rosie raced to the back door, growling, and the handle rattled. Max was so scared he thought he might vomit. It was lucky he'd locked the doors, or Jaden would be inside now, grabbing him by the neck and choking him. If he got in, Jaden might destroy the place and Max wouldn't be able to stop him. Jaden's black book of evidence meant Max couldn't defend himself.

Next door, Bonnie was still yapping, high-pitched and frantic. Max's back door had stopped rattling, so he crawled to the window and peeped out. No Jaden.

Max inched a little higher and saw Jaden on the footpath, hands on hips, staring at the house, mouth pinched, eyes hard. He stood there a long time while Max leaned against the wall, hardly breathing, too scared to move. His stomach was aching from being bent over. He wished Mum and Dad would come home.

Jaden walked over to Leon's place. What was he doing? Bonnie raced up and down, barking. The wire zinged as she threw herself at the fence and bounced off. Then all went quiet.

Max peeked out, trying to get a view of Leon's yard, but he couldn't see Bonnie. She should still have been yapping at Jaden. And Max couldn't see him either.

Then he noticed Leon's gate was open.

He was terrified, sick with worry. Jaden must have opened it and let Bonnie out. She was just a pup and didn't know about cars—she might run down to the highway and get hit.

He heard footsteps on the front porch again, and Jaden squinted in at the window. Max shrank into a ball.

When he looked up a few seconds later, Jaden was sprinting down the street.

Max raced out, looking for Bonnie. He ran to the footpath and glanced down the street. No sign of Jaden or the dog.

Max was crying now. He wished he'd been brave enough to tell Jaden to piss off. He wished he could tell someone what Jaden had done, but then Jaden would tell his policeman father about the stealing. Max saw himself in prison with bars on the doors. He would have to wear orange pyjamas, and live in a concrete cell with a hard, narrow bed.

Everything was messed up. Back inside, Max sat on the couch, feeling terrible.

It wasn't long before Leon's car pulled up next door. Rosie barked, so Max let her out and she dashed to the fence, yapping. Leon got out of his car like an old man. He had a limp and was covered in mud. He hobbled up the driveway, then paused. His walk sped up until he was running into the yard, yelling, 'Bonnie!' Then he rushed to the street and stared down it, like Max had just a few minutes ago.

Mum and Dad arrived at that exact same moment. Max saw Mum talking to Leon through the car window. He couldn't hear what they said, just Leon's lips moving and a worried look on his face.

Dad parked in the driveway, and Mum came into the house. 'Max. Where are you? Come quick. Bonnie's missing.'

Max slunk from the lounge room.

Mum frowned at him, hands on her hips. 'What have you been up to?'

'Nothing. Hanging out here.'

'Go outside and help Leon. Bonnie's gone. Someone opened the gate.'

'It wasn't me.'

Mum's frown deepened. 'I didn't say it was, did I?'

Max shook his head.

But Mum was suspicious. 'You wouldn't do something like that, would you?'

'No. I love Bonnie.'

'You didn't go round there to play with her and forget to shut the gate?'

'No, Mum. I always shut it.'

'That's what I thought.'

She came with him over to Leon's.

'I don't know how she got out,' Leon said. 'Maybe I didn't shut the gate properly.'

'These things happen,' Mum said. 'Let's start looking in the street. Max will go find some friends to help, and I'll knock on doors and ask if anyone's seen her.'

Max was glad Mum was in charge. She was the best. She always knew what to do.

He grabbed his bike and took off, pedalling furiously. It felt good to do something at last. He raced down the street, past Robbo's log truck, calling for Bonnie. Robbo's ute came up the hill, so Max stopped and waved. Trudi opened the passenger window and looked out at him with her sad eyes. 'Bonnie's gone,' Max said. 'Did you see a dog on the road?'

'No, but I'll come and help look for her.' Trudi clambered out of the car.

'Don't overdo it,' Robbo warned.

'I won't. I want to help.'

Max took off down the street again. He stopped at a house where a kid from school lived. When Max told him Bonnie was missing, he was keen to help. Soon they were riding up and down on bikes, yelling Bonnie's name.

Callum joined in too, but not Jaden—he was nowhere.

All over town, people came out of their houses to help search for Bonnie. Everywhere Max went people were calling her name. Nobody wanted her to be lost or hit by a car. Especially Max.

He stopped at the highway with his heart thumping. He was on his own now. The other kids had split up and gone in different directions. He wasn't sure where to go next. If Bonnie had run down the highway she could be halfway to the next town by now. She could be sniffing around on somebody's farm, or hiding under a car. She could be anywhere.

The main street was full of people and cars because the footy had just finished. Max checked the rubbish-hopper behind the hardware, but Bonnie wasn't there. Maybe she'd gone exploring down one of the lanes. He rode to the takeaway, dropped his bike on the footpath and ran in. 'Have you seen a dog?' he asked Miki. 'Bonnie's missing.'

Miki turned towards him and shook her head. It was the first time he'd noticed her face was shaped like a heart.

'Can you come and help look for her?'

Kurt was big and dark like a bodyguard. 'No, she can't. She has to keep working.'

Miki gave a sad smile and said sorry. Then she glanced past him and pointed. 'There she is.'

Max spun to see a grey shape slinking along the footpath. He raced outside calling, 'Bonnie.' The dog paused, but her eyes were wild and frightened, and she didn't stop—she was too scared.

Max heard running footsteps and turned to see Leon pounding down the footpath. 'Hey,' Leon called out. 'Someone try to catch that dog.'

People stared at him, but nobody moved. It was like they were frozen.

A car was driving up the street, and suddenly Bonnie flashed across the tarmac and there was a thud and she tumbled under the wheels.

Leon's yell was raw. He sprinted past Max and waved frantically at the driver, who'd already stopped the car.

Max saw Bonnie lying on the road. She was all stiff with straight legs and she was breathing hard with clamped teeth, and she didn't seem to know where she was.

A lady driver got out, someone from out of town. She was talking high and fast. 'Oh my God! What happened? Have I hit a dog? Is it dead?' She started crying, and then Max was crying too. He was sobbing, his body shaking.

He felt a hand on his shoulder and Miki was standing beside him. She was calm and quiet, even though her face was twisted with worry.

Max saw Leon bending over and gently lifting the dog. He had Bonnie in his arms, and she was huffing loudly. Her eyes had gone all quivery and weird.

'Is she dead?' the driver wailed.

'No. She's still breathing.'

'Maybe she's brain-damaged,' the lady said.

Leon was soft with the dog, like a mother. Max liked the way he was caring for her. Max was scared, but Leon's hands on the dog made him feel better.

'I have to get her to the vet,' Leon said, glancing around wildly. 'Damn! I'll have to run home for my car.'

Max wished he had a car so he could take Leon and Bonnie to the vet. He would drive fast like an ambulance. He would break all the speed limits, and he wouldn't care if the cops caught him and gave him a fine. He would tell them he was saving Bonnie.

Max heard Kurt order Miki to get back in the shop. He felt her hand fall from his shoulder, but he couldn't turn around because he was watching the dog. Who would take Bonnie to the vet?

Then Max heard a gruff voice. 'I'll take you.'

It was Toby. His F250 ute was just behind the crazy lady's car, and he was leaning out of the window, beckoning to Leon.

Leon carried Bonnie down the street, blood dripping from her nose. Toby swung open the door so Leon could get in with the dog. Then Toby banged his hand on the side of his car and shouted, 'Come on, lady. Move your car so we can get going.'

The lady bustled into her car and pulled over in front of the post office. Then Toby drove up the street, revving his engine loudly.

Max waved to Leon as they went past, but Leon didn't see him because he was bent over Bonnie. They were gone in a cloud of blue fumes.

When Max turned around to walk up the street, he saw Miki at the door of the shop. Kurt was a shadow behind her, his hand on her arm. He was like a bear holding on to her. She saw Max and waved, then Kurt tugged her into the shop.

31

In the back seat of Toby's ute, Leon shoved Coke cans and chocolate wrappers onto the floor, then sat with his broken dog on his lap. His hands shook as he stroked her battered head. She had scrapes and nicks everywhere, drops of blood from her nose. She was so unlike her usual self. How many times had he wished she would grow up and become quieter? Now his little dog was in pain.

Toby was concentrating on driving. They were already on the highway and heading out of town past the footy field, which was almost empty, only a few cars left—probably somebody cleaning the change rooms after the game. Toby was disregarding the speed signs.

'Thanks for taking me,' Leon said.

Toby hurled his ute around corners. 'It's been a bad day. How's she going?'

'She doesn't look good.' Leon ran a hand over Bonnie's shoulder. She was more settled now and the huffing had subsided, but it was as if she had wilted, all her puppy energy gone. 'I can't believe I'm so upset about a dog.'

'Part of your family,' Toby said.

Leon tugged gently at Bonnie's soft ears as they spun down to the river, following the road along the silvery water.

'Dogs are great,' Toby went on. 'Always happy to see you.' He chuckled. 'More than I can say for the missus.'

'I've heard your missus is a good woman.'

'Yeah.' Toby glanced in the rear-view mirror. 'Steph puts up with me.' He was fiddling with his phone while he kept an eye on the road. He handed the phone back to Leon. 'Want to call the vet and let her know you're coming? I've pulled up the number.'

Leon was relieved when Kate answered the call. He quickly explained the situation before asking, 'Is it okay to see us?'

'Sure. Just knock on the door.'

He reached forward and passed the phone back to Toby. 'Heard any more about Mooney?' he asked.

'Yeah. Has to take two weeks off.' Toby shook his head. 'Imagine Mooney at home for that long. Poor Liz.'

'Yeah, poor Liz.' Leon leaned on the words heavily, because she deserved all their sympathy—and maybe it was time for someone to acknowledge it. Everyone knew about Mooney, didn't they? Yet Leon had noticed the silence in town, and he knew it was wrong. He'd experienced the same silence in his parents' home: the denial and pretence that gave people permission not to say anything. It wore them away, killed their spirits. Like cancer.

In the rear-view mirror, Toby's eyes locked on Leon's then dodged away.

He knew.

Leon waited for him to say something, but the silence lengthened. Maybe Toby was going to brush off Leon's comment or ignore it.

Leon had given a slab of his life trying to make things right for his mum and protect her, but he'd been quiet in this town for too long. 'My dad used to hit my mum,' he said. 'I know these things can be tough to resolve, but maybe someone should look out for Liz. Keep an eye on things.'

Toby's gaze was fixed on the road, his brow a dark line, thunderous. Then he said, 'It's bullshit, that stuff. I'll talk to Steph and we'll work something out. Should've done it ages ago.'

Their eyes connected again in the mirror, and Leon nodded. 'It's never too late.'

At the vet clinic, Leon lifted Bonnie out.

'Want me to wait?' Toby asked.

'No thanks. I don't know how long it'll take. You're good to go.'

'How will you get home?'

'Catch a bus or a taxi. Depends on how long it takes.'

Toby grabbed a receipt from the floor and wrote a mobile number on it. 'Call me if you need a lift.'

'Thanks.'

Toby grinned. 'Reckon we're even now.'

Leon smiled. 'Reckon we are.'

32

Monday, Miki was up early, ready to go to the forest. But after breakfast, Kurt announced he was going without her. She felt herself deflating, and she followed him, dejected, to the door. 'Why can't I come?'

'Because I'm going alone, and then I'm going straight on to Hobart.' He seized his coat and keys, blocking her out.

'I want to smell the trees,' she pleaded. 'It helps me get through the week.'

'Fuck your week. You don't need to smell trees.'

She watched him slide his feet into gumboots and lift his pack from the hook by the door. 'Please, Kurt. Let me come.'

His mouth flatlined. 'Not happening.'

'Why not?'

He glared at her. 'You ought to know.' He gathered everything together and slammed the door on the way out. The lock clunked home.

He'd been sullen since Saturday. All she'd done was to comfort poor Max, who had been beside himself with distress, but Kurt had been furious that she'd defied him by going out onto the footpath. It wasn't such a big deal, and she was angry with him for being irrational. Why couldn't she help? Where was the harm in it?

She suspected something else was bothering him. Possibly the key. Every day she watched him, trying to detect in his body language if he'd discovered her deception. She studied his frown over breakfast and tiptoed around him. But she'd lost her ability to read him. The constant vigilance exhausted her: always holding her breath, always anticipating the moment he might confront her. It made her edgy around him. It affected her sleep.

But now he'd gone, her blood was stirring. Freedom and air were what she needed. Kurt could leave her at home, but he couldn't stop her from going out. She fetched the key from the hole in her mattress and went to insert it in the lock.

But the key wouldn't slide in. Her heart kicked. She tried again, but it still wouldn't fit. A chill spread through her as she inspected the key and the lock. They looked the same, but they'd changed.

She sat at the kitchen table, back straight, hands folded. She could barely breathe. All these weeks of wondering whether Kurt knew about the key, and perhaps he'd known all along. Her stomach crawled. Why hadn't he said anything? And how was he planning to punish her?

She stared through the kitchen window into the lane and her skin prickled with stress. What was bothering her, she realised, was the tight feeling of being caught out. The key had made her life larger; now everything would be constricted again.

She lay on her bed and stared at the ceiling. The room felt small and the walls pressed in as if they were shrinking. She couldn't lie still, tossing from side to side, jerking her legs. She was trapped, and the restlessness inside her was like a river welling over its banks. The more she couldn't have freedom, the more she desired it. She wanted to be outside: to feel the cold air, smell the wood smoke and cut grass, the scent of bread baking just up the street. She wanted to hear the sounds of the town. She wanted to stretch her legs and swing her arms and stride along the road—it didn't matter where.

She paced the rooms, searching for another way out. She considered the windows—apart from the shopfront windows, which couldn't be opened, there was only the kitchen window. When they'd moved in, Kurt had nailed it shut to prevent burglaries. Now she wondered if it had been more about keeping her in.

She tugged at the nail with her fingers, but it was too tight to pull out. She tried to slide a butterknife under the nail's head, but the blade was too thick, so she tried a paring knife that Kurt had recently sharpened. This was slightly more successful—she could at least insert the tip under the nail. Taking care not to damage the paint, she worked her way around the rim of the nail, prising it up a little. Then she returned to the butterknife and tried to lever the nail up. The nail-head was well embedded in the window frame, and at first she was discouraged. But she had all day. If she was patient, she would get there, a fraction at a time.

It was mid-morning before she had loosened the nail, and by then she was sweating with the stress of it, worried Kurt might notice the damage. If you looked closely, the nail-head was now slightly deformed and there were several small chips in the windowsill. Another twenty minutes of wriggling the nail and she was able to slide it out.

Then there was the window lock, which was fixed solidly and wouldn't budge. A pair of pliers would have been handy, but Kurt kept his tools under the house. For a moment, she was crestfallen—had all her work come to nothing? Mustering strength, she tried again to open it, but it was seized up from lack of use.

She pulled open the pantry and perused the contents, wondering what she could use. Olive oil as lubricant? She poured a small amount into a saucer and dipped her finger in, then applied the oil carefully around the lock, not wanting to make it look slimy. Taking a tea towel, she laid it over the lock, cocked her fingers and jiggled until the mechanism twisted and freed.

The window itself was jammed, of course, glued in by paint. She would have to knock it upwards, but how to do that without breaking the window and without tools? She inspected the contents of the utensil drawer, but nothing seemed useful. Then she thought of the meat mallet in the shop, which they used to flatten the minute steaks and chicken schnitzels. Retrieving it from the tub by the grill, she wrapped its metal head in a tea towel and knocked gently at the lip of the window. Slowly it loosened and inched up.

Fresh air rushed in. Miki inhaled it.

Leaning out over the sink through the open window, she peered down to the ground. It was quite a long way, but not a dangerous distance—she could slip down there easily. What about coming back in? The steps were too far to one side for her to swing across to the window from there, so she would have to find another way.

Once again she roved the rooms, looking for options. Near the back door was a crate of empty bottles and tins ready for the tip. She piled the rubbish on the floor, then cut four long pieces of string and tied one to each corner of the crate. Holding the strings like a puppeteer, she lowered the crate to the ground; she would use it as a step to re-enter. She had to be able to lift it back inside when she came home, so she knotted the strings loosely and hooked them over the kitchen tap. Finally, she crawled over the sink and onto the sill, squatting like a crab before leaping to the ground and landing in a puddle.

The air felt clean, the sky large. It had started to drizzle and she'd left her coat behind, but she didn't care; if it rained she would embrace it. Wet and cold and outside would always be better than warm and safe and locked in.

She tramped out of town, heading towards the forest. This was a risk, she supposed—there was a slight chance Kurt might come by. But it was already late morning, and she figured he would have already gone on to Hobart. As she marched along the verge, she drew in the chill air and felt free. Smoke hung like a veil and she could smell hay, rolled out for cows. She paused at a fence to watch gangly calves playing in a paddock. They stopped to look at her, and the bravest crept closer, ogling her through long dark lashes, extending its wet nose to sniff her fingers before swiping her hand with its rough tongue. Miki smiled and wiped the saliva on her overalls, then continued along the road. Pale sunlight bled through the clouds and lit the land with a misty glow.

She passed Toby's house with its mountain of firewood in the front yard, the paddock behind raking steeply up to the forest. Most houses in town had neat walls of wood along their fences, but not Toby's—his woodpile was a mess, dumped by a truck straight from the mill. He didn't seem to mind the disorder. He and Steph lived a life of chaos with their tribe of four children. But the children were happy; at least, they always were in the shop.

Miki was beyond Toby's and climbing the hill when she heard a car coming behind. Leon drew alongside in the Toyota. She was surprised to see him—usually he left for the park much earlier than this. 'Hey,' he called through the window. 'How's it going?'

'Okay. How's Bonnie?'

'She's home now. A bit sore and sorry for herself, but she's fine.'

'That's a relief. Does Max know? He was very upset when she was hit.'

'Yeah. He's been over to visit . . . Do you want a lift?'

Miki peered up the valley where cloud was beginning to descend, blotting the view of the mountains. 'All right,' she said. 'Just to the edge of the forest.'

Leon swung open the door, shifting a paint tin and a couple of brushes to clear the front seat.

'What's the paint for?' she asked.

'Someone painted graffiti all over the toilets up in the park. The boss wants me to fix it.' He reached to snatch a jumper from the floor and tossed it in the back. 'Okay, you're right to get in.'

Miki settled in the passenger seat and snapped in her seatbelt. The car was dirty: greasy takeaway wrappers and clods of mud on the floor. On the dashboard: scattered maps and a pair of sunglasses with a broken arm. Leon's work boots were muddy too, with patches of dried dirt on his trouser cuffs. His hair was ruffled as if he'd forgotten to brush it, and his shirt was creased; maybe he didn't own an iron.

'Crappy weather, isn't it?' he said, putting the car in gear and taking off up the road. 'Not the best for working outside.'

'Isn't it too wet to paint?'

Leon shrugged. 'The weather's supposed to break up.'

'Need some help?' Miki had enjoyed painting when she and Kurt had renovated the shop just after they'd moved in.

'It won't be much fun . . . But I suppose you're dressed for it,' he eyed her overalls, 'so if you want to help, many hands make light work.'

They drove into the forest, catching up to a tourist bus slowly ferrying a load of passengers to the sky walk. There were few safe places to overtake, so they were stuck behind it to the turn-off.

Along the road to the park, Leon stopped to pick up a Coke can and other rubbish that had been left on the road. 'Idiots,' he said, dropping the trash in the back. 'You'd think people who come up here wouldn't litter, but they're as stupid as everyone else.'

A Mars bar wrapper among the litter made Miki think of Max. He'd stolen one the other day. She'd been suspicious for a while that he'd been stealing, and she was worried about him, afraid of what would happen if Kurt caught him. She also knew Shane could be volatile. Leon lived next door to Max and they seemed to get along—maybe she should mention it. 'How's Max going?' she asked. 'Does he chat to you much?'

'He seems okay,' Leon said. 'We talk from time to time, when he comes over to see the dog and kick the footy, but it's hard to get much out of him. He's pretty closed up. I was too, at that age.'

'I think he's been stealing from the shop,' Miki said. 'I'm not sure why.'

Leon frowned. 'How long has that been going on?'

'Maybe a few weeks.'

'The family isn't very well off. Maybe he doesn't get pocket money.'

'Someone left ten dollars on the counter a couple of weeks ago. I thought it might have been him.'

'Could have been,' Leon said. 'I gave him ten dollars. Maybe he's trying to make amends. Do you think he could be stealing to impress his mates? Boys do that sometimes.'

'I don't know. It's not like him. Could you talk to him?'

'I can try.'

'That would be great. I'd hate him to get into trouble.'

The road had been climbing as they drove, and now it broke from the forest onto a rolling plain where peaks with jagged spines poked out of the heath like bones. Miki drew breath, and her thoughts about Max melted away. She'd never been above the tree line before, and it was like being lifted to another level, as if the lid had been peeled off the landscape. She could see the whole sky.

The weather seemed to be clearing. Tendrils of mist still clung to the tops, but most of the cloud had dissolved. The plain was studded with grasses and low bushes, the occasional white outlines of stunted dead trees. It was stark but beautiful. She loved the way the mountains seemed to graze their shoulders against the sky. 'It's amazing.'

Leon was smiling. 'You like it up here?'

'I love it.'

'Let me show you something then.' He pulled over at a turnout. 'Come on. We have to walk a little. It's not very far.'

She followed him along a trail that plunged through tall heath before opening onto a boardwalk, winding across the plain where the scrub grew low and spiny. Clumps of grass shivered and swayed, and Miki thought of the moors above Wuthering Heights where Cathy and Heathcliff had roamed. They had loved country like this; it had connected them. Jane Eyre had loved it too: she had traipsed the wild moors near Thornfield Hall where she'd met Mr Rochester and frightened his horse. Later, she had fled across the high country with a bruised heart after discovering his secret. Later still, she'd heard his ghostly voice on the wind just as St John Rivers was asking her to become a missionary. Now Miki could see why these characters had loved the high country so much. It spoke to her soul. She felt energy and strength in the wind and the rocks.

As Leon strode ahead, she noticed lightness in his gait. He must like it up here too. Maybe this was his place.

The track led towards a distant, mist-shrouded mountain. Ahead, light broke through the clouds in shafts, casting shadows on the land, and it was beautiful. They crossed tea-brown streams trickling over lichen-patched rocks. Up high, the slopes were needled with granite and the stunted shapes of wind-scoured trees. The track began to descend and then a lake appeared out of the mist: a silvery eye with zephyrs of wind ruffling its slate-grey surface.

'Wild, isn't it?' Leon said and she nodded. 'I love the cold air and the views,' he went on. 'When I look out, I see patterns of light and dark, colours in the scrub, places where the soil changes. It's like a story written into the rocks.'

Miki tried to see what he saw. When she looked closely, there were shadows and creases in the land, dimples and folds, shades of brown, grey and green. She thought how the land was made of many things: forest and heath, mountains and streams, plains, lakes, clouds, sky. The land had layers. Like people. Like trees.

Every element complemented the others, and every element was different. She liked how things came together to make a whole. A landscape. A country. A world. Everything was here.

Leon picked up a flat stone and skipped it across the steely surface of the water. 'This lake was carved out by a glacier millions of years ago,' he said. 'I like to think of everything covered in ice. Rocks being worn smooth. How old it all is.' He chuckled as if laughing at himself. 'It gives me perspective when the going gets tough. Sometimes I need that. I suppose we all do.'

Miki hadn't thought about Leon's life being difficult. But perhaps he was like her.

She remembered the little prince travelling the universe only to discover that what he had always needed were his home and the rose. Belonging and friends. Maybe it was the same for everyone. Only the details were different.

When they returned to the car, Miki sat in silence while Leon drove to the end of the road. It was windy in the car park: air gusting against the windows and rocking the car, clouds scudding overhead, the heath thrashing.

No one else was about.

'This is it,' Leon said. 'My office!' He grabbed a black garbage bag from the back seat and slid out of the car.

Miki opened her door into the wind. 'Should I bring the paint?'

'I have to do rubbish duty first. You can stay here if you want.'

She didn't want to wait behind, so she followed him to a large picnic shelter not far from the car park. Beer cans, bottles and other rubbish were scattered over the floor.

'Someone had a party and forgot to clean up,' Leon said.

Miki helped to collect the paper plates stained with tomato sauce, sausage packs, napkins, dented drink cans. It amazed her people could be so disgusting. Whoever had done this must have come to enjoy this beautiful place, and it would have taken quite some effort to get here, forty minutes on a dirt road. Then they'd left their trash behind—it didn't make sense.

Leon lugged the rubbish and tossed it into the back of the Toyota, then he lifted out the tin of paint and the brushes. 'All right. Time to tackle these toilets.'

The toilet walls were splashed with graffiti. *Greenies Go Home*, *Greens Cost Jobs* and *Fuck Off Green Cunts* in red capital letters. Miki was embarrassed but Leon didn't seem fazed. 'It's a spray-paint job,' he explained. 'A can of paint makes anyone an artist.' He paused. 'I think I know who might have done it . . .'

Miki thought she had a fair idea as well.

'I reckon it was probably Mooney,' Leon said. 'He's struck with his spray can before . . . He painted my car.'

'I think he wrecked our beehives too. In the forest.'

Leon shook his head. 'Wouldn't surprise me.'

'He's not a nice man.'

'No.' Leon was short. 'He belts Liz. I've spoken to Toby about it. Hopefully things will change.'

Miki hoped so too. She thought of Liz's sad eyes, that scared-rabbit look as if she was being hunted. Someone like Mooney could do that to you. He could make you live in fear.

Leon used a screwdriver to open the paint tin then mixed the paint using a broken-off stick. The paint was bottle-green, perfect for blending with the landscape. They got to work, dipping their brushes and running them up and down the walls of the toilet block.

'What's it like living with Kurt?' Leon asked. 'It can't be easy.'

'He's good most of the time.'

Leon chuckled. 'I reckon it'd be like living with a tiger. Fine so long as you keep him fed and make sure you don't stir the pot. Hard going if you let him get hungry or do something he doesn't like.'

Miki had never thought of Kurt as a tiger; she'd always thought of him as more of a bear. But perhaps Leon was right.

'Where is he today?' Leon asked. 'I assume he's not in the shop.'

Heat flushed Miki's cheeks. 'No, he's gone to Hobart.'

Leon paused to look at her, his eyes sympathetic. 'Do you need more time to get out?'

She bent quickly to dip her brush in the paint. 'I'm out now,' she murmured. 'Making hay while the sun shines . . . painting while the rain holds off.'

Leon laughed: a pleasant sound that rolled off the corrugated-iron walls of the toilets and rippled away over the heath. He was so different from Kurt, so much more relaxed and human. Not a tiger at all.

With two of them on the job, it didn't take long. The end result was a bit rough, but Leon seemed happy. 'That'll keep the boss off my back till they can get a professional painter.'

It was lunchtime by then, and Leon offered Miki hot chocolate from his thermos and half of his sandwich. 'It's a bit soggy,' he apologised. 'Lettuce and cheese. There wasn't much in the fridge. And I couldn't buy a pie—the takeaway was closed.'

They smiled at each other, sharing his joke.

Miki discovered she didn't mind soggy sandwiches. She hadn't realised how hungry she was. Working outside, you built up an appetite; she was never hungry in the shop.

When they'd finished eating, Leon packed away the paint and brushes. 'Okay,' he said, 'you've saved my arse today, so I'm donating my afternoon to you. It's on National Parks. I'll be tour guide. I thought maybe I could take you to the sky walk. What do you think?'

Miki hesitated for the briefest of moments. 'I'd like that.'

'Hop on in then,' Leon said. 'It's a bit of a drive.'

At the sky walk, they left the Toyota in the car park and bypassed the visitor centre. Leon paused to wave at someone inside then led the way down a raised boardwalk through wet eucalypt forest. A rain shower had just passed through, and everything was fragrant and dripping.

The boardwalk descended to a gravel path that wound down to a broad inky river. Miki stopped on the bank and contemplated the swirling water. The current was swift and strong. She could hear the voice of the water as it gushed through. She could smell the water too: fresh and clean, a hint of tannins and earthiness. As she stared into the depths, it seemed the river was alive with power. She wondered what it would be like to fall in, imagined coldness sufficient to take her breath away, the grip of the current pulling her under, brown water pouring over her head, the hint of light way above as she sank.

They walked across the concrete causeway, and Miki paused to dip her fingers into the river. She was mesmerised. Everything seemed to be drawn towards the water, magnetised by its energy. Thickets of lime-coloured scrub and tall white-trunked trees crowded the banks, as if trying to leap in. It was the movement that captivated her. The sense of the river going somewhere. Purposeful, as if it understood its reason for being.

Leon led the way up a formed path through wet, moss-covered forest. The track wound among giant trees with thick, riven bark, past slick fallen logs, scattered carpets of ferns, rough clumps of wire grass, tree ferns with spreading fronds. At the top of the path, a steel walkway projected out into air. They stepped onto it, their boots scraping on wire. Beneath them, the ground fell away quickly, and they were up among the mid-storey tree crowns, looking down into fans of ferns below, the lower layers of the forest and beds of rotting leaves.

Miki had never been so high before, and she was dizzy and had to cling to the rail. The transparency of the wire gave her vertigo, the ground looming below. For a moment she felt she might fall, but she forced herself to look up and out, breathing in the views and the air that nipped her ears and nose and hung in vapour puffs in front of her.

The vista was magnificent: rolling waves of forest and hills where caterpillars of mist clung and shifted slowly with the breeze. The stark silver trunks of old trees protruded from the canopy and bristled against the sky. Miki had a sense of what it must be like to be a bird flying over the landscape, an idea of what they would see—such a different perspective on the world.

The trees grew close to the walkway, and she was amazed at their height. There was a stillness in them that spoke to her, a timelessness that hinted at endurance and longevity. Her lifetime made up only a few centimetres of their girth, and they would remain long after she died. There was something reassuring about that.

Leon paused to point out a flowering sassafras tree almost within reach. Miki could smell the white bellflowers, like daphne or jasmine, surprisingly sweet. She followed Leon along the walkway as it traversed layers of forest. Ahead, she could see flashes of silver between trees, hints of light reflecting from the river. Slowly, she gained enough confidence to lean over the edge and peer down to the forest floor, so far below, and then up the straight trunks into the canopy, so much closer now but still unattainable.

The final elevated viewing platform swayed as Miki stepped onto it. The movement was only slight but the way it bounced took her breath away, and made her pause and grasp the handrail, trying to block out the dizzying height. They were now walking towards the dark river that swept in a wide arc below. Further away, she could see where two rivers joined to form this broad torrent.

She stood at the end of everything, suspended over nothing but air, looking out across the landscape to smudges of cloud sliding along contours. Even way up here she could hear the roar of the water. It felt like she was on the edge of something much larger than herself. The river brought movement and scale. She could see into its black depths. She wanted to know what was higher up, where the landscape had collected all of this water. What was up in those misty hills? What would it be like to walk there, to struggle through the undergrowth, then climb and climb through the present and the past, to understand what the river and the world were made of?

In some ways, standing on the cantilevered platform was like standing in the shop looking out, because what she could see was only the beginning of things. But here she felt excited and free, full of sky and air and river and hope.

'Have you been up there?' she asked Leon, pointing to the mountains beyond the river.

'No, but people do go. You drive deeper into the forest, and from there you can walk into the mountains. It's wild and exposed and windy and dangerous, but I've heard it's also amazingly beautiful. I'd like to do it one day.'

Miki stood in the air above the river and forest and realised how much she liked the water and trees together. She thought of the forest, steady and patient. And the river passing through, strong and deep, carrying secrets beneath its dark skin. River and forest belonged together, needed each other, and were one. Even at this grand scale, everything was interconnected.

She smiled. The key and her deception had been discovered, but she was still out here, connected with trees and sky, reaching for life. This was the way of the world.

PART IV
Understorey

33

Some days you have energy for dealing with other people's problems, and some days you don't. This is what Leon thought as he pulled up at home after work and saw Max sitting on his front doorstep with Bonnie sprawled in his lap. The issue wasn't the fact the boy was there—it was the look on his face that made Leon feel weary: that particular lopsided, fragile look kids get when they're about to cry.

Leon had had a long day. He'd left for the park early that morning to meet a minibus-load of volunteers, then spent seven hours organising them into jobs and making sure they enjoyed their work and felt useful. It had been a tough call because of their varying ages and fitness. A few had been young and able uni students on holidays, wanting to do something worthwhile, but the rest had been either overweight or old and arthritic, and one was so ancient that Grandpa might have been more efficient. Leon had given the young people spades and barrows while designating lighter tasks to the oldies. They were all supposed to have brought their own food, but he knew from experience that volunteers came with different levels of preparation. Luckily he'd dropped in at Miki's this morning and stocked up on lollies and chocolate.

And they'd been fortunate with the weather today. Up in the mountains, even in spring, wind could whisk in a cold front in minutes. Bad weather had been forecast, but the rain held off most of the day, and the views had been excellent—to the east, the lowlands on the coast and the steely blue sea; to the west, the rumpled blanket of mountains. In the end they'd completed a reasonable amount of work before the weather came in: big purple clouds rising up from the ocean and marching over the mountains.

Now Leon was tired and hanging out for a shower, and he didn't feel up to dealing with Max. But there was no dodging it. The kid looked upset. Leon remembered the discussion he'd had with Miki last week. Maybe Max had been caught stealing.

'You okay?' Leon asked, approaching the boy and the dog. He hoped Bonnie had been working her magic. Dogs were good at mood-reading; they seemed to know when you needed company.

Max's voice wobbled. 'Yeah, fine.'

Obviously not fine but trying hard to be brave. 'Do you want to come in?' Leon glanced at the ominous clouds; it could rain any time.

Max shook his head.

'How about I bring some food out then?'

'Nah. I've had afternoon tea.'

'Want to kick a footy?' They hadn't kicked balls in a while.

'Yeah, okay.'

Leon grabbed a footy from the laundry, and they knocked it around out the back. Bonnie kept trying to run off with it, and Leon tried to distract her with her own mangled ball, firing kicks at Max in between. It wasn't much fun. Max was quiet, even when Leon asked questions.

'How was your day?'

'Good.'

'Anything interesting?'

'Nah.'

'Any problems at school?'

'Nup.'

Something was bothering the kid, but he wasn't ready to talk. Leon tried to remember how his mum had wrangled things out of him when he was young. Or maybe she hadn't; maybe, like Max, he'd kept everything tied up inside. Leon tried biscuits and hot chocolate, hoping to draw the boy out, but Max ate in silence. In the end, Leon decided simply to wait. If the volcano was rumbling, eventually it would erupt.

They sat on the back doorstep, and Bonnie snuggled up beside Max. The boy's hand rested on the dog's head as he stared up towards the bush beyond the fence where the trees were tossing wildly in the wind. He looked hollow and gaunt.

Leon was worried. 'Are you sure everything's okay? You won't get in trouble if you tell me. I'm here to help.'

Max said nothing.

Leon could hear wind scooping under the eaves. A door banging somewhere. Shane's shed rattling. 'Is anyone hassling you?' he probed. 'Anyone hurting you? Is it a friend?'

Max shook his head.

'I saw Miki the other day,' Leon continued carefully. 'She said someone's been taking stuff from the shop.'

Their eyes clashed and Max's face blanched. He glanced away and his shoulders slumped as he murmured something.

'What did you say?' Leon asked.

'Jaden made me do it.'

'That big boy who hangs out with you sometimes?'

'Yeah, him. He's not my friend. I hate him.'

They were getting somewhere at last. 'What's been going on? Has he been hitting you?'

A small nod.

'Has he been making you take things from the shop?'

Max's eyes, large with fear, flew to Leon's face. He looked as if he might jump up and run.

'Don't panic.' Leon said. 'Miki and I want to help. It's not like you to steal. You're a good kid.'

But the boy was still cowering.

'How long has it been going on?' Leon asked. 'This stuff with Jaden.'

'A while.' Max kept his eyes averted. He seemed so small, so closed in on himself.

'Did something happen today?' Leon asked gently. 'Can you tell me?'

A long pause, then another incoherent mumble.

'What was that?'

'I took some beer to school.'

'For Jaden?'

A nod.

'Did he drink it?'

'He said he was going to save it till he got home,' Max blurted. 'He said he was going to tell his mum I made him do it.'

Leon put a hand on the boy's skinny shoulder. 'His mum won't believe that. As if a small kid like you could make a big kid drink beer!'

Max started crying. 'But I got it for him.'

Leon didn't have to ask where Max had got the beer—Shane was rarely without one in his hand. 'Okay,' Leon said. 'What's Jaden been doing to you? Tell me everything.'

It all came out then, the boy clinging to Bonnie while he talked. Smoking. Stealing. Bullying. The dog helped him. He stroked her head as she lay draped over his lap in her favourite position.

It was all starting to make sense to Leon. Max taking things from the shop. Not wanting to go to the footy. Jaden letting Bonnie out after the semifinal. The bullying must have been going on for weeks, and Leon felt terrible—why hadn't he noticed? It appalled him that Miki was the only one who'd suspected. From the small world of her shop, she had been far more aware than he, who was the boy's next-door neighbour and supposedly his friend. Leon had been so caught up in his own troubles, he hadn't actually been looking. He'd let the kid down. It was pitiful.

In a show of support, he patted the boy's leg, but Max winced. Why was he so sore? 'Can you show me?' Leon asked.

Reluctantly Max tugged up the leg of his trousers. Purple bruises on his shins.

'Jaden did this to you?'

Max cast down his eyes and nodded.

'Okay.' Leon stood up. 'We have to do something about this. We have to tell your mum.'

Max grabbed Leon's arm and shook his head violently. 'No, don't. She'll kill me.'

'It's okay, I'll do the talking. Jaden shouldn't be doing this to you.'

'Please don't tell her,' Max begged.

'You should come with me. Mums are good with this stuff. She'll be on your side.'

Max just kept patting the dog's head, soothing himself.

'We have to tell her,' Leon said. 'It's the only way to make things better. And schools have bullying policies—they'll stop all this crap with Jaden.'

Max curled around the dog and shut down. Clearly, he was too terrified to tell his mum. That was why he'd come to Leon.

'Wait here then while I go,' Leon said. 'You'll be okay. I'll make sure of it.'

Max didn't look up. He had gone into a cocoon.

'Promise me you'll stay put. You can go inside if you want. Watch some TV. I won't be long, then this will be over. Everything will be fine. Bonnie will look after you.' That was a dog's job: to be with whoever needed them.

Leon hurried next door. It probably wasn't a good time—he could hear Suzie shouting somewhere inside the house. But this wouldn't wait. He knocked.

Wendy came out looking hassled, Suzie at her heels, still yelling.

'Sorry,' Leon said over the din. 'We have to talk about Max. He's just told me some things you should know.'

Wendy frowned and stared at him for a moment, then turned to Suzie and told her to shut up. Surprisingly, Suzie went quiet—she must have sensed something weighty in her mum's voice. 'Come in,' Wendy said to Leon. 'Don't look at the mess.'

Leon followed her down the hallway, which was wall-to-wall junk. The kitchen was a shambles: dirty dishes, overflowing bin, filthy windows, used pots on the stove.

'We had a hard weekend,' Wendy said. 'Shane went on a bender.' As if this explained everything. 'He's not home yet. He's got a long way to drive. The new logging site is miles away.'

She put the kettle on and gave Suzie a bag of chips while Leon talked. He recounted everything Max had told him: the stealing, the cigarettes, the bruises, the escaped dog and the beer. Wendy listened, pale-faced and tense. Her lips compressed when he mentioned Jaden. 'That explains a lot,' she said. 'Where's Max now?'

'At my place. He's waiting for us.'

'Let's go then.' She grabbed Suzie's hand and led the way out the front door.

But Max wasn't in the yard; the back doorstep was empty. Leon checked inside the house, but Max wasn't there.

Wendy's face was haggard when Leon told her the boy was gone. 'I'll phone some friends and find out if anyone's seen him,' she said. 'Then we'll call the police.'

The irony wasn't lost on Leon. The policeman's son was the bully.

34

Miki was wiping the counter when she saw Max run past. He was puffing and red-faced, possibly crying. Was someone chasing him?

She hurried to the door and leaned out into the street. There he was, dashing down past the visitor centre, veering left at the bottom of the hill.

'What are you doing?' Kurt barked from the back of the shop.

'Max just ran past and he looked upset. I'm going to see if I can catch him.'

'No, you won't. Stay here.'

For the first time, Miki ignored his command and took off down the hill. At the T-intersection beyond the last shops, she peered anxiously along the road towards the forest. No sign of Max. Maybe he'd taken a side street.

Then she saw him: a small figure stumbling along the verge. Where was he going? It was wild out here and he needed to be home. Since mid-afternoon the weather had been building, clouds muscling against the horizon, the sky darkening.

She hastened back to the shop where Kurt was waiting in the doorway, steel-faced, arms folded. 'What do you think you're doing?'

'Max is in trouble. I should let his family know that I've seen him.'

Kurt scowled. 'It's none of our business. Let them sort it themselves.'

But Miki knew it wasn't right to do nothing, and she felt a wave of strength rising: the courage to stand up to Kurt. 'He's a nice boy,' she said. 'I'll run up and tell his mother, then I'll be back.'

Kurt's frown was as threatening as the approaching storm. 'No, you won't. You'll stay here.' He reached out a paw to grab her, but Miki dodged it, heart thudding.

'Please, Kurt, it won't take long.'

'Don't you go,' he growled.

'I'll be as quick as I can.'

The heat of his glare stabbed her skin as she raced across the road and up the footpath. Glancing back, she saw his thunderhead frown, then ahead the thunderhead clouds over the mountains.

At the highway, she paused to let cars pass. Then she crossed the road and ran along a side street, turning the corner and puffing uphill past Robbo's log truck to Max's house, next door to Leon's. She knew where to go from her night-time walks.

Everyone was on the doorstep: Wendy and Shane, Leon, Suzie hanging on to her doll. Miki felt their eyes on her, full of questions. Wendy's face was riven with angst, and Miki was sorry for her—she had a look of smallness about her.

'I saw Max go along the road to the forest,' Miki puffed. 'He ran past the shop and I followed but I couldn't catch him.'

Wendy turned to Shane, who already had his car keys out. Miki saw her put a hand on her husband's arm. 'Don't be angry when you find him, Shane. Just bring him back home.'

Shane frowned and nodded gently at his wife. It was the first time Miki had seen softness between them. 'It's okay, love. I'll leave the telling off to you. But I'll tan Jaden's arse when I see him, and I'll give Fergus a piece of my mind. Bloody copper's kid, bullying my son. We'll see about that.'

'I can come too,' Leon said. 'Two sets of eyes are better than one.'

Miki could tell by the tussle that worked on Shane's face that this offer was unexpected. He tightened, then relaxed and exhaled. 'Sure, mate. I could use a hand. We'll need torches and wet-weather gear. There's a storm coming.'

Wendy rushed inside and came out with packets of chips and chocolate, a bag of spare clothes. 'In case he gets wet,' she said, thrusting everything at her husband.

Shane shoved the food into the bag then held Wendy's gaze for a moment before leaning in to kiss her cheek. 'No worries, love. We'll make sure he stays dry.'

The wind tore at the men as they strode to Shane's ute—Miki saw the way it pressed their trousers to their legs and flung their hair about. They took off in a cloud of diesel fumes, the engine roaring while Shane revved down the street. When they were gone, the hollow sound of the wind seemed to intensify, butting against the house and moaning under the eaves. Wendy had sagged a little. She lit a cigarette then laid an arm around her daughter's shoulders and stroked the child's hair, a look of immense devotion on her face. Miki couldn't remember snuggling with her mother like that. There had never been much physical affection at home; love had been reserved for God. It was sad. This kind of intimacy looked so comfortable.

'I'd better call the police and let them know you've seen Max,' Wendy said. 'I rang them just before to say he was missing.'

'I'm sure you'll find him now,' Miki reassured. She imagined the men overtaking Max on the road, Leon jumping out and jogging back to him, leading the boy to the car.

Wendy took a drag on her cigarette, cheeks hollowing as she sucked in the smoke. There was something desperate about it, as if she needed the nicotine to help stop the shaking of her hands and maybe also her heart. Her free hand kept stroking Suzie's mop of dark hair. 'Thanks for coming.' Her eyes connected meaningfully with Miki's. 'That can't have been easy with Kurt.'

Miki thought of her brother in the shop. 'I have to get back.'

Wendy shook her head. 'He's like Jaden, love . . . only bigger. Just you watch out. If you ever need help, you know where to find me.'

As Miki passed Robbo's log truck on her way down the hill, she wished she could climb into the cab and drive away. A whole world of roads was waiting out there, a universe of choices and decisions. But the only way to go right now was back.

35

Max jogged along the road with Bonnie trotting beside him. Trot, trot, jog, jog—they were both breathless, but they kept going. Every time a car came past, Max grabbed the dog's collar and pulled her off the road. She still had no road-sense, even after being hit by a car, but it was good to have her with him. If Max looked after her, maybe she would look after him. When the cops came to get him, she could be his guard dog.

He'd decided to go up to the forest and then on to the mountains. You could live up there—he'd seen it in movies. He could make a spear and catch fish in the river, and Bonnie could help him hunt kangaroos. Dad had told him about people finding gold in the mountains, so maybe Max could find some too. Then he could pay for all the things he had stolen, and everyone would forgive him.

But the forest was still a long way away, and he was already tired. He saw the road to the tip. Maybe he would find something useful there.

The gate to the tip was open and no one was around, so he went exploring. It was amazing what people threw out. He climbed a pile of rubbish and dragged a blanket from under some tin. He found a backpack with broken straps. Some knotted string. A rusty bike with no tyres. An old loaf of bread in a plastic bag; there were green bits on the bread, but he kept it anyway. He rode the bike around but it was slow and the wheels squeaked—it wouldn't be good enough to take to the mountains.

Bonnie was in the garbage, pushing things around with her nose. She found a tin and started licking it, her pink tongue going in and out. Max surveyed his pile of potentially useful stuff, then checked out the weather. The clouds were thick, and fat raindrops had started to fall. It was dark and windy. The rubbish was banging and creaking. Any minute now, it was going to piss down.

Within moments, the skies opened like someone had turned on a tap. In seconds, his clothes were drenched and stuck to his skin, and he was shivering. He ran through the tip looking for somewhere out of the rain. Down the back, he found a dead animal on the ground. It had a huge festering lump instead of a face, like a zombie out of *Call of Duty*. Max's legs stiffened and he couldn't move. What if it came alive and chased him? It could eat him and suck his blood.

Suddenly his legs were working again. He raced through the tip to escape the dead animal, but he was lost and couldn't find a hiding place.

Then he saw it again. Had it moved? Was it following him? He screamed and ran away, and then Bonnie came out of the rubbish. He ran to her, sobbing. She had blood dripping from her mouth. Had the zombies already got her? Was she turning into one too? But she was his friend; maybe he could save her. He grabbed her and tied string to her collar so she couldn't leave him. They needed to get going. He would have to find his way out of here and walk to the mountains. They could do it. Even in the rain. On the way he could eat that loaf of bread, and when the rain stopped he could make his spear for hunting.

He pulled on the string, and the dog followed him through the tip.

36

It was close to midnight when Shane and Leon drove down from the forest. They had assisted Search and Rescue until the weather became so bad the search was called off. Shane hadn't wanted to stop. 'Fuck it. Let's keep going. My boy's out here somewhere.' But the authorities insisted it was too dangerous to continue. Dense cloud had enveloped everything, snow falling higher up. 'Sorry, mate,' the coordinator had said. 'I know you're worried about your son, but we can't risk people's lives.' For a moment there, it looked like Shane was going to hit the guy, and Leon had placed a calming hand on Shane's bony shoulder. He didn't have to say anything, but he felt the fight go out of Shane. They agreed to continue by themselves while the others went home. Leon had never figured Shane for a friend, and friendship wasn't the right word for it anyway. It was more accurate to say the missing boy had bonded them.

It was freezing up in the mountains, but adrenaline and concern had driven them both on. Visibility was zero in the fog and rain, and there certainly was a high risk of getting lost, so they'd largely stayed in the car. In the forest, the cloud was so opaque that direction was meaningless and the landscape was alien. Every way you turned it looked the same: banks of mist and trees. Enough to give you vertigo. Leon couldn't stop thinking about hypothermia.

Wendy had been on the phone several times, seeking updates. Whenever she called, Shane hung his head, his pain and anguish tangible. 'Sorry, love. Nothing.'

Leon and Shane had tried brainstorming where Max might have gone, but Shane hadn't taken his son up to the forest often, so there were no favourite or familiar places to which the boy might gravitate. If Max didn't want to be found, it would be easy for him to hide; roads were everywhere, and he could have taken any one of them. All they could do was comb the edges of the wilderness, with Leon leaning out of the window, head in the rain, calling the boy's name.

Driving back to town was slow going, the headlights bouncing off the swirling mist. Shane was quiet; Leon assumed he was thinking about arriving home empty-handed, and how devastated Wendy would be. The longer Max was missing, the lower his chances of survival, especially in conditions like this.

As they approached the outskirts of town, Leon saw the sign to the tip. 'Maybe we should have a quick look,' he suggested, not holding out much hope.

'Max hates the smell of that place,' Shane said, but he took the turn-off anyway, and drove into the yard.

The fog was even thicker down here. Leon strode between piles of rubbish, probing with his torch. He almost tripped over a dead Tasmanian devil—it had to be Miki's poor male. Using the side of his boot, he pushed it over and saw the ulcerated mass on its face. He found a rag and dragged the corpse to the nearest garbage heap, then covered it with a sheet of tin and a few cardboard boxes. It was a burial of sorts. At least Miki wouldn't see it when she came here with Kurt.

It didn't take long for Leon to do a circuit of the tip, and there was no sign of Max. No kid in his right mind would come here anyway—Shane was right: the trash stank. Leon was about to return to the car when he spotted the rusty old excavator down the back, with its bucket resting on the ground. He paused. Kids liked machines; he had climbed all over them when he was a boy. He should take a quick look, just to be sure.

Close up, he flashed his torch through the window, but the glass was cloudy.

Then he pulled up short, hope shooting through him like electricity. Cloudy glass could be condensation. Maybe someone was in there. He climbed the ladder and peered in. Through the misty glass, he could just make out someone curled up on the seat.

He tried the door, but it was locked, so he yelled and knocked on the window, banging frantically with the flat of his hand. He could break the glass—but maybe he shouldn't, machines like this were expensive.

He climbed down and sprinted to the ute, shouting, 'Shane, come quick!'

The police were at the tip within minutes: a siren and flashing blue lights. Fergus was driving, his assistant, Ken, in the passenger seat. Leon met them at the gate while Shane waited by the excavator, pacing with anxiety and tension.

Fergus rolled down his window. 'I've got the key for the excavator,' he said. 'Picked it up from the tip manager on the way.'

By the sheepish look on his face, Leon knew Fergus was feeling guilty about his son's role in this drama. Good, Leon thought. Hopefully Jaden would learn a lesson and leave Max alone from now on—that was the benefit of things coming out in the open. 'Shane's waiting.' Leon said. 'He's not happy about almost losing his son.'

The big man nodded uncomfortably. 'I don't blame him. Awful when your kid goes missing.'

Their eyes connected. They both knew Fergus would have to tread carefully.

Leon directed the police through the tip to the excavator where Shane hovered impatiently. By torchlight, Fergus unlocked the door of the machine and swung it open. Leon couldn't see any movement in the cab, but there was blood. Lots of it. Fergus went to mount the steps but Shane grasped his arm and held him back. 'Don't touch him, you bastard. That's my boy. Your son did this to him.'

Before the situation could escalate, Leon pushed through. 'Let me do it. I'm first-aid trained.' He leaned into the frigid excavator where boy and dog were huddled together. Reaching over Bonnie, he groped Max's neck, feeling for a pulse. The kid's skin was cold and moist, clammy like plasticine. What if he was dead? What would they tell Wendy? Leon laid his fingers in the groove where the kid's pulse ought to be and found a weak, thready beat. 'He's alive but hypothermic. We need to call the ambos. Shane, are you ready to take him?' Leon couldn't disentangle the boy from the dog. 'Hang on,' he said, 'Bonnie has to come first—she's on top of him.'

Scooping up the limp dog, Leon handed her down to Fergus, then lifted Max, who was all skinny limbs and felt as flaccid and absent as the dog. The boy's clothes were wet, his lips blue.

With arms of iron, Shane reached for the gangly body of his son and clutched him firmly to his chest, a few choked sobs escaping him.

'Ambulance is on its way,' Ken said. 'We'll drive to meet them. Save some time.'

Shane carried Max to the police car and laid him inside where the heater was blasting. 'We need to get his wet clothes off,' he said to Fergus. 'Got any blankets to wrap him in?'

Fergus shifted self-consciously. 'We came down in a rush and forgot the kit.'

'Can you get that bag Wendy threw in?' Shane asked Leon, obviously exasperated with Fergus.

While Shane stripped the boy's sodden gear, Leon grabbed the spare clothes. Naked, the poor kid looked even more vulnerable. Leon helped tug dry clothes onto his frozen body.

'Get going,' Shane instructed Fergus, settling in the back seat of the police car beside his son.

Leon said, 'I'll take your truck home and tell Wendy.'

Shane looked at him and nodded, the strain showing in his face—a mix of anger and fatherly love and concern. But he mouthed *thank you* to Leon as the police car pulled away, blue light whirling, the boy lying limp across his father's lap.

It was almost one in the morning when Leon arrived at the vet clinic. 'Sorry,' he said, as Kate opened the door and ushered him inside. 'I'd better buy a cage here for my dog.' He laid Bonnie on the table, and Kate began her examination.

'It's all right,' she murmured. 'These things happen.'

In the bright lights of the clinic, Leon could see his dog properly, and it didn't look good. Bonnie was a mess. She had crusted blood all over her, and even though Leon had the heater up high all the way here, she was weak and dozy. Kate's silence worried him. 'She's a good dog,' he said, filling the void with words. He explained that Max had run away with Bonnie, then said, 'We found them in the excavator at the tip. They kept each other alive, cuddling up.'

Kate inspected Bonnie with competent hands. She opened the dog's mouth and pointed to a jagged gash on her tongue. 'That's where the blood's coming from. She must have caught her tongue on something sharp. Lucky she didn't cut it right off.'

'There's plenty of sharp stuff at the tip. She might have been licking out tins.'

'That's possible. She's lost a bit of blood, but it looks worse than it is. Her main problem is hypothermia.'

Leon helped Kate set up a drip, then they shifted Bonnie onto a heating pad and placed hot water bottles around her.

After the dog was settled, Kate glanced at Leon. 'Are you okay?'

'Yeah, just tired.'

'You look like the walking dead. Let's have a hot chocolate before you go home.'

'That would be good,' Leon admitted. 'I'm pretty cold.'

Kate directed him to the bathroom. 'Why don't you clean up while I heat some milk?'

In the mirror, Leon saw the shocked pallor of his face and the spattered blood on his cheeks, more blood on his jacket. With dampened paper towels he cleaned his face, but he couldn't do much with his clothes.

Kate had two mugs of hot chocolate ready when he came out. She seemed so bright and clean and orderly compared to his dishevelled appearance. 'Not much improvement,' he said. 'I need a serious shower.' She smiled and handed him a mug, and they sat in the waiting room beneath the harsh lights.

Leon felt fatigue washing over him. 'They should be at the hospital by now,' he said. 'I hope Max is all right. You should have seen the fog—a real pea-souper.' He ran a hand through his hair and told Kate more about the search. She listened attentively; she was clear-eyed and vibrant, but she also seemed relaxed and at ease, so patient and thoughtful. Leon was still jittery with stress. It was helpful to debrief, good to connect with someone who actually wanted to hear him.

'I need to know how Max is going,' he said eventually. 'Do you mind if I give his parents a call?'

'Go ahead,' Kate said. 'I'll check on Bonnie.'

Leon tugged his phone from his pocket and discovered he'd missed a text from Wendy. *Hi Leon. Max is on a drip in hospital and being warmed up. The doctor says he'll be fine. Thank you so much for your help. Shane and I are so grateful. Max might have died if it wasn't for you and Bonnie.* Leon felt a rush of relief, as if a mountain had been removed from his chest. When Kate came back, he read the text to her.

'Same as your Bonnie,' she said, smiling. 'She'll be fine too.' Then she chuckled. 'Maybe I should have been a doctor. I'd get better pay.'

Leon was embarrassed—here he was rabbiting on when maybe Kate would prefer to be home asleep. 'I can settle my bill now, if you want,' he offered.

She brushed it off. 'I'm not worried about that. I'm just pleased Bonnie's looking so much brighter.'

'Thanks for your care.'

Kate shrugged. 'That's okay. It's my job; I like helping animals. But what about you? You're so busy saving everyone, who saves you?'

Leon was startled. Wasn't it his job to look out for others? If he didn't do it, who would? 'I save myself,' he said. 'Isn't that normal?'

She laughed. 'I wish more people had that attitude.'

Leon was starting to wind down now he knew Max was safe, and Kate was an excellent conversationalist. She led him into talk about work, life in town, the footy and dogs. In the warmth of her company, Leon revived and became almost light-hearted. She was easy to talk to, so laid-back and interesting. While they chatted, she sat on the chair with her legs folded beneath her, hands wrapped around her mug, ponytail swinging as she talked, eyes sparkling even at this hour of night.

'Which park do you work in?' she asked.

He told her.

'It's pretty up there. I've walked some of the trails.'

'I've been fixing those trails,' he said. 'It's hard yakka. They give me volunteers, but it makes my job harder—a bit like herding cats. Sometimes it's easier to do the work yourself.'

She laughed again, and the way she shifted in her chair and tipped her head back made him appreciate the smoothness of her throat. 'We should go hiking sometime,' she suggested. 'I don't mind walking on my own, but it's good to have company.'

'Sure. That would be great.'

When he'd finished his hot chocolate, she reached to take his cup and their hands brushed briefly. She smiled, their eyes connected, and Leon felt a part of himself turn to liquid. He should organise something with her soon. Go for a hike, like she'd said. Maybe she would like to try sea-kayaking.

He stood to go. 'Thanks so much for everything.'

She smiled again, her face crinkling pleasantly. 'That's fine. I hope you've warmed up a bit now.'

Yes, he was definitely warmer.

37

On Tuesday, Miki was alone again. It was no surprise. Kurt was angry with her for defying him and running up to Max's house. When she came home that day, she had expected him to explode. But not a word. Tension was building inside him—that familiar humming of bees. Too many things had been left unsaid, and Kurt was not one to store things forever. He still hadn't mentioned changing the locks. An eruption must be coming, but its timing could not be predicted.

Sitting at a table in the shop, she gazed out to the street, where clear light poured with the promise of spring. Weather like this should have made her feel positive, but loneliness descended like a cloud. How many weeks now since she had visited the forest? She missed the trees and the breathy rustling of leaves. Missed the way the light fell through the canopy. Missed the scent of the leaf litter connecting her back to the earth. But she had no regrets. Taking action to help Max had made her feel powerful.

To dispel loneliness she decided to read—maybe *Wuthering Heights* today; in her present mood she felt closer to Cathy than Tess or Jane Eyre. She admired Cathy's passionate liveliness, the way she stood up for herself and announced her feelings, the strength that drove her to follow her will, no matter what others thought. There were things Miki could learn from Cathy.

But when she went to her room, her books were not on the bedside table where they belonged. They had been there last night—she had read *Jane Eyre* before going to sleep. That meant Kurt must have taken them this morning. Was this how he would punish her, by removing her privileges in small insidious ways?

She wondered where he might have hidden the books. He wouldn't take them up to the forest, so they must still be here. Methodically she searched all the rooms, riffling through cupboards and drawers.

Then, in a panic, she checked the bins. He wouldn't have thrown them out, would he? He knew how much she loved those books.

Baffled, she considered other hiding places. He could have put them in his room under the shop, or perhaps he'd stashed them in his filing cabinet where he kept everything else. The storeroom had always been inaccessible, of course—Miki's key had never worked in that lock. And the cabinet was likely to be out-of-bounds, too; Kurt had changed all the locks. But perhaps she should at least try to open it.

She retrieved her key and entered Kurt's room. The cabinet stood beside his desk in the corner. She slid the key into the lock but, as she'd expected, it wouldn't turn. She pulled it out then tried again, jiggling it carefully in case the teeth hadn't engaged.

With a soft click, the lock released.

Her chest tightened. Why hadn't she tried this before?

The cabinet rattled as she drew out the top drawer. It was a mess—Kurt clearly wasn't organised. Papers had been shoved, overflowing, into torn manila folders. When she eased one out, a shower of scrunched receipts spilled to the floor like autumn leaves. Aghast, she dropped onto hands and knees, gathering them up. Surely there'd been no order to the way they'd been crammed in—hopefully Kurt wouldn't notice.

At his desk, she shuffled through the receipts. They were ordinary purchases he had made for the shop, all essential for tax. She replaced the file and pulled out another. This one contained a ledger with records of income. The figures weren't great, but they were similar to her regular mental calculations, and they showed what she already knew: that Saturdays and Sundays were by far their best days, thanks to the tourists and Mum's Night Off. They weren't getting rich; it wasn't easy to make a fortune out of fish and chips and hamburgers.

She slipped the file back in the drawer and wondered if she should stop her search. It was wrong to go through Kurt's papers without his permission. But shouldn't she have the right now she was eighteen? Feeling justified again, she drew out the next file, which contained the monthly rental payments. She scanned the numbers, and her stomach clenched in surprise. Their income covered the rent, but the profits were slim. How had they managed to keep afloat? And how had Kurt bought the ute and the boat, which he had ordered last week?

Beneath the shop rental documents, she found another rental agreement for an address in Hobart, and sweat pricked her armpits. Kurt must have access to another property he'd kept secret from her. Was that where he stayed when he went to the city? He'd always said he rented a room in a cheap hotel. She thought of Wendy's comments, months ago, about Kurt keeping everything for himself. All these documents were in his name, Kurt Muller—no mention of his sister Mikaela.

She returned the file to the drawer and removed another folder that contained printed banking statements. She could see the monthly rent going out to both properties, and also regular payments to their suppliers, like Coca-Cola and the supermarket in Hobart where Kurt made purchases for the shop. She could see his weekly cash deposits from the till, and the cash card and EFTPOS income. But there was also a significant monthly deposit coming in from another bank: two thousand dollars a month. Miki was perplexed. After the fire, when Kurt had taken out the lease on this shop, he'd said there was nothing left over. So where was this extra money coming from? It must be tied up with his business interests in Hobart—and perhaps this second rental property was part of that too. Miki felt a twinge of annoyance. Wasn't it time Kurt started sharing information about these things with her? Wasn't she entitled to know?

Agitated and uneasy, she flicked through the rest of the cabinet, but there was nothing of interest. More receipts for items purchased. Warranties and instruction manuals for appliances.

Then she searched each drawer for her books—but they weren't there. Neither was Father's black leather folder.

Carefully, Miki replaced everything and locked the cabinet. She needed time to think and work out what to do. She needed to get outside in the air.

In the kitchen, she tugged the nail from the sill and opened the window, then lowered the milk crate and leaped out into the lane where the spring wind whipped her ponytail and the air smelled of cut grass.

Wound tight, she tramped the side streets, stewing over Kurt's files. He'd always said he had her best interests at heart, but the evidence indicated she didn't figure in his intentions at all. She should have seen it before. The new ute and boat were recent examples of his self-indulgence, while he'd never bought anything for her. And the farm she'd dreamed of—the replacement for their loss—was never going to happen. She was an irrelevant bystander. An unpaid worker in his shop, with no rights. She was powerless.

Misery spilled over her. She couldn't live in Kurt's cave anymore. Couldn't live with being excluded from everything. But what could she do? She ought to confront him about those files, but she couldn't—he would shout her down—which meant she had no recourse other than to leave. But he would never let her go. And where would she flee, even if she could? She had nothing.

On autopilot, she walked into the visitor centre where Geraldine smiled in welcome from behind the information desk. 'Hello, stranger. Where have you been?'

Now was the moment Miki should share everything with this kind, friendly woman, but the habit of keeping it all locked inside was too strong. She tied down her shutters and returned the smile. 'It's been hectic at the shop. Kurt keeps me busy.'

'Lucky the locals are hungry,' Geraldine jested. 'Soon you'll be rich.'

Miki smiled as if sharing the joke, but the irony of Geraldine's comment was a knife in her chest.

'How did you go with *The Old Man and the Sea*?' Geraldine asked. 'It feels like I gave it to you ages ago—shows how long it is since I've seen you.'

'I loved it. But I've forgotten to bring it today. I'll give it back next time I see you.' Miki was relieved Geraldine's book was safely hidden under the jumpers in her wardrobe. Pity she hadn't hidden her other books too, but Kurt would have noticed.

'Hemingway's a great writer, isn't he?' Geraldine was saying. 'One of the best. His work is deceptively simple, but everything is there. That book won him the Nobel Prize for Literature, you know. Only one hundred pages but it's magnificent. I'll bet it didn't take you long to get through it.'

'Not long. And I read it more than once.'

'Fabulous!' Geraldine's eyes were squirrel-bright. 'Tell me how it made you feel.' She looked hopeful, as if expecting the book to chisel open some secret passage in Miki from which everything would gush out.

And it almost happened. Miki was hovering on the brink of confiding in Geraldine. She felt as if an ocean was trapped in her chest, surging to escape, but she couldn't let go. 'It's about freedom,' she managed.

Geraldine nodded encouragingly. 'The fish is fighting for freedom, and the old man is fighting for his reputation as a fisherman—which is a kind of freedom too, isn't it? Freedom is worth fighting for. It's being able to choose what you think. Not being told there's only one way.'

Miki knew Geraldine was referring to Kurt. But Geraldine didn't know the barriers Miki faced. She couldn't know how completely Kurt controlled everything.

'The book is about power too,' Geraldine went on. 'The power shifts between the fish and the old man and back again. Does anyone win?'

'The old man beats the fish in the end,' Miki said, gaining momentum now she was on safer ground.

'But is he proud of that?'

'He is, until the sharks ruin it.'

'And how does the old man feel about the fish?'

'He loves and respects it. And he admires the fish's will to fight and live. He loves its strength and beauty.'

Geraldine sat back in her chair, the corners of her eyes creasing into half-moons. 'So perhaps Hemingway is saying that you can love something, and respect it, but still wish to be free. Maybe he's saying you can love someone, and not agree with them. That it's okay to be yourself.'

Miki's breath locked in her throat.

'Kurt keeps you under a tight rein, doesn't he?' Geraldine said. 'I know he cares about you because you're his sister. But you need more freedom.'

Miki felt she might break. Geraldine wasn't telling her anything she didn't already know. She began to retreat, stepping towards the door.

Geraldine reached under the counter and called after her. 'I have another book for you.'

But Miki felt the walls collapsing around her. She had to get out. She couldn't breathe. 'Thank you, but I can't take it today.'

As she fled through the door, the last thing she saw was Geraldine's soft face, wrought with sympathy.

38

When Max came home, everyone in the street was asking about his three days in hospital. 'How was it?' 'Were the nurses nice to you?' 'Did you eat lots of ice-cream?'

He'd had a pretty good time and would have stayed longer if he could. The food was the best! Three courses for every meal in so many little containers. Rice Bubbles in a box for breakfast. Meat and mashed potatoes for lunch. Ice-cream and jelly. He'd been too sick to enjoy it at first. He'd had a drip in his arm, an oxygen monitor on his finger, and a nurse to help him go to the loo. But once he began to feel better, he ate everything and watched TV all the time and nobody stopped him. It was better than home. The nurses were kind, and they gave him snacks and unlimited milk.

Back at home everyone was acting strange. Suzie and Rosie were the only normal ones. Max had expected Mum and Dad to be furious about all the stealing, but Dad hadn't said anything, and Mum was being too friendly. 'Are you all right, Max?' she kept saying. 'Do you need anything?' 'Are you hungry?' 'It's so good to have you back.' She was always giving him chocolate and hugs. He wished she would either leave him alone or tell him everything was okay.

He was terrified about going back to school, but it worked out all right. The teachers made a fuss of him, saying it was a miracle he was alive.

Jaden and Max had to go see the principal, Mr Merrick, in his office. Max sat in the corner looking at the floor while the principal made Jaden say sorry. It sounded fake. But when Mr Merrick told Max to look up, he saw Jaden was scared. Then Mr Merrick told Jaden to get out—just like that. When Jaden was gone, Mr Merrick said, 'Jaden's not allowed anywhere near you, Max, do you understand? And he's not to speak to you. Not any time. You're safe now, son.'

Max nodded. He wanted to tell the principal he wasn't his son, but decided not to. Mr Merrick must be confused.

At recess Max hung out on his own. He sat on a bench and ate the chocolate Mum had put in his lunchbox. Jaden and Callum kept away, but they weren't the only ones. *Everyone* kept away. Did that mean Max didn't have friends? Jaden stared at him from across the playground, and Max's heart started thumping. Then Jaden looked away. He didn't smirk or poke out his tongue. He didn't do anything.

Lily Moon came over with her halo of blonde hair. She sat down beside Max, and he didn't know what to say so he gave her a piece of chocolate. 'Can I see your bruises?' Lily asked. 'Mum said Jaden was kicking you.'

Max pulled up his trousers and showed her. The bruises were fading.

'Jaden's a fuckwit,' Lily said. 'Mum says he made you steal stuff and smoke cigarettes. Is it true?'

Max nodded.

'If he comes after you again, let me know and I'll punch him.'

Max was impressed. He'd never talked much to Lily before, but now she might be his friend.

'I heard a dog saved you,' she said.

Max shook his head. 'We saved each other. We kept each other warm.'

'Mum said you hid at the tip. Were you going to live there?'

'No, I was going up to the mountains.'

'Will you run away again? If you do, I'll come with you.'

'Not for a while.' He was pleased she had offered. 'But when I do, you can come.'

The school bell rang; it was time to go in. Max picked up his lunchbox and started back alone to his classroom. But Lily Moon grabbed his hand and walked with him.

Just outside the classroom, she said, 'Are you going to the rally on Sunday?'

'I suppose so.' He'd forgotten about that.

'Good.' She leaned in and kissed him on the cheek.

Mum had given Max some money to spend at the takeaway on the way home, but he was anxious about going because he hadn't seen Miki since everything had come out in the open. Mum said Miki had been really nice, and he should be grateful she was such a kind person. All the same, when Max entered the shop, he stood back from the counter, feeling awkward, and let the other kids crowd forward first to buy lollies.

Miki was serving alone, and when she saw him, she smiled. 'Hey, Max. Are you okay? I was worried about you.'

Max dropped his head, glad the shop was empty now. 'I'm really sorry for nicking stuff.'

Miki nodded. 'I know Jaden put you up to it. And I know you're not a thief, so I'm sure you won't do it again. Kurt might find out next time . . . and we don't want that.'

No, Max didn't want that at all. Kurt was as scary as jail.

But the apology was over with, and he was ready to move on. 'Can I have a Mars bar?' he asked, grabbing one. Then he thought twice about it and placed the chocolate back on the shelf. He opened his palm and left Mum's scrunched five-dollar note on the counter. 'Actually, I don't need anything. But you can keep this. I'm going to pay for all the things I've stolen.'

Miki smiled. 'How's Bonnie going?' she asked. 'All recovered from her adventure?'

39

A week later, on a sunny spring Tuesday, Miki tidied herself in front of the mirror and pulled her hair back in a ponytail. She needed to compose herself because today Leon was taking her to see her devils at the sanctuary, and she was almost erupting with enthusiasm. Three hours in a car! The furthest she had ever been. Three hours of talking to Leon. She studied herself in the mirror, rearranging her features until she looked normal. Calming herself wasn't easy. It required capping internal wells and damming psychological rivers, but she knew she had the strength to do it. Wasn't this something she did every day?

She left through the back window then strode down the lane. Moving fast gave her confidence. It was time to embrace the day. Kurt wasn't the only one who had secrets—this was an adventure beyond his control.

She met Leon in the car park behind the visitor centre, and they took off towards Hobart in the big white Toyota.

'How are you?' he asked, raising his eyebrows.

'I'm good. How's Max?'

'I think things are better now they've sorted out Jaden.'

'Max still looks pale. It was lucky you found him.'

'Bonnie's the real hero,' Leon said. 'Who'd have thought my pup could be so useful!'

Miki hadn't visited the city since Father lost his fingers. Back then, Hobart had been exhausting and frightening, but this time she was alight with excitement. Eleven years had passed, and so much had changed. She had changed too.

She had forgotten how the mountain frowned over the town, the way tall buildings lined the streets. Home was so quiet in comparison, so small. Maybe one day, she would visit here by herself and walk all these streets. Maybe she could go up on the mountain, and see the city spread out in front of her. She tried to take everything in as Leon navigated the busy streets: a church, a stone-walled park, old buildings, rows of shops, occasional glimpses of the sea.

Soon they were out of the city and heading north. Leon drove fast, sometimes breaking speed limits. Miki knew he was worried about getting her home before Kurt, but for once she didn't care—she was doing this for herself.

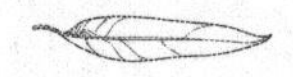

When they pulled up at the sanctuary car park beneath towering trees, Miki slid out into cool air that was tangy with the aroma of eucalyptus. In the shop, her eyes grasped everything, forcing it into her memory. People trying on T-shirts. Children nagging parents to buy things, just like in the takeaway.

Leon told the receptionist they'd come to see Dale, and she smiled and made a phone call. Dale soon appeared, striding into the office and reaching to shake Miki's hand. 'Hey, Miki. I'm so glad you've come.' His smile widened as she accepted his hand. Then the two men greeted each other, relaxed and familiar. Miki could see they were friends, and she was pleased for Leon.

Dale led them through the sanctuary to the breeding pens, which had waist-high corrugated-iron fences and had been erected beneath gum trees to make the most of the shade. They stopped at a pen and looked in. It was large and grassy with strategically placed logs and ferns for shelter. A scrappy-looking devil was loping along a worn track around the boundary. He did one circuit without stopping, then another, round and round, eyes empty and fixed straight ahead. His behaviour made Miki uneasy, reminding her of how she felt staring out of the shop: the same blankness. He must be miserable, and this made her fearful. What if her devils were unhappy here?

She glanced at Dale and caught a flash of empathy in his eyes. 'This is unusual,' he said. 'Most devils don't do this kind of stereotypic behaviour. We try to make the enclosures safe and interesting, but he isn't suited to captivity. We're going to release him soon. Probably onto Maria Island. But he's important genetic stock, so we need to breed him first. Maybe we'll match him with your female.'

Miki watched the devil doing laps. Did he ever stop for a break? Maybe the laps eased the pain of boredom. How long had he been here? Did he remember how it felt to be free?

Another devil appeared from beneath the pile of logs, and the first devil stopped and hissed. The two faced each other, hunching and snarling. Now that the second devil had arrived, the first devil's behaviour was more normal. Miki was relieved. Creatures weren't meant to be isolated. These devils didn't have a choice about being held captive, so she wanted them to be comfortable and contented, at least. It would be wonderful if they could be returned to the wild, but the disease was so prevalent that perhaps they could never be completely free. And maybe complete freedom wasn't possible! She thought of her eagles, riding the updrafts above the forest. They were the freest creatures she knew, and yet in some ways they were captive too—tied to their nest tree and their young. People considered themselves free but they were also restricted by rules and commitments, the shackles of ambition. Maybe that was okay so long as you could exercise your free will. The devils couldn't do this, but they were unable to fix their problems without the assistance of humans, so captivity seemed like the only solution. She smiled at the irony of humans trying to save devils, when the humans were the cause of their decline.

'How about we see your devils now?' Dale suggested.

Miki tried to conceal her anxiety as he led the way to another pen. 'Here we are,' he said, leaning over the fence. 'This is your female. She's doing well. Come and see.'

Miki advanced slowly and peered in. There was her devil, stretched belly-down on the grass, busily gnawing the bloodied rib cage of a dead animal. Her coat was thick and glossy—better than it had been at the tip. And when she squinted up at them, blinking in the light, Miki felt a surge of relief. The devil's face wasn't blank, and she didn't seem frightened.

'I have some good news,' Dale said. 'Her tests were clear and she's nearly finished quarantine, so we'll pair her up with a mate soon.'

'When will she have babies?' Miki asked.

'Once we put her in with the male it might take a few weeks. The young are tiny when they're born—little kidney beans that have to climb into her pouch. They won't emerge for a few months.'

'Would it be okay if I go in with her?'

'Sure. I'll open the gate.'

Moving quietly so as not to frighten the devil, Miki crept into the pen and perched on a flat log. The devil paused from eating to glance at her then went back to the food, apparently unperturbed. Miki slithered off the log, squatted low and shuffled closer. The devil raised her head and stopped chewing, testing the air with her nose then blinking before returning to the business of eating. Miki listened to those strong teeth grinding on ribs and crunching through bone. The devil focused on her again as Miki crabbed further forward. She could smell the devil now: not the rank odour of anger, but the musty scent that she loved. The devil was not afraid; Miki could see her whiskers twitching, the moist shine of her eyes. She was healthy—no wounds on her face.

This was all that was needed. Miki's devil was safe; it was fine to go home.

She was about to retreat when the devil dropped the carcase and stepped towards her. Miki extended her hand, and the devil walked up and snuffled it. Out came the pink tongue to lick Miki's fingers: three short swipes.

Miki couldn't see through the blur of her tears, but she knew she'd made the right choice. Her devil would be cared for here, and she would make babies that didn't have the disease. This justified the cost of giving up the devil's freedom.

Dale was smiling as Miki came out of the pen and he closed the gate behind her. 'She knew you,' he said. 'No one's been able to get that close since she arrived.'

They visited the young devils next, who were in a smaller pen near the entry, on display with two other little devils. They were all running around together like wind-up toys, their stiff tails cranking.

'You might not believe this,' Dale said, 'but devils make good pets when they're young. Not so good when they're older though—they become less tame and more unpredictable. But sometimes the staff have to hand-raise little orphans, and they fall in love with them.'

Miki didn't like the sound of devils as pets; they had wild temperaments and deserved to be free. 'Being here is a good step on the way back to freedom,' she said. 'This is a nice place, but it's not where devils belong.'

Dale regarded her thoughtfully. 'You're right,' he said. 'Having healthy wild devils is what we're working for.'

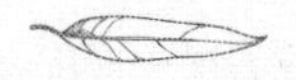

On the way home, Leon wanted to discuss the wildlife park and the breeding program, and Miki was happy to go along with it, weighing up the costs and benefits. Leon was convinced the devils would eventually be restored to the wild, but Miki wasn't so sure. 'I'd like to see them all free again,' she said. 'But how will we get rid of the disease?'

'Vaccination.'

Leon was confident humans could solve the problem, while Miki hadn't the same faith in humankind. 'Have we managed to eradicate all human diseases?' she asked.

'Point taken,' he said. 'I'm trying to be optimistic. I don't want devils to stay in zoos and sanctuaries forever.'

Neither did Miki. This led to a discussion about zoos. Leon told her about the trade in wildlife to supply zoos around the world and how this had led to pressure on wild populations. Miki found this abhorrent. 'Why do people even go to zoos?' she asked.

'Because it's easy. They can take their kids and see wild animals close up.'

'Can't they just look in books?'

'These days you can buy a David Attenborough movie or look up YouTube clips.'

'I don't use the internet,' Miki said.

Leon glanced at her sideways. 'Because Kurt won't let you?'

She let the question slip by. Leon was right, of course, but this wasn't a discussion she wanted to have, and fortunately he didn't press. He was a good listener, and she was enjoying herself. It was the most she'd spoken to anyone since Mother died.

As they drove along, Leon cast a quizzical look at her.

'What's wrong?' she asked. 'Have I said something funny?'

His mouth twisted into a lopsided smile. 'It's interesting to hear you talk about devils and captivity. Has it occurred to you that maybe you're a bit like that devil running circles in his pen? Don't you feel like that in the shop?'

'I do get out,' she defended, unnerved by his perceptiveness. 'Like today.'

'But you have to sneak out, don't you? What if Kurt finds out and stops you?'

Miki didn't have an answer to that. It was her greatest fear.

'What do you want for yourself?' Leon asked. 'What are your hopes and dreams?'

'What are yours?'

He paused, as if considering. 'It's a big question, isn't it? I think about it a lot. A few more months in this job and I'm hoping they'll give me more responsibility. I want to take tour groups into the park—teach them about nature . . . But longer term? Maybe I'll do some more study. Get married, have a family.' He laughed. 'Not that I'm in a hurry for all that. It can wait till after I'm thirty. How about you? You must have plans.'

Miki's throat locked.

'I get the feeling you want to finish school and go to uni,' Leon said. 'You're bright enough . . . so maybe you need to leave. Kurt doesn't let you be yourself. He doesn't let you live.'

'I can't leave,' Miki said, tightly. 'I don't have any money.'

'Kurt must owe you something. You work harder than he does.'

'But where would I go?'

'There are options. How about Geraldine? She might have a spare room.'

Miki thought about this. It was one thing to dream about going, another to actually do it. And the hardest step on any journey was the first. Kurt would never release her—so would she always remain in his cage?

'He doesn't own you, Miki,' Leon said. 'You are your own person.'

She stared at the white lines flicking beneath the car, the grainy texture of the tarmac, the blur of fence posts flashing by, the looming presence of clouds, cars whizzing in the opposite direction. She thought of the accounting books and the strange cash deposits, and her eyes shimmered with tears. 'Money is coming into our bank account from somewhere,' she told Leon. 'It's not our regular income. I can't work it out.'

'Doesn't Kurt have business in Hobart? That's what you told me.'

'Yes, but there's a regular payment coming in from another bank.'

'Maybe he has a separate account to make transfers.'

'Maybe . . . That does make sense . . .'

'Perhaps you have to ask him,' Leon said. 'You're entitled to know.'

But Miki wasn't entitled to anything where Kurt was concerned. 'I'll think about it,' she said, already knowing she wouldn't.

40

On the day of the loggers' rally, cars poured into town while Leon escaped in the opposite direction. He knew he wasn't welcome at the rally, but he had come up with a plan, and now he was enacting it. He swung the curves down to the water then drove along it, past farms and green paddocks on the way to the old people's home.

Grandpa was waiting in the foyer in collar and tie, an uneven attempt at a Windsor knot clasped at his throat. Leon helped him into the car, and they retraced the journey. By the time they landed at the bottom of the main street, the rally had begun.

The way was blocked by Robbo's log truck, skewed from one footpath to the other. Leon parked downhill from the truck and ushered Grandpa up the footpath. The old man obliged like a puppet, willing to accept assistance when it was needed. But Leon knew Grandpa had a will of iron, even though he was physically fragile. You didn't cut trees all your life and burn down a timber mill to protect your wife unless you had plenty of gumption.

Just beyond the log truck, Robbo was standing on the tray of a smaller truck with a microphone clamped in his hand. Further uphill, the road was packed with loggers and their families from all around the region. Everyone associated with the industry would be here. This was their chance to protest against the government for *locking them out of the forest*. It was an overreaction, Leon thought because, in truth, the government was only resuming a small patch of land.

He led Grandpa up behind Robbo's truck where they remained concealed by one of the wheels. Robbo was announcing the morning's agenda. He and Toby would speak first, he said, to outline general concerns about recent local developments, then the microphone would be opened to the public. After that, everyone would vote, by show of hands, on a strategy to achieve the best outcome.

It was clear that Robbo liked the sound of his own voice. He started banging on about how loggers had cut trees since time immemorial, and how there wouldn't be any forest at all if it wasn't for them, because the land would have been cleared for farms. Loggers, he concluded, were the ultimate conservationists. This triggered cheers and laughter from the crowd. Leon wasn't laughing—since when had loggers been conservationists? Even his dad would find that amusing.

Robbo was becoming louder, shouting into the microphone as if he was addressing the footy team. 'This is our town and these are our forests, right? And these are our jobs under threat. Bob Brown might waltz in here and say we're doing it wrong, but what would he know? Has he worked in these forests? We're the ones who know about trees. And we should be able to use them however we bloody well want.'

The crowd chanted *hear, hear* like politicians in parliament. Leon noticed Robbo's disciples were mostly big-bellied men in checked flannelette shirts, and women supporting their husbands.

'What Bob Brown and the greenies don't understand,' Robbo went on, 'is that this industry is our livelihood and our future. It's our jobs and our homes. It's food on the kitchen tables. We're not going to sit back and let them have their way—we're going to make noise and let them know what we think. And we won't be giving up any more forest. Not without a fight.'

He made a fist and raised it high, and the crowd copied him. Then they began punching the air and hooting like baboons. Robbo was grinning as if his team had just won the football premiership.

He offered the microphone to Toby, who monkeyed onto the truck to take his turn, sleeves pushed up as usual. 'Thanks, Robbo.' Toby's voice was surprisingly smooth over the microphone. 'I'm Toby Carter from the local mill, and I just wanted to remind everyone that this town has suffered enough. Some of us remember when there used to be four mills around here—now there's only one. The others were shut down because there wasn't enough sawlog. And everyone lost their jobs. That's greenies for you—they lock up trees and don't give a stuff about jobs.'

People murmured and shook their heads as if Toby was giving a eulogy.

'None of us want to be on the dole,' he said. 'And for all of us to get work, our industry needs access to trees. The government stopped the boys from logging near here, and now they have to drive an hour and a half to get to work. It's tough on the wallet and tough on families. This new reserve means more forest locked up, which is bad for our industry. And bad for jobs.'

'Greens cost jobs,' Mooney shouted over the crowd. 'Greens cost jobs.'

Through the sea of heads, Leon saw him up near the takeaway with his fist in the air, punching out the rhythm of his chant. Other people joined in, a small group at first. Then it grew until everyone was shouting, 'Greens cost jobs. Greens cost jobs.' The voices were like a drum, beating out the words. Toby leaped down from the truck, and all the people kept shouting, 'Greens cost jobs!'

Then Robbo declared an open mic, so anyone could speak. His wife Trudi was the first, and the audience quietened as she huddled on the back of the truck, wide-eyed as a rabbit. 'I don't know about all of you,' she said softly, 'but most people I know in this industry aren't getting rich. It's hard to make ends meet. Our men work long hours with high overheads. They're away a lot. Many of us women have to work to keep food on the table. The greenies just don't understand.' She placed a tentative hand on her husband's arm, and everyone cheered.

Other people took turns at the microphone, and all the stories were the same. Nobody was rolling in money; everybody was struggling. Each time someone concluded their speech, the crowd exploded with applause.

When the queue of speakers waned, Robbo took the microphone again. 'We need to talk about what we should do,' he said. 'Anyone got any suggestions?'

People began calling out. 'Burn down that old tree.' 'Shoot the eagles.' 'No, shoot the greenies!' That made everyone laugh.

Robbo held up his hand and waited for the crowd to quieten. 'Okay,' he said, 'all good ideas. But now I want to hear something sensible. We don't want a war.'

'We've already got a war,' Mooney shouted.

'Not quite, mate,' Robbo returned. 'We're trying to find a peaceful strategy here.'

A murmur ran up the street like leaves in the wind.

Leon grasped Grandpa's arm, then propelled him around the truck and up to Robbo. 'This old feller here wants to have a word,' Leon said. 'He's my grandfather. Can you give him a hand to get up there?' The disdain on Robbo's face showed what he thought of this proposal, but Leon wasn't backing away. 'Come on, Robbo. I'm asking for help. I can't lift him up there myself.'

Whispers swelled to a crescendo behind Leon's back. He could sense everyone craning to see what was happening. The mumbles converted to words. 'Who's that?' 'Why's he here?' 'He's got a nerve.'

Mooney's sneer was loudest. 'What the fuck is Parkie doing here? I'll fucking smash his head in.'

Leon waited, glaring daggers at Robbo, but the truck driver didn't move.

Then Max emerged from the crowd. 'I'll help,' the boy called out. 'I'm strong.'

A hush descended.

Leon locked eyes with the boy and nodded. 'Thanks, mate. That'd be great.'

He showed Max how to link hands to make a step for Grandpa and then, together, they tried to lift the old man onto the truck.

But Max's hands gave way, and Grandpa slumped against the tray and hung there with his feet off the ground. It would have been funny if it wasn't so desperate.

The crowd rumbled as Leon struggled to think of a solution.

Then a harsh voice rasped over the crowd. 'Get out of the way. Let me through.' It was Shane. He sounded angry, and the crowd sank away from him as though he was Moses parting the sea. He stood in front of Grandpa and stared at him, expressionless. Then he nodded at Leon. 'Okay. Let's give him a leg-up.'

They shot Grandpa skywards with so much momentum, Robbo had to stick out an arm to break the old man's trajectory. Now Grandpa was up there, Robbo's continued obstruction would look petty. His mouth turned down at the corners, and for a moment Leon thought he wasn't going to let the old man speak. Then he slowly handed over the microphone.

Pride surged through Leon as his grandfather wrapped his warped hand around the mic and peered out at all those unsympathetic faces. The old man looked as if his scrawny legs wouldn't hold him for long. But Leon knew Grandpa had the strength of a tree, all on the inside. Now he had the stage, he would use it.

'Sorry for barging in on you folk,' Grandpa said, 'but I'm an old logger from way back and I thought you might benefit from hearing my perspective. Name's Thomas Walker, and I know the industry well as you do, probably better, because I've been around these parts since Jesus played fullback for Jerusalem.'

A few people chuckled.

'I've lived most of my life in the forests. Close to forty years on a chainsaw. Mostly Bruny Island, but also around here. My father and grandpa and my great- and great-great-grandfathers were loggers too—you can see them in the history books. They worked the timber tramways on Bruny Island. Helped set it up right back at the start. Those are my credentials. Generations of my family working in forests.

'I know there's been some trouble round here lately. My grandson, here, Leon—he's filled me in. And I've seen it in the newspapers. Front-page news! That's got to make your knees tremble if you work in the industry. Fact is, I know your big tree. I remember it from when I was working down here. There's no other tree like it. Thirty, forty years ago, we logged all around it. Could have cut it down, but we didn't because it was the biggest tree for miles. When you're working in the forest, and you find a tree that huge, you can't help thinking about all the things it's survived. And you respect it. Anyone who's seen that tree and stood underneath it will know what I mean. It makes you stop and listen to the forest. Most days when you're on the job, picking off leeches and trying to keep dry, you don't even think about what's around you. But when you get that rare perfect day, and you go into a patch of old-growth and the sun's out and a breeze is blowing, there's no better place.'

While Grandpa talked, Leon studied the crowd. They were listening—he could see it in their quiet attention, the way their shoulders and mouths had eased. Bringing Grandpa here was a coup. He was speaking a language they understood.

'Way back forty years ago,' Grandpa was saying, 'we decided to leave that tree because we couldn't bring ourselves to cut it down. And it's my belief that you fellers can turn it into something useful. A showcase for the forests, like the festival and the sky walk, so the punters can come and have a look. They can see it right here, close to town. And if you do it right, it's a win–win situation. From what I've heard, the authorities only want to take a small bit of land. Maybe you can be obliging this time, so you're ahead when it comes to bigger fights in the future.'

'You're being naive, old man,' Mooney mocked.

Grandpa frowned and straightened his back. He was skinny as a willow branch and looked like he might snap in the wind, but he was still game to stand up to Mooney. 'When you're my age and you've spent your whole life in the industry, you're not naive, sonny. And I've still got contacts who go up to the forest and tell me what's going on.'

'Who? Parkie? What would he know?' Mooney sniggered.

'Back off, Mooney,' Shane growled. 'Let the man finish.'

'Gone soft, have you, Shane, since Parkie saved your son?'

'He saved you too, Mooney. Everybody knows that. Pull your neck in.'

Mooney scowled but backed off.

Grandpa's voice was like ripples going out on a lake. 'I'm not trying to tell you folk what to do. I know you'll make your own decisions. But I'm encouraging you to think carefully. I've seen my fair share of forest fights, and I know how fast things can turn bad. As I've already said, I reckon you'll end up in front if you're accommodating on this one. You show them you're flexible, and next time you'll have more bargaining power. Two small reserves around two trees—that's all they're asking for. If you fight this, you'll end up with no support from the rest of the community. I'm talking Hobart and the rest of Tasmania. You'll seem like bad sports.' He raised a gnarled hand and waved. 'Thanks for listening.'

He passed the microphone back to Robbo, then grasped the younger man's hand, forcing a handshake. Robbo looked as if he didn't quite know what to do. He mumbled something into the mic about everyone taking some time to think things over and talk it through before they reconvened in ten minutes. Then, almost bashfully, he helped Shane set Grandpa back on the ground.

Leon was impressed. Grandpa had earned the crowd's respect—and, in doing so, he had constructed a bridge between Leon and the town. He had achieved this in a hostile climate: quite a feat!

Leon leaned close to whisper in the old man's ear. 'Thanks, Grandpa. You were a champion. And you didn't even let on your real opinions. Lucky you didn't get started on what you think of their machines, or tell them you've turned conservationist.'

'That's the art of persuasion, lad,' Grandpa murmured. 'You have to learn what to hold back.'

'I didn't know you were so good at public speaking.'

Grandpa winked. 'There's a lot you don't know about me. But we've got plenty of time for talking. You won't be moving away any time soon?'

'Not a chance.'

Grandpa gripped Leon's arm. 'It's been good having you around, lad. You've given me life.' He turned to the others, eyes sparkling as he shook hands with Shane and then Max.

'Can't say I agree with everything you said,' Shane declared, 'but you do have a point.'

'Call it experience,' Grandpa said. 'You fellers need to choose your battles. Otherwise the whole world's against you.'

Robbo was listening too. 'I suppose you've seen a few changes over the years.'

'More than a few. I can sure tell you some stories. Maybe I will sometime. Do you blokes drink beer?'

Shane laughed. 'Is the Pope a Catholic?'

Grandpa straightened his tie and tilted his head at Leon. 'We'd better go now, and let these folks get on with their vote. We don't need to be here for that.'

Leon nodded thanks to Shane and Robbo, then gently scuffed a hand over Max's head. The boy had been the trigger for all this; if he hadn't offered to help, the outcome might have been different.

At that moment, a thin little girl with hair like sunshine rocked up and hooked arms with Max. She had to be Mooney's daughter—she had his face without all the bitterness.

'I'm bored with this,' she said to Max. 'Where's your dog? The one who saved you. She must be clever. I want to meet her.'

'She lives next door to me.'

'Okay. Let's go.'

As the girl took Max's hand and they weaselled off through the crowd, Leon saw that the glint of sunshine in her hair had transferred to the boy's face.

It was the colour of happiness.

41

A few weeks after the rally, the boss gave Leon the task of transporting signs up to the forest, with instructions to leave them beside the timber that had already been dropped off for the boardwalk. Once the signs were there, everything would be ready for work to commence. The sooner it got under way, the sooner the area could be opened to tourists.

At the rally, the locals had voted to let the reserve go ahead. They'd decided it made sense to link it with visits to the sky walk. Mooney was the only one who'd voted against it; he was the sort to choose conflict over compromise every time.

Before leaving the Parks office, Leon checked the weather so he knew what he was in for. The forecast was grim: rain and storms were predicted, which wasn't unusual for spring—this time of year was always unstable. Leon hoped to drop off the signs and be out of there before the cold front hit the mountains. He checked that the signs were secure, then he headed off in the Toyota with the trailer rattling behind him.

On the way, he lobbed in at Miki's to buy hot chips and coffee. But Kurt was the only one serving, and he glared as Leon put in his order.

'Where's Miki?' Leon asked.

Kurt's face soured. 'Out the back. I don't like her being familiar with customers.'

Prickliness was normal for Kurt, but for some reason Leon was especially unsettled by him today—something to do with the venomous twist of his mouth. He was a caustic bastard; Leon pitied Miki having to live with him. It was clear he inflicted emotional abuse on his sister, and Leon wondered if he also physically hurt her.

'What are you up to today?' Kurt asked.

This was definitely out of character: Kurt never asked questions. Leon paused in surprise before he answered. 'Dropping some signs at the big tree.'

'They started work up there yet?'

'Not as far as I know. But it should be happening soon.'

As abruptly as the conversation had begun, it was over. Kurt turned his back, and when the chips were ready, he slapped the package on the counter. Leon paid up and left.

On the way to the forest, he noticed the weather changing. Heavy grey clouds were congealing, and wind was tossing the trees. He would have to unload the signs quickly.

He drove through the logged area and on past the eagles' nest to the big tree. The track wasn't as overgrown as the first time he'd come here; someone had cut back the bush to make access easier—maybe the men who'd dropped off the timber for the boardwalk.

Beside a pile of treated-pine poles, Leon parked and got out. The weather was worsening. Trees and shrubs waved wildly around him. Leaves whipped, bark slapped, and the canopy was flailing. He hoped nothing would fall. Days like this you could imagine being crushed under a tree.

He lowered the tailgate and tried to haul the signs off the trailer, but they were too heavy, so he climbed onto the tray and lifted them one at a time. By the time he'd unloaded, he was sweating. Recent rain had softened the ground, and his boots dug in the mud as he leaned back to pull the signs off the track into the scrub.

The track was too narrow for him to turn the car and trailer around, so he unhitched the trailer and pushed it back to a rough grassy track, then swung it to face the right direction. He was about to vault into the Toyota and re-hitch the trailer when he noticed footprints on the trail—not his own. They were heading along the track, deeper into the bush, and he paused to inspect them, wondering who'd been there. Maybe the men who'd dropped off the poles. But it seemed strange that delivery men would bother with a walk in the forest, unless they knew of something worth seeing.

Leon's curiosity got the better of him. He followed the boot prints along the track for a few minutes, until they disappeared. Looking around, he noticed bark flapping against a nearby tree trunk, the clouds sinking lower. Rain was coming, and he'd left his coat in the car—perhaps he should head back.

On the cusp of retracing his steps, he saw another boot print: man-sized and deep. It was beside a decaying old stump and seemed to lead onto a faint trail into the bush. He decided to check it out. It wouldn't take long. The trail was vague, maybe an animal pad.

As he shoved through the undergrowth, drizzle began to seep from the sky. But now the track was more definite, so he went on, following it uphill. Shouldering aside wattles and shrubs, he made his way along it, stepping over logs and sticks, streamers of bark. It was wet underfoot. Several times he slipped and almost lost his footing.

The trail forged upslope, and soon he came to a thick patch of young trees where the track wove among the chaos of trunks for a couple of hundred metres before breaking out onto an open area, logged sometime in the past few years. He stopped to scratch a leech from his neck and flick it away—part of the scenery.

He crossed the clearing and followed the track into forest again. Now the trail was more obvious; the vegetation had been cut back to make progress easier. To one side, he saw patchy areas on the ground where it appeared someone had turned over dirt with a shovel. Ahead, the scrub seemed less dense, as if there might be a break in the canopy. He thought he could see some kind of barrier, so he went on.

As he came closer, he saw a fence of star-picket posts with chicken wire pulled tight. Within the enclosure, rows of plants waved in the breeze. Just short of the fence, his skin started to crawl.

It was a dope plantation. Fifteen metres by fifteen, worth a lot of money. He crouched down. Whose was it?

A crash in the scrub made him jump, but it was just a wallaby. Even so, he was edgy. Before, the forest had felt friendly, but now it had alien vibes. The trees were leaning in as if they were watching him. He pulled out his phone and tried to call the police. No reception. He would have to take photos and drop in at the police station on the way home. He walked around, snapping shots. The fences had clearly been designed to keep wallabies out, and the forest had been thinned to let in the light, leaving just enough trees so the planting wouldn't be seen from the air. Whoever had planned it was clever.

He took photos from several angles then headed quickly downhill; there was no point hanging around.

On his way along the track, he came across the dugover area again and decided to take a look. He went closer, elbowing through scrub. The diggings were strangely uniform with squared-off corners as if something had been buried there. Curious, he kneeled and started to scoop with his hands, pulling away clods of dirt. It was filthy work and soon he was coated in mud, so he found a fallen branch to poke and gouge. He struck something and squatted to shove his hand in the soil. He felt plastic but couldn't pull it up—there was still too much soil—so he dug until he started to expose a transparent plastic bag with cream-coloured cloth bags inside. The cloth bags had an imprint on them. Were they bank bags? He tugged the plastic bag free, undid the loose knot in its neck and pulled out a cloth bag, opening the ties to reveal bundles of notes.

Something was skipping in his chest now: a feeling of dread. This could be quite a stash. He knew he should cover it up straight away and get out of here. Hand over to the police. The dope plantation probably belonged to some loggers who'd put it in after cutting the forest nearby. They would kill him they found him here. What the fuck was he doing?

As he replaced the bags and began to kick dirt over the hole, another possibility occurred to him, and his heart ratcheted. He remembered Miki saying that Kurt often came up here shooting while she stayed at the car. Leon's mind was clicking over quickly now. Miki had mentioned unexplained money going into one of Kurt's bank accounts.

Everything began to make sense. If it was Kurt's marijuana plantation, no wonder he had business in Hobart: he had to sell off his crop. It would be hard to hide all the takings, and he wouldn't be able to spend the money in town—too obvious—so maybe he had buried some of the proceeds here. He could also be laundering his drug money at the casino on his weekly visits to the city. It tied in with the cash deposits Miki had noticed. Leon was shocked by the logic of it all.

Thunder rolled as he hurriedly covered the hole. The drizzle was thickening, and any time now he would get drenched. Another crack of thunder sounded. Hopefully he would make it back to the car before the bottom fell out of the sky.

42

Miki wasn't sure why Kurt had banished her from the shop. Whatever the reason, it worried her. She hovered behind the door, trying to work out what was bothering him by seeking clues from the way he spoke to the customers. Wendy and Steph came in for coffee after the school drop-offs, their voices mingling with the hiss of the espresso machine. A while later, she heard Leon ordering chips while Kurt attempted a half-friendly conversation, which was unusual.

After Leon departed, Kurt called her back in to serve. She was wiping benches when Mooney arrived. He glanced at her coldly then beckoned to Kurt, who followed him outside. Miki felt a twinge of anxiety. Why would Mooney want to talk to her brother? It wasn't as if they were friends.

The men stood on the kerb looking at the street, so Miki couldn't see their faces. Kurt was taller than Mooney, thicker through the shoulders, slimmer at the waist, muscular from weights training under the shop. Mooney was doing most of the talking, and whatever he was saying upset Kurt: there was tightness in his squared shoulders and short nods. When Mooney was done, they shook hands—another aberration—then Mooney stared at Miki through the window, something victorious and mocking in his eyes.

Kurt came in bristling with anger. 'I'm going to the forest,' he snapped. 'You will look after the shop.'

Sweat pricked her armpits. 'Can't it wait till Monday?'

'No. I have to go now.'

In the past she would have let it go, but not today. 'Is anything wrong?'

His gaze was so harsh, she couldn't help shrinking away. 'Mooney said he saw you in Leon's car the other day. Driving somewhere. What the fuck's going on?'

Her gut lurched, but she kept her face very still. 'He must have been mistaken,' she said, stiff with fear. 'I was here.'

'Don't lie. I know you have a key and you've been going out. I changed the locks, but you've still been escaping. Mooney's telling the truth. How are you getting out?'

Denial was the only option. 'It's not true.'

Kurt's face was storm-dark. He was like Father in a rage. 'Get out the back,' he spat. 'We'll talk there.'

Miki had no choice but to go. She heard him lock the shop doors.

In the kitchen, he pointed to a chair. 'Sit.'

She sat.

'The truth,' he growled. 'I want to hear it.'

She remained silent, quaking inside.

He slapped the table hard. 'Speak, Miki. I'm waiting. What's going on? Have you been fucking that guy?'

She sprang to her feet, outraged. 'Of course not.'

Kurt pressed her down, nostrils flaring. He gripped her arm, nails digging into flesh. Pain flashed behind her eyes and she looked away.

'Sometimes I need to get out,' she said. 'It's like a prison here. You lock me in like an animal.'

His fingers gouged deeper. 'To stop you behaving like one.' He loomed over her, his breath on her ear as his hands encircled her neck. 'What have you been up to with that red-headed bastard? Did you let him shove his dick in you?'

'No.' Miki was truly frightened now. If Kurt thought Leon had stolen her purity, there would be serious trouble. Father had taught that it was the most precious thing, and Kurt considered it his role to defend her honour.

'I can't believe this,' he snarled. 'I saved you from the fire, and this is what I get in return!' He released her and she almost tipped off the chair. 'I'm going to find him and I'm going to smash him into next week.' He flung a chair aside and strode to the back door.

'No!' Miki raced after him, reaching for his arm. She'd overheard Leon telling Kurt he was going to the big tree. She must not let Kurt leave. 'Where are you going?' she cried. 'I haven't done anything. He hasn't touched me.'

Kurt flicked her off, slamming her into the wall. 'I've always trusted you, and you've betrayed me. It ends right here.'

He grabbed her shoulders and pushed her against the wall, then let go so suddenly she staggered. Then he hit her twice: a hard backhander to the cheek and a fist in the eye. She crunched backwards, stunned, a rusty taste in her mouth. When she touched her lips, there was blood on her fingers. He snatched up his coat and keys, and she reached for him once more, still trying to prevent him from going after Leon.

He shook her off and hit her in the face again, hissing, 'You belong here with me.' He left her hunched on the floor. She heard the lock ram home.

Her face was afire with pain, but adrenaline drove her to her feet. She ran to the window and saw Kurt go under the house and come out with his rifle, which he shoved in the back of the ute. From the driver's seat, he glared at her through the windscreen, so angry she could almost see sparks flying from his skin. His lips formed words: *I'm going to kill him.* She had no doubt that he would. In a spray of gravel, he revved the ute and roared from the yard, spitting stones at the fence.

For a moment Miki was paralysed, but she knew she had to move fast to get help. First, though, she had to cover the damage Kurt had inflicted.

The mirror revealed a puffy-faced stranger with a bloodshot eye and a fat lip. Her tongue had three cuts where her teeth had gone in, and she had a mark on her cheek, a crimson splodge like a rose. It was as if a bear had attacked her—a big brown bear with rough paws. A raw sob rasped her throat, and one of her ears buzzed like bees in the apple blossoms. There was no time for self-pity. She wound a scarf around her face so only her eyes were showing, then grabbed a knife and dug the nail from the windowsill—no need to be careful anymore. She tipped the recycling from the crate, leaving cans all over the floor, then she dropped it from the window without bothering about the string. As she clambered out, her face was pulsing with pain.

It had started to rain outside, and she was thankful nobody was around as she raced up the street. She had no plan except to go to Wendy who knew about Kurt and had offered to help. But Miki pounded on Wendy's door to no answer. Next door, Bonnie was leaping at the fence. As the rain thickened, Miki hovered on the doorstep, stressing about what to do, desperately hoping Wendy would arrive. Max's dog Rosie came from behind the house and snuffled Miki with a wet nose. She pushed the dog away firmly—her mind was elsewhere. She couldn't suppress thoughts of Kurt speeding up the forest road and taking the turn-off to the tree. She could picture him bouncing along the track, stopping at the tree, pulling out his rifle and loading it. She'd worried before about the risk of him losing control with that gun. And now, enraged and shamed over his belief a man had tampered with her, he wouldn't be rational.

She decided she couldn't wait any longer. She would go to the visitor centre, and if Geraldine wasn't there she would head straight to the police.

Her face throbbed as she hurried downhill, and by the time she opened the front door to the centre she was soaked through with rain. Geraldine was at the desk with a book in her hands. She looked up, surprised. 'Is that you, Miki? Take your scarf off. Don't worry about being wet.'

Miki quickly shrugged off her coat and unravelled the scarf.

Geraldine's features contracted. 'My God! What's he done to you?'

'We need to call the police,' Miki said. 'Kurt's gone after Leon.' Her voice was husky and her speech slurred because of the cuts in her tongue.

Geraldine grabbed the phone, dialled a number and passed the handset over the desk. Miki had never used a telephone before. They hadn't had one on the farm, and since then their only phone was Kurt's mobile.

Fergus answered her call and asked how he could help, and she explained the situation, amazed the words came out calmly, as if someone else was speaking, someone who knew what they were doing. She described to Fergus the exact location of the big tree, then read out coordinates from a map that Geraldine spread in front of her. It was almost like a dream; Miki felt as if she was flying up near the ceiling looking down on herself with her ruined, bruised face.

'Thank you,' Fergus said. 'I'll get onto it immediately. I'll call the special operations group and they'll have someone up there soon.'

Miki handed the phone back to Geraldine, whose eyes overflowed with pity as she hung up the phone. 'What are you going to do?' the older woman said. 'You can't go back home.'

Tears tracked warm down Miki's sore cheeks, stinging the skin. Geraldine pushed past the counter and laid a gentle arm around her shoulders. This simple gesture broke Miki open. The great well of her suffering burst from her in a paroxysm of sobs.

'You poor thing,' Geraldine said. 'You need to be free of that man.'

'I'm worried about Leon.'

'Me too.'

Geraldine hugged Miki in a way she hadn't been hugged since she was a child, and it felt good, a release. Geraldine was soft but strong. She was warm and loyal, a friend to lean on.

'Now,' Geraldine said, slowly withdrawing. 'We need to get you somewhere safe so you can calm down and get cleaned up.' She gave Miki an umbrella and key and directions to her house. 'You can sit in the kitchen and make a cup of tea. I'll be home as soon as I can, but you must promise not to leave, because then I won't know where you are. Have a shower and warm up, turn the heater on. The drying rack's in the laundry. Put your clothes by the heater and use my dressing-gown.'

Miki hesitated. 'There won't be anyone home?'

'I live on my own.'

Miki took the key and wrapped the scarf around her face again before heading out into the weather. The wind tried to flip the umbrella inside out, so she pointed it into the rain and hurried down the street.

Geraldine's house was a little blue weatherboard with white window frames and a line of rosebushes along the footpath. A playground stood across the road near a grassy drain: two swings and a slide, deserted because all the children were at school. Around the back of the house, Miki collapsed the umbrella and unlocked the door. It was strange entering Geraldine's space; she felt like an intruder spying on someone else's life.

In the laundry, she shed her wet shoes and paired them up near the washing machine, then peeled off her coat and hung it on the clothes rack. The pain was almost unbearable as she removed the scarf, which had glued itself to her face in the rain.

For a moment, she thought she would faint, but slowly the burn subsided to a dull throb.

It was quiet inside except for the sound of rain on the roof. The house felt calm, though Miki did not. She was cold, shivering, her clothes wet, her head filled with worry about Leon and Kurt. She lingered at the laundry door, not quite bold enough to go in. Somehow it seemed wrong to impose, even though she'd been given permission. She'd never been in anyone else's house before. But she couldn't stand there all day. After stripping down to her underpants, she carried the clothes rack through to the lounge room, tiptoeing on the cream-coloured carpet, then set the rack in front of the gas heater and switched it on.

Geraldine had said to use her dressing-gown, and now Miki went to find it, creeping tentatively through the house. Everything was neat and fresh-smelling, like washing powder and soap. The kitchen was small and tidy; no dishes on the sink, everything wiped and put away, just like at home. On the table, the newspaper was folded as if it hadn't been read, and even the fruit in the bowl was neat.

Miki slunk through to the bedroom. Geraldine had a double bed, and on the bedside table sat a reading lamp, a packet of mints and a pair of reading glasses on top of a book. The bed was neatly made with a folded mohair blanket on it, and Geraldine's slippers were on the floor peeping from under the bedspread. The dressing-gown hung from a hook behind the door—it was pale pink with red roses like the ones in the garden. Shivering, Miki put it on. The bathroom was old but clean, like at the shop, but with a nice deep bath. Miki took a towel from the linen press in the hallway and showered to warm up as Geraldine had instructed. She kept her head bowed so she wouldn't have to look at her face in the mirror. Everything felt swollen and wrong. If she saw her reflection she might cry and the tears would sting the grazed skin.

Afterwards, wrapped in the dressing-gown, Miki sat in the lounge room facing the street. She was edgy, waiting for something to happen, but she wouldn't know anything until Geraldine came home, and who knew when that would be?

The rain was still falling, and the day felt interminably long even though the small crystal clock on the mantelpiece said it was only ten o'clock. She couldn't control the kaleidoscope of her mind and knew she'd go mad if she didn't distract herself. Geraldine's bookshelf was by the sliding door into the hallway. Miki went to inspect it—maybe books could save her once more.

The books were carefully lined up from tallest to smallest. The top shelf had spines all the same. Among them she saw *Wuthering Heights*, *Jane Eyre* and *Tess of the D'Urbervilles*: her favourite, familiar titles. But there were so many others: *Emma*, *Pride and Prejudice*, *Persuasion*, *Les Misérables*, *The Picture of Dorian Grey*, *Great Expectations*, *The Mayor of Casterbridge*, *Anna Karenina*, *The Portrait of a Lady*, *Madame Bovary*, *Frankenstein*. A whole world of books she might borrow one day. On the lower shelves, Geraldine had a collection of newer books. Miki scanned the titles and longed to read them.

Even in her fear and pain, she felt something opening inside her. Her life had changed. It had started with finding and taking the key. And from the moment she'd launched out of the kitchen window this afternoon, it had altered irrevocably again.

There was no going back.

43

Leon was hot-footing it down the trail from the plantation when he heard a loud crack. Everything had gone quiet before the storm hit. He could feel thickness in the air, an eerie silence, and the sky was brooding, lightning sparking somewhere in the distance. The thunder was closer now. But something wasn't quite right.

Another crack. Bark sprayed from a nearby tree, and instinct hurled him to the ground. It wasn't thunder—it was a gunshot!

He knew immediately it was Kurt. Who else would it be? Back at the shop, Kurt had asked where he was going, and stupidly Leon had told him. He had no idea why the guy had followed him here. But now he had discovered Kurt's secret, there was plenty of reason for Miki's brother to track him down and shoot him—of that Leon was sure.

He squatted in the damp scrub, listening with every cell in his body. Rain began to patter softly on leaves, and a breeze shivered in the canopy. Birds chirped. Bark rustled. Leon couldn't tell where Kurt was, but he knew he had to move or he would end up in a grave beside that buried money.

Staying low, he crawled across-slope away from the track. The understorey was a rubbish heap, and everything was out to get him. Sword grass snagged his skin. Twigs crackled. He manoeuvred carefully. Kurt would be waiting on the trail. One loud snap and the man would know where to find him.

Leon couldn't believe this was happening: it was simultaneously terrifying and surreal. He was an animal cowering in the undergrowth and Kurt was the hunter.

What had triggered Kurt to chase him? People had been visiting this part of the forest for weeks now without Kurt going after them, so it didn't make sense. Something else must have happened.

Leon puffed as he struggled through scrub, and the forest breathed too. Then the rain eased and stillness settled again. He was aware of every sound, every tiny movement, every nuance of the bush. The peppery scent of the shrubs. The dense smell of wet earth. The misty light. The touch of leaves on his cheeks. He saw how cloud had settled over the forest like a coat. He heard thunder rumble.

When his knee snapped a stick, the noise radiated through the quietness. A loud crash downslope told him Kurt was coming. Instinct commanded him to run, but sudden movements would give him away. He fought to calm himself so he could think. There must be eighty metres between them, so he had some time.

A shot rang out and slapped into a tree somewhere. Not very close. Kurt was just guessing; he didn't know Leon's location. Stooping low, Leon crabbed over a slippery log—then skidded and fell, vegetation collapsing beneath him. He paused and held his breath, hoping Kurt hadn't heard. The crashing stopped: Kurt must be listening too.

On hands and knees Leon went on, trying to increase his distance from Kurt. Soon the way opened a little and, semi-crouching, he ran. The terrain was awkward and uneven, and he worried about making noise as he shoved through the scrub. He needed to find somewhere to hide.

He came to a thicket of grass and wriggled in. Fern fronds waved overhead, and through them he could see the dull sky. He groped for his phone to check for reception, but the screen was smashed and the phone wouldn't work—it was useless. He slipped it back into his pocket. Squatting, he waited, listening for Kurt.

Now that he'd stopped moving, his mind started racing. Thoughts and images flashed at him like fireworks. He saw himself lying dead on the forest floor, eyes glazed, a bullet hole in his head. He saw his mother's face as she phoned him again and again, to no answer. His father sitting shrivelled and yellow in bed. Grandpa in his lonely room staring at a door that never opened. Bonnie running circles in the yard, racing along the fence then sitting quietly watching the road. Food rotting in his fridge. The Parks staff waiting for him to return this afternoon; Terry helping to organise a search party.

Life wasn't meant to be this: fleeing in fear from a predator. It was meant to be so much more than what Leon had achieved so far in his twenty-six years. It wasn't meant to be stolen.

His breathing slowed and his mind refocused. All around he could hear the sounds of the forest. He was like a rabbit, ears and eyes tuned to detect the approach of his hunter. Each crackle of bushes could be Kurt. Were those footfalls—that steady, even crunching? Should he flee?

He couldn't bear to wait any longer. Worming out from his hiding place, he scraped free of ferns and took off, quicker this time and panicky, stumbling across the contour and then down, making too much noise, forcing through banks of vegetation, wattle flowers dehiscing yellow dust as he shoved past. If he could somehow get to the main track, he could sprint to the Toyota. But which way to go? His sense of direction was skewed. All the trees looked the same.

He came to an area of tall regrowth trees and bashed his way through, turning uphill to confuse Kurt. Sticks and litter crackled underfoot, but he couldn't afford to go slower.

At a recently logged site, he stopped to listen. The open space ahead with no trees was a risk—he had to reach cover. He sprinted downhill, leaping over debris, dirt and piles of dead branches, smashing through tree crowns and bark mounds. A stick caught between his legs and he fell, grovelling, stabbing a twig into his palm. Adrenaline launched him back to his feet and sent him racing towards a patch of bushes lower down where he could go to ground and catch breath.

As he reached the edge of the clearing, a loud crack cut the air and dirt splattered near his feet. Kurt was shooting at him again. Leon leaped into the air, crashing over a log and skewering his shin on a fallen branch as he dived into the scrub while more shots pinged around.

Kurt's voice echoed across the logged coupe. 'You fucked my sister, you bastard. Now I'm going to fuck you.'

In the cover, Leon squatted and gasped for air while bullets smacked into trees. What the hell was Kurt on about? He hadn't touched Miki. This guy was so crazy he didn't know his own sister. Leon tried to think what to do next. He was wet with sweat and fear, and he could smell himself: sharp and rank. He considered his position. He was mud-caked and covered in cuts, a blood-soaked sleeve from a gashed arm, a shredded shin. The reality of his situation almost drew a sob from him. He had to stay calm or he would break.

Through the leaves, he could now see Kurt out in the clearing, studying the bush with the fierce, clear-eyed focus of a predator. He was in a red coat, easy to see, and Leon was thankful that his khaki uniform provided some camouflage. He inhaled and held still. Kurt was scanning for minutiae; one small sound or movement would give him away.

The drizzle was changing to rain: intermittent fat droplets splashing on leaves. Leon knew the downpour was coming. When Kurt started striding downhill, he moved too, slipping from the thicket and weaving through trees, ducking under tree ferns, past the tipped-up end of a fallen tree whose buttressed roots made a wall he could hide behind.

Working his way across the contour, he came to a gully where myrtle grew shady and dark. It was boggy, and he slithered down a steep slope to step through a stream, soaking his boots in black mud. The other bank was strewn with debris, and he stumbled across it. His foot punched through a rotten log, caught in a crack—and he fell, slopping into the mud and twisting his leg.

Something gave way in his knee, a sharp pain, and it took him a while to kick free. He imagined Kurt creeping towards him and aiming the gun. Then he heard a noise nearby: Kurt just across the gully, coming downhill.

Leon burrowed through ferns, releasing a shower of spores onto his head. His leg wouldn't support his weight properly, but he hobbled on—if he couldn't run, he was done. Hiding behind ferns, he waited to let Kurt pass, alert to the sound of footsteps crunching through undergrowth, flashes of red coat only twenty metres away, the long shaft of the rifle, the grim set of Kurt's mouth. Leon froze and held his breath.

When Kurt had gone past, he moved on again, weaving downhill. Tall trees gave way to rainforest where it was softer and quieter: myrtle and ferns, sticky expanses of mud. Moisture made everything slick, and he skidded on a log and slammed to the ground, winded. As he tried to drag in air, his head was enveloped in dangerous lightness. If he fainted now, Kurt would shoot him and leave him to rot. No one would find him.

He forced himself up on astronaut's legs, unhinged from gravity. Then he saw Kurt again and lowered himself slowly into the mud. Kurt had crossed the gully and was stalking uphill, scanning as he went. Leon lay along a log, then thought twice about being caught and the difficulty of getting up to run. But Kurt was so close it was risky to move.

He could see Kurt's legs as he came by. What if Kurt bent down and looked under the log? Should he wait for that moment, or should he do something to defend himself now? He could knock Kurt down and try to wrest the gun from him. But if he hit Kurt, he had to do it properly.

Leon's mind had never been clearer. Now was the time.

Lashing out with his feet, he kicked Kurt hard and it was like hitting a tree. The man went down, and Leon scrambled out, looking for the rifle. It was on the ground beyond Kurt, who was facedown in the mud. Leon knew he couldn't get there first, and then Kurt rolled over, snarling as he scrabbled for the gun.

Leon leaped up and took off again because he knew Kurt would quickly be after him. Like a startled wallaby, he ran, smashing through shrubs and wattles, somersaulting over a log. Somehow his knee was still working. His feet flew and he stayed upright, riding on adrenaline. Kurt would be running too; there was no point worrying about noise.

A shot bit a tree behind him and he thrashed through bushes, ducking, dodging, trying to stay out of sight. At the edge of another logged area, he paused. In the empty wasteland, three trees stood like soldiers, and the ground was bundles of bark and branches. He had no choice—he had to run across that raw open space. Committed, he sprinted, completely exposed, barrelling wildly over the terrain, stumbling and falling. If he made it to the forest he would gallop downhill, try to find the track back to his car.

Air sighed around him, and down came the rain. It sounded like a river pouring from the sky, water rushing over stones. He was drenched in seconds.

He saw the edge of the clearing and strained to reach it. He was sodden, clothes glued to his back. Leaping into the arms of the bush, he slithered and fell, catching on sticks and tangling in a snarl of grass. His right leg folded, caught in a web of bark, and his shoulder slammed into a log: the pain wrung a cry from him. Staggering, he forced himself up and thrust on downhill. He would make his body work and to hell with the agony.

Through the rain, he heard shouting. 'You bastard, where are you?'

Then Leon broke from the bush onto the track and ran, pumping his arms despite the wrenched shoulder, rain streaming down his face. Thank God for the footy training. His legs were hard and his mind was strong. But once Kurt hit the track, he'd be fast too.

As Leon ran, he found a rhythm of sorts, puffing with each stride. Through the curtain of rain, he could hardly see where he was going. Any time now, Kurt would be out of the bush and shooting at him.

A loud crack from behind kicked up mud at his heels, and Leon launched sideways, diving like a goalkeeper into the bush. He churned uphill, windmilling as he shoved aside shrubs. Wire grass tore at his skin and caught round his legs, slowing him like fishing line.

Twenty metres uphill he hid in a patch of daisy bushes, buying time and breath. At first he could only hear his own rasping inhalations and the patter of raindrops on leaves. The downpour provided cover of sorts and he was thankful for it, but how long would it last? He had no idea how far he was from the Toyota, twenty metres or two hundred. And now he'd stopped, the cold began to eat into him and the shivers took hold. He was wet, torn and bleeding, bits of bush in his hair, leaves down his back, bracken in his boots, a leech in his eye. He plucked it out: swollen and oozing blood.

Kurt must still be on the track. Shouldn't he have appeared by now? But time had become strangely warped since Kurt had first shot at him, and Leon couldn't tell how long that lunatic had been chasing him.

As he waited, he had a feeling of being outside himself. He was an eagle up in the canopy, looking down at his filthy tattered self, hunched on the ground. He saw his own terror as if it belonged to someone else, right down to the blanched look on his face and the spots of blood from the leech bites. Visions spiralled and flashed in his head. He was sea-kayaking on the calm channel near Bruny Island, dipping his paddle and weaving between swans. He was riding the ferry across the water—no, he was a cormorant skimming low over waves. He was fishing off the rocks below Fluted Cape. He was sprawled on a blanket on the Cape, losing his virginity to a young woman, her kisses like butterflies on his face. He was kicking footballs on the beach with his dad. He was at the lighthouse looking out over the great Southern Ocean. He was up on the cliffs, yelling into the wind.

Then a flash of red snapped him back into his body—Kurt was creeping along, far too close. Slowly, Leon eased through the bushes, wiping water from his eyes. Branches pulled back, dousing him as they recoiled. He stopped. Between bundles of grass, he watched Kurt searching the forest. Then Kurt swung his way, and Leon breathed through his teeth, telling himself to hold, hold . . .

A racket came from upslope, directly in line with his hiding place. Probably a wallaby. Such rotten bad luck. Kurt trained the rifle and took a shot. It smacked into a tree. 'Move again, you bastard,' Kurt yelled. 'I'm going to get you.'

Three more shots, then Leon heard him reloading. Now it was time to go. If Kurt came into the forest, he would be an easy target. But how to shift without drawing attention?

Kurt moved first and continued along the track, passing just a few metres away. On his back, Leon squinted into the falling rain, almost hysterical with relief. His hands were trembling and his chest was tight, his nerves shredded. He crawled uphill, dodging sticks and rustling through grass.

Then he slipped and fell on a branch with a sudden sharp snap. Through the tumbling rain he heard the thud of running footsteps on the track—Kurt was onto him.

A loud crash pinpointed the moment Kurt plunged into the bush. Then a volley of gunshots hit a tree trunk just downslope. The wallaby startled from its hiding place, scarpering frantically along a runway to Leon's right, hind legs beating the ground. Kurt veered Leon's way.

Frantic, Leon scrambled uphill, pushing through clumps of grass that raked his neck and flayed his hands. He managed to stay ahead and out of sight while Kurt cast back and forth, firing into patches of undergrowth. Each rifle crack made Leon flinch.

As Kurt progressed uphill, Leon started down again, staying low over rocks and fallen logs, nests of sticks and grass. Ahead the bush thinned; he saw an opening and drove himself towards it. He was noisy now, relying on a delay before Kurt broke after him.

Then he was out on the track. But he'd come too far! Past where he'd parked the Toyota. And Kurt was following fast.

He bolted along the trail. No one could catch him on the footy field, and he had never had more motivation than now. The only thing he couldn't beat was a bullet.

The tall tree loomed ahead, Miki's tree. But Kurt's ute was parked on the track, and there was no way Leon could get the Toyota around it. He was gutted—he would have to go bush again.

Then it occurred to him to check Kurt's car in case he'd left the keys behind. He jerked open the door. The keys were in the ignition. With racing heart, he clambered in and turned the key, and the engine roared to life. But he had no choice other than to drive towards Kurt and the gun; the Toyota and trailer were blocking the track in the other direction.

Leon shoved the ute into reverse and swung it round so he could get the hell out of there. Grinding it into first, he revved the engine, his foot slipping off the clutch. The ute jerked forward, and he crunched it into the next gear, gaining speed. He rounded a corner.

There was Kurt, crouched on the track, rifle aimed at him.

Huddling behind the wheel, Leon floored the accelerator. He had to drive straight at Kurt; he couldn't stop now. The shot smacked—not through the windscreen, as he'd expected, but into a tyre—and the vehicle faltered and swayed, slewing sideways. Leon tried to correct, but the wheels were slipping.

He felt a sickening thud as he hit something before slamming into a tree trunk at the side of the track. The vehicle tipped. Glass tinkled. The side door sheared off. Leon slumped in the driver's seat, disoriented by the sudden halt and a blossoming pain in his ribcage. He couldn't breathe, couldn't move; he could die here. But instinct propelled him out through the torn door and into the scrub.

On hands and knees, and buckled over with pain, he crawled uphill, trying to distance himself from Kurt and the ruined ute. Eventually, he stopped to inspect his injuries. He was a wreck: lacerations everywhere, a massive abrasion on his abdomen where he'd rammed into the steering wheel. Was he bleeding internally?

He couldn't hear Kurt, so he lay down among dripping bracken fern while the trees spun in a vortex above. The rain eased, and he still couldn't hear anything. Had he escaped? Why wasn't Kurt following him? Had he given up, or was he being deliberately silent, planning to ambush Leon if he headed back to the Toyota?

With a sick feeling, Leon realised it was possible he'd hit Kurt on the track. But he couldn't think about that now. He couldn't go back. If Kurt was waiting for him, there would be no second chances.

He hauled himself to his feet because that was what he had to do. He couldn't stay here. It was quiet now, but Kurt might still come for him. He stumbled forward on rubbery legs. He had to get through the forest and find another way out.

44

It was Max who saw the white Toyota go past. He was in the playground at recess, hanging out with Lily Moon down by the fence during a break in the rain. They had just seen a helicopter fly over, and then Leon's LandCruiser swung into the street. 'Hey,' he said to Lily when he saw the Parks logo on the driver's side door. 'Here comes Leon.' They climbed onto the fence to wave, but Leon didn't wave back. He was bent over the steering wheel and driving fast, so maybe he didn't see them. But Max thought it was weird. Leon always waved to him, and he and Lily had been easy to see, jiggling like crazy on the fence.

The bell rang and they trudged back to class. Mum had come in for reading. She'd been doing it every week since she found out about Jaden. She said it was to make sure Max's reading was on track, but he knew she was keeping an eye on him. It was annoying because he could look after himself. The principal was watching out for him now and the teachers were too, and he had Lily Moon for a friend, which was good because she was tough. Whenever they ran into Jaden, she glared at him and he walked away. 'He's scared of me,' she would say. But

Max reckoned it was Lily's dad that Jaden was scared of, because Mooney was frightening—all the kids thought so.

Mum had brought Suzie with her to reading, and Miss Myrtle gave Suzie colouring-in to do. Mum wanted to hear Max read first, before she listened to other kids.

'Can't you listen to someone else first today?' Max asked, as Mum sat down beside him. He could smell cigarette smoke on her jumper, mixed with the sweetness of her perfume.

'Come on, Max,' she said. 'Let's just get started.'

He couldn't concentrate because he was thinking about Leon. Then Max realised—it hadn't been Leon driving the car.

Mum was getting impatient. 'Come on, Max. Try a bit harder.'

'Mum,' he said urgently, 'Lily and me saw Leon's work car at recess, but it wasn't him driving.'

Mum's brow furrowed and she shrugged. 'There are lots of people who work for Parks.'

'I think it was Kurt,' Max said. 'I think Kurt was in Leon's car.'

Mum looked bothered then. 'Couldn't be. You must have got it wrong.'

But the more Max thought about it, the more certain he was. 'Kurt shouldn't be in Leon's car, should he?' Max said.

'No,' Mum replied. She stood up and tugged her phone from her big pink handbag. 'I'll call Fergus. Even if you're wrong, he should know.'

She went out of the classroom, and Max sat staring at his book instead of reading. Why would Kurt be driving Leon's car? How would he have got it? And where was Leon? Why had he let Kurt take his car?

When Mum came back, her face was white, even under all her makeup. She went to Miss Myrtle and they had a quiet talk. Miss Myrtle glanced at Max, then Mum came over and said she was leaving.

'What did Fergus say?' Max asked.

'He said thank you, and that he was going to look into it.'

Max knew she wasn't telling him everything. She was giving him a fake smile to make him feel good, but he could see tightness in her eyes. 'Is Leon okay?' he asked.

'I don't know. I'll tell you later.'

'No. Tell me now, Mum.'

Her face was serious. 'He's missing, Max. The police special operations group has gone out to find him.'

Max thought of the helicopter he and Lily had seen flying over. 'Is Leon hurt?'

'He might be.'

Max was worried now. 'Can I come too? I need to know what's happened to him.'

Mum's eyes locked with his again. She knew how important Leon was to him. 'Okay,' she said. 'I'll talk to the teacher.'

Outside, the rain had stopped but the sky was murky. Max could smell smoke in the air. Usually rain washed all the wood smoke away, so Max wondered if there was a house fire somewhere: they happened sometimes around here. Mum said it was a bad thing in Tasmania that so many houses burned down. It was because people had open fireplaces and weren't careful enough—not everyone had fireguards round their hearths. People knew it was a problem, but they thought it wouldn't happen to them.

Max, Mum and Suzie were walking towards the school gate when he heard the siren go off at the fire station. He raced out the gate and looked up the road. Brown smoke was billowing into the sky.

'That looks close,' Mum said. 'I reckon it might be in town.'

She picked Suzie up, and they walked fast towards the main street. Toby's ute raced past them to the fire station. Not long after, the fire engine lumbered out, lights flashing, siren wailing.

The cloud of smoke was ballooning up into the sky, and it smelled so bad Max wasn't sure he wanted to go any closer. But Mum was rushing as though she was being pulled by a magnet.

She took a short cut across the park, dragging Suzie like a dog on a lead.

Max jogged along with them, crossing the footbridge and hurrying up the gravel path into town. By the time they reached the main street, he heard roaring as if a dragon had been let loose, like in *The Hobbit*. The smoke was black and seemed angry.

'It's one of the shops,' Mum said.

Across the road, people were standing on the footpath, watching the fire. Max felt a jerk in his guts like he'd been shot. Miki's takeaway shop was burning, flames whipping and clawing like a wild beast, dancing in the windows, pouring from under the roof. The fire engine was in the middle of the street, and Toby and the other volunteer firemen were rushing around hooking up hoses.

'Is anyone inside?' Mum called out. 'Has anyone thought about Miki?' She had Suzie perched on her hip, and Suzie was crying but you could hardly hear her above the noise of the fire.

Shocked faces turned to Mum: Trudi, her eyes as big and sad as an owl's; Lily's mum, Liz. Other people too.

'She might be inside,' Mum yelled. 'Kurt locks her in.'

'No one's alive in there, luv,' a man said.

'Why aren't the firemen going in to save her?' Max asked Mum.

Her face was dreadful when she looked at him. 'They can't go in yet.' She laid a hand on his shoulder. 'It's too dangerous.'

Everybody was staring at the fire in horror. It was hot and terrible. Max held on to Mum's hand.

Toby and the firemen had the hoses set up now, and they shot jets of water and foam onto the shop. Max heard glass breaking, water hissing, flames roaring. He wished he'd stayed at school. He wanted to hide his eyes, but he couldn't look away—it was like he was hypnotised.

A fireman was putting witches hats on the street to stop people getting too close. Then the local police car pulled up. Fergus and his assistant Ken got out.

'Why are they here?' Max asked Mum. 'Shouldn't they be helping to look for Leon?'

'A special squad has gone out to find Leon,' Mum said. 'Fergus and Ken aren't trained for that.'

'What sort of special squad?' Max asked. But Mum didn't answer.

Fergus and Ken made people move further away from the fire so no one would get hurt. Max's heart thumped. When were they going to save Miki? Mum was crying. Did that mean Miki was dead? He didn't want to think about it. There was a knot in his throat, and tears like a sea waiting to come pouring out.

Up the street near the hardware, a pale-blue car stopped on the side of the road. Max knew that car—he knew all the cars in town. It belonged to the lady from the visitor centre. He saw Miki leap out, but she was staggering like a drunk, and her face was all swollen. One of her eyes was half-shut and she had a big red bruise on her cheek.

Mum had seen Miki too. 'Oh, thank God she's alive!' she breathed. 'But Christ! Look what he's done to her! That bastard.' She gave a small sob and shoved Suzie at Max. 'Look after your sister. I'm going to help.'

Max held on to Suzie while Mum rushed over to Miki. Suzie was like an octopus in his arms; she wanted to stick with Mum, so she hit him and it hurt, but he didn't let go. He saw Mum put her arms around Miki and say something to her, but Miki stared at Mum like she was a stranger, then pulled away and ran towards the shop.

Toby blocked her, clamping the hose under his armpit while he used his other arm to stop her. Miki scanned around like a wild animal. Max wanted to go to her but he was stuck with Suzie, who was screaming now. He was glad when Mum looked towards them, because he knew she was coming back for Suzie, so he dropped his little sister to the ground and took off after Miki.

She was heading downhill to get around all the people. She stopped near Trudi and Liz, staring at the fire. Further down the street, Max spotted Leon's Toyota.

And there was Kurt, limping up the hill, shoulders hunched, face hard as nails. He looked terrible. His trousers were bloody and torn, and he had a gash on his face, and blood in his hair and all down his neck. Max was the only one who had seen him. He saw Kurt grab Miki's arm and drag her down the street like a ragdoll. She didn't want to go: Max could tell by the way she leaned back, like she and Kurt were in a tug of war. But even though Kurt was hurt, he was still strong, and he made Miki go with him.

Suddenly Max knew what to do. He squeezed between all the people, pushing them out of the way. Past the witches hats he felt the heat of the fire against his skin, the flames leaping at the sky. He was looking for Fergus, screaming his name so loud his throat felt like it had been scraped by one of the rasps in Dad's shed.

There was Fergus with Toby. Max raced up to them, hesitating a moment as his eyes were drawn to the gear hanging from Fergus's belt: gun, baton, handcuffs, radio, Taser.

Fergus looked down at him, and Max yelled into his ear.

Then Fergus's eyes shot down the street, and he pulled out his gun and moved faster than Max had ever seen him go. All the people stepped back like a snake had been let loose.

Down the street Fergus ran towards the Toyota, Ken following. Miki was in the passenger seat; Max could see her lopsided face in the windscreen. Fergus and Ken were shouting and pointing their guns at the four-wheel drive. It was like in the movies, but it was happening here. Max was scared there might be a shootout because he knew Kurt had a rifle—everyone knew it. He wanted Miki safely out of the car before the shooting began.

Some sort of struggle was going on inside the Toyota. Miki was trying to grab at Kurt's arms, maybe to stop him from getting his gun. Kurt's hand flew at her face, and she cowered like a dog. More shouting. Fergus roared almost as loud as the fire.

Then the driver's side door opened, and Kurt stepped out slowly with his hands in the air like a criminal.

Fergus was yelling at him to turn around and put his hands on the roof of the car. Max thought Kurt wouldn't do it—his lip had curled, and his eyes were hard and shiny like bullets. But he obeyed. Fergus locked handcuffs around Kurt's wrists. That's when Max's legs went all wobbly; he wanted Fergus to drop the handcuff keys down the drain so Kurt's hands could never be free again. Not after what he'd done to Miki.

Fergus and Ken hauled Kurt up the street to the police car and pushed him inside. Miki swayed out of Leon's Toyota and stood on the footpath, hands hanging by her sides. Max couldn't tell if she was happy or sad about the police getting Kurt. Maybe she didn't know how she felt about it yet because her home was burning. Max wanted to go up and hold her hand, but he felt awkward—she didn't look like her normal self with her face all bruised. Then he felt bad, because he knew she would do it for him.

He put his hands in his pockets and walked over and stood beside her. She didn't seem to realise he was there, so he slipped his hand out of his pocket and took hold of hers. Her fingers were cold and limp, like the blood had stopped flowing into them, even though the fire was pumping out heat. He squeezed her hand and she looked down at him, her bloodshot eye like something from a horror movie.

All the while, Toby and the other firemen were pouring water and white foam onto the shop, and the flames were flicking and writhing like they were never going to stop.

45

Toby was rolling out hay for his cows in the early evening. It had been a big day and he needed a beer, but the cows were cold and hungry and they wouldn't wait. He was tired. Things had been crazy since he was called to the fire station this morning. So much had happened. Kurt chasing Leon with a rifle. The police special operations group flying in by helicopter, followed by a ground crew. Kurt being caught in the main street.

While all this was going on, Toby had spent an hour fighting the fire in Kurt's shop, then he'd joined the search to find Leon. By then, Search and Rescue had taken over, and another helicopter and handlers with dogs had been mobilised. Volunteers were needed for a search line, so Toby had put his hand up, along with many other people from town. He'd looked around at them all and been proud. They were a motley crew—but together they were a supportive and close-knit community.

Up at the big tree they'd passed Kurt's wrecked ute. Then they'd made a line and combed the bush, calling Leon's name, fearing the worst. Shane had found Leon's phone in the forest not far from Kurt's ute, nothing else. Toby hoped the poor bastard wasn't bleeding to death in the forest somewhere. He had a strong feeling Kurt had shot Leon.

Late afternoon, Toby had excused himself then gone home because there were things to be done. Kids to be picked up from after-school activities. Dinner to be cooked because Steph was working late. Wood to be chopped. Cows to be fed. He'd felt guilty leaving the search, but there'd been plenty of other helpers and he knew they would be okay without him.

Now he finished unravelling the last bale and bent over to collect the twine; he didn't want the cows chewing it and causing a blockage in their guts. Usually being out in the paddock cheered him up, but not today. He was worried about Leon, and disappointed in Mooney for not joining the search. He knew Mooney's attitude shouldn't bug him, but it did. Mooney was selfish—Toby shouldn't have expected anything else. Fact was, Mooney's wife and kids were his only redeeming features. But Leon was part of this town now, and it was time for Mooney to get used to it. People weren't going to tolerate his crap anymore.

As he was stuffing the twine behind the tractor seat, Toby caught sight of something on the ground up near the forest. He wasn't sure what it was. A blanket blown from the washing line? A cow lying down? It didn't look right.

He revved the tractor uphill, tyres spitting chunks of mud in the soggy paddock. Two gates had to be opened and closed before he was near, and it wasn't till he was almost there that he recognised the shape of a man on the ground. Something turned in his chest.

Parking the tractor sideways across the steep slope, he jumped down and leaned over the body, a sick feeling in his throat. On the footy field Leon had checked Mooney's pulse, and that was what Toby did now, pushing his fingers into the cold skin of Leon's neck. Relief poured through him as he felt a beating pulse and saw Leon's chest gently lift and fall.

He pulled out his phone to ring Steph, who was home now and down in the house with the kids, out of this infernal wind. He would get her to call the ambulance, and then he would work out how to ferry Leon to shelter.

46

Two days after the fire, Miki was allowed access to the ruins of her shop. She stepped into the bed of ashes and debris on the concrete slab, and it was as if she was a ghost shifting between the present and the past. Her mind skidded in and out of her body, remembering a different ruin and comparing it to this one. In less than two years, she had completed a circle—twice now, finishing up with nothing except the clothes she was standing in.

She wasn't the same person this time. She was older and stronger now, and had friends, new knowledge, more confidence. She knew she could start over because she'd done it before. She also knew that the important things in life couldn't be seen and couldn't be burned. Freedom. Choice. Friendship. Self-determination. Courage. All things Kurt had denied her. Yet she still cared about her brother. He was all the family she had. Her only friend in childhood. Her saviour from the farmhouse fire. Her guardian. Her guide. She wondered how he was faring in the remand centre: whether he was angry with her, or just angry at life. She would visit him soon. But not now. Not yet.

She scuffed through the ashes, astounded that the firemen had prevented the flames from spreading to the neighbouring shops.

The margins of her shop were defined by the edges of the concrete slab. Like when the farmhouse had burned down, there was little left: the molten metal remains of the fryer, skewed tin from the roof, soot-scorched beams, a few bits of buckled furniture. Their home—the rooms at the back of the shop—had been annihilated. All the walls destroyed. Kurt's filing cabinet gone. Everything erased. A stranger looking at the wreckage wouldn't be able to tell what it was. They wouldn't know what had gone on here. They wouldn't be able to tell she had been locked in. They wouldn't know Kurt had hit her here.

Miki was surprised by the emptiness inside her, the lack of emotion. Last time, she'd been crushed by the loss of her parents. Back then, she'd known so little of the world, but through the shop and its customers she had grown wiser. After the farm, she'd looked forward to a new beginning with Kurt, but hope hadn't delivered. This time she was somehow calmer.

While Geraldine waited in the laneway, Miki wandered through the rubble, reflecting on the life she and Kurt had shared between the lost walls. It hadn't all been bad. There had been moments of light in the darkness. There had even been times when she was happy. But that seemed long ago. Nothing was as it had seemed. She suspected Kurt had never really wanted to buy a farm. And maybe he didn't even love trees. She doubted everything about him now.

She couldn't claim to understand him, and there was sadness in the fact she knew him so little. Like her, he had suffered from a restricted upbringing, and it had harmed him as it had harmed her. Isolation wasn't healthy, of that Miki was sure. People needed each other, and they needed an opportunity to make their own choices and mistakes. So why had it been so important for Kurt to control her? Had he been trying to recreate their past life on the farm? Trying to emulate Father? Or had he enjoyed the power he'd held over her?

For too long, Miki had allowed herself to be contained and dominated without challenging him. She'd done it for a peaceful life, as Mother had taught her. And yet it hadn't brought her peace—quite the opposite. It had caused her grief and sadness, restriction, suffocating loneliness.

But now she had to let it all go. Loss and grief, she realised, were the ingredients of rebirth. She had to pass through them before she could grow.

She could begin again.

Feeling strangely unburdened, she ventured through the back door, which was no longer locked: it was gone. Then she walked slowly down the concrete back steps. The only part of the damaged shop she really wanted to see was Kurt's room underneath, the only place spared by the fire. But the police had already emptied it. She was disappointed; anything left that mattered would have been among Kurt's hidden things. She had hoped to find something that explained his reasons for the way he had treated her. She had hoped to find her precious books, but perhaps he had disposed of them after all. She had hoped to find Father's black folder—who knew where it was now.

She saw the vacant room, and turned away. Hope was in new beginnings and what she could make for herself.

In the afternoon, Fergus came to Geraldine's house to ask questions. Miki's face was still sore, but the swelling was starting to settle. Even so, she noticed Fergus's discomfort as he lowered himself into a chair in Geraldine's kitchen. He obviously wasn't sure which eye to look at: her right eye was bloodshot and her left one was fat with a purpling bruise. The graze on her cheek was bad too—Kurt had done a good job, nothing by halves with her brother.

She wrapped her hands around the cup of tea Geraldine had made to help calm her nerves. She'd been feeling anxious, because she knew Fergus would outline all the charges against Kurt. Geraldine was certain Kurt would do time in prison and she thought he deserved it, but Miki didn't like to think of her brother behind bars. When she'd mentioned this to Geraldine, the older woman had guided her to the bathroom mirror. 'This is what he has done to you,' she said. 'He'll do it again.'

Feeling a strange sense of calmness, Miki now looked at Fergus. He was a big man like Kurt, but softer: dough instead of muscles, chins instead of a jawline, handlebar moustache instead of clean-shaven. He cleared his throat. 'Sorry for what you've been through, Miki. I can see you're in a bad state. Kurt shouldn't have done that to you.'

Geraldine was at the kitchen sink, furiously wiping her hands on a tea towel. Her mouth was set hard and Miki knew she was angry. Geraldine would have preferred Fergus to wait longer before presenting himself here with all his *important information* about Kurt and the fire. But Miki didn't really mind. She wasn't afraid of the policeman, even though she'd never spoken to him except to serve him in the shop. There was nothing he could say that would surprise her. While she waited for Fergus to speak, she was thinking how there would be no more fish and chips in her life, no more locked doors.

'I thought it was best I come and tell you what we've found out about your brother,' Fergus said. 'Then I'll need to ask you some questions to make sure you're in the clear.'

'She's not an accomplice, Fergus, if that's what you're implying.' Geraldine glared at him, screwing the tea towel into a ball in her hands. 'And you shouldn't be conducting a meeting like this in my kitchen. It could have waited till next week when Miki was better. You could have done it down at the station.'

Fergus looked bashful. 'Thought it would be less threatening for Miki here, but it can wait if she's not up to it.'

'I'm all right,' Miki said. Another week wouldn't change anything.

He fixed her with serious eyes. 'Did you know about your brother's room under the shop?'

'Yes, but this morning was the first time I ever went there,' she said. 'He kept it locked.'

Fergus nodded. 'Thought as much. We had to cut open the padlock. Do you know what was in there?'

She shook her head. 'It was empty today. I know Kurt kept his gun down there and his gym. And the spare supplies for the shop.'

Fergus folded his big hands on the table and his face was grave. His fingers were fat as sausages. His hands red as his hair. 'He kept some of his drugs down there too, Miki. Did you know about that?'

How could she have known?

'And he had a house in Hobart where he's been preparing his product for sale: a drug lab with irrigation and drying rooms for marijuana. Leon found his plantation in the forest the other day. We've found links to a drug-trafficking ring.'

Miki felt everything piling on her like clouds on the mountains. Fergus began listing the charges against Kurt. Drug-related offences. Assault. Intent to murder—Leon had made a statement from hospital about how Kurt had shot at him many times, trying to kill him. Arson, for setting fire to the shop by igniting the fryer.

By the time Fergus finished, Miki was exhausted. Her vision was blurry, and Fergus's uniform shimmered in the bright light of Geraldine's kitchen. She was about to excuse herself so she could lie down and rest, but then Fergus reached into his satchel and drew something out: her three books and Father's black leather folder.

She stared at the folder, a sudden fluttering in her heart. Fergus had surprised her after all—she had thought these things were gone. He placed the books and folder on the table and pushed them towards her. 'We found them in the storeroom.'

Miki couldn't examine the folder while Fergus was there, so she thanked him quietly. Somehow it was important to appear calm, even though she was in turmoil.

Geraldine must have understood. She escorted Fergus to the door, and Miki heard him say, 'Tell her to call me if she has any questions. It's probably been quite a shock for her.'

Miki heard Geraldine return to the kitchen, felt the touch of the woman's soft hand on her shoulder. 'I'll be in the garden if you need me. Take your time.'

The house lapsed into stillness and Miki sat staring at the black folder. She could hear Geraldine's crystal clock ticking on the mantelpiece, the low grinding hum of the fridge, the background buzz of the fluorescent light in the kitchen.

She lifted her hand and placed it on top of the folder. She'd never touched it before. Both Father and Kurt had locked it away. But she'd always known it was important. With quivering fingers, she slowly unzipped the cover and laid the folder open.

The top sheet of paper was the rental agreement for the shop, and Miki heard herself sigh—at least that much had been legal. The next document was more interesting: a photocopy of an agreement for a monthly transfer of two thousand dollars into an account under Kurt's name. It was signed in a scrawl Miki couldn't read. Something opened inside her, a vault of hope. This was a relief: the extra money hadn't all come from Kurt's drugs.

Scanning through the agreement, she saw her name embedded in the typing. *These payments are for the care of Mikaela Gretel Muller, payable monthly until she attains twenty-one years of age unless she elects to establish contact earlier.*

Establish contact? Miki's heart tumbled. Who could be paying her?

Her hands shook as she shifted the document aside. Beneath it: her birth certificate. Register of Births. Her surname: *Muller.*

Given names: *Mikaela Gretel.* And below that, the names of her parents: *Klaus and Heather Muller.*

Miki slid the birth certificate aside and found an envelope beneath it with her name written on the front. She turned the envelope over and found that it had been opened and resealed—Kurt must have read it. She drew the letter out, unfolded it and read the first words: *Dear Mikaela, I am your grandmother, though you may not know of me.*

It was handwritten, dated a month after the fire in which Miki's parents had died.

Tears welled, and she couldn't go on. She was trembling, as if a great wind was blowing over her like it did up in the forest.

Taking a moment to compose herself, she set the letter down and rested her hands on the folder. There was a bulge in the back pocket. Something more? She slipped her hand in and tugged out a bundle of cards tied with blue ribbon, just like the ribbons Mother had used in Miki's hair when she was small.

The cards spilled onto the table when she untied the bow. They were birthday cards with glittery numbers on the front. Miki flicked through them. One for every year of her life up to sixteen. She opened one and recognised the same scrawl as the handwritten letter: *To dear Mikaela on your 6th birthday. With love and best wishes from your Grandma.*

Closing her eyes, Miki tuned in to the sounds all around her, the hush and quiet, movements outside the house: a car going by in the street; wind buffeting at the windows; the thump of Geraldine hacking at something in the garden with a hoe; the sound of children's voices next door, arguing and then unexpectedly breaking into laughter.

That was life, wasn't it? Tears and then laughter. Knocks and recovery. Injury and healing. Loneliness and then friends.

Miki breathed into the enormous wave of emotion that had taken hold of her, knowing she was about to discover what she had always wanted to know. She lifted the letter again and read:

Dear Mikaela,
I am your grandmother, though you may not know of me.

I have no idea what your parents told you about me, but I have always wanted to meet you, and I hope one day you will read this letter. I was close to your mother until she met your father, and then everything changed. She separated herself from the family and I've had little contact since. As a young woman, she developed her own set of standards and principles, and she thought the way your grandfather and I lived was too materialistic. So she turned away from us, and dedicated her life to her husband and her faith. This was very sad for me, but I have respected her choice and kept my distance, despite questioning the wisdom of this many times. It feels like I have had no other option.

As a parent, you want to help your children, even if they reject you, so I have assisted the only way I could—by making financial contributions to your upbringing. Sadly, I lost your grandfather from a heart attack when he was forty-two, but we were fortunate in our careers, and this has enabled me to continue to provide for you. Your mother never declined money. I'm sure she wanted what was best for you, and I'm happy I could help.

When your parents died, Kurt informed me that he was taking over your guardianship, and that you did not wish to meet me. I've never known if this was true, so I have decided to keep making payments in the hope that some of the money will find its way to you, or at least make your life more comfortable.

I have also set aside a lump sum for your education. It troubled me that your mother didn't pursue further study once she converted to your father's religion. But I've always believed education is important and liberating for girls, and I've long sensed your upbringing might make access to higher education difficult.

If you do receive this letter, Mikaela, I want you to know that I would like to get to know you—on your own terms of course. I would make no demands.

With much love,
From your grandmother,
Brenda Jones

Miki sat with the letter in her hands while tears tracked down her cheeks and spilled onto the paper. The pain of Kurt hitting her was nothing beside this. So much sadness was exploding inside her. Why hadn't her parents told her she had a grandmother? She couldn't understand it—had it truly been because of their religion, as this letter suggested? But God taught of love and acceptance, the importance of family. If her parents had been close to God, how had they cut family out? And how had her mother felt about losing contact with her own mother? It was tragic. Miki couldn't imagine erasing such an important bond. If the house fire hadn't taken her parents, Miki and her mother would still be connected. She would always grieve this loss.

And where did this leave her relationship with Kurt? He had been receiving money that was meant to be hers and spending it all on himself. No wonder he hadn't wanted her to leave home, because his regular payments would have ceased. The income from her grandmother had been financing the shop and his other acquisitions. The two utes. The new boat. The gym equipment. So, why the need to sell drugs? Was that his strategy to sustain himself after Miki became independent? She was beginning to understand many things.

She wondered, now, if Kurt actually cared about her, or whether she had simply been a means to an end. A source of income? No, he must have feelings for her. They'd shared so much. Their childhood. The loss of their parents and the farm. The forest. Didn't that count for something?

And then, with a surge of sadness, she realised Kurt would never have told her about her grandmother's letter and the money. He would have taken the income as long as he could, and maybe, eventually, he might have let her move on. It was clear to her now, that he'd burned down the shop, not just to hide the evidence of his drug dealings, but also to get rid of this letter.

So why hadn't he disposed of it earlier? And why had he held on to the black folder? A shred of guilt? It wasn't enough to absolve him.

She glanced down at the birthday cards, wondering why her mother had kept them. Surely she must have wanted Miki to read them one day and learn the truth.

This was her mother's gift to her. A grandmother. Someone who cared.

Leaving the letter and cards on the table, she stood and walked out of the front door into Geraldine's garden. After the rain, the roses along the front fence had rebounded, their pink heads bobbing in the quickening breeze that gusted up the street. The cold front had passed, and though the sky was grey it was lighter now, heading towards warmer weather.

Turning to face the mountains where the clouds hung steely and low, Miki saw the faint suggestion of a rainbow. Real, or imagined through the mist of her tears, it didn't matter. All she knew was that the river running through her, like the waters of the river up in the mountains, was rich and deep with life, anticipation and hope.

Epilogue

A month after the episode up in the forest, Leon racked his kayak on the roof of his car and drove down to the water. It was only five minutes from home, but somehow he had neglected to do this in all the months he'd been living here. Today, however, the water was calling to him and he couldn't wait to put his boat in.

The drive took him past the footy field where so many dramas had played out this year. It took him through grassy farmlands springing with growth, past an old disused sawmill, an orchard bursting with lime-green leaves, and down a gravel road to the river. The estuary was so wide here it didn't seem like a river at all—more like an inlet or a lake. He pulled up on a grassy bank and wondered if he had ever seen water so still and glassy, the clouds and sky so perfectly mirrored.

The river had been here all along, and he wasn't sure why he hadn't taken advantage of it. Perhaps he'd been afraid of stirring his homesickness for Bruny Island, because he had missed it dreadfully when he first came here; he could admit that to himself now. He'd missed the quiet hiss of wavelets collapsing onto the flat grey shores of Adventure Bay. The wild Southern

Ocean frothing against the cliffs down near the lighthouse. The peaceful paddling expeditions on the Channel, drifting among swans. He'd even missed carrying his boat across mudflats seething with crabs at low tide. But now the time was right to put his boat in here: on the other side of the Channel, where his new life was finally forming. He was still bruised and sore from his ordeal in the forest, but he was healing.

After parking close to the water, he hauled the kayak from the roof-racks and lugged it down to the shore. The river was like glass, and as he heard the soft swish of boat contacting water, it felt like coming home. He realised that putting the boat in was part of belonging; until now it hadn't felt right.

Hanging on to the cockpit, he manoeuvred into the kayak and sat down gently without too much rocking. The boat dipped beneath him as if greeting his weight. They had forgotten how to be with each other, but it was coming back quickly.

Taking the paddle in both hands, he pushed off and the boat glided out. It was still, so still, and the water was waiting. He dipped the paddle, making soft splashes as the blade broke the surface. It was fluid and good; the kayak wanted to move.

As he paddled out, a cormorant startled from a tree and beat its way along the shoreline. A breeze rippled over, and he paddled into it, soft fingers of wind on his skin. Silver light reached across the river to the distant hills, picking out the white trunks of the trees and igniting them. All was quiet except the sounds of the birds and the rhythmic dip of his paddle.

For a while, Leon followed the shore, gliding beneath scraggly gums that held out their arms. Then he paddled onto the open water, finding his rhythm, warming up, his muscles switching on to the task. Later this afternoon he would call that nice vet and organise something. He was ready for new friendships.

This was his place now.

Acknowledgements

I am sincerely grateful to poets John Karl Stokes and Jane Baker for the epigraphs at the beginning of this novel. Thank you for allowing me to cite your fine words.

Writing a novel is mostly a solitary journey, but it could not be completed without the support of friends and family, or without the insight of others.

For bringing light to this novel, I thank the fabulous team at Allen & Unwin. Special thanks to Jane Palfreyman for pushing me to find the heart of the story, and Angela Handley and Kate Goldsworthy for providing detailed editing suggestions. I also thank my French publisher, Sarah Rigaud at Les Escales, for giving timely and perfect advice about the ending of the novel.

The final draft was written while I was an Artist-in–Residence at the Boyd Property, Bundanon, near Nowra. This was a valuable window of time to immerse myself in nature and art, and I thank the Bundanon Trust for this opportunity. I also spent time writing at the Cairns Bay Waterfront Retreat on the Huon River in south-eastern Tasmania.

For moral support and encouragement during difficult times, I thank Fiona Inglis at Curtis Brown Australia, and the wonderful Deb Stevens, my confidante and friend. Thank you also to the members of the Ramekins writing group for accepting me into your midst and giving thoughtful and caring advice on writing and life. Biff Ward, Robyn Cadwallader, Jenni Savigny and Dianne Lucas, I am grateful to have you as my literary friends.

Technical advice was provided by several friends and colleagues: Stephanie Robertson enlightened me about bees and bee-keeping; Judy Clarke shared insights into trapping and research on Tasmanian devils; Andrew McKee answered my questions about policing; Denise Kraus checked my medical facts; and Mandy McKendrick proofed my Tasmanian colloquialisms.

Several books inspired and informed the writing of this novel, including *Engaging the Giants. A history of sawmill and tramways of Tasmania's southern forests* (Scott Clennett); *Following their Footsteps: Exploring Adventure Bay* (ed. C.D. Turnbull); *A Short History of Tasmania* (Lloyd Robson); *Voyages to the Southern Seas* (Danielle Clode); *Into the Woods* (Anna Krien); *Tasmania's Recherche Bay* (Bob Brown); *A History of Tasmania* (Henry Reynolds); *Into that Forest* (Louis Nowra); *In Tasmania* (Nicholas Shakespeare); and *The Forgotten Islands: One man's journey into a truly gothic Australia* (Mike Veitch).

Many other friends have supported me during the writing of this book, including Cindy Trewin, Alex Sloan, Jane Hodder, Marion Halligan, John Stokes, Kaaron Warren, Sarah Mason, Nigel Featherstone, Dan O'Malley, Sulari Gentill, Karly Lane, Kelli-anne Bertram, Craig Cormick, Jack Heath, Sarah Coleman, Heather Scott-Gagan, Alice Kenney, Sara Toscan, Jill Petherbridge, Sarah Toohey, Stella Clarke, Arianne Lowe, Deb Williams, Fiona Starr, Charlie Webb, Jess Winsall, Lynda Newman, Jeanne O'Malley, Denise Kraus, Felicity Sander, Emma and Mark Tahmindjis, Marina Tyndale-Biscoe and Lynne Whitehead. I thank you for your friendship and patience, for listening to me and for encouraging me.

Thanks also to my Facebook and Twitter friends for all your conversations and comments, and for distracting me when I needed to be distracted (and sometimes when I didn't).

For proofreading and helpful suggestions I thank Marjorie Lindenmayer and Jim Viggers.

A major leap forward for this novel came about due to the incredible perceptiveness and understanding of my sister, Fiona Anderson, who read earlier drafts and tactfully pointed out what was going wrong and gave illuminating suggestions.

Above all, for endless patience, love and encouragement, I thank my family: David, Nina and Ryan. David read the manuscript more times than anyone should, and picked up my pieces when they were shattered; I owe a great debt to him. Nina and Ryan have journeyed through this book every step of the way, even though they may not have realised it at times. Their humour and humanity kept me in touch with the world.